PENANCE

PENANCE

SJ Alawine

Book cover by SJ Alawine.

ISBN 979-8-9985500-4-1 (paperback)

First edition January 2026.

PENANCE

CARY AND LOUISE stood a few yards away, tense, watching Sara for the cue to leave. Nathan Bedford Forrest glowered behind them on his pedestal, as he had for about a century. Sara glanced at him, and at the Black woman holding her toddler, sitting on a bench nearby.

Nate was coming down pretty soon. It hadn't been one of the new voices on the planning committee that suggested he take a permanent vacation, but an old friend's—Don's; and opening that conversation had somehow given permission to others who'd kept still for years to speak up also, say they didn't like the vibe Nate brought to the area. It was one of the first small pebbles rolling down the hill; and Sara hadn't been sorry about it...just surprised.

Still, for now, there he stood. The minute the woman had strolled through with her child and sat down, Sara considered sketching them, with Nate behind. The visual irony was sublime. But right now she had to deal with this other man, the flesh and blood one in front of her; and if he wouldn't just go away, sketching would be done. She'd end up having to leave, herself.

When she'd started allowing Cary to go into stores on her own, or hanging out downtown with a friend or two on a Saturday afternoon, Sara had preached: Just walk away from scary people. Run, hide, fight, like they tell you at school. Emphasis on "run." She felt bad now, doing the opposite. But I'm old; I've learned when to run, she thought as she met his gaze and he stood quietly, patiently, several feet away, holding a parcel wrapped in white paper. Another gift...something else to deal with today, along with the old lady and whining teenager she'd dragged along to the park over their objections.

He nodded. "Afternoon, Ms. Wells. Don't want to interrupt."

"But you just did." She stowed her pencil in her briefcase and considered her next words. She'd learned the hard way. "Can I help you?" had once prompted a man to tell her how she could, and she'd had to walk briskly away, and he'd finally wandered off, talking to himself. "So—?"

Louise, eyed the man, inched nearer to Cary.

He shifted his feet. "This's a gift to express appreciation for your books and your volunteer work around town." And on cue, he held out the parcel. Obviously rehearsed.

She scoffed.

"Seriously, I was sent to give you this and tell you, people appreciate your volunteer spirit."

" 'People'? Somebody I'd know?"

"I realize it seems weird. There's a note with it. His compliments." He set the parcel on the bench next to her.

"Who's 'he'?"

"My boss. He wants you to open it before I leave."

"Thinks I might throw it away, straight off?"

"Something like that."

And, usually, it's what she would do. She'd thrown away many odd gifts through the years. She put the drawing pad onto her briefcase and stowed the loose pages to keep them from falling out. She did it slowly, hoping he'd take a hint and leave. But he didn't. If she were alone, she might have sworn at him, yelled a little: I'm scarier than you are.

But there was Cary, and there was Louise, watching, waiting for the cue. She shoved the pad and case under her arm. "I can't just open stuff that strangers hand me. You understand."

"I do. I expected that. So I'll open it myself. It's just a gift. Really. That's all."

"I appreciate the thought, but I don't take gifts from people I don't know."

"Well, it's not from *me*, I said."

She smiled a little in spite of herself, at the aggrieved tone in his voice. He picked around carefully for an edge to start a tear. "It's just from a person, my boss, who felt like you don't get the credit you deserve for volunteer work."

"I get the idea somebody doesn't want me to know who they

are, for whatever reason. Maybe this person thought I wouldn't listen to you if I knew who he was…am I right?"

"I told them it'd go this way." He was still grumbling. She began to enjoy it. "Look, there's a note here, it'll explain." He talked fast, unhappily, ripping the paper. "They told me to open it if I had to—what you think, it's a bomb or something?"

He lifted the lid and offered the opened box. There was an envelope inside; she plucked that out. Folding back tissue paper, suddenly gentle and cautious, he lifted a small sculpture, cradling it. It was perhaps porcelain, she thought, maybe acrylic, a midnight-blue hemisphere on one side, and as she turned it in her hand, it changed into a tumble of cubes falling upon each other.

"No bomb, huh."

"Why would anybody want to blow up this piece of art?"

"Looks like it's already gone off," Cary suggested.

"So who's it from? You said it's 'he', sometimes you said 'they'… Which is it?"

"You got the letter." He turned to leave.

"Nope, not doing that. Just hang on." She tore open the envelope. "I don't guess you or 'they' gave much thought to how people have to be cautious. But I learned the hard way not to take a gift at face value."

"That's a shame."

For a couple of seconds Sara pondered this. "It is what it is." She scanned the page. "There's no name here."

He shrugged. "Meant to be anonymous. Not my idea, but like you said, it is what it is. They asked me to bring it, I did. I have to get back to work now. Good afternoon, Ms. Wells."

She put the sculpture into the tissue paper and sat down, watching the man stride unhurriedly across grassy picnic grounds, past all the recent alterations which could not be overlooked in the park, and just for a moment or two her mind went there: New faces at planning committee meetings, once conducted in a rote manner; different accents interrupting the slow drawls in the economic development commission. Last fall another transplanted citizen had suggested work should be done, more sidewalks to make it accessible. Then again people who *had* been here for years added complaints, things they'd noticed for a long time but held their silence about, when the budget was tight; but now they could get grants from the new company—from MTE—to pay for it all.

Community improvement. So, renovations on the old pavilion, dirt pathways between the softball fields paved, bedding plants installed at the exits. Today, at the main entrance, Parks Authority employees were yanking lantanas and salvia from plastic pots, shifting them here and there to check out how they looked before permanently installing them. And Nate had been decommissioned. Where he'd finally end up was anybody's guess. Some closet, she hoped.

The man walked fast and was out of sight in the time she thought about those changes. Louise and Cary bent over the box. "That was strange," Louise grumbled.

"But, a gift, there's that." Cautiously, Cary dragged the sculpture out of its nest of rustling white paper.

A red car came into view and maneuvered the wide curve at the park's gate. "Your daddy had one of those. Long ago," Louise said.

"I guess everybody and their brother saw that interview this time, Louise, so maybe you're right. Maybe I should stop doing them for a while."

Vindicated, Louise gloated. "I won't say I said so."

Cary turned the sculpture around and around, hefted it as if it were a bowling ball. "Sort of like a geode. You know, Aunt Louise. Those rocks that you break open, and inside it's all crystals." She rotated it. "But it's not a geode. It's a made thing. So read the note."

"I bet it was somebody at the historical society. And the handwriting's awful."

Louise started to say something, probably to tell her again that she did too many things for free; but, not wanting to hear that sermon, Sara plowed on: "I mean, we get along. Individually. As a group they have some problems with me. Could be Nora's idea of a joke." But she knew Nora found very little funny. Jokes would be beneath her.

Cary rolled her eyes and seized the twice-folded paper, poring over it. "Like a doctor's handwriting. Ego," she grumbled. "Not much to say." She read aloud, haltingly: " 'Saw your interview, purchased your latest book, found it charming. Glad to see there are still people willing to volunteer time to worthwhile organizations and speak up for things they believe in, without reward. I respect that, and I also prefer anonymity'," Cary dropped her voice piously and rolled her eyes. "Geez. Saint Whoever."

In spite of herself, Sara laughed.

"Doesn't look like a big deal," Louise added. "You've got this kind of stuff before."

"I know. 'Without reward,' huh? Guess he didn't consider those TV gigs helping me sell books."

"Doesn't seem to bother him," Cary said.

Strangely unhappy, and with those words—"That's a shame"—going around in the back of her mind, Sara crammed the note into the carton with the sphere and snapped the locks down on her briefcase. "I've lost my focus. Let's go home. You mind?"

"I didn't want to come here, anyway, you know. I wanted to go straight home, but you didn't ask me."

"Give it a break. You sound like an old lady."

"Like you," Cary muttered, ignoring the glare Louise turned on her; Louise found that kind of snark disrespectful.

"Yeah, like me," Sara agreed. "We'll get some ice cream. Since work's done for the day." She knew Louise had turned the glare her way, now.

Cary took Sara's briefcase and they headed toward the parking area. "Hot fudge sundae. Chocolate's always good."

The park was on the west side of town, not too far from where she and Rheta had grown up. Driving home every Friday after her routine trip to sketch, Sara always remembered one particular year when, sitting on the front steps of their parents' house on the warm spring evenings as night approached, the two of them watched a string of lights switch on, not smoothly like Christmas-tree lights, but erratically, one here, one there, the others slowly filling in outward from the street where they lived. It was the year Rheta was a senior. She and Sara would watch as far as they could see across the flat farmland, and when the mosquitoes got too thirsty, they would retreat inside.

The lights were Ransome Moore's. His brother Wilburn had financial interest in their agricultural enterprises, and one day, on the farm, as they stood at the foot of a long, even row stretching far, far to the treeline at the horizon, they paused the desultory bantering they'd been having over the year's potential profits and stared, both of them, at the converging crop lines. After a while Wilburn said, "Time, Ranse," and their eyes met, and they went to their homes. Neither of them ever spoke a reason to each other; maybe they didn't have to use words, or they couldn't. But that was the day the farms shut down; and soon after, the lights shone.

Ransome's political enemy David Burkes had theories about the four miles of lights: Ransome just wanted to shock people again, David said; or maybe he was writing it off on income tax. David would do that, so he figured Ransome would. Maybe he'd got death threats and was scared, wanted illumination to scatter the shadows.

All of that was wrong. Before the next year arrived, just as abruptly and inexplicably as he'd turned them on, he had all but a handful of the lights shut off. David Burkes sneered, to anyone he thought might tell Ransome, that the old fart had found out Mooresville wasn't paying attention to him anymore. And, within the year, Ransome hired a team of tree-planters to fill some of what had been his soybean, corn, cotton, rye fields with pine seedlings, and over time a forest grew between his house and the town.

SHE REMEMBERED, AS she drove on streets that angled to a point near the heart of town, where the old railroad depot stood. Several decrepit buildings put up in the 1920s and -30s huddled over downtown streets. Once, long ago, they wore bright-colored paint, gargoyles, inviting canopies over heavy doors that slid open into department stores cooled with fans whirling overhead. No longer: Now they were painted in more practical hues. Right before Ransome shut down his operations, David Burkes and Reginald Griffin—men who didn't think about what they might do with the buildings, but could afford them—had bought them at fire-sale prices. Now the unbeautiful hulks squatted, decaying, occasionally occupied by somebody who wanted a small, cheap space for a pipe dream business that closed quietly within a month or two.

She drove past the ice cream store, where she and Rheta had eaten chocolate cones long ago—so many customers now that it wasn't fun anymore. Past the building where the old bookstore had been—the two of them used to pass half an hour now and again, giggling in the historical romance section, leafing through bodice-ripping books until they found the racy parts, reading those aloud. One of the several clerks who knew them by name would approach: "You two gonna buy anything today?"

The bookstore had shut down. In its spot was a jewelry store that specialized in trendy, high-end things: Morris Jewelers. The traffic light changed red; and, as she waited, Sara wondered briefly if the shop owner could tell her anything about the sculpture. She glanced across the street at the building where Neil's office was. The light went green, and she drove on.

"You're awful quiet," Louise remarked.

"Just thinking about some of the things Rheta and I got into when we were girls. Looking at these buildings in human terms, like, they're showing their age, they need to get facelifts, that kind of thing."

"You're hanging out with those old preservation ladies too much," Cary remarked. "You know they've all had facelifts. Botox."

The town's genuine Italian place, Liberto's, was where she and Rheta would sip soft drinks at a table near a window, feeling misunderstood and trapped, the same way Cary probably did now. The canvas awning over the restaurant entrance flapped gently today in the wake created by the passing of cars. To the right and left of the building were plainer, grey, hulking structures shouldering up together as if to chaperone the restaurant, the outlier, the crazy old great-aunt of the three who wore bright colors to a funeral where the other relatives were dressed in black.

Plaques stood near intersections. "Mooresville Historic District." She remembered when, a few years earlier, several important men had retired almost simultaneously, and their wives founded the Mooresville Preservation Association, extending invitations to carefully-selected gentlemen and matrons—and she'd got one, too, not because of family or money but because she was a local celebrity of sorts. The society's officers attended city council meetings once in a while, begging for grants. Or they approached the mayor as a group, their White Shoulders wafting around his head, a suffocating aroma of old money, their fingers and wrists heavy with antique jewelry. In self-defense against this assault, he would remind them of the unlikelihood of additional taxes to finance a project. "You ladies go ask MTE," he told them these days. "They got money, and they're always trying to give some of it away." And at that, they would exchange glances and shake their heads, leaving the matter tabled for a few more months.

"Maybe I should ask Neil's opinion about this thing," Sara mused aloud.

"I thought we were going to get ice cream," Cary complained.

Sara turned at the next light and circled the block. "How about an early dinner instead?"

"I've already fixed supper," Louise told them ominously. "It's in the slow-cooker. I just have to heat it up."

Cary rolled her eyes, but from the back seat Louise couldn't see that. Sara parked in an empty slot in front of Liberto's. "We'll just get one of their sorbets, something light. I did offer, and, anyway, I want to think about some things."

"Then you ought not to go *there*—you know who'll hang around running his mouth, there'll be no peace and quiet," Louise grumbled; but she ordered two scoops and even chatted amiably with Don. Cary called him by his given name, as if he were a brother, and he lingered near their table and talked, simultaneously watching his other customers.

CARY OPTED FOR the non-Italian choice of a sundae after all, but Sara and Louise enjoyed the sorbets. They left, feeling companionable again for the moment, ambling down the sidewalk in the late-afternoon spring chill to where Sara had parked.

"You have big homework this weekend?"

"Nah. I actually did, the other day when you made me go to Dad's." She gazed at Sara for a moment, coldly, fidgeting with her phone. "When can I have some input on that?"

"Sorry. You're not there yet. Do you not like Jennifer?"

"She's OK. But it's so lame. I mean, I'm just visiting, but they don't want me hangin' by myself; they want me around them all the time, so they can say we were *together*. Fake." Cary's mouth curled downward. Sara remembered that age; she'd tried to keep up with how Cary felt about things now. Parents had to do that, she'd told Louise, trying to get her to learn this new language, too; but Louise wasn't going there. In her day the elders told you how it was to be, and that was that. Sara knew sympathy wasn't what Cary wanted: She wanted the choice of going or not, and that was legally still a year from now. And they knew Matthew wouldn't give in on his allotted visitation. Cary said he thought it showed Jennifer he was a committed, involved father; and she was probably right about that.

Cary took the front seat again; Louise sniffed disapproval and climbed stolidly into the back. Sara glanced over—was Cary crying?—but she'd turned her face away, the purple streak she'd dyed in her hair framing her profile. Sara looked in the rearview mirror reflexively to see her own grey, and felt old.

"You know, I wonder..." Louise paused, her door still ajar.

"Wonder what?"

"That man at the park...he didn't have any trouble finding you. He came right up to us. How would he've known we were there?"

"Maybe he just asked around." Where, though, and whom? she wondered. And then she recalled, and admitted: "Oops. I mentioned that. Deborra always asks me about what she calls the 'artist's routine.' And I told her I go there on Fridays."

"Geez, Mom," Cary complained. "So he or somebody else listened, and then they stalked you there. *Us* there," she added accusingly. "Thanks a lot."

"So I guess I change my schedule. No more Fridays at the park. Have to do it another day. Big deal."

Louise sighed loudly.

Sara froze her expression in neutral. Best to put that particular worry into the back of her mind, filed with all the other frettings. She drove on home.

BROADCASTING HER PERSONAL life had never bothered her before, but, today, Louise's often-replayed warnings gnawed at her. Because, possibly, she had screwed up this time.

She didn't have to be reminded about safety, and she knew she was doing a lot—she told herself as much, in the privacy of her bedroom. There was the library-sponsored literacy campaign. The preservation society and their professed goal of saving the old downtown area. The night classes she taught at the college. The TV announcements she'd taped for the fertility support group that met in town once a month. She knew all the organizations she'd signed on with were using her name, and mostly she was okay with that. Everybody liked it when famous people had the same problems they did.

Louise hadn't been the only doomsayer. "Saw you were on TV again." When Matthew arrived Wednesday to pick Cary up for his dinner-out evening with her, that was what he said first to her, and she waited for the jab that always followed—she knew him well, knew he'd punch a crack or two in her confidence when he could. He opened the door for Cary, and then: "Deborra Anderson knows sex sells," and he smiled at his comment, and Cary made a gagging noise as she slammed the car door. Sara wanted to be civil, for Cary's sake; but before his car was at the stop sign at the end of the street, she was on her phone with Rheta, unloading on her.

"Yeah, sex sells," Rheta agreed, "and he's scared you might tell people one day he ain't got a lot of inventory, and, look, it would be on TV! And maybe his current girlfriend might be watching!"

"Ouch!" Then she'd laughed. Like him, Rheta knew where to hit, and she'd never particularly cared for him and delighted in throwing a punch herself.

Deborra Anderson had her on her late-afternoon program every two or three months. It was soft news before the real stuff at six, and they both knew the drill—P.R. for Sara to sell books, easy interview for Deborra. She asked versions of the same questions, knew she'd get versions of the same answers. This last time had followed the usual script. They'd memorized the skit, the cues and the responses:

"Thank you for coming by again today. We always enjoy having you. What's new?"

As if a neighbor dropped in with a different recipe.

They fed each other a couple of lines about the weather; and then, glancing at notes of things she'd asked Sara on other afternoons, Deborra said: "So remind us how you got involved in the literacy campaign."

"Well, you know about my daughter, everybody in my house is a big reader. I want everybody to love books."

"Because that's your living: people buying your books!" —A soft laugh paired with a twinkling eye.

"Yes, but also because people should read. So we were checking out some things at the library one day, when she was younger..."

And so it went, the prompts:

..."So I think the library has reading circles. How does that work? Have they started a new one?"

..."I see they've scheduled some local writers to read their books aloud—will you be doing that again?"

But this time Deborra had deviated from the script: "I've been told MTE's sponsoring a different sort of program this summer for kids. What do you know about it?"

She and Deborra had what people called "history," and the camera was rolling, so she froze her face to impassive. "Nothing.

News to me. I'm not sure why we need another program competing with the one the library has, but, you know, if they're funding something good, more power to them."

They looked pleasantly at each other. "By the way, what are you currently working on? Can you tell us?"

...And later, as always, "Everybody likes to think you just live in pajamas and drink coffee and tap away on a computer and draw. But what's an artist's, a writer's, daily routine, really?"

The literacy campaign plug properly done, and Sara having managed to publicize her own current project, Deborra would sometimes lean in a little closer, like an old friend discussing her latest menopause symptoms, and would bring up the fertility support group. Station polls had confirmed viewers perked up when this subject arose. Sara played along, repeating what she'd said on other occasions: She'd had trouble getting pregnant, knew what people went through, knew the toll it took on you psychologically, emotionally, financially, wanted to offer support where she could, because it had helped her feelings whenever a prominent personality had talked about their own issues, someone who was successful in other ways but not in that one. —And so on and so forth, until, smiles frozen on their faces, they waited for the ON AIR lights to go off, and a commercial rolled and another guest was brought out.

There'd been nothing unusual about the last week's interview, until near the end of the segment, when Sara recited again (how many times through the years?) the day and hour and place the group met, and she paused just a brief moment, realizing she'd done the whole show and didn't remember a lot of what she'd said. Sometimes they recorded a day ahead of broadcast, but this time it had been live, and neither of them had changed the routine: an easy eight minutes of treading water. She was inexplicably still annoyed about the MTE question thrown at her earlier and thought Deborra looked bored. So she added, "Anyway, the clinic has good help, and who knows—one day even you might want their services."

"Maybe so." She blinked as if she'd been dozing off.

"You don't know how big a deal it can be until you go through it. You, you probably couldn't imagine it would dominate your whole life, take over all your thoughts, make you a little psychotic."

Deborra smiled, smoothly awake again. "That would be

depressing! Good to know there are groups like this. Thank you again for updating us."

They kept smiling at each other as the commercial break was announced. Sara removed the lapel microphone. "Appreciate your having me back."

"Always a pleasure." She looked intently at Sara, her black curls framing deep hazel eyes set in her brown skin. She'd been the obvious choice for a broadcaster at the station—local girl, parents involved in education, and the town considered her *theirs*, they owned her. "You know, I don't think I want kids."

"Sorry for throwing that at you. Feel free to edit it out."

"It's fine. Shake it up a little! Besides, I did it to you, didn't I. You really haven't heard anything about MTE's program?"

"No. I just wish they'd quit—" She had paused, knowing it would sound petty, aware Deborra was watching, no, *assessing* her response. "I guess I wish they didn't try to barge in all the time and take over. It makes us look inept."

"Maybe we are inept."

"We did okay."

"I think they're trying to help. Make up for all the changes they caused."

"You know, it was a really big deal—all the perks and concessions, tax deals. You remember. You reported on it. Then they just brought that one division, that does all computer work, online stuff—they could all work from home, they wouldn't even have to be here. Everybody figured they'd bring jobs."

"Manufacturing," Deborra suggested.

"Yeah. And they didn't. They didn't even use the labor pool we had. Maybe it wasn't much to brag on. But they just moved some of their specialized people here."

"People *were* hired, some were trained. You have family yourself working there, I think you said one time."

She scoffed. "Former family. Yeah. But, others, just maintenance and low-skills things."

She stopped. Deborra had a watchful, interested look on her face.

"One minute," somebody said.

"You remember when I interviewed their financial guy," Deborra went on, "Ken Thomas, and I asked him if they'd thought about jobs for people with lower skills, and he admitted they wouldn't have many of those at first. He was candid about it. You remember he said they intended to use all local suppliers, though, and he hoped that would help?"

"I remember the interview." And she remembered, too, that Neil had been invited to present an opposing view that day.

"Mr. Thomas pointed something out to me I hadn't thought about. He said bringing their fabrication division here would disrupt the economy back home. He said they'd eventually get to that, here, and train another unit in Mooresville. But the designing would come first. He said being here might make other companies wonder what was good enough about us to lure a corporation like them, and others might take a chance on us. It made sense."

"What 'lured' them was all that money thrown at them," Sara said.

"Well, they have put a lot back in."

"Maybe."

Not wanting to provoke Deborra further, Sara had left, speaking to a few of the front people she was acquainted with.

Louise always fussed after each interview. Somebody was going to send Sara a pair of used underwear in a little package one day, she warned. E-mail her pictures of himself naked. —And other things she'd seen on cable TV programs. Sara reminded her of the book signings, the personal appearances, where nothing had ever happened—but that was different, Louise said, because she faced those people, whereas this was available to anybody with a TV or a computer or just a phone, even, and who knew what might go through their crazy heads.

"You're right. But it's how I make a living. Can't be scared of everything." But every time she said that, Cary shot her a skeptical glance, knowing as teenagers do when they discover the truth: She never did anything scary or different or unusual.

And now somebody'd told her she looked as if she'd been sent a bomb. A bomb. And a tiny part of her almost wished it had been. Something, just anything, to knock a few holes, make the stones rattle a little. Maybe some people wanted that, once in a while, to get the whole bloody event done and finished at once, instead of living the gradual, continual bruising of the slow-motion ones that defined their real lives. But in real life, bombs didn't go off every day. At least, not the real ones, that made the news with flames and smoke boiling up into an eerily blue sky, just out of nowhere.

2

CARY RETREATED TO her room, and Louise went to the kitchen and dialed up the heat on the slow-cooker. Sara sat alone in the living room, opening again the box with the sculpture, looking for the artist's name, a company, any identification. As Cary said, it was something like a geode, but not—made of porcelain, stoneware clay...she wasn't sure. She held it in front of her face, and from one side it was a plain sphere, inky blue, but glazed with something that made it look like a ball filled with profoundly deep water. She rotated it slowly, and it became ocean but not, round and oval-shaped crystals tumbling out of the depths, gradually becoming cubes; and then, as she kept turning it, the cubes softened again and climbed up into the sphere that was the water.

She played with it a few minutes. Cary, phone in hand, wandered through towards the kitchen. "It could just be a paperweight. It'd make a nice one."

"Yeah."

In a moment Cary appeared again in the living room, now with a juice box. "I mean, if you don't want it, I'll take it."

"I think I better find out a little more about it, if I can."

"Google it," Cary suggested and returned to her room.

In college she'd been dilettantish about art—a semester of art history, a course of pencil and chalk drawing, one of oil painting, basic ceramics, nothing steady; she wasn't "committed," an instructor once scoffed haughtily. But, now, in her TV appearances, once in a while, she managed to get in a dig about the value of a liberal arts education. They don't advise those anymore, she'd say; they expect students to specialize right away. But she, Sara, had tried all sorts of subjects. "And look how I make a living now—not at all what I started out in," she'd say to Deborra, who would flash her smile and appear fascinated.

From all those courses long ago, Sara knew original art when she saw it and didn't think she'd find this piece on the Internet.

She started to place it on one of the bookshelves, changed her mind, and wrapped it up in the tissue to go back into the box. She'd figure it out tomorrow.

She should probably relent and concede to Matthew that Cary didn't cooperate with her all the time, either—it was just the age. Right now Sara would have appreciated her being in the room, even if she did tap on her phone incessantly and answered questions with, "Hm?" a lot. Tonight there was no one to talk with. And the trouble with having a housekeeper, especially one so closely related, was that she herself was rendered useless sometimes in her own home.

It was about half an hour before Louise usually set dinner on the table. She smelled beef stew, the aroma of basil and sage mingling with vegetable juices. Louise was pretty quiet in the kitchen; not many clangs and bumps, just a soft bustle and footsteps as she moved around. Sara thought to be grateful for Louise, who moved here when Cary was a toddler and Sara a newly-divorced mother. Rheta had never got along with her, though she was their father's sister. It was her damned prissiness, Rheta said; she wanted to be right there with that first stone.

But how would I have managed without her.

And yet she was restless tonight, useless in her own house, and with thirty minutes to somehow fill. She thought of turning on the evening news, but called, "Getting some fresh air." Louise answered, "Hm," and it was like Cary: It was a syllable of assent, of permission, as if she needed it. She picked up a jacket and went out the door.

"That's a shame," the man had said.

She perched upon the bannister, remembering the times that summer when she and Rheta had sat and watched Ransome's string of lights come on. But this house wasn't on that side of town, and the only thing she saw now was that cars were moving too fast to suit her, and the neighbors' cat seemed to have a death wish as it crossed the street. She waited outside half an hour until the sun set, and obediently went in when Louise called to say their supper was done.

AFTER THEY FINISHED kitchen clean-up, the three of them usually went to the living room for just a bit, sometimes awkward moments, lately, but it was a custom that had started when Cary was a little girl, and they hung onto it because stopping would leave a void. Cary hunted down the white cardboard box and took out the sphere to hold it near her face. "See, it would match!" She fluttered her eyelashes. Cary had Sara's blue eyes.

Louise looked skeptical and rustled the pages of the newspaper around.

"Good try. But no. I may just return it, if I find out where it came from. So what do you think it means?"

"End of the world," Cary guessed.

"Or it could be the beginning of the world. Turn it around."

" 'Things fall apart,' " she went on. "We read a little of that in English class last week." She balanced it her left hand.

"Powerful… 'Creation,' " Sara countered.

"Glass half empty, half full." Louise snapped the newspaper, folding it. "Depends on how you want to see it. One of those artsy things meant to confuse you."

Cary and Sara gazed at her for a moment. "Conversation starter," Cary said cheekily, and laughed.

"Now I advise you both, if you're ever able to return it—which I think would be a good idea, if you asked me—I think you ought to put it back in that box so it won't chip or break. Sara, here's the paper if you want it." She passed it over with another snap. "You're making awful light of that thing. I'd still like to know how long that man had been waiting today, wasn't in a hurry, knew who you were."

"You already have that answer, the last one, anyway: I've been on TV too much, like you said. And not careful enough about what I say. This thing—" she took it from Cary and repackaged it in its container—"I agree we shouldn't be playing with it. I'm going to do a little research on it tomorrow. Good enough?"

Cary rolled her eyes as she ambled back to her bedroom. Sara heard the door shut. "I wish you wouldn't scare her with all that talk. You said yourself, I've got things like this before."

"But not delivered in person," Louise insisted. "People call that 'stalking,' like she said."

The paper was thin today, the front page devoted to a new state education initiative and a legislator who had been diagnosed with cancer. A color photo of children in the library. She looked to see whether Rheta's byline was on any of the stories, then turned to the inside, where obituaries ran on the same page as arrests. Sometimes she thought it seemed unfair that people arrested but not yet convicted had their mugshots published, but Louise saw it as justice: They'd done something bad to have their pictures on that page and should be exposed for it, was her opinion. Sara scanned the faces, read the names.

"How have I heard of Stephen Logan before?" she asked.

"Why? Where do you see him?"

"Right here..." She bent the paper down to show. "Didn't you notice?"

"Lord, I don't look at that unless I do it accidentally. I'd have nightmares thinking of them people out on bail, running around with the rest of us."

"You never look? Don't you wanna know who to watch out for?" —But it was dangerous to poke too much fun at Louise about these things. Sara had awakened to find her checking door locks in the middle of the night after watching a thriller with Sara before bed, hours earlier. "Well, anyway, he's in the news."

"What's he done now?"

"It says he was arrested for threatening behavior and simple assault. How do you know him?"

"You ought to remember...I'm surprised you don't recall. Didn't you or Rheta, one of you, go to school with him? It was those church-burnings," she said impatiently as Sara gestured for her to continue. "You remember he was a suspect. Long ago. He never was any good. Into things all the time."

Sara stared at the face she now did recall. It wasn't your usual criminal face, or druggie caught in a sting. The face in the photo seemed mildly amused, but pissed, anyway. Neat hair, Polo shirt. The vibe was businessman-with-one-too-many-parking-tickets.

Not at all the Stephen Logan of back then. She hardly heard Louise's final comment: "Once bad, always bad."

SHE POURED HERSELF a tall insulated mug of coffee in the morning. Louise, who went to bed by eleven o'clock and was up by six-thirty, watched silently as Sara capped the thermos. But she turned down breakfast. "I'll grab a bite in town with a friend," she said. "I'm taking that little piece of art, so it'll be out of Cary's reach. Maybe I can find out something about it. I'll text and get Cary up around nine-thirty. Let her sleep till then, okay?"

Louise scoffed, quietly.

"And why don't you take it easy till she gets up? You've been going all week, yourself," Sara added as she pulled the back door shut and heard the distinctive click of the deadbolt behind her.

She'd heard Louise shuffling softly to the kitchen this morning, as always, heard the quiet noises of water running, the coffee canister being opened, the gurgling of the pot as it brewed. Sometimes she didn't hear all that in the morning, but last night fragments of dreams—unconnected images, really, snippets as from a longer video—had roused her more than once. Resigned finally to being awake, she'd got up at dawn to watch sunlight brighten her room. Finally, around seven, she'd got the answer to her text.

See u @8:30.

Somehow the shortcut message made her unease go away, so that now she could snicker a little about Louise turning the deadbolt and fastening the chain.

Up until a couple of years ago, early on a Saturday morning you might only have seen a vagrant or two hunched around the doorways of shuttered buildings, a few cars lined up in front of hardware stores; you'd have waited a long, long time for a crowd to pick up. But it was different now, and she wasn't the only person up and about: Joggers in running shorts crisscrossed the downtown blocks, because they'd been used to doing that in places where, a year before, they had rented third-floor apartments over urban parks. Other people brought their newspapers and frappuccinos to the permanently-installed cement outdoor tables.

Liberto's wasn't open yet. But if she was willing to put up with the sun slanting down the street until someone arrived with Don's red, white and green umbrellas, she could sit there; he didn't own the tables, as he'd remind you—the city did. Still, he was glad they were there, and you were always welcome to order from his menu…a waiter would happily serve you outside.

The aroma of cinnamon drifted from a kiosk on the next block. Sara bought two of the rolls and an extra-large coffee. The clerk helped her tuck the bag with the rolls into her tote and sling it over her shoulder, and she crossed the street gingerly holding the extra-large coffee and her own mug in her hands.

She settled onto a bench convenient to a table and poured into the thermos cup some of the fresh, hot coffee she'd just bought. A cluster of pansies were struggling a little, but the river birches had decided last year to thrive and were now leafing out.

Liberto's had been on Main Street for at least eighty years. Vincente had hung the first striped awning over the door, and over it a hand-painted "Liberto's." When times had been bad, his grandson Don had the name changed just to "Ristorante," because, he said, it might not at last be "Liberto's" someday—his face had been grim when he'd told her that.

And when the new people arrived, it was almost a private joke: Tell someone you were going to "Liberto's," watch them try to find that on Google.

Don had been glad to see all those newcomers arrive in Mooresville. Like his pop Dominic, he bragged on having the only good place to eat in town. He owned his Italian background even though the little Italian he knew came out of his mouth in deep Southern redneck.

Movement in the restaurant caught her eye: lights on. Someone was inside—Don, sitting at the bar with one of his managers, the two of them discussing something. Don had his back toward her, but as she motioned to the manager, he pointed, and Don swiveled. The two men said a few more words to each other, and Don unlocked the front door and came out to sit with her.

"Weren't you just here?"

"Yeah. We would've got a full meal last night, but Louise had already fixed something at home. But I'd promised Cary ice cream, so we stopped anyway."

"Always glad to see you."

"And my money."

"Also that…Do you think the flowers will live?" he asked.

"Maybe. Probably not. It'll be too hot in a while, but if they die, the city'll put something else in. It looks nice, Don."

A few more people had appeared pushing strollers, speed-walkers with earbuds dangling off their heads, waiting at the cinnamon kiosk.

"Except, not right next to me," he grumbled.

"It'll happen sometime, maybe."

"Doubtful," and he stood up. "Shit. Is *he* coming over here? Why?"

"Something happened yesterday that I felt like I need to run past him. He *is* my lawyer, you know."

"If you say so. Well, it's a public street. Neil, you know jaywalking's illegal."

"What're you doing here so early this morning, Don? Trying to compete with that cute little chick selling sticky buns? She's gonna get that clientele, man, give it up."

Don smiled tightly. "That's Lisa's niece."

"Oops! Sorry. Didn't know." He hunched his shoulders a little and sank down upon the bench which Don had just vacated. "Did you make this coffee for me?"

"That cute little chick supplied your caffeine today. You know we don't open till ten. See you later, Sara. After you take care of business or whatever it is, come in and we'll talk a while, if you want to." He went inside and relocked the door, casting a grim look at her.

"Neil, how can you make a perfectly innocent remark, and it sounds nasty?"

"I have the talent. Actually, I just wanted to get rid of him. Didn't you know he and Lisa own that kiosk? They bake those biscotti and sweet breads, all that stuff, and get that girl to sell it on the weekends and Fridays before school. They set the place up over there, away from the restaurant, so people think it's new and different. I just didn't know the kid was related to Lisa."

"I didn't know *any* of that."

"You should keep up. He's your friend, and you don't know whose bread that child's peddling? Well, anyway—did you buy me something?"

She retrieved the paper bag and handed him one of the rolls. "And these are delicious," he said. "Actually, I admire Don. He knows how to make money."

"If you'd do something about these old white elephants here, he'd be happier."

"Not my job to keep Don Liberto happy. I see you siphoned off some of my coffee. Nice, assertive touch. Now, sweetie, what's on your mind?"

But she hedged: "There are a lot of people out these days. I wonder if something's going on this weekend."

Neil finished the cinnamon roll, watching her as he ate. She pretended to be interested in the line of traffic waiting for the light to change; she had a feeling Don might be glancing out from time to time.

"That was very good. I doubt there's any special event this morning," he said. "And surely that's not why we're sitting here at this godawful hour on a Saturday: just to talk about how many people are out. Why'd you get me out of bed to sit in the cold air and breathe exhaust fumes? You could've come to my office. You haven't, in a long time."

That was true. For a while she'd just been dropping off her small contracts and documents and asking his paralegal to have him look over them, and Jean would call her later and tell her what he'd said. "I want your opinion about something that happened yesterday."

"Matthew giving you trouble?"

"No, it's not him, it's Louise. Well, it's not her fault, really. It's me. She worries a lot about people, criminals, being around everywhere. But I'm responsible for letting her get to me this time. Normally, I don't." She dug into the tote and brought out the white cardboard box, opened it, folded the tissue back.

He watched her face, and, beyond an uninterested glance at the sculpture, seemed to forget it as she told him about yesterday. When she finished, he shrugged. "Keep it. And I wouldn't worry about it. You might find out, sometime…this is still a small town. Sooner or later somebody'll probably want to take credit."

"I suspected…I wondered if *you* got it for me." It had been in the back of her mind, part of the stream of little thoughts during her restless night.

"Oh, no—you know I'm going to hold it over your head if I do something like that. I'd definitely let you know if it was from me. So Matthew's not the problem?"

"Not him. Cary doesn't want to see him as often as the court said. But she doesn't kick about it too much."

"That's good, because you know I got what the judge allows. She'll be able to decide for herself in a year or two. So, then, today it seems you just wanted to ask me out!"

She had been staring pensively at the little kiosk. Now she laughed. "*Somebody'd* think that. Hate to let you down, but it was about this thing. I'd feel better if I knew what it's worth, or who made it, or something."

They both turned as Don unlocked the door and held it open while two of his employees brought out armfuls of striped umbrellas and began setting them up over the tables. The process seemed to require a lot more than the usual clamping, adjusting, moving the frames, setting the poles into oversized containers filled with sand. Don supervised the kids and ignored Sara and Neil.

"A hint for us to buy something or move on," Neil suggested loudly. "But you don't open till ten."

"You want a menu?" Don retorted.

"Sara, we have a few minutes before Morris'll arrive. I know his routine, I know everybody's on this street. Yours, too, Don. And your schedule's off."

One of the helpers stopped working and turned to gaze at him. Don mumbled something in Italian.

"If it makes you feel better, we can have him take a look at it. He might be able to guess what it's worth, or tell you about the style, or something. He sells some pieces like this. You through with your sweet roll? Let's cross over and wait in my office."

Don seemed to have been listening. "I don't own the tables. Sit as long as you like. Sara was a paying customer last night, at least."

It wasn't the first time a Liberto had more or less rescued her or Rheta from an awkward situation. She lowered one eyelid slowly at him.

THE SPRING RANSOME quit farming was the spring Rheta dated Frank Moore. They rode Frank's horses at the farm, swam in the pond, for a few weeks reveled in the sensual pleasures of youth on the verge of adulthood. One day she vaguely noticed the weatherbeaten sharecropper shacks on the way out of town; and then, one evening, as the sultry glowing sun fell so slowly down in the sky, she saw someone puttering around the rickety porch of one of the cabins.

"People live there?" It burst from her, and her face burned in the light of the declining sun.

"I don't know. Maybe." He glanced back in the rearview mirror a few times.

"Shit! How could you not know? You own this place!"

"I don't own it, and I don't intend to," he retorted. "I can't wait to get out of here, and when I do, I won't come back!"

She glared at him, inched away to put her back against the door. "You don't mean that. You're rich: People always go back to rich."

"You got a short fuse," he mocked—she didn't forget that: People didn't laugh at her, and she told him so, and they cursed at each other. But they were in the driveway by then, and they were expected—his mother had asked Rheta to supper. Ransome ignored her sharp questions, told her not to worry about the houses, and Frank squirmed. She got through the meal Regina had prepared, stared at those houses again on the way back, didn't answer Frank's calls anymore.

Then she spent a couple of weeks pacing the sidewalk in front of Wilburn Moore's "Fresh Grab Go." The hand-painted sign she toted said, "BOYCOTT." She knew but didn't care that people rolled their eyes when her name was mentioned. She stayed with it until Don Liberto told her she was making a fool of herself—the only old man who lived in any of those houses had been born there and said he intended to die there. "He don't even work for Ransome! You look like an idiot!"

She'd take that from Don, but not from Frank.

The ridicule got Chris riled up; he told Don to shut up. But she asked around, on the sly, and found he'd told her the truth. In secret she disposed of the sign.

She graduated and looked for a summer job.

"Well, sure, Hal, what'd she expect?" Dom said. "Most of 'em probably wonder if they'd be next if they hired her, figure she'd look around and see things *they* do she doesn't like, and she might go out in front of their store, too."

The two of them were chatting after eight-o'clock Mass. Hal shrugged: "And she might. Her heart's in the right place, though."

"I mean, if she'd do it to her boyfriend's uncle, she'd do it to anybody," Dominic added. "That's what they're thinkin'."

Dom always went to the earlier service on Sunday mornings, and Hal joined him in a middle row, and they nodded at each other, one nod, as if checking "Present," before they began the usual liturgy. Afterwards, as Dominic left, he'd fuss about having to get ahead of Mooresville's Baptists and Methodists, who showed up when they got out at twelve, expecting him to feed them.

"Dependable customers," Hal would remind him. Customers of any sort that summer were welcome.

Their words were the closing lines of the Sunday liturgy.

Dominic seemed in no hurry that day, Baptists' appetites notwithstanding, because another thing he liked to do was talk with Hal about their families, while the kids lay asleep at home, and today in particular he had something to say. Funny how they'd both ended up with just the two each, good Catholics though they were. Dominic knew about Connie's emergency hysterectomy years ago; and, as for him...well, he'd never wanted to remarry after his own wife departed for Italy when Chris was seven. Mistake, falling for somebody just because she was also Italian, just because Vincente feared the nature of assimilation and wanted him to stay with his own. So Giulia had returned to her grandparents' hometown, and he'd stayed single, raising the boys, shipping them to Europe every summer, if he could afford it, to visit Giulia and their other relatives.

He'd be willing to have Rheta working for him, and he knew Chris couldn't keep his eyes off her. But he'd heard from her lips one day, right there in his place when she and Sara dropped in, swearing how she wouldn't have any of these losers in this shithole town, Sara telling her to quiet down. She'd talked loud enough for him to hear it over the pass-through to the kitchen.

But Dom didn't say any of that to Hal. "You know she was some right about Ransome," he went on, instead. "Him closing down did hurt the town, but then old Mr. Sam'd been letting people go for years before Ransome inherited the place."

"Guess it was bound to happen sooner or later."

"Yeah... People around here, their consciences bother 'em a little more, now, thanks to her." Dom snickered. "But even if she was right, nobody wants to go through all that themselves."

"What about you? Would you hire her?" Hal had asked him suddenly.

"Me? Tell her come talk to me. My conscience's fine. I'm kinda on her side. And nobody's gonna boycott the only good place to eat in town." He was relieved Hal had brought it up on his own, and he hadn't had to.

By the time he forgot not to, and told her that Hal had asked him to give her a job, Rheta was grateful enough to only say, "Shit!" and stalk off to the kitchen.

Chris let his breath out—"Whew!"

LONG BEFORE MORRIS Jewelers opened, many more people had bought sweet breads and coffee to take home for breakfast or to enjoy under an umbrella in front of Liberto's.

"Nobody seems to know them," Neil said quietly. "These people. Who are they, anyway? Shall we?" He held out his arm as if to squire her, the way things might've been done a hundred years ago in town.

"Please!" She rolled her eyes and disposed of the napkins and his cup.

Morris unlocked the door when Neil tapped. Then, "Sara, show him," and one more time she dragged out the sculpture. The jeweler took possession of it; she wandered away to look in a display case full of earrings but listened as Neil told him a much-shortened version of what she'd said earlier. Morris peered through a loupe at the sculpture and rotated it, inspecting it slowly as the midnight-blue globe disintegrated and rebuilt itself into a whole as it turned—it was almost mesmerizing. He packed it up again. "I'll make a few calls. There are some marks, could be the way the artist signed it. I'll keep it till Monday and get in touch with a friend of mine who's more up-to-date on this kind of thing."

He pushed it carelessly, dismissively, to the side, and something about it—how they'd left her out of their quick examination, hadn't showed her where the supposed marks were—hit her wrong. Reaching past him, she took it and opened her bag. "No, I think I'll ask around, too. I know some people at the college. Why don't you get a picture and text it to your connections," she added, realizing Neil was smirking at her, barely hiding his mirth. Morris seemed pissed off; but he took a fast shot. Laid the phone down without looking to see if he'd focused.

"I'll find out what I can, if I have time." He actually sniffed a little.

"You know you were the one who ambled off. If you'd expected to be consulted, you shouldn't have obsessed on those earrings," Neil murmured as they were leaving. And that was true, and she didn't like it. "See something you want me to buy you?" he added. "Get back into your...affections that way?"

"And you didn't have to go all 'Little lady doesn't understand' on me, either." When he laughed at that, she hurried her pace. "It's almost ten o'clock. I told Louise I'd be back sooner to help her get the cleaning started"—a lie, and he probably knew it was.

"Whatever you say. What a weird date this was."

The bag swung heavily against her hip with every stride. Someone he knew stopped him, and she didn't wait to be introduced, which seemed a thing he had in mind when he turned to her. "I have another stop to make. Send me a bill," and waved backwards and left them behind. It was what she and Neil always said to each other.

CARY AND LOUISE had had words. In the same way the air feels thick before a summer thunderstorm, the atmosphere in the kitchen was heavy, charged with electricity. "Thanks for telling me you were going somewhere," Cary said accusingly, sipping from her cup. Louise had her back to both of them; she suddenly slammed a handful of clean spoons into the drain board.

"I thought you'd rather sleep."

"Yeah, I *would've* enjoyed that...."

Another clatter at the sink. "You didn't get up till nine-thirty. That's late."

Damn: She'd forgotten to text Cary. She considered offering an excuse, decided it probably wouldn't help.

"Sara, there's still some coffee in the pot."

"I've had plenty. I brought you both a pastry, still warm."

Louise rolled her eyes at being placated with food, but she took the roll when Sara served it to her on a saucer; and so did Cary, perched on a barstool away from them. She told them about the kiosk and Lisa's niece as they ate.

"Well, that was delicious," Louise said in a while.

"Yeah. Dominic taught his boys well, didn't he. He'd be proud."

"He'd've been prouder if the older one'd stayed with the business," Louise muttered.

"You know he does still work with Don."

"Paperwork," Louise scoffed. "Upstairs in his 'office.' Not where he's needed. But, oh, well, kids gotta do their own thing."

Cary glowered at her, and the moment was tense again.

"Like how *you* ran off to Mexico for a while when you got out of school, worked in resort hotels, hung out on the beaches. Yeah," Sara went on, "Dad told me all about that years ago."

Louise chuckled.

"Mexico? Really? Why'd you come back?" Cary asked.

"Ran out of money. Wasn't making much cleaning rooms, and the gal that lived with me got tired of the work and quit, and I couldn't afford it any longer. That, and I grew up," she added primly.

But Cary ignored that sermon. "So you learned Spanish?"

Louise thought a moment. "*Sí, un poco.* That was a long time ago. Don't you get any ideas."

They divided the chores. Sara volunteered to clean the bathrooms, Louise to fold laundry, and Cary—in a moment of overly-emoted sacrifice—to vacuum. Sara opened the windows to keep from suffocating on bleach fumes and scrubbed vigorously, though nothing was very dirty, and congratulated herself on her diplomacy, on having successfully manipulated them. Cary could be such a pain in the ass; but then so could Louise. She needed them to get along, to keep their routine stable. They'd started looking to her as the referee. She was tired of that role. She'd had to do it when Rheta was a teenager; she'd tried it on Matthew. It had never worked with him.

Louise was so gratified seeing Cary doing something useful that, finishing her own chore early, she'd fixed tuna salad sandwiches for lunch and arranged them on trays with chips and cookies and lemonade. "It's a pretty day," she said. "Why don't you two go outside and eat on the patio?"

Cary, also feeling generous now, said, "What about you?"

"I believe I will stay in, thank you. We all need a little time to ourselves," she added, lifting her brows meaningfully.

THE SPRING BREEZE blew strands of her hair around her face, and as she brushed them back Sara was reminded again of the grey. And it's too long, she thought, reflexively pushing it behind her ears, gazing at Cary's shoulder-length golden-brown locks, with that streak of purple. I could do that, Sara thought—put a color in it. She considered Matthew's expression if she showed up one day with blue locks.

"Why're you staring at my hair? I know you don't like it, but I do." Cary twirled a purple strand.

"Actually, I was admiring it. Maybe I should do something to mine instead of putting up with the grey. Or maybe just cut it off."

Cary eyed Sara's hair. "Old ladies do that," she said disdainfully. "Look at Louise. You're not old. Leave it long."

"Speaking of Louise...I wish you'd try not to annoy her all the time."

"I don't! Oh, I don't mind her, but she fusses at me too much. She fusses about everything. And it's getting worse."

They looked guiltily at the back door and found it closed, but nevertheless spoke more quietly. "And you're getting older. She did things for me when you were little. I could leave you with her when I wasn't here, and feel safe. I could teach those night classes because I didn't worry about you."

"And she's always been here when I get home from school. Always," Cary emphasized. "What's the deal with you two? I know her, so I know there's got to be one. I never asked but I've wondered lately."

They were veering toward that one certain area where their words, picked out so carefully, always went awry anyway. She drained her lemonade to give herself time to think. "When I knew I'd be raising you by myself, mostly, I didn't know how I could get it to work. Mother got a job after Dad died, and I couldn't ask her to quit and stay with you...and Louise, you know, never married. She was living in a retirement community, not because she was particularly old; she'd been hurt on the job, and they retired her. But she hated the retirement village."

"Golden Acres. That place she goes to all the time. So why does she go if she hated it?"

"Don't know. Maybe you should ask her. So, anyway, it just kind of fell together."

"You pay her to be here? You don't have to; I could do what she does."

"Oh, you wanna cook for us?"

"Never mind."

Sara laughed. "Well, here's the 'deal.' She had a settlement, because of the injury, you know, and she had her retirement, which wasn't too bad, and so she really just needed people. Family. Dad was her only brother. She missed him. She was paying rent at the place, so she insisted on paying *me*, or she wouldn't come. Said it would be 'charity.' But then I told her I'd have to pay for child care anyway, so guess what."

"It evened out," Cary said. "What a coincidence. Do you still pay her?"

"Yeah, and she still pays me. We square up every month. We've never raised our prices. It suits her. It suits me."

Cary giggled. "So she's here, like another Italian grandma, hangin' over our meals, tellin' us to eat, eat, it's good for us." Her mood shifting suddenly, she watched Sara's face closely, "Dad didn't really want me, did he."

And there it was, what she thought they'd avoided this time.

"Oh, my God, we've covered this before; why do you keep bringing it up? Is it something he's saying? Your dad did 'want' you—he just—" She'd used many words explaining this over the past few years; none of the words were very good. "We just couldn't live together. Not even for you. You're better off with us apart. He probably tells you this himself."

"I don't ask him."

The wind, just like that, blew cold. Sara began picking up the remains of the sandwiches, the plates and cups. Cary silently helped her, and they took everything inside, rinsed the eating ware, stowed it all in the dishwasher. Louise had gone to the living room with the newspaper. As Cary walked toward her own room again, she said, "Thanks for lunch, Aunt Louise, it was good," then hurried out before she had to suffer a response. Sara heard the door close.

"She's a good girl," Louise remarked.

"But a late riser."

"Hm. Look, you asked about that man last night. There's some more about him. Some things just never go away, do they. People are always the same." Louise handed her the paper, folded to showcase a particular section. "I'm going to visit the old folks at the home. Y'all start adding the menu."

She had changed into nice slacks and a white pullover with a screen print, because, after all, it was Saturday, and every Saturday afternoon she went back to Golden Acres to see people who still lived there, whom she hadn't really liked all that well while she was there herself. Like Cary, Sara did want to ask why, but wouldn't; maybe instead of flaunting her independence, she was just remembering she'd once been like them. And that "old folks" stuff: Some were younger than she.

"Watch out for traffic; it was picking up when I was in town earlier," Sara told her. She began reading.

WITH LOUISE GONE and Cary in her room, the house was very quiet again. Sara heard an occasional mumble from the back which meant Cary was on her phone, but the sounds were indistinct and infrequent. In the stillness she shifted uncomfortably. Had Louise locked the back door? —No, she would not do that to herself. It was Saturday afternoon, for God's sake; broad daylight, people driving and walking all over the place.

She glanced at the story Louise had pointed out: Local Man Arrested for Assault. Byline, R. C. Whitson. "Stephen Logan, a Mooresville resident, was charged with assault in an initial court hearing. Officers who responded to the assault call said witnesses testified that Logan pushed a resident down as he exited a local business on Tuesday. The resident, a manager at Music Monster, had told Logan to leave, referencing signs posted banning loiterers. The manager, who asked not to be identified at this time, fell and suffered a sprained ankle as a result of Logan's actions.

"Judge Diandra Williams refused at this point to upgrade the charge to assault with special circumstances. Some customers told police officers that Logan used a racial slur as he pushed the manager. The manager is Black.

"Logan was considered a person of interest in the arson of the Mt. Pisgah Missionary Baptist Church twenty years ago. He was convicted of other misdemeanors several decades ago. Because of that, District Attorney Daniel Lamb says, he could face incarceration under the habitual offender law.

"Judge Williams asked Logan if he required a public defender. However, from documents obtained through a public records request filed by this news outlet, it was learned that local attorney Neil Griffin will be representing Logan."

Sara put the paper down on the sofa and went to the kitchen to make more coffee.

She hated him when he defended jerks like that.

3

WHEN SHE GOT home, Louise went straight to the kitchen to start supper. Cary had told Sara more than once, lately, that every Saturday evening, having entertained herself that afternoon, Louise took it as her duty to attend *them*, and she did it with energy but not cheerfulness. Sara watched her patting out hamburgers, slapping them down onto the griddle where in a moment or two they were sizzling and filling the air with savory aroma. A couple of years ago she'd insisted they begin writing down things they wanted to eat the next week. "I'm just cooking. I'm not the chef," she told them. At first Cary was enthusiastic, jotting down "pizza" or "Mexican" on about every fourth day of the whiteboard calendar Louise hung in the utility room. Louise told her vegetables had to be there somewhere. She'd already wiped off last week's menu, so now they had to consider the next seven days. A small thing; but, looking at the huge whiteness of the board, Sara knew she'd avoid doing it until Louise again ordered them to.

Louise silently flipped the burgers and took out clean plates and silverware from the cabinets, condiments and pickles from the refrigerator, as Sara watched, thinking she should talk, but not having much to tell. She was the one who'd written in "hamburgers" for tonight, but just lately Cary'd gotten squeamish about beef, one of her rebellions. Sara got three russet potatoes, scrubbed them, punctured them.

"These will be good with the burgers," she said. And Cary could pick around on the meat and, ultimately, probably leave it but still have something to eat. She wrapped the potatoes in foil and shoved them into the oven as Louise watched wordlessly.

The newspaper story bothered her. Earlier, before Louise got home, she'd taken coffee to the living room and tried to absorb other articles, but she found herself wondering if she'd misread a word or two in that story that concluded with Neil's name, and she'd flip back to glance over it again and again, Louise's words resurfacing in her mind every time: "I guess some things just never go away."

Eventually she threw the paper into the trash can and went outside with her sketch pad and pencils. And then Louise drove up and passed her on the way into the kitchen: "It's dark and cool. When you have to turn on the lights to see," she'd added, "time to go in."

At supper Louise doled out details of the lives of the retirement home residents, none of whom they knew and none of which they cared about, possibly even Louise. Cary was quiet, and Sara wondered about social media, and friends. But she was too preoccupied by the newspaper story to ask Cary anything just yet. And she probably wouldn't get an answer, anyway.

The meal finished, they retreated to their own parts of the house. Louise turned back: "I'm going to church with your mother tomorrow. Either of you want to go?"

"Ugh, no," Cary said immediately. Then, before Louise could express her disapproval, "Wait. Yes. I'll go. What time? I mean, I'll go if it's not the early one."

Louise didn't wait for her to change her mind. "Be up at ten if you go with me." They looked expectantly at Sara.

"Can't. I have some things I need to do. College."

Most of that wasn't true, only the last part, but they accepted it. She watched an old Tom Hanks rom-com to make her mind quieten. Once or twice she heard Cary's voice grow a little louder and more animated as she talked to whomever; but she forced Tom and Meg's problems to override Cary's for the moment. The movie played, the nagging questions about Neil were pushed into a corner of her mind, and she did sleep.

SHE WROTE AND left a note in the kitchen telling Louise that since they were going to Mass, she'd fix their breakfast herself. She knew Cary would wait till the last minute to get out of bed—she did—and the aroma of biscuits and sausage would speed her up. They ate, Louise glaring instead of speaking her disapproval of what Cary wore, and when they were gone, she cleaned the kitchen and took the blue sphere in its box and left.

She could have just asked Charlie to meet her downtown, as she had Neil, but Charlie was an old boyfriend from college, and *she*, not Charlie, had been the one to earn money and some local fame and success, even though *he* had the art degree. She taught the writing classes, but her kids' books sold as much for the art she put into them as for the text; and, then, he'd acquired the rep of being the art teacher from hell, his more disgruntled students posting savage online reviews, doubting he even liked his own subject matter. Once in a while, on the evenings she was there to teach, if he was late leaving his classes, or she, early arriving for hers, they'd run into each other and speak—"Doin' okay these days?"—and he'd have a querulous look on his face, as if the question had an obvious answer that irritated him, and they'd hurry on to get away from each other. Sometimes she ran into Susan, the former student he'd married. Susan worked in an office there; and just to keep things straight, she texted her first, asked if they would both meet her today. It felt stupid: She had nothing for Charlie anymore, and she doubted he had anything for her, and yet there was that resentful glance he shot her sometimes....

They'd stopped dating when it seemed inevitable they'd end up sleeping together sometime or other and she found that pitiful: He was just too grateful for the possibility.

They were waiting for her in his office. She dragged the sculpture again from its box.

"That's a nice piece." Susan took it from her, stroking the smooth side.

"You told him the story, I guess…so have any of your students done this kind of thing, Charlie?"

"They don't show me what they do on their own time. I imagine it's probably beyond any of *them*. How'd I know?"

Susan rolled her eyes. "He hasn't had enough coffee. What he means is, it's a mature expression. Very polished."

"Yeah. That. Look, Sara, off the top of my head, it doesn't look like something they could do. But who knows. They might have hidden talents I'm unaware of."

That was aimed at her; but she ignored it. "Maybe it's one of a kind, not mass-produced. What do you think it's made of? Is there an artist's mark? Is there something significant about it that could indicate where it was made, or who did it?"

Like Morris, Charlie carefully turned it around and around. "It's clay, porcelain, possibly, hand-sculpted, I guess. Nice job. Color's intense. That took patience and time, several firings. Might be original. The glaze's pretty. Did I answer everything?"

The sarcasm annoyed her, more so because he probably thought he'd get by with it with Susan there. "You talk to your students that way? I had somebody else look at it already, and he said he saw a mark, but he wasn't sure, and I don't want to tell you where, because it might not be anything."

He shrugged. Susan took the sphere from him and stood under the glaring fluorescent light with it, turning it around, her nose almost against the surface. " 'X V I I I' on one of those little things there. Lower down, 'X I I I.' Roman numerals."

"Eighteen and thirteen. 1813, the year?"

"It wasn't made in 1813. An eccentric way of numbering, like a print?"

"Eighteenth of thirteen prints? That's not right," Sara disagreed.

"Thirteen of eighteen, though…"

"People don't do sculptures like they do prints," Charlie interrupted. "You through guessing? It's probably just something the person who made it put there. Maybe he just made the one. Or maybe not. And since it was given without a name card, you'll probably never find out, unless that person wants you to. So toss it, or donate it, or just enjoy it."

She turned from him to begin the repacking when Susan took it from her.

"That how you've been hauling it around?"

"That's how it was given to me."

"Okay, well, don't keep hauling it around in that flimsy box. I'll find something better."

She vanished into Charlie's studio classroom; cabinet doors slammed, opened, as she rummaged. Charlie kept touching the sphere, gently, as if it were a small animal he was stroking; he glanced at her with that bemused expression. She always felt sympathy followed by irritation when he looked at her that way, passed her in the hall and frowned as if she were a student who'd not finished a project on time for him. I'm not responsible for your life, she wanted to say but never did. It wouldn't change anything now, for either of them. And at any rate maybe he wasn't comparing the two of them....

"Do you need help?" she called, but Susan was already returning with a sturdy carton.

"If you're gonna keep dragging it around with you, do take care of it. Charlie didn't say so, because apparently he's on the rag today." That wrung a quick laugh from Sara. "This could've been done by someone who's got a reputation already. Or maybe it's an older piece, somebody who's not around anymore, and the person *was* noteworthy. So it might be valuable. It wasn't thrown together by a child. So you don't want to break it."

"But maybe I do."

A malicious smile crossed Charlie's face. "Do it now. I'd like to watch."

Susan carefully packed the globe inside the carton; they walked outside, commenting about the sky and the weather as the panic doors clanged shut behind them.

"I'm sorry I asked you to drive out just for this, but I did want another opinion."

"We didn't mind driving over this morning, but this's a doodad, not a bomb." The embittered tone was in his voice again when they paused beside Sara's car.

"Funny you say that—it's what that guy told me: 'It's not a

bomb, lady!' Something like that. So you're thinking I wasted your time on it. I don't know why it bothers me. I'd be less anxious if I knew even who it was from. It just makes me feel…"

"Stalked," Susan suggested. "Like someone *wants* you worrying about it."

"Yeah."

"Then, donate it or something, like Charlie said. Out of sight, out of mind. But it really is lovely, and I think, myself, I'd just enjoy it. Take it as a joke on whoever gave it. Maybe if that person did want you uneasy, it'll be payback if you're not."

"But they'll never know that."

"Or they might. They could be somebody you know, waiting for a reaction from you. Expecting a 'thank you.' "

"Oh, that definitely makes me feel better." She remembered what Neil had said; what he'd have done. "I don't like sneaky things. There's so much stuff going on right now."

"Oh, so you heard. What a piece of shit," Charlie remarked.

"Louise says she doesn't even read the 'Arrests' section. She says she doesn't want to know who's out on bail, or what they're accused of. Once in a while I feel that way, too. Is that wrong?"

"Yes, it's wrong," Charlie said. "You have to know. You have to find out these things. You realize, he's been talking up a run for councilman? Go home and read today's online comments. Lynne Houston's got plenty to say. And that lousy lawyer defending him…"

Sara wanted suddenly to leave. "Let's all eat sometime with the kids. Thanks for letting me talk it out, trying to make me be sensible." Leaving the parking lot, she waved, and relief washed over her to be going. At one time Charlie had been Matthew's friend.

THE COLLEGE WAS past the east edge of town; to get back to the little house she'd bought from Neil after Cary was born—the one he always liked to hold over her head, as he'd suggested yesterday—she returned through Mooresville, past the fabric and hobby shop Lynne Houston owned. Past the music store Andy McGowan operated. Andy had an agreement with the high school and college bands, tuning instruments, supplying parts, which had kept him afloat some years ago, when things had been really hard. Past a couple of new boutiques, shoe stores, the ice cream shop.

The grocery that William Sykes, Lynne's brother, had managed to keep open and which was now flourishing again.

Impulsively, she circled around a couple of blocks and cruised slowly past Liberto's, where the Sunday-after-church crowd had taken over the sidewalk in a pleasant scene of temporary camaraderie. She waited for the light to change. The two hulking, plain neighbors loomed on either side. Both owned by Neil, both officially for sale but not really: If your price was high, too high, you weren't trying to make a sale. She'd never asked Neil about that, so he might not realize she even knew, but she did; word got out in a small town.

Someone behind her beeped impatience. She drove on through the green light.

Ever since the first book was published—years back, not long after Cary was born, so she liked to think of the two events as connected genesis—she'd been uncomfortable wearing what Louise called her "famousness." Every two or three months someone asked for a public endorsement from her. Neil, in his lawyer mode, had said she should let herself be used—he'd raise his brows suggestively—and offered to vet every request for her. And she'd let him do the early ones.

When the Preservation Association approached, she waved him off. His mother Sally was involved with the group, and it felt too conflicted. She read everything she could—regulations, suggestions, requirements...all easily-found documents. She asked for minutes from two previous years, so she could see who'd appeared at the meetings requesting help. The officers grudgingly let her go through those things. They'd have been happier if she just lent her name to the list of board members and showed up, silent and smiling, at an occasional meeting. She knew this because Neil had told her. He'd had dinner with his mother and Reg one evening when it came up:

"All you old broads see each other every day, got a club for everything. Same old same old. You should take advantage of local talent."

"Such as that woman you're seeing?" Reg asked him.

"Not just her, but, then, why not. She's lived here as long as we have."

"We don't want people who're all about self-promotion." Sally's glare was frosty. "They only interfere with us."

"She won't interfere," he said.

Sara suspected he hadn't told her everything about that meal. "Sweetie, they just want your name. You don't have to do the work. In fact, they don't *want* you to do the work. And they'd *really* like you to stay out of the files. When I told you to do your research, I didn't mean go this far."

But she'd ignored him and made copies of the minutes and showed up for every meeting, alarming the members for a while until they realized they could shove onto her now the job of explaining restoration, rehabbing, preserving. If you wanted a historical designation, you had to work your way down a long list of forms, maps, descriptions, significance, condition of the building. Sara studied and learned about all of it, repeated it to people who attended meetings and wanted to find out how to redo one of the old places....

Back home, she found Louise reading the Sunday paper and Cary moping around the kitchen, opening cabinets, the refrigerator, the pantry. She fended off the complaint before Cary put it into words.

"Today'd be a good day to eat in town."

Cary's face brightened, and, actually, so did Louise's. She laid down the paper, went to the hall mirror, and patted her hair.

"Italian?" Sara asked.

Cary had sauntered toward her room to gather up whatever she thought she needed, but stopped, turned an odd look her way. "Again?"

They formed another triangle, she realized, three points angling off in separate directions. "Well, where, then?"

Cary frowned. "I don't mind, I guess. Another family meal." She flipped her hand as if swatting away a bug. "Whatever." She went down the hall to her room.

"We'll just have a salad for supper." Sara turned to Louise. "Did she tell you what's bothering her?"

"I'll let *her* say."

Louise had a code of ethics: She'd raise hell at Cary about leaving her shoes in the living room, or picking up her dirty clothes, but she wouldn't rat her out on serious stuff.

A cool rain began drifting out of the sky after they ate; and as if the drops sliding down the car windows offered sympathy to Cary, she blurted out her problem.

There would be another company picnic next Friday, when she'd be at Matthew's house, and he expected her to go with him and Jennifer. She'd done those things when she was a kid—this meant three years ago, when Matthew started working there, Sara knew, but she said nothing about that. Sometimes there'd been other people Cary's age, which made it bearable, but now, no other parents made *their* teenagers go, and it was unfair for Matthew to expect it of her; she'd be the oldest of the younger people, she was sure, and she wasn't going to babysit all the toddlers whose parents turned them loose, as they did at the picnics. And she'd talked with her friend Allie to see if she'd go, because her mother worked there, too, but Allie didn't want to, and her mother wouldn't make *her*; so it appeared she, Cary, would be the only teenager. And Dad had insisted she *was* going, and it was just to make him look like an involved father.

Louise, sitting in the front with Sara, was silent.

"Let me think about it."

Cary seemed shocked, then aggrieved, at Sara's failure to offer her a way out, and lapsed into sullenness and took sanctuary again in her room when they got home.

Louise sorted the ads from other sections of the newspaper and rustled them about. The rain had picked up a little, making the living room darker, too dark to read without a light. Sometimes Louise would take the circulars, the community sections, and withdraw to the brightly-lit kitchen on Sunday afternoons, but today she stayed with Sara and shifted the pages around. At last Sara brought it up: "So what's *your* opinion?"

"I'm not her parent; I don't have to make the decisions," Louise retorted, as if Sara had poked her.

"OK, sorry." She made as if to leave the room, knowing how they played the game, what move to make next.

"But if I were, I'd agree with her," Louise added. "You know how it felt when you were fourteen. To be made to hang out with the old folks."

Sara waited. Louise moved a cell-phone ad to one side and studied it carefully.

"But," she went on, "she has to figure out sometime or other you just do some things you don't want to do. This is one of 'em. It won't kill her to spend the evening over there."

"She'll be horrible this week, brooding about it."

"Not if you tell her you'll go somewhere on spring break. Let her bring her friend, too."

"That's bribery."

"Yeah." Matter-of-fact; and that was the end of it. She began picking up the widely-distributed pieces of newspaper.

"OK. I'll talk to her."

"You do what you think you should." And in a moment, Sara heard her leafing through the circulars in the kitchen. The sound complemented the patter of the rain upon the windows, gentle little noises as if fingers outside were also touching the house.

She took her phone and tapped out a message to Matthew: ***Cary's going to the picnic and won't argue anymore, so back off and act grateful to her; that's how to handle her.***

He'd always made himself pleasant and indispensable to his bosses but dropped the act with her and Cary, because it was an act and not a natural thing to him. He'd worked for MTE ever since the CEO quietly bought up most of Ransome Moore's pine plantation and built the small engineering branch here. All of Mooresville, maybe except Ransome himself, had been incredulous to learn its package offer, with tax incentives and agreement to upgrade the infrastructure, had been accepted by a large corporation; and, like Matthew, employees had discreetly submitted resumés, defecting from the local companies.

Ransome, still trying after all those years to atone for sins he'd committed, moved with his wife to one of the other places he owned. He told her he'd done the best he could for the town now, with this sale; it was up to MTE and the sons and daughters of the people who used to run everything to figure it out from then on. Just as she'd always done, Regina heard him without thinking too much about what he meant, and nodded and moved on with him. Wilburn closed his "Fresh Grab Go" market and took over one of those businesses he and Ransome owned near Tennessee. Frank married a woman he met in college, and left the state; Emily moved to the capital and worked for a lobbyist there.

Waiting for Matthew to reply to her text, Sara considered the irony for a moment: Nobody of the family that had named it lived in the town anymore.

Her phone buzzed. **I'm not going to baby her.**

She shouldn't have to tell him how to parent. She shook her head impatiently and tapped back: ***Just do it, and everything'll be***

OK. Do you really want another fight? Pick your battles.

There was no response that time. She scrolled down through the calendar and reminded herself of the Preservation Association meeting tomorrow at lunch. It was Monday again.

4

CARY WAS OLD enough to know she was being manipulated, Sara realized when she started talking about beaches. She saw the unyielding look on her face and changed tactics: "Matthew wants you to go to that thing on Friday. You'll already be at his house. If you can't negotiate him out of it, try to have a good time, and I'll take you and Allie, if her mother'll let her go with us."

Cary was skeptical. "No strings? No matter what?"

"I said we'd go if you went to that picnic. I didn't put conditions on it." Oh, boy, will he regret this, Sara thought, watching Cary's eyes get squinty and the edges of her mouth lift a little. "But instead of being obnoxious, there're ways you can make him think twice next time about making you go."

Cary gave her a sideways glance as she left the kitchen to brush her hair one more time. Sara took her to school every morning, a concession to Louise's anxiety, and either she or Louise picked her up in the afternoons. Five years ago Cary would emerge from the car, smiling modestly towards the envious faces of her little friends, whose parents made *them* ride the bus or walk a few blocks; but now she was counting days if not minutes until she could drive herself. And she had Sara drop her off down the street a little.

Sara always went straight home afterwards. Waiting for inspiration didn't work, as she'd prated to Deborra over and over; she had to keep a routine, but some days she had to force it—as now, when in spite of her resolve she found herself pulling from the shelf the carton Susan had given her. From above, the sphere looked like an eye, staring at her...nice image to put into her thoughts—and probably, tonight, her dreams. She closed the carton and put it back in the closet.

Louise edged past her open door at the sound of the closet shutting. "I have an appointment in town this morning. See you later."

Sara drank more coffee and graded papers she'd assigned the small class; it wouldn't take too long to finish them. Matthew had mocked her stipend. But he was shortsighted, and she was playing the long game: If she kept teaching until Cary graduated from high school, Cary'd get free tuition. That was something to think of. College was expensive.

Cary'd probably end up wanting to go somewhere else....

In a while she dressed for the meeting. When they'd asked her to join, six or seven years ago, she'd been intimidated. Nora Burkes, Sally Griffin, Regina Moore, Lindsay Mason—those women were the officers, people she'd never been around, growing up, had nothing in common with now. She'd suspected Neil had something to do with her invitation, even before he admitted it. It had bothered her for a while, knowing they wouldn't have considered her if he hadn't—they wouldn't have; she knew that, and sometimes she thought she ought to decline, on principle.

Eventually they realized they'd have to invite a few men, too, because it was the way things worked now, they were dismayed to learn: Begging regular people for project money meant those people would expect to be represented in the organization. So, a retired educator; a former vice president of the college; Don Liberto, after they first inducted Lisa, because, after all, he did own one of the buildings in the downtown revitalization area... These people and a few others dropped in now and again to find out if anything was going on. Don seldom showed up, nagged Lisa instead to attend and give him a report; and Sara knew Lisa made him ask her about it several times, later, payback for having to go. Don's excuse was he had a restaurant to run. But Dominic had disliked David and Reg, whose office loomed on the other side of the street, and who, he believed, had just as soon he not live in Mooresville, if it were not for his eatery.

After Regina and Ransome sold their land to MTE, people said the group *should* include some of those people, too. Nora couldn't think up a legit reason not to. It went down as it had at Parks and Recreation: longtime citizens smiling, concealing resentment, at unfamiliar faces.

"But, after all, our goal is preservation of the older parts of our community at large," Nora intoned in a private executive session. "The new folks are part of the community now and that's that...."

Then she moved that the meetings be changed to a daytime hour, so a light lunch could be served—as if this were an unrelated item. Lindsay pointed out in her breathy voice that it was inconvenient for those new people to get off work and drive into town.

"Well, we can't please everybody, can we?" Nora said.

Sara found out about that meeting only because Nora told David, and he'd never been able to resist gloating about something he considered a win, and told it to Mark and Reg, who passed it on to Neil.

She glanced in her closet, peeking upward at the box on the shelf, then away. She could wear a suit, as Nora and Sally generally did, but that wasn't her image, and she didn't want them to think her a sycophant, or that she'd been *grateful* for their allowing her membership. And the hair...she gazed at it and decided to let it hang, the big grey streak blazing on the front. Maybe they thought that was what artists did. Maybe she should get that part bleached out even wider. That would get their attention.

Louise returned as she was leaving. "Do I need to get Cary from school today?"

"No. I should have time; not much on the agenda."

Hearing the locks click on the door behind her, she smiled.

THERE WERE CANAPÉS from the new little diner on the other side of town whose owners were willing to cater to small gatherings. Canapés and, of course, sweet tea, and coffee. Sara chose water.

She always carried a notebook in which she'd scribble from time to time; it gave her the look of being busy, and resulted in her being left alone. She knew the routine, anyway. At some point Nora would ring a little bell that meant grazing time was over and the officers and board members present that day should take their places at the head table. The secretary would read minutes of the last meeting. Nora would go through excruciatingly correct parliamentary procedure to get the minutes accepted into record. She'd beam at everyone in the room and ask about the status of old business. It always made Nora happy when form was followed.

Old business today, as usual, included funding and how to grow the association's bank account so they could actually award grants themselves to projects they decided were worthy. Sara'd heard this many times and always tuned out most of it. Through Neil she knew the officers could fund an entire small project themselves—they had the money—but they'd been advised it would look bad, would seem they'd bought control. So fundraising was a pointless item of every meeting's agenda, and Nora always brought up that topic with the mien of someone making funeral arrangements.

Once, early on, Sara assumed an innocent-of-politics expression and addressed Nora: "Get David to donate that little storefront he owns on Third Street to us, he could take a charitable deduction and a loss on it and we'd raffle it off, sell tickets statewide, with a minimum bid required, and the buyer has to rehab it and run a business there. David would get tax credits himself," she'd added, "and so would the new owner."

The silence following her suggestion that day had been profound. Nora gazed uncomprehendingly at her.

"Could they do that?" Lindsay wondered, her eyes wide.

Sally smiled: "David could've already had tax credits if he wanted to open a shop. So could Reg."

Sara had at first thought her point was misunderstood. "Yes, but we're always trying to find fundraisers, and this would be one, it might stir interest from businesses outside the area, and we'd have a visible example of how to use an old building—*another* example, besides just Lisa and Don's," she'd added, motioning towards Lisa, who was in attendance. Lisa tilted her head sideways, knowingly, her lips just slightly upturned in a smile.

"We'd have to accept whoever won the raffle," Nora answered smoothly. "It might not be a situation we were comfortable with. What if the owner wanted to open a strip bar?"

Several people murmured.

"Yeah, I know what you mean, but you could avoid that up front by stipulating what the winner couldn't do. We do have zoning laws."

Nora's gaze was unwavering. Sara felt uneasily that she hadn't communicated somehow. She glanced at Lisa who lifted her brows a little.

"Well, it's an interesting idea. Maybe we'll try it sometime. I'll mention it to David." Nora moved smoothly to discuss other strategies.

"Silent auctions, little crystal cups that have 'Mooresville

Preservation Association' etched on them," Lisa scoffed later that day as she and Sara sat in Don's upstairs office, drinking wine. "I knew that was coming. And you should've. You gotta understand, they don't *want* outside businesses here, and they're also not keen on new ideas, either. They're just delighted with how Don and his pop fixed up our place, but we've been here all along. They think we don't have any surprises for them. Surely you knew that, before."

She had. And ever since that meeting, she'd kept silent during fundraising-discussion time. Lisa drove her home a little drunk that afternoon, and she hid from Louise on the patio, nursing a mug of coffee till the wine wore off.

So today when the group finished thinking about raising money, and no decision having been made, she looked up to face the twenty or so people in the room and ostentatiously closed her notebook with a soft rustle of pages. That was her way of letting them know she was listening now, a sort of quiet protest statement, but if Nora took the hint, she didn't let on, and with only the tiniest squint of her eyes did she acknowledge she'd heard the notebook close. There was an official agenda. By the rules, people were supposed to have requested time to make a presentation. But after fundraising discussion, protocol wasn't always followed if Nora didn't feel like it, and it seemed today would be one of those times. "Does anyone have something to bring up?" she asked cheerfully.

A man raised his hand; Nora nodded.

He and his wife were new to town. They'd bought the old Jenkins place on Windsor Avenue. They'd always wanted an older house to live in—they had such character. They wanted to know how to get a historic designation, what kind of work they could do to the house, what could they not do...

Nora froze her smile on her face. She hated those bureaucratic details; she only wanted to hear about people's interior decorating. And she resented new people buying the old properties, anyway. She turned to Sara, who leaned forward and began the spiel, the process of documenting historical significance, uniqueness, the questions of whether the structure was in jeopardy, which, oddly, might help, she told them: Things might move faster if it was. She broke the bad news that there wouldn't be large grants from the government, something everybody always seemed to think they'd get. The couple's faces fell. But there were tax credits under certain circumstances. They looked hopeful. She mentioned where to get the forms, said if they wanted to pay a consultant to do the paperwork and research, there was a list. They interrupted to ask if she could do the job. "I could if I had time," she told them, "but I don't."

There were other things: They could alter the inside of their building, except not too drastically and not changing the original footprint. Outbuildings should be preserved, if possible. And if they were going to do the paperwork on their own, there were online examples they could follow. She gave them a sheet she'd prepared herself, a list of resources and people who'd do the documentation. They were grateful.

So was Nora. "Anything else?"

Several people she wasn't used to seeing on a regular basis were there today—not just the usual spectators who dropped in for the canapés and conversation. One of them raised his hand slightly, actually, just his forefinger, almost pointing at the front table. Nora nodded coolly at him. "Yes? Please tell everybody your name."

Sara knew his face from the couple of times he'd been on TV. Seated three chairs to Nora's right, she realized Nora's body went stiffer as he said, "Ken Thomas, with MTE. Glad to attend today." He smiled around. "Just came to ask if any other work's been scheduled in the downtown district."

"Happy to finally meet you face-to-face, Mr. Thomas. I'm not sure what you're referring to. The district went through that a few years ago, you're aware, and last year this association was instrumental in placing markers downtown—"

"Yes, I know all that," he interrupted, "but I mean, what's been done *lately* to get the owners of those derelict structures in the district to do something about their buildings? I mean, I understand the group here has no legal authority, but are you putting any pressure on the owners to motivate them? Or giving them incentives?"

Lisa was very interested in her nails and kept her eyes down.

Nora had slowly raised her hands to the table in front of her and clasped them together, interlacing the fingers as she continued to stare at Thomas. Sara watched her face in profile: no movement, no expression. "We've covered this before with your company."

"First, it's not 'my' company, but—"

"With Mr. Matheson. In writing. And with you, by phone."

Sara saw Nora tap her right forefinger one time against the back of her left hand, as if tallying something up.

"Yes, your organization did send a letter. I have it with me." He produced a black portfolio and began removing some documents.

"We have copies, of course," Nora said, and tapped once more.

Thomas glanced at her, his chin lowered—a baseball pitcher staring down the batter before the windup, Sara thought. "I'm sure you do. But I have them right at hand, and I believe you said..." He held a page in front of him. "Let me read..." He adjusted his glasses downward a little. "Says, 'The Mooresville Preservation Association does not retain authority to enforce compliance of the owners of these structures with our goals and guidelines.' Now *there's* a good legal sentence for you. But then, you do have lawyers handy to run these things past."

The whole room had become quiet and absorbed; even the people who'd wandered in today for refreshments were attentive.

"I'm not sure what your point is."

He smiled, laying the paper down. "We know you can't make people do things. And you know MTE isn't trying to push this organization around. No matter what you may want people to think."

"We don't—" she started indignantly.

"I've heard the talk, maybe not from you or the other officers, but it's out there. We have our own interest in the community, too; improving things helps MTE as much as it does Mooresville. I'm just wondering if some incentives might motivate, help, people do the work, admittedly hard work. Like, maybe these folks." He gestured at the owners of the Jenkins home, who smiled at him and perked up.

"We've discussed *this*, as well."

Sara wondered when they'd discussed it; she attended all the meetings, to keep her board membership authentic. She'd never before heard it brought up in a public manner—well, Nora and this man *had* alluded to letters, phone calls.... She opened the notebook and jotted down a question about that to bring up later. Nora turned a meaningful glance at her before continuing:

"Every individual in the historic district is free to do what they can with the buildings, within Department of Archives guidelines, you know. Some have. Don and Lisa did it on their own. We wish we had funds to give owners—"

"Sure, everybody loves Liberto's. We all eat there, don't we. But, then, the others you mention…MTE's offered several times to provide grants to help with them. Under your auspices, not ours. It's a community thing for us—"

"We all know about MTE's plans to improve us. Our position, which we've explained, is that to maintain our independence, we can't accept money from a corporation with local ties."

Sara wrote that down, too.

"Are records of donations available to the public?"

Nora unclasped her hands, then entwined them again quickly.

"I've seen the quarterly statements. But, lists of who actually contributes. You *are* a nonprofit, so I believe you're required by law to give those documents to people who ask for them. Freedom of Information Act, or something?"

"We don't have to do that if privacy issues are involved."

"But are they?"

Nora brought her hands up and rested her chin on them. "We don't have deep, dark secrets, Mr. Thomas."

"Excuse me, Nora. If you'd like, let me explain to Mr. Thomas what we can and can't enforce."

Nora's hands went to the table, palms down as she turned a cold look at Sara.

"Oh, it's not necessary," He gestured, as if brushing it away. "I'm sure I can find what I need without bothering any of you. And thank you all the same, Ms. Wells. Actually," and he stood up, glancing at his watch, "I have to get back to the office. I just popped in to hear if anything had changed. MTE's sincere about the offer." He faced each officer and board member. "A vibrant, revitalized downtown can't do anything but help us, all of us. MTE's brought employment into the community where it was experiencing high unemployment for a number of years. We're not going anywhere. It makes sense to work together and grow the area."

"Was this the presentation you planned to give?" Nora needled.

He smiled again. "Thank you for your time."

But he paused and approached Sara, laying down near her water glass a business card and a sheet from a notepad bearing the letters "MTE," on which there was some handwriting; then he left the room. Sally and Nora looked at each other, rolled eyes. Chairs shifted, scrubbed lightly on the floor as people squirmed. Sara stowed the MTE items in her notebook.

The meeting was off the rails. Sara intercepted cold glances as Nora wrapped everything up and took a step towards her; but Lisa was fast: "Nora, I need to ask you about an idea Don hatched the other day, those planters and the tables; he wanted your advice." Sara raised one finger to let Lisa know she owed her, and escaped before any of the officers could waylay her.

LATER, ON THE way to the parking lot, she read what he'd scribbled on the notepad page: "We'd like to commission you to do some artwork needed for a project that's stalled at the moment. I arrived too late to discuss it beforehand and didn't know if you'd be there, anyway. We'll be in touch." She clambered into the car and dialed the number he'd circled underneath his name and title: "Ken Thomas, Chief Financial Officer." A pleasant switchboard voice transferred her to the extension on the business card by the time she'd made the first traffic light.

"Well, I haven't been here even ten minutes. I appreciate your calling so soon."

"Did you show up today just to get me in trouble, Mr. Thomas?"

He laughed uneasily, but she was not mollified.

"I mean, first, I don't do commission work anymore. You'd know that if you'd done some research. And it didn't help for you to single me out. You could've sent me a letter, or just got my number by asking my former husband, who works there, I'm sure you know."

"I do know Matthew's one of our accountants. And, yes, he's mentioned you were married at one time. So, yes, I could've got your number from him. Would you've wanted him involved?"

"I don't know what you mean."

"Since you aren't married anymore, I guessed you don't share everything with each other. Maybe I guessed wrong. Maybe you'd prefer I pass things through him."

"No. But I don't do—"

"Yeah, you said—'commission work.' Just like that preservation group doesn't want outside funding."

She didn't like the dismissive tone in that. "I can suggest another artist I know." And Charlie would probably appreciate the job, she thought.

"I'd rather not go there yet. I tell you what, Ms. Wells. I'll make an hour on my schedule right now. Would you please—"

"No point; I'm not interested in—"

"Yes, you said, but would you please, as a favor, in return for my battle with Scarlett O'Hara a while ago, just drive out here and see what we need?"

She was sure he heard the chuckle that slipped from her, because he added, "You have another name for her?"

"Sometimes, but that one's pretty good. What makes you sure you don't want someone else for this job?"

"If you'll come out, I'll show you, you'll understand."

She checked the time. "I teach a class at college tonight, and I have to prepare, but I'll give you thirty minutes. But I'm leaving now, so get everything out for me to look at."

"Absolutely. I'll let them know at the gate. And, by the way, we recognize you're an established professional, so payment's negotiable."

She thought about that as she headed out: Was that meant to flatter her into doing this "stalled" project?

The drive to MTE took her down the highway that bisected Ransome Moore's old fields; but of course they weren't cultivated anymore. For a while, after Ransome had the trees planted, people watched the seedlings grow taller and gradually fill in the empty, flat land stretching away from town toward the west. But pines grew fast in the South, and in ten years a forest separated the town from the farm his family had owned so long. For what some people called a "pine barren," it was a pleasant departure from the endless crop rows that had ribboned from Moore Farms outward, and the developers for MTE's physical plant had left most of it alone, clearing out only near the approach to the main buildings. And, even there, the impression was of a group of structures that had long stood in that very place, with pine straw wisping over the sidewalks, and carefully-positioned plantings, set off by hauled-in boulders. They had wanted to blend in, Sara thought. And they did that part right, at least.

Ransome had kept horses, just to give Frank and Emily meaningful chores to keep them out of trouble—so he used to say as he had his lunch salad with friends downtown. The horses were nothing but a financial pit, and, he'd add, he wished somebody'd tell him why he kept hanging on to them, eat him out of house and home. But they'd seen him riding the animals in high-school homecoming parades through Mooresville, had watched him slip them treats and pat their flanks; they knew the truth. He'd kept the pastures green and manicured and, long ago, built a pond, which the CEO of the new company had decided not to fill in and even enhanced with more of the plantings and some picnic tables, and a pavilion under the pines.

Sara had driven out this way before, a couple of times, indulging in a sort of nostalgic indignation, the way she felt whenever a lovely old Victorian house was demolished: This had been Moore Farms, and now it was gone, even the decades-old house the Moores had occupied, and the barns, except for the last one Ransome had added. But parking in the visitor lot, she glanced around and wondered why Cary objected to being here a few hours one night. Free food—that's what she'd tell her when she got home: You'll get free food and have nice scenery.

And the trip to the beach.

During the euphoria of having an actual business move into the area instead of out—and the resentment that that company had got breaks the old ones never had—Rheta'd done a profile on them, had described some of their personnel policies. "Weird shit," she separately remarked to Sara. "Everybody has to work reception duty sometimes, I was told, to keep them socialized. Like taming feral cats." No one she interviewed wanted to own that rule, and more than one person had stolidly stared at her, grimly praised it, even when she lifted her brows in disbelief. Rheta could adopt a bland, neutral expression that emanated trustworthiness. She'd gone to Ken Thomas and got him to admit it was his idea, after years of having to clean up his boss's diplomacy failures. Twenty minutes with her smoothly abetting, nodding him along, encouraging his betrayal of confidential company policy, had softened him up, and he told her what he'd preached at Matheson: "They have to deal with the public sometimes! And so do you, and I'm tired of covering your ass, and theirs. It won't hurt 'em to sit up front for one damn hour once a week, learn to be nice to whoever comes in, meet people in the area."

Rheta had published the last sentence, as Thomas ruefully discovered on reading the newspaper profile (at least she'd left out the "damn")—and the piece confirmed Mooresville's suspicion that the new company was run by a bunch of elitist old hippies from the North; who else would make perfectly good engineers suffer in a receptionist's job?

Sara wasn't surprised when the guy today was uninterested when she approached him, simply taking her name and repeating it questioningly on the phone: "Ken? Sara Wells?"

So much for her "famousness," she thought wryly. And if she told Louise about this, her aunt would be contrarily angry that she *hadn't* been recognized.

Thomas had a presentation laid out on a long table beside his desk. He greeted her and stood aside, let her glance over everything for a few minutes. He'd pulled back both of the wide doors that opened into his office; that made it seem like an extension of the spacious hallway. She noticed a few other doors open as well and wondered cynically if that, too, was a company policy.

Seeing her glance at the corridor, Thomas appeared to understand: "We like for people to come in and give input on projects."

"Couldn't that become chaotic? I couldn't work that way."

"Well…it's not for every stage of every project. We encourage it at certain points…the beginnings, for instance. Or if we have a problem later on. Otherwise, people could sit at a desk all day and never say one word to anybody."

She picked up a sheet from the table. Deborra's rumors had been correct. "Okay, so I heard about this last week."

"How? We haven't started publicizing—"

"Yeah, well, a friend of mine…you know, things get out in a small town…" She didn't want to tell him, and paused, thinking she'd sound pretentious if she said, *I was doing an interview…* "So as I see it, this'll be a sort of book, for company families?"

"Yes. For children, actually. That was why—"

"You wanted a kids' book person." She scanned one page. "Activities to do as they read."

"Yes, and online things—you see the links we've put in—" he pointed—"and, here, we want to foster a little reading competition. The idea is, they complete the activities, and we'll get some outside group to judge winners, offer prizes after everybody's through…"

"…so you have some books suggested. And with the titles you'd want illustrations…"

"Something like, a child imagining what he's reading from the books. Yes."

"And this?" She pointed to the "Last" section. "What does 'Paint Pots' mean?"

He grimaced. "Me, I don't really see how this'll work. But the boss wants it and he's willing to spend the money to do it. If it can be done." He hesitated, shrugged. "He remembers from his childhood having little, um, coloring books, with dried embedded watercolor paint, that he says he used right on the page…"

She laughed. "Mr. Thomas, you didn't do that kind of thing, am I right?"

"Ken—call me Ken."

"No, if I get used to that, I'll slip up one day at the preservation meetings and they'll all think I'm colluding with you. After today, they probably will, anyway. Now, about this: I see what he wants. It'll probably be expensive. But doable. Will the kids use their fingers to paint?"

"No. Each of the books will come with—"

"—a little paintbrush in the spine," she interrupted. "So they'll be spiral-bound, and the final page'll be heavier paper, and the kids'll pull it off after they paint and—"

"—we'll put it on display for a while. Exactly." He gestured at the table. "You understand the vision."

"Good presentation. Easy to see."

"You're grudging about it."

"Not at all. It's good. You could even include a cheap little tray of actual watercolors with each book, instead of doing the paint chips. Might be less expensive. You should look into that."

He took a pencil and scribbled a note. "So you might agree to do illustrations?"

"Maybe, yes. It's, what, a summer thing for the employees' kids or something? Keep them learning and creating while they're not in school?"

"Not just our kids. We plan to distribute copies in the community, too."

"Oh, my God, that's gonna cost a fortune!"

He grimaced. "Yes, it will."

"Why would he do this—tax write-offs?"

"There *will* be advantages there, but it wasn't his first goal." She met that assessing look head-on. He continued: "There're kids who don't get the benefits that parents who work here can take home. Mr. Matheson's…committed to this town."

"I know it's part of your job to rep him as well as you can. I don't have a problem with that, I have to do that, too. But it really does start to look like an ad campaign selling *him*."

"But if it is, you say you understand…."

"Is that what it is?"

She knew what crossing your arms meant, knew he didn't like the question.

"If I told you it was not, would you believe me? I don't think so."

"You know the library has a summer reading program."

They had come to the moment, she thought, and stared each other down. "We're not trying to crowd that out," he said. "Kids can do both."

"But yours'll be flashier and more fun."

"That's a bad thing?"

"Likely to cut into the program at the library."

"They can up their game, too. We actually talked with them about all this, and they got on board pretty fast."

"Oh, did they." No one had mentioned it to her the last time she'd done a reading there.

"Do they usually sign *you* on to do things with them?"

And that tilt of his head meant he suspected she resented losing her place. "Are you asking if they pay me? They don't. I volunteer."

"We know."

She started to smart back, "Oh, you know—" But, if she was to believe the note with the little blue sculpture, it seemed everybody did know. "Okay, well, you're aware a lot of kids, especially out in the country here, they don't all have access to computers, right? Or Internet?"

"We've thought of that. We have a few ideas."

She wished she hadn't had breakfast with Neil on Saturday, didn't remember he'd warned her against being exploited. "I have to think about this. I don't sign onto everything people want me to do. A lot of times, it turns out a group just wants to use a name to trade on."

An impatient sound escaped his mouth. He reached as if to take the papers she held. "Considering this isn't a money-making enterprise for us—in fact, the opposite; I'll tell you, I've used up a lot of paper showing what it's going to cost—considering that, I'm not sure how 'using' your name—" she could almost see the quote marks—"is relevant. If you don't want to do it, give me your other person's name, and we'll talk to her, or him. But me, I'm getting tired of everybody always suspecting our motives. Mr. Matheson wants to be a partner in the community, that…it's his motive, if I can use that word again. I'm tired of the town putting on this show of being bought, against their better judgment. Like a kept woman."

" 'Kept woman'? Wow, that's inappropriate."

"I guess I'm still in Scarlett mode. I'm sick of hearing it from y'all."

" 'Kept woman.' Please. And don't try that 'y'all' on me," she scoffed.

"You know what? I grew up outside Atlanta. Go, Bulldogs. For years we *owned* Scarlett. The good and the bad, you know. I make no apologies. I am what you see."

She winced. "Sorry."

He took the pages from her and began spreading them on the table again, keeping his back to her. "So you can jump to conclusions, too. The idea here is to give something of value, a community-wide thing for as many kids as we get interested in it, participating in it. And, by the way, we're going to donate some computers to the library for kids to check out, who don't have one at home to use."

"That's commendable. Really." She looked at him carefully for the first time: nice button-down shirt, tie, crisply creased pants. Graying hair, thin on top. Wire glasses. A nerd.

"My wife and I would've loved having this kind of thing for our kids, when they were little. I never thought I was artistic. Maybe I just didn't get exposed the right way or something. That's not self-pity; it's just a fact. Not everybody has access to art—you know that, like not everybody has access to their own computer, as you said. Maybe as a kid I would've loved painting, or whatever. But here I am, now…. They hired me a good many years ago, before there was talk about moving a branch down South. It was under, let's say, different management then. Different philosophy, work environment. So on this project, they asked me what would be a good thing the company could do, something for community involvement, fun, but also beneficial. Since I was Southern, I'd have an *insider's* opinion." She heard cynicism in the word, as if it had been spoken to him one time too many. "This—" he nodded at the table—"was to be—no, *is*, because it'll happen whether you're involved or not—it's us showing we belong here as much as you. We just need..." he fumbled for a word: "The old people used to call it a 'proper introduction'."

"That's what I said—why you need me. Famousness."

"What?"

She gestured randomly. "That's what my aunt calls it. Is that why you were there today at the meeting—you want me to endorse *all* your plans? Not just this, but the ones involving them, too?"

He approached a large window and adjusted the blinds, darkening the room a little. "You bring that up. I said, I didn't know if you'd even be there. But can I ask you, why's nothing happening downtown? Why's everything just stopped? We've donated to Parks and Recreation, helped with the historical district, other things you wouldn't know about, and, now, nothing. We don't get it. What're we missing? I see you don't know, either.

"So, why'd I go today? Because, again, they think I know how to get along with y'all. With 'all of you,' excuse me. We made Nora Burkes and your group a generous offer. She turns it down. Every time."

"You did call her husband out."

"Mrs. Griffin's, too, and *her* son. Though I didn't mention names, actually."

"But, 'lawyers'? Everybody knew who you meant."

"Or maybe it's because I don't look like them."

"Because you're a Black man? I don't think that's it."

His gaze at her was cold, stolid. "Whatever. They can have their little club, and keep their attitude, too. It's just gut resistance. Not even with a good reason behind it. Sooner or later something'll give. We'll wait it out. It could take a while—doesn't matter. We aren't going anywhere. However..." He paused. "This project means too much. We want it to work. So who's the other artist?"

"This is firm—it'll happen, regardless?"

He took a folder off his desk, brandished it at her. "Contract."

It was very quiet in his large office. She remembered the open doors and wondered how many people were listening. "Your card says 'CFO'," she said, "not 'artistic director.' I mean, the historic district, and now this…"

"The accountants answer to me, including Matthew, you know, and they don't need direction 24/7, and that frees me to do some things the company wants to sponsor. Some things I'm personally interested in. That's the way we work. And you're stalling." His smile was wry. "So, you or your friend?"

"I'll do it. I like the idea. And don't be concerned whether I'll do a good job."

"I won't. You're getting paid. We expect a good job. You okay being a bought woman?"

There was a sort of relief in his voice, and she rolled her eyes. "Sure. It'll be a first for me. And by the way, don't say that kind of thing to just anybody. I don't care if Scarlett, or your mama, or the owner of this place would've said it. And do me a favor. Don't come to the next meeting. I'll do what I can, but it can be hard sometimes to tear down a wall."

"Somebody just has to start plowing through." He handed her the folder after she gathered the pages again. "Look it over. Be sure, before you tell me definitely."

"Negotiable, you said?"

"To some degree. Read it. Get your lawyer to look at it. You must have someone for your book contracts, right? I'll have a copy emailed to his office, or hers. Who is it?"

"Neil Griffin."

Facepalm, she thought, as he wiped a hand slowly down from his forehead. She knew the word; Cary'd told her.

"He's a good lawyer," she added. "You need his email address?"

"Oh, I've got it."

Chuckling quietly, she put the descriptions into the folder with the contract and left through the pushed-back doors. A sudden busy-ness told her people had indeed been listening. Thomas had stepped in behind her; she waved him off and found another man escorting her out instead, a man with unruly gray hair hanging too long on his suit collar. Another of those socially inept engineers.

"Neil Griffin, huh?" His face was unsmiling. He held the door and followed her out to the parking lot, maintaining a couple of paces' distance between them so that she knew he was there but couldn't actually see him unless she turned around, which she would not do. She laid the folder on the passenger seat of her car, remembered she could be intimidating too, and turned on him.

"I didn't get your name," she said bluntly.

"Ron Matheson. Happy to meet you. I hope we can work together. Doesn't look promising, does it." He went back inside.

ON MONDAY EVENINGS when she was preparing to teach that class, she always made her own sandwich in advance and ate at the table by herself. Louise and Cary respected the routine, aware it helped her focus on the lesson she'd be teaching. Sometimes she'd come home afterwards and find the two of them watching a movie, eating popcorn, nothing to show they'd had anything like a nutritious supper, but she didn't lecture.

Tonight Cary met her at the door. "Are we still going to the beach?"

"One day, and you think I've changed my mind? Yes, we'll go. Have you talked to Allie? Should I talk to Allie's mother?"

"I'll do it."

Sara took a bottle of water from the refrigerator and picked up an apple. "If I halve it, you want some?"

"Sure."

One way to get fruit into a teenager. Cary slumped into the chair opposite Sara, eyeing the apple as Sara cored it. "I went out to MTE this afternoon." She told a summarized version of what had happened, just the part about the project. "...And long story short, I think I'd go, if I were you, for the food. And it's peaceful. So, yeah."

Cary bit into the apple. "It is kind of nice."

"So what's the problem then?"

She looked downward as she ate. "I'm not a baby, and I'm tired of him telling me things he thinks I have to do, just because he said them."

"You're almost there. Age-wise, legally. Maybe when you can choose, you'll decide you *want* to do some things with him."

Cary scoffed. "So how'd it go? What'd they do tonight?"

"Incorporating research into their stories." This class was about writing for nonfiction outlets, and she knew the college had hired her because of her famousness—she flinched at the thought again.

"Ew. Sounds like a term paper," Cary said. She yawned. "I'm going to bed, Mom. And I'll talk to Allie."

"So how was everything while I was away?"

"Oh, you know—same old same old."

She ambled off, calling backwards, "Oh, and Aunt Louise left the paper out. So there may be something you need to look at, or, something, I don't know. She's already in bed. It's what we do on Mondays. We have a pretty boring life, you know. I guess you'd say that's a good thing. Don't bother. I just did for you." Sara heard her mumble, "Love you," and her door shut.

5

SHE TOOK THE newspaper to her bedroom some time later, laying her satchel down in its usual place on her desk and stacking the papers from the other class on top, as she always did; to remind herself to grade them. After the rain on Sunday, the weather had turned chilly; she donned an old robe from the closet, glancing up at the closed box on the shelf.

"That's a shame," the man who gave it to her had said. She'd told him she didn't take gifts at face value, and he'd said that.

Leaning back against pillows in bed, she turned pages distractedly without reading more than the headlines. Cary said they had a boring life. She looked at the students' papers lying on her small desk. She did it that way every time she had things to grade, every single time. And her mornings, taking Cary to school. And her afternoons.

Oh, my God, she thought suddenly in a paroxysm of desperation, hands over her eyes.... Who had she been all these last years: Cary, or at least a copy of her, trying to think like Cary, talking like her so that—she told herself—she could communicate; or Louise, with her in-your-face bluntness, her rules, her routine.... She'd pushed back parts of herself to keep the schedule running, had managed to hold Neil at a very certain distance by not letting thoughts of who he was disturb her mind...and so who had she turned into—a part of all of them? Wasn't that what you had to do, to juggle the necessaries of the people in your life?

She breathed deeply and picked up the paper again.

Matthew had been almost pathologically OCD, straightening his shirts on their hangers in the closet so they made an absolutely symmetrical pattern, lining his shoes up by colors, each toe not a quarter-inch ahead of the next one. If she accidentally moved these things and he found them slightly off, he'd nagged her—never threateningly, just in that aggrieved tone of his. And sometimes she reacted to that by leaving her pants askew, the shoulders of her dresses almost but not quite sliding off onto the floor.

And that kind of thing hadn't helped; she knew it now. Escalating pettiness eventually got you to the War of the Roses. Kathleen and Michael hanging from the chandelier.

She looked down to find she'd gripped the edge of a page and torn the newsprint.

After the divorce a counselor trying to be relevant with catchy analogies had told her, "Cut the line. Quit reeling in your failures. Think of the good catches. Think of Cary."

…Cary, who, she suspected, was busy texting with Allie in the dark right now. Sara glanced at her watch: eleven o'clock. She'd check on her in ten minutes, tell her to go to bed. …Cary, conceived after all kinds of tests and several drugs had failed, making Sara feel it was her failure—and Matthew thought that, too. …Cary, whom she discovered growing inside her the same week she packed bags with Matthew's clothing and invited him to go on a long vacation, alone….

She was staring sightlessly at the newspaper again, her legs tense and stiff. She squeezed her eyes shut for a moment.

Cut the line. She started again on the first page.

An update on the representative's decision to begin his cancer treatments and his optimistic state of mind. A vote on building a skateboard ramp at the park. She turned the page to the obituaries and police reports. Nothing new there. In the section right after the editorial page she saw at last what must have drawn Louise's attention: Rheta's byline, R. C. Whitson.

"Businessman Has Questions for Local Preservation Group Meeting Today.

"Ken Thomas, the Chief Financial Officer of Matheson Technology Enterprises wants to know why some buildings in the historic district downtown remain in poor condition two years after the district was designated. 'People visit Mooresville when they have business with MTE, and they see the markers and the historical district and come back and ask us why we haven't assisted in rehabbing the area. We offer help, but help has to be accepted. And so far that hasn't happened.'

"MTE was instrumental in the district's receiving its historical designation. Thomas cited mutual benefits to the company as well as to the county and municipality."

In the quiet of her room Sara wondered when this story had been done. Rheta hadn't been at the meeting. She remembered identifying the faces that afternoon and, in the back of her mind, being relieved it was Jared Brown and not Rheta covering it. Pretending they weren't related was hard whenever they both showed up at the same place sometimes. But Rheta'd probably had the conversation with Ken Thomas several days earlier, maybe waited until today to file this story, so it would run after the meeting and prompt a little curiosity about what had happened. Then there'd be a piece tomorrow describing today's actual events. It was a strategy Rheta used to hook the repeat readers.

Thomas had asked her this afternoon to explain, if she could, why nothing was happening in the district. She'd started to tell him that he should *know*, being from the South, too; but he was from Atlanta, and Atlanta was just different from a small, inbred, rural town. And she'd never known for sure who was pulling the strings in Mooresville. She wasn't in that crowd.

She laid the newspaper down and went to get Cary off her phone. Padding softly past the desk, she glanced at the papers arranged over the leather case, and reached out to disarrange them just a little. Which was ridiculous. As if that would do anything to change her life... She gathered them up, tamped them into a straight rectangle and shoved them inside the satchel, and as she did, she saw the folder with the project materials and that contract. She hadn't even looked at it, not as she ate her sandwich earlier, not since she'd returned home from the class. And it wasn't because she'd forgotten about it: It had been irritating her like a tiny sore on the tip of her tongue. Did she just want to put it off, not think about it, let the decision to sign it, or not, evolve to the default "no" of missed deadline?

She hesitated, staring at the folder, then went down the hall to Cary's room and tapped on the door. "It's late."

"I'm *in* bed!" was the aggrieved response. Actually, too aggrieved—false grievance.

"I don't doubt that. But you have to sleep. Get off the phone."

The histrionic sigh could be heard through the door.

"Really, I mean it. Love you."

"All right." There was a brief silence, then, grudgingly, "Love you too."

The contract was standard stuff. She'd signed enough of them to know what it would have: a deadline, an amount payable to her, penalty if the deadline passed before she got done. A clause reserving the right of MTE to cancel if the work was unsatisfactory. In this one she was pleased to find a bonus if it was finished ahead of the deadline. The rest was a summary of the presentation Ken Thomas had put on that table earlier.

She decided not to have Neil look at it. She knew what she was doing, and, really, this one wasn't his business. She thought about that for a moment, knowing the truth was she didn't want him to find out yet.

Before turning off her lamp, she looked around the room one more time, reminding herself that without Neil she probably wouldn't have this house. Cary'd never known another.

But maybe they'd be all right somewhere else, too.

THOMAS CALLED THE next morning.

A few pleasantries, then: "Ms. Wells, I want to be sure you're going to do the project, because, if you're not, I need somebody else, right away."

"You remember, I did say yesterday I would. Haven't changed my mind."

The enthusiasm in his voice bothered her: "Great! The deadline won't be a problem? And can you do a few sketches for us to confirm we're on the same page?"

"Absolutely."

"We know everything's going fast. We intended to get it started before now, but—well, things came up. So here's something else you might think about: We have spaces in the child-care building that aren't being used right now—"

"Child-care building?" she interrupted. "What are you talking about?"

Her queasiness returned as he explained with scarce-hidden pride that MTE provided care for the employees' kids, if they chose to use the facility, and most did, he added, since it was on-site and excellent.

"Another of Ron Matheson's projects, huh."

The silence was terrible.

"I'm sorry. That was snarky," she apologized. "Go on."

But he waited a few more seconds before saying coolly, "That one was actually mine. My wife and I struggled to find good child care, back in the day. You do want to do this? Because we want commitment—"

"No, I didn't intend it to come out that way. Let's say…let's say it's a new thing for me, corporations being so concerned about their communities. Or maybe—" *Reboot*, she told herself silently. "Sorry. Go on, please."

"Hm." She heard a murmur in the background and realized someone else was in Thomas' office. "I'm disappointed you haven't already heard about the facility. But here's what I was *going* to say. There are a couple of spaces where kids can do inside things if the weather's bad. You could use one of them. They're not carpeted, they have access to bathrooms, water—industrial sinks in one of them."

"I usually work at home."

"I understand. I just thought, in light of the deadline, the time crunch…and would it be helpful to have real-life subjects to draw from? Wouldn't the work go faster that way?"

"Probably. All right. I'll bring the contract out later today, and I'll look at the rooms then. And, yes, it might be better to have a structured setting, since there *is* deadline pressure."

"Today? You've had Mr. Griffin look over it already?"

She heard another murmur in the background, and a grumbled laugh—not as if someone were amused, but scoffing. "I didn't ask him to look over it. It's straightforward. I know what I'm signing."

As soon as she'd said that, she hated the words—as if she were trying to convince herself as well as Ken Thomas.

"I have a couple of meetings I can't avoid, so I'll get someone from the front to show you around when you get here."

"Be there about four," she said and immediately disconnected, then thought, Damn, Louise'll have to get Cary.

Later, she drove out into the country again, past the pine forest, past the gatehouse, skirting the landscaped lake, into the parking lot with the wildflower plantings. She gave her name to the young woman at the reception desk, who did recognize her and buzzed someone else, handing her a "Visitor" sticker with her name. In a moment her guide appeared, Lillie, her ID said, and she was talkative. She had two children who came to MTE with her most days and stayed in the child facility, which was so handy because she could check on them if they didn't feel well, and it was peace of mind when the spring weather brought tornadoes because there was a shelter in the basement of every building.... Sara nodded now and then as the monologue continued. Lillie glanced at her watch before they walked outside, around the main building, and then into a cream-colored brick unit with large glass windows and colorful flat rugs. Children played under the supervision of workers wearing jeans and T-shirts that identified them as "MTE Kid Kare." Sara winced.

"This's one of the places they think you'd like," Lillie said, ushering her into a moderate-sized room with not much in it except a large utility table, a couple of stools and a chair or two, and the industrial sinks Thomas had mentioned. The outer wall was mostly glass; the view was into the pine forest that loomed beyond a trimmed lawn where a few older kids were climbing on playground equipment. Sara opened a door beside the sink and found a storage closet with other tables and chairs folded and stacked.

"This room doesn't have a door, you see," Lillie said. "But, on the other hand, any of these cabinets—" she gestured at the sink surrounded by storage units— "can be locked, and they'll get you a key."

"And the other room?"

Lillie checked the time. "I'll unlock it, Ms. Wells, but I have to be in a meeting with the other engineers in a few minutes. You feel free to look around. I'll fix the lock so you can just shut the door when you leave. Could you find your way out when you're through, please? Ken said for you to let him know tonight, or tomorrow. He said you have his card."

She thanked the younger woman. She could work here, in the room with the glass wall—clean, well-lighted.... There'd be kids' chatter and cries and goings and comings, but Thomas was right: There'd also be plenty of life models, and she wouldn't have to worry about messing up anything at home. She glanced into the second area, just to say she *had*, closed that door and went back to the larger one, imagining being in that space for hours at a time. It would get her out of the house, would make it impossible for her to leave her work and find Louise or Cary to chat with, as she did too frequently. And she'd have all those kids to draw.

That framed, doorless opening—it was a problem, but she

could live with it. She rolled her eyes: It seemed the whole place abhorred privacy.

She crept silently along the wide hall bisecting the building into crafts space on one side and play and nap areas on the other. When she walked by a room where a sign noted that three- and four-year-olds were there, one of the T-shirted supervisors looked up and smiled. Sara waved back. Passing another area marked "Toddlers", she saw six or seven babies playing with large blocks, stuffed animals, sturdy toy trucks and cars. She wondered if there was a nursery but didn't want to roam about too long: The Kid Kare workers in the Toddlers room had also stopped to stare at her. She pointed to her "Visitor" patch and hurried outside.

She wasn't sure she needed to sign out before she left. She probably just looked lost right then, standing aimlessly by her car. And there were windows, many windows on the front of the building, too, so at least some people were probably watching her indecision, perhaps even Matthew.... She threw her bag onto the front seat, returned to the main office, and asked the receptionist for a piece of paper and an envelope.

On the way home she thought about what she'd written and hoped it wasn't either obsequious or too demanding.

Mr. Thomas, I toured the two areas you suggested, and I think I could work well in the larger one, for the reasons you mentioned. I'll be here tomorrow after my daughter leaves for school. Here's the contract, signed. We didn't discuss supplies. Should I expect to buy them and provide receipts for reimbursement, or would you prefer I give you a list (it won't be long) and have the purchasing department get them for me in advance? Yours, Sara Wells.

She already had what she needed, really, and the pay was more than enough to cover what she might use up of her own— especially if she beat the deadline and got the bonus, which she planned to do. But she didn't want him to think her a bought woman.

SHE DROPPED CARY at school the next morning and went home to get the folder Ken Thomas had given her, her briefcase, the pencils and inks she figured on using. Louise wandered into her room, watching silently. She wouldn't ask about things that weren't her business, but she'd hang around until Sara explained;

so, sighing, she told her about the project. Stolidly, her expression unchanging, Louise said, "That sounds interesting," and left.

Another thing not mentioned in the contract was the media they wanted. But it wouldn't matter much right now, she thought; she was just supposed to do the trial sketches today. And maybe nobody there really knew about that kind of thing, anyway. She could always run back into town and get anything they wanted her to use.

And then I can bill them mileage, she thought grimly.

She dabbed on a bit of makeup and tied the too-long hair back into a ponytail. She was halfway there when Neil called her.

She could ignore it. She could tell him later she'd been driving, traffic was busy. But he might call while she was at MTE, working, and no telling who would overhear that conversation, all those open doors. Well, she could silence it again, there, if that happened…. Impatient with herself, she answered.

"Neil! What're you doing this morning?"

He didn't say anything immediately; maybe, she thought, he wasn't expecting her voice to be bright, upbeat. Maybe he'd been expecting penitence because she hadn't returned to discuss the gift in the white box.

"Well, I was fine until I opened an email from Ken Thomas."

She'd forgotten about Thomas emailing him. "You know, I didn't think it was necessary for you to look at it, but *they* did. It's a simple contract. I read it and there wasn't anything wrong with it."

"Don't get defensive with me. The contract's fine. I was just a little—"

"Surprised that I didn't ask your permission?"

"Didn't take your meds this morning, I guess."

Gripping the steering wheel with both hands, she forced a laugh she knew sounded phony. "Too much coffee. So here's the thing: After the meeting on Monday, Mr. Thomas got in touch with me about working on a project for the company. An art job. But you know, right, since you saw the contract."

"Mother said he passed you a note *during* the meeting," he contradicted. "I had dinner with her and Dad last night. She told me he showed up and tried to hijack their precious agenda and then left you something before he went away."

"Don't play gotcha with me." She cleared the main entrance

and wanted the conversation over before she parked, and she was pleased that, for a moment at least, her remark had silenced him. "He did all that, yes, and then later we discussed this thing. And it's pretty straightforward. The pay's good. You didn't need to look over it, I already did. I'm sorry they sent it to you. I didn't ask them to. I didn't ask *you* to read it."

"No, you didn't," he said, that tone of accusation she hated hearing in his voice. "And you didn't ask my opinion, but I'll give it anyway. Yes, it's clear and simple. Yes, the pay's generous, in comparison to a few other things I've looked over for you in the past." That was like him, reminding her he'd once or twice negotiated a better deal. "Here's the advice: You've heard about the place. I'd be careful getting too involved with them. They probably just want your name on whatever they're doing. But they can be relentless about getting their own way."

"It seems they just want this project finished."

He scoffed. "You don't give them an answer they expect about some little thing, you'll find out about 'relentless.' Just watch out, that's all. Ever since they got here, they've been trying to infiltrate every board, every organization in town. I've told you this before, about other things. Don't be a fool about it."

While she was thinking that over, he went on: "So, you find out anything about your little gift?"

"No, and I'm not wasting any more thought on it. And you don't need to, either. It's nothing."

"I only mention it because you did bring it to me, you know. Whatever. I have to get busy. I'm talking to a new tenant for my building, the one next to Don's."

"He'll be glad it's not vacant. A good tenant, I hope…"

"Good for me; not my problem how Don feels about it."

The answer—somehow displeasing, disquieting—wasn't what she wanted. "Look, Neil, I'm at the company now, so…"

"Oh." She could almost see him lifting his brows, the corner of his mouth going up a little sardonically. "They told you to work there?"

"No, but if I want to, they're giving me space, and since I have a deadline, I'll probably do it faster away from the house. Text me if you need to tell me anything else. Send me a bill. Talk later," and she disconnected the call. It felt good cutting him off.

6

SHE STALKED INTO the room and sat down on the floor against the glass wall, drawing, at first oversized black-and-white nightmarish things. Trees with bare limbs. Long arms ending with thin hands and grasping fingers. Ghouls.

She glanced up when Ken Thomas appeared.

"You need some other furniture, Ms. Wells?"

"I sit on the floor a lot," she snapped.

"Okay..." He stared at the discarded sketches beside her.

Relenting, glancing at the gargoyles and grim, anthropomorphic trees, she laid the paper and pencils down and stood. "I was warming up. Not a great morning at home, but I guess you can tell."

The smiled a little. "I spilled coffee down the front of my shirt. Had to change."

Distractedly, from nothing, she brought up the lack of contract guidance about style and media, and they talked about that for a moment. He suggested she sketch in several different ways to give them an idea of what she would do with the text. She was still angry at Neil, and Thomas frowned at her curt answers. "I have a headache, not bad, but still," she lied. "But the equipment here's absolutely adequate." A silence fell, and then he left.

He emailed later telling her to buy her supplies, as only a handful of people would know what she needed, said to provide receipts, and Mr. Matheson would okay the expenditures himself. Any other requirements she had should be forwarded to him immediately so delays wouldn't slow her down.

Pretty impersonal, she mused: Get finished on time and then get out. But she was responsible for that, with her own terse words earlier.

She watched the children the rest of the day, sometimes through the glass as they played out back, and sometimes as she sat on the floor in the hallway across from the toddlers and older kids in their indoor spaces. All the care providers wore those matching T-shirts she'd noticed. She'd read *The Cat in the Hat* over and over to Cary when she was a baby, and watching the energetic pair in the older kids' room now, she mentally named them Kid Kare

One and Kid Kare Two. The one with the braids questioningly pointed to a chair and pantomimed through the glass, and Sara shook her head. She was mostly unnoticed with her back against the corridor wall, her sketch pad propped on her raised knees. The kids weren't interested in her, and that was what she wanted. She did realistic drawings, stylized drawings; line drawings, shaded ones, some with no background, some with context. The kids took a snack in the rooms at ten; and then, around eleven-thirty, someone called, "Centipede!" and a line formed that marched out of the building to some other place, from which they returned in a while, the older ones clutching juice boxes, the toddlers' workers bringing more in a crate. Kid Kare One paused at the entrance to the projects room, where Sara had moved, and held out a white bag.

"Nobody knew if you'd made arrangements for lunch, so Mr. Thomas asked me to bring you this."

Inside were a turkey sandwich, an apple, a bottle of water. Safe food: Everybody liked turkey, apples were good for you, and water had no calories, no sugar—no caffeine, she told herself wryly. Maybe he thought she didn't need any more caffeine.

As she ate, she wondered what other facilities the company had on site. She hadn't known about Kid Kare, and now it seemed that there was either a catering deal with someone or, stranger possibility, a cafeteria.

No one returned to her space that afternoon. Around three she went to the reception area and asked that a group of sketches and a note she'd written be sent to Ken Thomas. She called Louise to remind her to pick Cary up again, but she'd decided she wouldn't stay until their closing time of five or so. Neil's warning had rankled all day; she wasn't going to let them own her time, she decided. The chair she'd used off and on she moved back into a corner. She turned off the lights and drove home, thinking Neil should have at least texted an apology. But she knew he wouldn't; not yet, anyway.

On Thursday, still smarting from the things he'd said, she rose early enough to dress before taking Cary to school. They'd be surprised to see her at eight o'clock, and she'd leave after lunch: The other college class was that evening, and she'd need to prepare. Ignoring the dim glow at Cary's partly-closed door, she'd stayed up late grading the papers she'd shoved inside the briefcase on Monday.

"I'll swing by the school myself this afternoon," she said.

Louise glared at her: "You're running too much; you need to slow down."

That's probably true. "I'm okay. See you about three-thirty."

"We'll eat *before* you go to class tonight. I'm cooking that soup today, the one you wrote down," Louise warned, standing in the doorway as she and Cary headed for the car.

Cary didn't want to talk. Sara figured she was still sulking about having to go to the company picnic tomorrow evening, and Matthew's house for the whole weekend. At the school gate she said, "I hope you're not sick; your period come early?" but Cary shot her a disgusted look.

"No, and don't worry about it all day."

"I won't!" Sara told her with a laugh.

Cary rolled her eyes. "You always do."

Somebody didn't get much sleep last night, Sara mused as she drove on. Traffic was heavier—well, she was arriving with the employees, so it would be. She parked at the far end of a row and dashed inside to avoid the drizzle of rain just starting up.

"Several of the kids are home with a stomach bug," Kid Kare One told her pleasantly. "Better use lots of hand sanitizer today, try not to touch the doorknobs."

"I don't have one," Sara laughed from the entrance of the large room she claimed, then turned back, her conscience bothering her a little. "I'm sorry; I haven't asked. What's your name? I'm Sara Wells."

"It's fine; we could see you were busy. Mr. Thomas told us about you and what you're doing. We didn't want to interrupt, but, anyway, I'm Kathy." She gestured to Kid Kare Two. "She's Liz. In the toddler room, you have Laura and it's usually Sue, but sometimes Anna's here and Sue isn't."

"I doubt I'll be working more than another couple of weeks, maybe not that long, but nice to meet you."

On the utility table she found a large sticky note asking her to let Thomas know when she'd arrived. She peeled it up, headed next door, showed it to the receptionist, told her not to bother buzzing him, and strolled past, feeling empowered. Thomas, standing in his office doorway with a cup of coffee in hand, chatting with a couple of people, held the mug in the air when she walked up unannounced.

"I'm keeping different hours today." She stuck the note down to his desk. Bemused, he gazed at it for a moment as she waited.

"I don't know what to say. I didn't leave that in your room. I don't know what it means."

"Who did?"

"Probably Ron, maybe, or Caroline, that's his assistant. Looks like her handwriting. He's not here yet. Maybe he took your sketches with him to the visitors' cottage and looked over them last night. I'm here sometimes before he arrives. Let me see if he's in yet...." He dialed an extension.

So they have a "visitors' cottage," too.... She turned away, pretending to ignore the half-sentences Thomas mumbled into the handset. Half-closed blinds covered the large window at the left of his desk; she stood beside it, contemplating the lake in the distance, remembering Ransome's horses, and the pasture that used to be here.... Rheta coming home from a date with Frank, having ridden some beast she'd said was spirited and hard-to-manage.... Rheta saying Ransome had dressed Frank down for not properly grooming the horse after they'd brought it back to the stable....

"...Let me repeat that to her. Go with the more stylized approach, some background but not too much, don't get it cluttered." He paused and listened, continued: "More line drawing, color wash if she wants to. Did I get that right?" He listened, then nodded to Sara.

"Please put him on speaker."

He gazed at her. "Can we go to intercom?" he said into the receiver, then pressed a button; and she sat down near the phone.

"Mr. Matheson, I have a question or two to keep me from wasting your time and money. When you say 'color wash,' do you mean with ink? How's that going to work when the print's run? Will it be a problem?"

The voice sounded mildly irritated. "I don't think so. I farm out the processes when we have to do manuals and those things. We can't always get the result I want here on our machines. They'll figure it out. I imagine ink would be safer than watercolor, right?"

"Maybe. Is there a particular kind of paper—"

"Again, I doubt it. Look—" and this time she knew he was getting impatient—"I'll tell you who to call, if you're anxious, but, really, I think it'll be fine. You can look over the galleys later, before the printing's done; I'll tell them to have you do that. I liked what you sent over yesterday; you know what you're doing and have a vision I approve of, in terms of our own vision, and so, go for it. I pay people to figure out what we send them. They'll manage."

"But…" she chose words carefully. "You understand, this is my work, me, the artist, my name on it, and I don't want it to turn out badly and then have to own it."

She glanced at Thomas to remind him of the word, and caught him flinching; and it prepared her to give some blowback herself. A few seconds passed before Matheson responded.

"Good point. I'll make sure you see those proofs ahead of the print run. You invested in the book now? I had doubts about that."

Thomas winced again.

"I am, and glad you care about the community. So, since we're on the same page, is there anything else you thought of as you looked over the sketches?"

"Not really. I liked, liked very much, actually, how you treat the subjects, the children. If you want to go whimsical and put in fantasy things here and there, that's fine with me."

"Mr. Thomas mentioned that on Monday."

"Then, if you don't have any other questions… He told you to buy your supplies and bring the invoices?"

"Yes."

"Then just keep doing what you're doing, and stick to the deadline."

"I intend to. Thank you." She nodded at Thomas and walked out the door, but the hallway was wide and empty and picked up sound too well:

"So you see, I told you so: Artists are hell to deal with. You don't want to, tell her to run it all by me."

"I believe I'll do the better job," Thomas answered.

His comment was broadcast as she poked her head around the door and glared. Guiltily glancing her way, he turned the speaker off and picked up the handset. She rolled her eyes at him and went back to Kid Kare to do some more sketches.

ON FRIDAY SHE went early again, intending to leave after noon to take Cary to Matthew's herself. No one bothered her today, and, again, there were fewer children. The drizzly rain had stopped, but there was no sunshine. On the utility table she found the sketches she'd given Ken Thomas on Wednesday; he'd put them into a nice portfolio with her name printed on the outside. She spread them on the table, looking carefully at each one, and picked up three to redo in pen and ink.

She worked on those all morning, finishing the second just before Kathy herded the children to the cafeteria for their lunch meal. "Would you like a sandwich?"

"I've something to do this afternoon, so I'll be going home to eat. Although," she added, "if you don't mind, a water would be nice. Plain."

"Will do. Centipede!" she told her kids, and each child immediately put his right hand on the shoulder of his neighbor in front, and the line began shuffling out the building.

She worked through lunch and was almost finished with the third drawing redo when Kathy brought her a cold bottle. The sun was trying to peek through a skyful of soggy-looking clouds as she stepped out to the playground area. The tables there were the same sort as those downtown, in front of Libertos's and in other places. That brought a question to her mind. She sipped the drink and stretched, rolled her shoulders, arched her back: She'd been sitting too long.

So many windows overlooking this area—every one of the five floors of the building had windows, and the employees could actually look out to see their children here: Kathy, or maybe Liz, had told her that. She stared at the glass panes, wondering how many people did it, every day. She would've, if she worked here.

There was a recycle bin nearby for the bottle—another point for Ron Matheson, she told herself, and went back to work.

Presently Liz knocked timidly on the wall and leaned in. "Hate to bother you, but they'll start getting the tables and chairs in about an hour."

It puzzled her. She'd counted on no interruptions.... She wasn't quite through with the third drawing; they wanted to see a color option.... She cleaned the table, and her pen, took the last finished page to a copy machine in the main office. A sense of hurry had replaced the laid-back tone she'd noticed before, people walking a little faster down the corridors. And Fridays must be casual days: Everyone was in board shorts or jeans. She waited at a copier where a woman about her age tried to get a quick look at Sara's drawing, then took her own sheets and trotted away. Sara made the copy and checked the time: She still had about an hour before she'd leave.

In her work space several people were hauling out the folded tables and chairs from the closet while she colored the photocopy she'd just made. She'd wondered at first, Why all the fuss about tables and chairs?, and then remembered the picnic that evening. The picnic...she wanted to talk to Cary a little before sending her off, wanted to remind her to be as mannerly as she could force herself to be.

Thin copy paper was terrible for color washes. She'd known before starting that the edges were going to curl—she didn't have masking tape to fix it down, or anything to fix it to. She should've asked for thicker paper.

The screeching noises of chairs being loaded onto dollies and the goings and comings were distractions. She frowned at everyone who came in and loaded the equipment and left, with clatters and bangs; but if they noticed her glares, it didn't reduce their noise.

Finished at last, she laid the drawing on the counter to dry, packed her tools into the plastic box and her briefcase, glanced up, irritated, when two men came and stood patiently, silently, by the utility table.

Kathy stepped in: "They need it outside. You through? I told them not to bother you if you're working."

"Nope. I'm finished," she snapped. Then, "Sorry. It's not them, it's me: I should've worked faster. Intended to be done before now."

The men lifted the big table and hauled it through the opening into the corridor and outside. The room seemed extraordinarily empty and echoing. Kathy noticed the paper on the counter. "Nice. Look, if you want to dry it fast, here's what we do when the kids finger-paint." She brought in a box fan from the older kids' room. "Low-tech, but it works. Looks like they've finally got all the stuff out of here, so maybe you'll have a little peace and quiet for a few minutes. Turn it up to 'hurricane'," she advised.

Sara held the damp drawing vertically in front of the fan. The wash had soaked in and wasn't running downward, but it wouldn't be dry by the time she wanted to leave. She waved it back and forth for a few minutes, glanced impatiently at her watch.

"You hot-natured?"

She heard the question, coming from behind her and asked loudly, over the roar of the fan.

"I mean, it's not that hot today," he added.

"I'm actually—" but she stopped, seeing that he knew and was just mouthing off at her, not a hint of smile to turn the words into a joke, either. "Kathy tells me this is how they do it over there. Pretty good trick. But I need to leave right away, so you'll have to take it—it's still damp."

Matheson reached for the page and stood in front of the fan himself as she fumbled with box and briefcase and portfolio and hauled her purse from the cabinet.

"Lots of stuff," he said.

She arranged it all near the opening to the hallway and came to touch the wet page—drier, but still soggy in places. He was stolid, as if intent on watching every drop of moisture leave the page. She fidgeted, looked outside, not liking the silence.

"This used to be a pasture, with horses. Did you see it before the company bought the land? Or did you not get here yourself until afterwards?"

"I looked at it with my own eyes before I recommended the purchase."

She glanced up at him. "I didn't mean anything by that. I was just wondering. Everything's so different from then. Ransome Moore, the man who owned it, do you know him?"

"We've met."

"Ransome had horses here, I said that. He made his kids take care of them. He was particular about them, the horses. I was thinking about it yesterday morning, when I drove in. My sister used to date Ransome's son. Long ago."

There was still no remark.

"You don't have to dry it completely. Just take it and put it between two pieces of paper. Or in a folder."

"I'm fine." He turned what she thought was a pretty grim look at her. "Nobody knows where I am right now, and I like that. So I'm just fine drying this paper. Tell me some more about Ransome's horses. Maybe I haven't heard this story from him."

She glanced at her watch. "Frank and my sister'd come out and ride the horses. Except one time, they didn't put them up to suit him, and that was it. I don't think he ever let them ride again, or not for a while, anyway."

"He didn't like them not being brushed down right. You know that old thing about riding them hard and putting them up wet."

"He told you?"

He scoffed. "No, but I know Ransome, and I know the kind of things that get him mad. By the way, what I said: Let that be between us. That's not what it means today, is it. But I'm old and tactless; I just blurt out what I think. Oh, and I need to say this, too: Ken told me you two had discussed 'bought women'? That's what he said, right?"

She sighed in exasperation, looked at her watch. "So he told you about it. He said 'kept,' if I recall, and I warned him about saying it in front of anybody else. Like you just did, that horse thing," she added pointedly.

"He came into my office and called it 'complete disclosure.' Said he might've used some words he shouldn't've that day. He didn't mean to be crude."

"I took it for what it was. He was trying to make a point."

He scoffed. "Yeah, Ken can make points. He told me which ones he was working on. 'Complete disclosure,' like he said." He was still flapping the paper in the backwash of the fan.

"I'm through with three of the drawings." She opened the portfolio and pulled them out. "That one you're holding is an example of color on this one." She lifted the original. "A poor example, by the way. Copy paper. But you can judge which you'd like."

"And I will," he told her, "later. Would you take all four of these to Ken and ask him to lay them on my desk, please. I'll look over them tomorrow morning."

"Tomorrow's Saturday."

"If something's going wrong, I'll be here."

His face was grim; she almost felt sorry for him. "You're the boss; you could make yourself some free time."

He glanced impassively at her, turned off the fan, and pushed it against the cabinets. "You want to stay for the cookout?"

For a moment she considered how much fun it would be to agitate Matthew, watching him wonder why she was there— payback for his nagging Cary. But that was just *like* Cary, she told herself. "I don't think so. My daughter'll be here with her dad. I don't think either of them'd be happy seeing me hang around. Each for different reasons, you know." She hesitated. "Do your kids come to these things?"

"My son's grown. My grandchild sometimes comes with him, when they're visiting. They're down, this week, but I don't think they will, tonight. Why wouldn't your daughter want you here?"

She stared him down.

"Okay. Not my business. I'll help you with these. Where'd you park?" He picked up the box of supplies and her briefcase.

Gathering her purse and the portfolio and damp copy, she let him follow, since he'd insisted, and she wouldn't look back to see how he was managing the supplies. She swung the rear door ajar, pointed for him to set the box on the floor and the briefcase on the seat. "Hold these for me"—and she gave him the four completed pages, positioned the nice portfolio beside her on the front passenger seat, locked the doors again, took the drawings from him, hesitating, mildly ashamed of herself.

"Cary doesn't get along with her father very well right now," she said. "You may know how it is, or maybe not; girls are different from boys sometimes, when they're teenagers. Matthew wants her to come here with him and Jennifer tonight, and he got really adamant when she said she didn't want to. She thinks she'll be the oldest of all the kids here. She thinks parents'll expect her to babysit their children. Her weekend's ruined. Her life's over," she added sardonically.

"Maybe I should—"

"Oh, no, don't do anything, don't say anything to him. That'll only make it worse. He'd believe I'm trying to undermine him in his job here."

"So Cary's not the only one not getting along. Also not my business," he added, as she started to speak. "He surely knows you've been here this week. He's probably seen your car, maybe even seen you outside. By now everybody knows what you're doing."

"Yeah, but he won't take it well if you tell him to back off, with his own kid. Would *you*? And then he'd probably end up blaming me, but take it out on her. Let it go. I've bribed her, anyway, so she's going to do it, and maybe she'll even enjoy a few minutes, if she can just get over being fourteen."

"What if I find a special job for her—" he stopped her objection— "not saying anything about this conversation, but just something for her to do, something with a little prestige? Would that be okay?"

She looked at the time again. "I have to pick her up now, right now, from school. I'll give these to Ken, and, yes, if you can get her to be happy, that would be a big favor, to me and Matthew both." She took a couple of hurried steps toward the main building.

"Go get your kid," he said, taking the drawings from her, walking away. And she realized she'd said "Ken."

SHE TEXTED MATTHEW she'd bring Cary to his house herself. There wasn't much to be packed into a bag—her phone charger, her computer, personal stuff; there were plenty of clothes and some sleepwear already at his house in the closet of the room she refused to call "hers." She wouldn't talk to Sara on the way home from school. Louise was waiting for them with the new windbreaker, the kind Cary liked, which Sara had sent her to get today as one more incentive. Cary said, "Thank you," shoved it into her bag, and glared at Sara as they occupied the space in the car. That was what it felt like tonight: "occupying the space."

"I've wondered about something this week," she began so the whole short trip wouldn't be made in silence. "You went to Mass on Sunday with Louise, but you didn't plan to at first, then changed your mind."

"Geez, Mom, that was last weekend! Do you have to obsess about things?"

Sara twisted her hands on the steering wheel and held back a retort.

"I mean, look," Cary went on in a quieter voice, "I just felt like going. A prayer now and then couldn't hurt. It was nice seeing Nana. And, well, you know I won't be going this weekend, probably, so I just figured, 'Why not.' I mean, Jennifer's okay, but she's not interested in church, and she drops me off, and picks me up, but it's not the same. So I don't ask her to take me anymore."

"I get it."

They were near Matthew's house, and Sara couldn't think of anything funny to tell her, the way she usually did before Matthew arrived if he picked her up. She swerved into a parking space on the quiet street. "Look, you know I've been out at MTE this week. Today the boss pointed out your dad *had* to know I was there, probably saw me, and so if he says anything to you—"

"I'll tell him to fuck off," she said.

"Um, no, you won't. You'll say he should take it up with me, or maybe Mr. Matheson. That'll probably shut down anything. In the meantime, I'll ask Mr. Griffin if we can work on your dad to get you more control about when you have to visit."

"No, Mom, just drop it. I'll remember what you told me to say if he asks, but, really, you know there's no way he's gonna give up this visitation thing, and, honestly, so long as Jennifer's around, it's okay." She heaved a dramatic sigh. "I can manage. I'll try to get him to take us to the movies or something. And we're still going to the beach, right?"

Sara kept herself from smiling. She turned back onto the street and pulled into the drive at Matthew's house. As if she'd been watching—and probably she had—the door opened and Jennifer came out.

"We have time for an ice cream float before we go over there, Cary, if you want to!" Sara heard another sigh behind her. Jennifer still didn't have the hang of talking to Matthew's daughter. "I hope you brought a jacket. I think it's going to be cool tonight."

"Yeah, I got one." She pulled out the new windbreaker. "It's new. Mom gave it to me."

"Oh, nice. I like it."

"Yeah, she knows which bribes work."

Jennifer looked away and fidgeted.

"You know they'll move everything inside if people get cold. They always do. But, anyway, yes, I have a coat." Cary dragged the backpack from the car. Jennifer took a step or two nearer Sara, then backed off and fidgeted. Sara was amused, even felt a little sympathetic, and old. Jennifer never knew whether to shake Sara's hand, or fake-hug her the way schoolgirls did, or just tell her goodbye and move on. Sara decided to be generous:

"Take care of her, and tell Matthew you should all go to the movies this weekend. Word it so he'll think you came up with it on your own. I know how contrary he can be."

Cary grinned suddenly and hugged her. "Love you, Mom. I'll text you later."

7

WHEN CARY WAS at Matthew's, Sara and Louise dispensed

with routine. Louise reheated the soup left over from the day before, and that was supper. Sara knew she'd made a double recipe so they could eat it tonight, and nobody'd have to cook. They took crackers straight from the box. Louise spread the paper out next to her plate, and began to read, a thing that violated her principles when Cary was home. Sara had showed Louise how to read the online version, so she didn't have to think about recycling; but as usual Louise claimed to be too old. So there it was, to be thrown away later.

They cleaned the kitchen.

"She gonna be okay?"

"She's fine." She said it firmly, knowing it was true. "She'll probably even enjoy it if she just quits sulking. So now I have to plan spring break."

Louise checked the kitchen door lock and put the chain on. Sara picked up the paper, and turned the lights out before going to her bedroom. Then they left each other alone—that was another thing, when it was just the two of them in the house: After supper, that first evening, they went their own ways, reclaimed the parts of themselves they'd pushed aside.

She stood there a moment and looked around.

God knows she had work she could do, ought to do, the art project and the courses and developing an idea for a new book.... So it wasn't boredom.

What'll you do when she does go off to college?

She laid the paper on her bed, sat cross-legged to read.

It was thin again today. Fridays, they were. On Tuesday Jared Brown had bylined a tiny piece about the preservation meeting. She'd had to look for it, buried in the "Lifestyles" section; it was nothing but the barest facts; she'd tell Rheta to educate him.

The meeting had been held; several community figures had attended; an owner of one of Mooresville's older homes had requested advice on rehabbing; an officer from MTE had asked about progress in the historic district. Generic stuff.

She noticed the framed banner at the bottom of the front page: "Stagnation in Mooresville's Only Historic District. In a three-part series beginning on Sunday, R. C. Whitson takes a look at the history of the area, its status, and its future."

Sara realized she was staring at letters without seeing words. Every story Rheta ever did about Mooresville brought up something from their past, hers and Rheta's, and she told herself to cut the line, and shook off the reverie, threw the paper to the floor, went to the closet to get the box with the blue sphere.

She sat on the bed; there, it wouldn't break if she dropped it, and she gazed deeply, feeling like a fortune-teller, chagrined she'd let others examine it but hadn't herself. Under the lamplight she slowly turned it, admiring the deep glow in the color and the way the artist had carved the shapes tumbling from the watery-looking side. She looked at each one of them until she located the "XIII" and "XVIII," very small, etched after the final glazing had been done. Most people would miss them or think they were just flaws in the piece. 13, 18. 18, 13.

It was heavy for something half the size of a bowling ball, the bottom flattened just enough to keep it from rolling. Instead of being hollowed, the way some people molded a big round piece, the artist had kept it thin enough from every side to just escape exploding in the kiln. Subtle variations in the color on the solid side hinted of deep water; on the broken side, of light, of crystals glittering in a cave. Like a geode, as Cary'd said.

She started to put it back; but it *was* a lovely piece, and she might as well keep it out. Her dresser was too cluttered; the desk, too small, and she might push it off and break it one day, if she was in a hurry. Shrugging, she laid it on the night table under the lamp, where its depths gleamed dark bluish-purple.

It was only ten o'clock: too early to sleep. She hadn't heard from Cary…that meant she was probably doing okay at the picnic, if it was still going on. She wanted to find out. But that would be helicoptering, and Cary'd already let her know what she thought about that. She heard the TV. Louise was probably watching an old movie, and maybe she should be sociable and join her, but, then, Louise hadn't invited her. Louise might enjoy the company. But, on the other hand, she liked sappy old 40's romances, which Sara'd mocked a time or two; and then they'd snapped at each other next day about trivial, unrelated things.

Really, just find something to do…. But she didn't want to work on the sketches tonight. She'd done that too much lately.

She threw the newspaper away in the kitchen trash, guiltily remembering the recycle bins at MTE.

"Going to bed early."

Louise paused the movie, mumbled, "All right," and the noise resumed as she closed her bedroom door.

But she didn't sleep for a long time, and then poorly.

SO IT WAS nine o'clock before she awoke, and Louise was knocking gently. "You okay? You don't usually sleep this late," she said when Sara told her to come on in.

"I guess I was tired from the week."

They had toast and coffee—"Big change from last Saturday," Sara remarked.

"Can't eat rich food all the time."

Laundry, vacuuming again, sweeping... Sara emptied the dust pan and stopped. "Nothing's dirty, Louise. We're just going through the motions."

Louise turned a discerning gaze on her.

"What're you doing today?"

"Old folks' home. Like always. What about you?"

"I'll be busy. The new thing. Other stuff."

Louise departed early for her visit, but not before asking once more if Sara was just going to stay home all day. Sara shooed her off, then took the folder and portfolio to the kitchen and spread the drawings out on the table.

Still nothing from Cary. On Matthew's weekends Cary sometimes messaged or called, but sometimes not, depending on what they were doing at his house. She shuffled the sketches around, wondering if Cary'd flip out if she texted her. She decided not to, grimaced and picked the sketch with the most detail; it would be an exercise in self-discipline. She'd have to focus on it or she'd end up doing it three times, not just two. She was almost finished with that one when her phone buzzed. The late-February afternoon was trailing itself out into a cool dusk, and she hadn't noticed how much time had passed. She read Cary's text:

Hi, Mom, did you have a good day?

She answered, and waited.

But then minutes went by. Her concentration broken, she sighed and capped the pen. *So what'd ya do?*

She waited again for a while before Cary responded, sending a flurry of messages one after another. She'd actually had an okay time at the company cookout—a grudging admission. The food was good, but the evening did get cold, so the meal was served inside, she knew it would be, and the babies got cranky and whiny.

She *had* been the oldest kid there! Or at least she thought maybe she was. But the boss had gone around talking to everybody and stopped at their table, and asked her if she'd do him a favor on the computer in his office. Weird! Why her? But she'd done it.

Sara broke in: ***Had you rather just call?***

No! Cary didn't want to be interrupted by Matthew or Jennifer, and they'd just listen in. First the boss asked her to get the crayons and markers out and then he asked her to go to his office with another dude—

Sara had a question: So there *were* other people her age?

Maybe one or two, Cary conceded. Then: In the boss's office she'd used his computer to print some coloring pages off the Internet for the little kids. She made copies, and the babies got happier, and so it wasn't too bad.

Sara asked what she'd been doing today.

Matthew and Jennifer had taken her to the movies, she responded. It was OK. At least it wasn't a G movie. And they'd let her sleep late that morning. And they were driving out to some barbecue place in the country for supper, so she had to get dressed because Dad didn't like her T-shirt (a frown emoji here), but she had something freaky to tell Sara tomorrow when she got home.

About what? Sara asked.

Later. Bye.

She made herself finish the sketch and stored it in the portfolio. Louise wouldn't be back till at least six, and for once she wished it would be sooner. The house was too quiet this evening. She grabbed a jacket, locked the doors, headed out to walk a few blocks in the cool evening air. She was on the way back when Louise called to say she was going downtown with Harvey, her friend from the nursing home, and get supper, maybe do a movie, she thought she might get back about nine-thirty, did Sara want to come? Sara begged off, smiling, knowing Louise really didn't want her along on her "date."

But the house was still silent and would be, now, for even longer. She made a sandwich and ate it in the kitchen, cleaned up again, put the garbage into the bin outside. The newspaper peeked out of the top. The newspaper she'd tried to read last night.

"R. C. Whitson takes a look at the history...."

She texted: ***Can you come over?*** The answer was almost immediate: **Who's there?**

Sara rolled her eyes. *Louise went to a movie. Said she'd be back at nine-thirty.*

All right. See you in a few.

In the fridge there was nothing much to drink…juice, milk… She put on a pot of coffee and wished she'd gone by Don's kiosk and bought some pastry today. But Louise'd frozen a couple of leftover Danish rolls a while back; she'd thaw them.

If she drove the way she usually did, Rheta'd be there in ten minutes. Having her over for a visit had always felt like scheduling a family intervention when Sara and Matthew were married. Rheta'd needled him whenever she saw him. Behind her back he'd whine if she came over more than once or twice a month, would grudgingly greet her, then go off to a bedroom and watch TV, making ostentatiously unnecessary trips to the kitchen, clattering things on the counter….

Sara waited, wondering, as she always had, why she'd allowed that, one of a long list of things he'd found fault with: her sister, her sloppiness, her snacking at night. Sometimes it had seemed the only things he liked about her were those he'd badgered her into doing. And eventually she was glad for moments he was away, even as she found herself pregnant and packing his bags.

She'd never minded solitude until just lately.

She heard Rheta's car in the drive, the usual sounds of someone's arrival: the engine shutting off, a neighbor's dog barking as Rheta got out, the slam of the door and chirp as she locked it.

Inside, Rheta peered down the hallway. "So how'd you get her to go away?"

Sara laughed. "Sometime or other, you two have to come to terms. You can't do this forever."

"*I* can." Rheta shrugged. "She could, too. You underestimate us."

"Anyway, she didn't *want* to leave me here by myself. But I insisted. I think she feels sorry for me."

"Yeah, who wouldn't?"

Sara opted not to answer. She led the way toward the kitchen, where she'd arranged the mugs and plates on the table and, in a last-minute inspiration, stuck the sphere as a centerpiece. "Conversation starter," Cary had said. But she and Rheta had never needed that, until Rheta left for college and, then, lived in Atlanta.

For all those years they talked no more than once or twice a month.

And then she'd come home, back to Mooresville. People stopped Sara at church, pulled her aside in the grocery store, asked why Rheta'd do that—"Don't get us wrong; we're glad, but..." All the unspoken words, the raised eyebrows—why would anybody come back to a place where she'd been unwelcome? Was there more pain where she was *now*? "She'll be like Deborra Anderson," they'd eventually say. "Our local people just understand local things better than outsiders."

She'd helped unpack Rheta's stuff into an apartment on the other side of town. Told her what was being said.

"All of 'em need to get something to do instead of psychoanalyzing. Tell 'em if they wanna know, they can ask *me*."

Sara, taking a step backwards as Rheta flung a carton of sheets and towels into a room: "I'll do that. Stop throwing things around."

But, later, as exhaustion overtook them and they had to stop and eat, and the bottle of wine got lighter: "Why *did* you come back?"

"It's just, you can't go to sleep. And you realize your life's half done, and you have nobody with you and it's too late, you're too old to put in the effort. I mean, *you* have Cary. I won't, I won't have my, whoever."

"You might. You could."

"No, I won't. Oh, and when he hired me, Joe made it clear I wouldn't be doing any 'gotcha' things, as he put it." She scoffed. "He just wanted to say he'd snagged a big-city reporter, got her back home. But he doesn't want to lose readers, advertisers."

Sara stopped folding towels, stood akimbo: "You won't quit that kind of reporting, though. I know you."

"No, not even if I find out my little old first-grade teacher sold weed on the side, and she's eighty now, I'll write it. I'll sneak in work-arounds. Anyway, I'm home now. Whatever that means. Eventually, you go home, to do what you can, where somebody still knows you."

Next day they moved the furniture around until she was satisfied with how it looked. Connie and Louise brought sandwiches, commented approvingly on the décor; but Rheta ate and said nothing, as if choking down the turkey on rye required all her concentration—no words from her at all, which was ominous, and predictive of the surge that at last did pour out:

"Well, I gotta tell you some things I never have, because you're gonna hear from the local bitches, they may figure it out from the name I use now." Louise drew herself up into an outraged posture, and Rheta rolled her eyes. "Calm down, Louise. I was married, in Atlanta." She shook her head before Connie said anything. "No, I *was* married. Not anymore. Actually, twice. You don't know about these things, Mom, be grateful you don't; but you're somewhere by yourself, and you know absolutely not a soul, and just about any human being is better than none. And then you wake up in a week and think, 'What the hell did I do? I don't even know this guy!' And so that was Billy."

"Billy," Connie repeated.

"Yeah. We were friends, before," she mused, "but not after. I think he'd have been happy just going along with it, because he was a lost soul, like me, but I couldn't look at myself anymore. 'Cause I knew I wasn't going to stay. So when I left, he was really bitter.

"And I did take my time with Justin. I really did. We lived together a while before I married him. I thought it might work. Funny what you don't know about each other that you think you do. So, anyway, that's it, and I promise there aren't any others for those old bitches to find out about. Marriages, that is."

Louise glared at Rheta. Rheta glared back.

"So that name you use—"

"Justin's. For privacy. Everybody thinks I just made it up, huh. But the minute I have to write anything unflattering, you can bet they'll start digging around, so you should know in advance what they'll find out. Sorry about the cussing. You want me to go to confession?"

"No, don't. I like our priest," Sara said.

"Well, I'd do it once, for you, but it wouldn't turn into a regular thing," she muttered.

And later, just the two of them, when Connie and Louise had left, she'd asked: *When you run into them, any of those men, don't you feel something?*

I make it a point not to run into 'em, Rheta sneered. *You can't go to bed with somebody and not feel something. One more reason I'm here and not there.*

...She poured her sister's coffee; Rheta knew where creamer and sugar were if she wanted them. Two siblings could not have been more physically unalike: Rheta, with her almost-black hair, hazel eyes, scrawny frame; Sara, with the brown hair, blue eyes...and her meals at Liberto's, those sorbets and the pasta seemed to be showing up on her now, but they never had on Rheta. "Are you dyeing your hair?" she blurted out suddenly.

"What the hell? What, you think I oughta have a little grey, since you do? I wouldn't tell you if I did. But I don't." Rheta stirred her coffee, pointed at the sphere. "What's that?"

Sara went through the whole story again.

"Okay, so just another weird thing that happened to you. Well, it's different from some. I'll give it that."

They ate the pastries and finished one cup of the coffee; Rheta poured a second. Her eyes went back to the sculpture; she tapped it. "It reminds me of something.... How's stuff going with the kiddo?"

Sara told her about Cary's skirmishes with Matthew, ending with the company picnic. "The boss apparently tried to entertain her this time."

"He's a decent enough guy."

"You know him?"

"You'll find out on Sunday."

"I've met him. Not impressed."

Rheta shrugged. "Whatever. I figured him out right away. Great at diagramming it all on paper. Can't understand why people don't operate like diagrams, so he does weird stuff, like I told you. This thing tonight...Michael usually goes—I've been with him a few times. Matheson says it's an opportunity for the employees to vent, say whatever's on their mind, no consequences. He's got the idea it helps keep things open. Kumbaya. I don't know where he came up with it, and I get the feeling that financial officer doesn't like it at all."

"Ken Thomas."

"Yeah, him. I think they're friends, more than boss and employee. I was there when some real intense shit started flying at one of those picnics, and I could see that man get madder and madder, but it seemed to me like he was mad more at his boss than at the people saying the shit. You want the truth? I can see why Cary wouldn't want to go, if she's heard it."

"Is it dangerous?" Sara recalled Cary's sullen, resistant expression yesterday.

"Nah, I don't think so, just uncomfortable stuff. He has rules: before you eat, you can vent. After you get food, no more. Free speech...on his terms." She snickered, noticed Sara's expression. "Look, Cary's old enough that she probably didn't want to go because attending a company picnic's not cool. I doubt she's ever paid attention to the other stuff."

Sara wasn't mollified.

"Shouldn't have even mentioned it. Put it out of your mind. Nothing'll happen. It never gets very far. Change of subject: I weaseled Matheson's personal number from Ransome, so he was kind of surprised when I called him the other day. By the way, he can cuss like me. Just in case you ever need to know."

"You still in touch with Ransome?"

"He knows stuff. What he knows has always mattered." Her gaze lowered to the cup of coffee. "You *realize* the two of us made up finally. Hell, I got along better with him, later, than I ever did with Frank. So, about Cary..."

Sara knew Rheta's segues, knew to follow them. "If Matthew'd just remember she's not a child anymore, let her decide a few things for herself, she might want to do stuff with him."

"She might. But she may just be fed up with him."

"He's her father."

"You can love somebody without liking them," Rheta remarked. "Be real, Sara: He's never been involved in her life, really."

"He can't be, not daily."

"Even allowing for that. And she knows. He wasn't really *there*, was he, from the very first. It was never him."

They eyed each other over the mugs, remembering: The nurses hadn't blinked an eye when she'd told them she wanted Rheta, not her baby's father. Then, in labor and running out of time, wanting to show how strong she was: *I can do this.* Rheta: **Get pain meds, goddammit, who cares?** And finding out it was too late and she *had* to do it without anything, and Rheta, her face horrified and white, helping her with the pushing rhythm.

"So how's *your* life lately?"

"Michael's away on business, and I'm enjoying the peace. Maybe I should send the boss a thank-you note. I'm too old to want somebody underfoot all the time. When he comes back next week, it'll be good to have a warm body in bed. You know how it is, you did the same thing."

"No, I didn't."

"Sure you did." She talked on over the denial. "Michael'll come back, and I'll get tired of him, and luckily they'll send him somewhere else after a while. You got any more of that pastry?"

"Nope. That was all."

"I'm not really hungry. Just, it was pretty good, and I could eat some more."

"You don't need it."

"No, *you* don't need it. You better start jogging with me."

"Why didn't you write that little piece about the meeting? Why'd Jared do it?"

"I did the series. Starts tomorrow. Didn't you see the banner? And I guess you didn't listen to me, either." Rheta dragged her fork through the remaining crumbs on her plate. "I gave you a head's-up a few minutes ago, but you didn't listen. You don't pay attention to what goes on around here behind the scenes, never have."

Somberly she stared at the fork. Her brain warned her not to go there, don't answer that. What was forgivable when you were fifteen might not be when you were fifty. It seemed Rheta had the same thought: "Sorry. Let's just visit, like sisters're supposed to. So, you seeing anybody now besides your lawyer? Please say yes."

Sara denied, again, being with Neil anymore, and Rheta claimed, again, she didn't believe her, and so it went for another half-hour—Sara's lack of social life, how Rheta kept her weight off, should Sara put color on her hair. It was almost like sitting outside and watching the string of lights come on, one by one, towards Moore Farms. We just need some mosquitoes, Sara told herself, but she didn't say it, because that involved blood, and she felt there was enough of that already, and no joy, in their banter—it was just the sad smartmouth of middle-aged sisters remembering too many things, and it was what they always came to at the end. In the very back of Sara's mind there was Rheta, always on the top floor of a high-rise she herself had booby-trapped, and when it exploded—and it always did, sooner or later—she emerged upright but staggering, with her invisible bruises, daring the building to cave in around her, dashing out just in time, when it did.

…Rheta glanced at the microwave clock and said she was leaving Dodge before the sheriff returned. Sara saw her to the car, checking the back seat just in case. Rheta looked straight out through the windshield, wringing the steering wheel. "We're a pitiful pair, aren't we."

"Let's not go through that again."

She went on, as if the words hadn't even been said: "We're messes. You use Cary as your human shield, keep you from committing to anybody. And I wanna throw gasoline on every pisspot flame I get going, just to see how big a fire I can make. Shit. Couple of losers." She blew a kiss through the windshield and drove away.

"Your human shield…" Sara washed the mugs and plates and turned out the lights, leaving the chain off the door so Louise could get in.

RELUCTANTLY, SHE WENT to Mass next morning, though she always hated seeing her mother sitting behind Don and Lisa and their kids, and Chris, the few times he came. She hated that flicker on Chris's face when she sat down with Louise and Connie. She always just wanted to tell him, *Rheta's not coming to Mass again. Give it up.* He hadn't been to church much lately himself; but she could almost see Dominic and Hal in front of her, in seats where they'd always sat; she pictured them there, even though they'd gone to the early service most Sundays, the one she and Rheta, and Chris and Don, out of laziness, avoided.

Then: Connie'd baked chicken and rice, enough for the three of them; so Sara turned down Don's invitation to eat with his family at their house, which she'd rather have accepted.

She worked grimly on another drawing that afternoon. Louise riffled through the newspaper, advised she might want to read her sister's piece, retreated to the kitchen with the advertisements. Sara put the last ink on that sketch and laid it aside to dry. She walked around the neighborhood once more, the unsettled feeling building in her that always did while she waited for Cary to get back. She knew she couldn't read the article right then. Maybe at bedtime. Maybe tomorrow morning. When the pattern resumed.

In a while Jennifer and Cary arrived. Cary wanted to get a shower, do her hair, have a snack before talking; so she waited again. The weekend was done; the routine was resuming, and Cary was right: She *would* say it was a good thing. And Rheta'd say there was something wrong with her.

8

"SO I WAS working on the computer, printing out all this stuff, cartoon things, all that, and you'll never guess what I saw." Cary was sitting on Sara's bed a while later, brushing her hair. "I mean, this other kid, Carson, and I, we were trying to find stuff for the babies to do—"

"Babies?"

"Well, you know: little kids, anyway. And Carson left me, went to get all the markers in the kids' rooms. I was creeped-out by myself in the big building when he left."

"Was he snooping around? You should've told him not to."

"Nah. He didn't go far. Mr. Matheson gave me the key. They all use an ID card, I think, but I guess he didn't want me to use his, and of course I don't have an ID, so, anyway, I opened the building, and I locked the main door behind us so nobody else could get in, and we went upstairs, and I opened Mr. Matheson's office. He'd already told me how to get into his computer. So when Carson wandered off, he couldn't even get out of the building unless I unlocked the main door again! He didn't think about that. So he came back pretty fast. It's creepy wandering around someplace in the dark, having to go up elevators alone, or climb stairs by yourself." She laughed and kept brushing. The lamplight turned her hair reddish-brown, except for the purple streak. "But in the meantime I saw some of your artwork. I guess they've been looking at it, and then, you'll never guess: There was a little small, much smaller, version of *that*!" She pointed to the blue sculpture, which Sara had brought back to her night stand after Rheta left last evening.

Sara had paid half-attention to the meandering story, and now took a sharp breath. "Seriously?"

"Yes! It was a copy, a smaller copy. By then, Carson was back, scared to death, and we both looked at it. See...I took a picture." She thumbed through the phone. Sara looked at a miniature version of the sphere, held in someone's palm.

"It wasn't as nice as this one. When you make little cheap copies, it loses a lot, I guess." She gazed at the night stand, where Sara was comparing the picture to the actual thing.

"Anyway, so maybe you can ask somebody over there about it this week. Sorry, Mom, but I think there might be lots of copies. This one's probably just a large copy."

"So what about the rest of the evening?"

"Oh, you know.... Carson and I got those markers and crayons, and I made sure the doors were locked, and I gave back the key—I know you'll ask, so I'm just tellin'—"

"I didn't," Sara retorted.

"Yeah. And we got the babies busy, and people kind of grouped off to talk, and then we helped put stuff up, and we went home. Well, *we* did, anyway. There were still people there talking politics when we left."

"Politics?"

"Yeah. Who's gonna run for office, who's not. And then the barbecue last night, well, it was just barbecue. Take it or leave it." Cary shrugged. "I could've left it. And today we just stayed in."

"And Allie didn't go?"

"No, I told you she wouldn't. But it was okay."

She finished working on the hair, hugged Sara, and went to bed. "Ah! *My* room!" she exclaimed dramatically before closing the door.

IT SEEMED ALL the children were back and maybe the stomach virus was gone. She'd have plenty of subjects to sketch.

Things had been moved back inside on Friday night without much thought to where they'd been before. She adjusted the utility table and dragged up a stool, spread out the drawings she had done last week, and set aside the two new ones. She was about a third of the way done with all the work; maybe more than a third done. She'd resolved to ink one of the rough sketches, so she started there, instantly messed it up, threw the page away.

She was distracted. She wanted to go next door and look around Matheson's office, find what Cary'd seen. She could say she needed to get the four drawings she'd finished Friday; it was a reasonable pretext.

Kathy poked her head around the open doorway. "Need help getting things back right? I know they probably didn't put it where it should be. Everybody was in a rush to leave."

She shook her head: "It's good," and after just the smallest hesitation, Kathy left. Sara gazed unseeingly at the papers, inks, pens. There was no help for it; she'd use the excuse, get those other drawings and take a glance around. And then what? she scoffed at herself as she walked into the main office. Would she ask where the small sculpture had come from? Was it really anything to her?

She asked to see Matheson. The receptionist gave a quick, cheerful answer: "He flew to Michigan yesterday, won't be back till Wednesday."

Nonplussed, she wavered by the corridor. "What about Mr. Thomas?"

"Oh, no, Ken went, too; he usually does. But I think they did leave you something," and the young woman handed her a flat package.

No point in hanging around there any longer. She might as well try to do some work.

Inside the parcel were her drawings, each protected between sheets of paper, and a note: *These look great! Do the others like them. We decided not to use color. The kids can add their own, if they want to. See you Wednesday afternoon, and we'll hammer out anything else.* He'd signed, "Ken" in big script. He was determined about that.

Her curiosity about the sculpture unsatisfied, not likely to be for a while, either, she worked doggedly the rest of the morning, throwing away two of her first sketches, doing others to replace them. Everyone was used to her by now. She sat on the floor in the hall, peered through the glass wall as the older children blew bubbles and chased them; and later, as they gathered around Liz while she read to them. When the story was over, she went into their room and let them crowd around her, making guesses about who the stylized kids in her sketches might really be.

She hoped, then, the project didn't fall through.

She left after lunch. Lately, she and Louise hadn't been around each other a lot, she realized—whether by design or not, she wasn't sure—not *hers*, but maybe Louise's…. But, anyway, she wouldn't go home right now. She'd go downtown and get a drink and sit outside in the fresh air. Louise, careful not to mention the Sunday paper again, since that could be interpreted as being proud of Rheta, had put it on the kitchen table next to her plate, without comment; she'd shoved it into the briefcase. Now was a good time to read.

The front top photo showed one of Neil's buildings on a street that ran parallel to Main. The photographer hadn't tried to make it look good: brick façade with mortar falling out, door frames peeling, and signs of decay everywhere. Or termites. A smaller inset picture at the corner of the large one depicted the same building in a long-ago time, grinning shoppers in twenties-style clothing standing near the door.

She took her eyes from the grainy photos and looked down the street. The real buildings, right in front of her, looked even worse.

Just below the fold, another picture, this one a closeup of the official marker—Mooresville Historic District—and its description of the area's significance. This first part of Rheta's series was just a narrative of the people who had put up the original shops—the Macons, Hendersons, Browns. None of the current owners seemed connected to these original businesspeople, except for Don Liberto, whose grandfather Vincente had started his bakery after the turn of the century, Rheta noted.

The story continued to page six with a map of the district, the few renovated or restored buildings highlighted yellow. Rheta ended the piece: In its heyday the old part of town had been vibrant and colorful, in character and literally. What was going on now? Tomorrow's Part Two would describe the work required to attain the historical designation, and the resistance to that effort.

Sara reached toward a nearby trash bin, wincing as she remembered this was Rheta's work. Would the summer book with her art, and, eventually, the kids', too, end up in a landfill? She sat under a green and red umbrella and gazed at the ugly building to the left, until she finished the soda.

ROUTINE. IT *WAS* a good thing.

Cary was right: Somehow, sometime, it had become her mantra. But, then, her life preserver, too.

The Monday-evening students were all sleepy and dull this week. She let them go twenty minutes early, telling them to read the current series running in the paper. She figured few of them, maybe none, would know that R. C. Whitson was actually Rheta Collins, her sister. Why should they?

She'd kept Matthew's name because of Cary.

Monday's paper was on the table when she got home. She scooped it up, laid her briefcase down in its spot on her desk, then, contrarily, turned it thirty degrees off-kilter. Cary, twisting a strand of hair, fidgeting in the doorway, observed, and touched the satchel as if to straighten it, but seemed to rethink that.

Mildly irritated at the invasion of her space just then, Sara undressed and put on pajamas, slowly, exaggerating the process.

"Mom." Cary sounded decisive now. "You know, I'm not sure I'm going to hold you to the beach thing."

"Why?"

"Some of us've decided we want to do stuff around here the week we're off."

Sara sat cross-legged on the bed and gestured—the usual invitation for Cary to sit and talk. Tonight she shook her head.

"No. I mean, I don't have anything else to say, really, just we're going to hang out over the break. So—" she shrugged—"you don't have to bribe me after all. Can you cancel it without too much bother?"

She shrugged. "Haven't paid yet."

Cary sauntered to the bed and hugged Sara. "Night. I won't stay up too late. Got a test. Already studied."

A while later Sara crept into the hallway and saw no light, no bluish glow under Cary's door. She heard Louise's soft snores from her room. It felt odd, creepy, Cary'd say, to be the only one awake in the house. But a good time to read that article. She settled back onto the bed, pillow behind her back.

The tone was sharper, no nostalgia. It was the first time Sara'd seen anything so close to the older pieces Rheta used to do. A few decades ago, Rheta said, when Moore Farms began winding down, the town at first didn't recognize the connection between their prosperity and Ransome Moore's. With the closing down of his production came the closing down of many local businesses, not all of them directly tied to the needs of a farm.

Sara knew all this, remembered Hal talking about it sometimes, had even seen a blank, tired expression on Dominic's face. It wasn't just the grain elevator, but the hotels, other restaurants and stores. Downtown shops closed. Two strip malls popped up, Rheta continued, populated with check-cashing businesses and adult-video emporiums. During all that time, several people bought up the older, now-empty buildings. David Burkes and Reg Griffin accumulated the majority.

And then they left them to sit, some for more than twenty

years, fading, peeling, untenanted. People wondered why they'd bought them, only to let them fall apart. Rheta talked with a few former real-estate agents, whose finances had also suffered during those lean years while property values went down—more collateral damage, she pointed out. Asked if they remembered what motivated those buyers, the agents were willing to talk: Burkes and Griffin, in particular, were after a bargain, pure and simple. Nothing wrong with that, one of the agents added; if she'd had the money, she might have bought some property herself. When the shop owners weren't able to turn profits, and it seemed in those years that the town might endure the same slow death other little Southern hamlets had, the buildings sold for cents on the dollar. Who else wanted them? the agents asked Rheta reasonably. And, yes, it was a fact the owners had financial interests in the strip malls on the fringes of town, but so what? They were investments.

Rheta asked: When it seemed that Mooresville's fortunes were at last improving, what might be a hypothetical motive for why the owners weren't rehabbing the stores? Were they not willing to spend money to fix them, which would be a lot, no doubt? Did they feel they wouldn't get decent offers if they put them on the market right now?

The agents had left Mooresville a decade ago, but real estate people networked. Some offers were made, one of them said at last—just not high enough to suit the current owners, who had turned those down and indicated little interest in negotiation.

So is it all a tax write-off? Rheta persisted.

One agent her shook her head. Hard to imagine how it could be that and nothing else. But, anyway, no law required people to publish their tax information.

Then why might it be that no one seemed to want even to rent the places now? Had the owners tried to find tenants?

The agents didn't know that. How could they? Again: privacy.

Two more exterior shots followed, photos contrasting Liberto's with the neglected structures on either side. If one owner could maintain such an appealing building, why couldn't others? On this point, Nora Burkes had offered a comment: Liberto's had been in business many years, had always occupied its space. This was not true of the other places, which were purchased empty and for which no new tenant could be found. When asked to describe efforts to find such a tenant, Mrs. Burkes declined to elaborate.

The article ended with a teaser about the third part: Tomorrow readers would hear from Ron Matheson concerning the involvement of MTE in Mooresville; and Ransome Moore had a few things to say, too, about his namesake town.

IN THE STILL house Sara made a scoffing noise, so quietly that neither Louise nor Cary could have heard, even awake. So Rheta had chased down the father of her old boyfriend. It was going to be another glass of the ditch water Ransome had used as a stunt, long ago, in a supervisors' board meeting, and in front of the media. He knew how to get an audience even then. Those televised forums, where David Burkes's face had got red and you could see him clenching his teeth—they'd been priceless. She smiled even now at the thought of them.

But those memories of Ransome squabbling with David receded in her thoughts. She wished Rheta hadn't brought Matheson into it at all. If he really wanted the area saved, why hadn't he installed his company downtown? Rheta'd probably say things about safe distances and the cost of modernizing, and how it would be simpler to build new and hang onto the worthy older things at the same time...all true...

She swept the paper off her bed, onto the floor. She'd get a nice check from this little book, and nothing else was relevant. She'd be done with it, and maybe then she wouldn't feel any more as if she were being pulled, resisting but futilely, away from a sheltering, snug haven where for all her life she'd known the things she had to know.

9

STEPHEN LOGAN WAS on his best behavior, and on a schedule, too, walking down the street about every other day, stopping to chat with people he encountered, people who sometimes wished he hadn't renewed the acquaintance. Long gone were the days of hanging around town, getting into minor trouble, looking for a chance to argue with somebody. It was all replaced by a new mien, just as the sagging, torn jeans and acid-rock T-shirts of youth were exchanged for pressed slacks and sweaters or Oxford shirts. He strolled along like any other of the local politicians, glad-handing and greeting.

When Sara left MTE on Tuesday afternoon, she stopped so long beside her car that an employee walking by turned a curious glance at her. She'd realized with a shock she'd probably finish the project on Thursday. She'd absent-mindedly gathered all her materials and supplies, packed the completed drawings and checked them off the list. It was as she placed everything carefully in her car that she remembered the checkmarks going down the column, leaving only two or three more items. She scowled unconsciously as she drove. Getting through earlier than the deadline would get her that bonus, and yet it bothered her that this one little daily change in their routine was about to end.

She told Cary she'd spring for sorbets before they went on home, if Cary was in the mood. Cary was always in the mood for a sorbet. Ten minutes later they sat enjoying the early spring sunshine outside Liberto's when Stephen Logan strolled by in a nice pair of jeans and a lightweight V-neck sweater. He leaned over a nearby table and said a few words to someone; and at that moment Don emerged through the front door to rearrange several umbrellas, meanwhile casting glances towards the table where the trapped people smiled nervously as their uninvited guest rambled on about something.

The umbrella-adjusting was unnecessary; even Cary watched skeptically. Logan took his leave of the people he'd been hanging over and tilted his chin upward, a smirk on his face. "Don. How's life treatin' you?"

"I'm good. You?" There was no warmth on Don's face. He leaned against the decorative cast-iron railing that separated the tables from the actual sidewalk, but no one would have thought he was relaxed.

"Can't complain...you got something fit to eat on the menu these days?"

"You've seen the menu. Hello, Sara, Cary."

Logan glanced towards the two of them, turning a toothy smile in their direction. Cary recoiled.

"You gonna order today or just keep walking around, making people uncomfortable?"

"I'm on my way to see my lawyer. Pretty afternoon—why can't I chat with folks I know? It's a public place."

The three people at the table where he'd stopped got up and, carefully casual, took half a minute to throw napkins and a paper plate or two into the trash bin as they left.

Don noted their departure, "Your lawyer's on the *other* side of the street. And you're not on the sidewalk. You're on an extension of my restaurant. I don't like you running off my customers."

Logan held up his hands quizzically. "They were done! You saw they threw their stuff away. City hall said this isn't the property of any one business."

Don abruptly stepped away from the little fence. "Test it in court."

"No need to get worked up. I'll just be on my way."

"Yeah, I'd avoid any more run-ins with the law, if I were you."

Logan crossed through the passage that allowed patrons to return to the sidewalk. "I won't take that as a threat, but I should. You're touchy these days," he said, crossing in the middle of the street and glancing back over his shoulder at Don. Sara stared as he went into the lobby of the building that Neil owned and where he maintained his legal office.

"If you hang out with scum, it starts growing on you," Don remarked to Sara, looking hard at her. Not wanting to ask whom he was referring to—her, or Neil, or Stephen Logan?—she focused on the new river-birch leaves.

"Who was *that*?" Cary said.

AROUND LUNCHTIME ON the day after the fires, Stephen showed up for work as usual, on time and ready to adopt a persona that, in his mind, was politely deferential and got him bigger tips. He and the boss's sons served the lunch crowd that began arriving a little early today. They were busy enough for a while not to pay attention to the chatter as acquaintances across tables exchanged information.

"Darrell Parten says it's faulty wiring."

"I say bullshit. Two in the same night? Wiring? Gotta be kidding me."

"You probably right."

"Just look at it this way: Ransome gets rid of his field hands, kid pops off his mouth... Somebody decided to make a statement."

"Well, just *hope* it's faulty wiring. Lord God, we don't need nothin' like what happened back then, that kind of publicity again."

The crowd was large today. The waiters heard all of it over and over, in variations.

Stephen hauled a load of dirty dishes and silverware to the back and handed it over to the dishwasher. Chris came in with another armful: "Nice crowd."

"For all the wrong reasons," Don muttered.

They didn't ask what he meant.

"Yeah. You listening to 'em? Stupid assholes."

Dominic hovered nearby, glowering, and Chris knew what was next: "Watch the mouth!"

Stephen rolled his eyes at Chris. "Yeah, yeah. Manicotti plate ready? Where's the garnish?"

The cook cast a dark glance at him and arranged a sprig on the plate, then slid it back. "You're trying to push 'em out too fast."

"Fast is what they want."

"Let you try this job for a while," the cook muttered.

Stephen laughed and went back through the door with the garnished dish. Chris bent over the plates and stacked the clean ones away to help the dishwasher, who, like the cook, seemed overwhelmed.

"Wish I'd never hired him," Dominic said.

"Why *did* you?"

He didn't answer the cook but, instead, turned and kept his gaze on the young man who lingered near the table where he'd delivered the manicotti. It irritated Dominic to see him lean down into the customers' conversation and make comments himself, snicker, hang around a little too long. Dominic's fingers tapped an angry rhythm on the pass-through. Stephen returned to the kitchen after a few minutes.

"Don't visit with the customers when we're this busy!"

"And be rude? They wanna talk, so I talk. Get a bigger tip."

The lunch crowd mostly straggled out by 2:30. Liberto's was a small restaurant in the small town, and all workers helped when there were customers. The three servers and the dishwasher finished kitchen cleanup. Dominic kept an eye on the two tables still occupied, one by a teenage couple and the other by Lynne Houston and her brother William Sykes, who'd arrived late. He owned one of the three grocery stores in town, and she ran a tailor shop and sold yarns and sewing goods, and they both were struggling right now, Dominic knew. And so was he. He was glad for the business today, even with the uproar accompanying it. Things had been off since March, when Ransome Moore shut down his whole farm.

Every so often he mouthed, "Everything good?" to the occupants of those tables. And they nodded back.

The boys talked and cleaned. Eventually Stephen returned to his opinion of the gossip he'd eavesdropped on earlier.

"They call it bad wiring. Like it jumps around place to place. Like lightning," he laughed.

"Why you find that so funny?" That was Don.

"I don't find it funny. It's funny those idiots say it. That boy shot off his mouth, now people are riled up." He was at that moment turned away from Dominic, whose head swiveled toward them a little. Don felt anxious, knowing what was about to happen.

"Probably KKK, coming in, throwing weight around. Bad wiring." Stephen scoffed again. "Wiring don't light matches. Hell, they probably did it themselves to keep stuff stirred up. That's *my* opinion."

When he found out Stephen's mother had lost her job cleaning rooms at the motel, Dominic had sent word for him to come by. He knew about hardship, raising kids alone. Stephen had kept a smirk on his face while they talked—as if he was doing Dom the favor. The lowered eyelids, the smartass body posture...he knew Stephen considered it beneath him. He knew doing it would probably fester in Stephen, that he was working for somebody he considered less than he.

"You know something, go see the sheriff," Dominic suggested. "Or else keep your mouth shut."

Don glanced at Stephen and raised his eyebrows, a signal. They needed a third waiter, and he could do a decent job when he wanted to. But the excitement in town seemed to have hyped *him* up, too; he swaggered more than usual, and Chris, the hotheaded brother, always reacted to that kind of crap, and now Chris was getting agitated.

They'd all made a pretty good haul today in tips, and Stephen's new affluence got the better of him. "I can talk if I want to," he told Dominic. "It's a free country. Where your kind of people come from, maybe you can't do that. But here, I can express myself however I want to."

Don looked at Chris, who was staring at Logan, red-faced,

hands twitching at his sides. Don was the diplomatic one of the three Liberto men; Chris's temper was almost as bad as Dominic's. "Why don't you take off a while, we'll get the rest straightened up here," he started, but too late, though it wasn't Chris but Dominic who grabbed Stephen by the elbow and hurried him through the restaurant.

"Out, out, don't show up tomorrow! Don't show up next day, either!"

"Why you firin' me, old man?"

Dominic rushed him toward the front. Don trailed, worried about this public exit, wishing Dominic had gone through the rear of the building, where an industrial door guarded the kitchen from the back alley. Stephen railed at him as he was shoved out: "I'll talk what I want to whoever I want! 'S a free country! And get your hand off me, try to shut me up, no—" And, being pushed through the double doors to the sidewalk, a few last words as the teenagers at the one table and the shop owners at the other watched: "Fuck you, old man! I don't need nothin' from a greasy dago anyway!"

STEPHEN ENJOYED THE time off and the fame of being the first person Dominic Liberto was known to have ever fired. He combed back his hair and wore nicer clothing for a few days, strolling downtown, hanging around outside different establishments, now that he had no job to regulate his hours. A day or two later, he was lounging languidly on the concrete landing at the courthouse, soda in hand. The baluster was hot, but crepe myrtles hung over it and shaded, dropping tiny petals in the light breeze, like confetti swirling around after a parade.

Several spots on the west side of the courthouse were designated for Sheriff Darrell Parten and his deputies. Parten had just about had enough of seeing the Logan boy wandering around. He'd heard the faulty wiring idea himself; actually, he hoped for that, prayed for it, knowing, however, it was a desperate, half-assed theory proposed by people who'd made bad grades in high-school history. He and one of the deputies had been called to the first conflagration and stood wordless at a distance from the frame building ablaze in the dark night. Forget all that crap about a full moon making people do crazy stuff: All that light prevented things, didn't promote them, he believed. He and the deputy had actually talked about it, the deputy telling him, "Light drives out darkness," a thing Parten wholeheartedly agreed with, although he had to be told later where the thought originated.

The crackling, spitting orange demon created its own heathen light. He'd wanted to say something—the right kind of something—to the man beside him, gazing while two local engines wasted water. It wasn't as if the deputy attended that church; it was just the deep, sad symbolism of the whole thing, the two of them motionless there in the lurid, flashing light. Darrell Parten had been raised in the county, and the deputy was from two over—local guys. As the flames scorched all green things nearby, their being together was itself an ironic symbol.

When the second call came in, the deputy had turned to Parten, a sort of astounded, ancient fury on his face, and all Darrell could do was look down at the ground and shake his head. "Let's go."

Now, as he parked in front of the courthouse, he saw him: a senior kid whose primary ambition had long been just to be noticed, to feel more important than he was. Parten already knew that Logan's boss, who didn't like the boy much in the first place, had hired him because he felt sorry for him, trying to hang out with that rich crowd. The punk was either unaware or unconcerned that that group tolerated him as somebody who'd act on and maybe even take ownership of their pranks and mischief around town: their scapegoat. Road signs vandalized, high school entrance sprayed with graffiti—it was probably Stephen Logan and whoever he ran with, people figured, unaware of exactly who was in the group. Willfully unaware, Parten would've said. Deliberately unaware.

He walked heavily up the steps and glanced at Logan. "Employment office is down the street. Hear you need a job now."

Stephen stretched his arms upward. "You could invite me to your nice, cool office. Kind of hot out here," he said as Parten lumbered past.

The sheriff's mouth thinned a little. "Not concerned about your body temperature. But you ain't no petunia planter, boy. Although you are full of shit," he said, as if it were a joke. He'd figured out Logan was behind some of the minor stuff around town, but it was mostly too petty for him to get worked up to the point of confronting him about it. And he knew Logan, after months lying his way out of the minor things, had learned what two-bit criminals and upstanding citizens all learned sometime or other: When you lied with a straight face, vociferously, people would believe you. Sometimes you could almost believe yourself.

"You wanna come in and cool off, that's okay by me," Parten continued, walking away, "we ain't got no job for you, unless you volunteerin' for road work I know about that needs doing. Some signs replaced. And you might pick up that soft-drink can there. I'd hate to write you a ticket for littering, you such a fine young man and all."

Parten nodded once at the deputy sitting at a table near the door and led the way into the nice, cool office. Darius Clark followed him and took a chair near Parten's desk, where he could glare at Logan. In the past few years they'd worked out the routine they used on people like Stephen who always seemed puzzled by the relationship between the sheriff and the deputy—D and D, the other cops called them in shorthand, or sometimes "Darryl and his brother Darryl," after those guys on that TV show. One of the others started that, and it was a joke Clark and Parten found unfunny but ignored, because responding would only make the other cops lay it on thicker. Parten enjoyed the role of the dim, small-town officer, and Clark cultivated his angry Black man persona whenever he thought it helpful. They'd worked it on local druggies, petty thieves, shoplifters, and on Stephen Logan a time or two, planting two notions in his head: that Parten secretly sympathized with him, having had the same kind of hardscrabble upbringing he'd had; and that Darius was just your stereotypical disgruntled Black cop stuck in a small town, waiting for a promotion.

Parten directed Logan to a hard, wooden chair with just slightly uneven legs. It wobbled when he shifted positions, tapping on the terrazzo floor. Stephen raked his long hair out of his face with the splayed fingers of his right hand.

Parten never talked loud, and Darius, hardly at all; the deputy mostly sat and glowered—today at Stephen Logan—with contempt, sneering through a conversation as if disgusted by the waste of his time. The sheriff spoke briefly to the deputy about inconsequential things they needed to do, and then, sliding some papers around on his desk, asked, as if he really didn't care, "You know, I heard your boss didn't like you bein' late to work the other day. Guess that's why you don't have a job anymore, huh. They're looking for a janitor here," he added.

"He didn't fire me, I quit, I wasn't late. Go ask the others. They know. They'll tell you I wasn't late."

"No, it was one of the *patrons* that day remembers you rushin' in with the plates. Said they thought you must be late... Or maybe it was Mr. Liberto told me," he added thoughtfully.

"If he said that, it was a lie! I was never late for work. That day or any other day. He was always down on me because I'm not his race, nor his religion."

The deputy sighed deeply.

"So why'd he fire you, again?" Parten asked, frowning a little, trying to recall.

"Hell, I don't know—go ask him! He just don't like me. For *whatever* reason," he added, to mollify the deputy, who hadn't stopped looking at him.

"Lotta people at the restaurant that day, they say; why'd he fire a waiter when he needed 'im?"

"I don't know, I said! Go ask him! We *were* busy, very busy that day!"

"I know; I rode by a time or two," Parten agreed amiably. "Lots of people in there." He leaned across his desk, earnestness on his face. "You hear anything that day could help us out? Something to give us a start on these fires?" He didn't think Logan had figured that one out just yet. He knew what it was to be that age—thirty years ago, he'd been one of those boys himself: pissing your time away in a little town with nothing to make of yourself, wanting to find somebody to push around, just to show you could. And he'd never have dreamed then he'd ever have a Black deputy working with him, and he was willing to give Logan a chance to walk it back and do the right thing, get all those boys and himself some community service and suspended time, if they admitted it, turn 'em into better citizens.

"Well, people *were* talkin' about it," Stephen said, leaning against the wall in the wooden chair, the front two legs up. "Sayin' it must've been wiring."

The deputy rolled his eyes, a contemptuous rumble in his throat. Parten said, as if it were something he hadn't thought of, something he might believe, "Wiring? You think maybe it was wiring?"

"No, I said that was what people were sayin'. It couldn't've been wiring unless it jumped light poles two miles apart, could it?"

"I don't know...could it?" Parten asked. The deputy leaned forward and glared at Logan, who, thinking all at once that this would be different from the stop signs and the spray paint cans, suddenly got nervous.

"Look, I told you, it's a stupid idea, I said so all along. I told old man Liberto, I told 'em it was stupid. I think..." He glanced at the deputy.

Parten waited.

"You know that boy—that Black dude," he said carefully, changing his mind about the words he'd started to use, "that guy that smarted off about old man Moore, after he closed down his farm?"

"Yeah, what about 'im?"

"Where's *he*? Just suddenly gone, now, last week or two. I heard folks talkin'about somebody maybe killin' him. Sayin' whoever got rid of him maybe was tryin' to get back at his family."

"His family? They moved off."

Stephen anxiously tried to find another word in his thesaurus, failed. "His *people*."

"His 'people'? What 'people'?"

"You *know* what I mean," Stephen hedged, another glance at the deputy, who spoke sardonically:

"He means us Black folks around here, Sheriff Parten."

Logan was beginning to feel nervous, no longer sure he was ahead of them. "I think it was people trying to scare *them*."

"Who'd be tryin' to scare them?"

"I mean, segregationalists, KKK, somebody..." The chair wobbled a little. He corrected it. "Or maybe they did it themselves," he suggested.

"Now, who do *you* hang out with, Stephen?" the sheriff said, all easygoing familiarity gone from his face.

He thought he might have said too much, and in his agitation he leaned a little too far to the right, and one side of his butt slipped off. He landed on a knee on the floor. Laughing softly, Darius Clark offered him a hand up.

Stephen pushed back. "I can get up. Leave me alone."

"We'd like to leave you alone, not see you again, but you got a big mouth, and this whole business ain't like stealin'a six-pack from William Sykes. This is big-time felony."

"Why you after me and not care about who killed that Black dude?"

"Haven't heard he did anything but leave town. You the first person's mentioned 'killing' to me. So try not to fall off your chair or wet your pants, and tell us about *that*."

"I'm done. You call me in again, I'll have a lawyer."

"You can have one. It's your right," Parten told him pleasantly. "And you might recall you offered to come in on your own. But if you're ready to go, get on out now, go find you a lawyer, before I decide to arrest you for vandalism."

The deputy sneered. "We got more important things to do than listen to your shit."

"Vandalism of *what*?"

"Got plenty of possibilities," Parten said, advancing on him. He'd never touch him, of course; just with his bulk and Clark's height they could intimidate most of the characters they brought into the office. Logan grabbed the doorknob and left, remembering to swagger out onto the first floor of the courthouse.

A newspaper reporter had had a slow day in the courtroom and was willing to listen to him.

"They brought me in, kept me there askin' stuff, but I didn't do nothin'," he told the reporter, who snapped a photo. It was Stephen's first public appearance: ***Local Boy Claims Innocence in Arsons***.

The fire marshall eventually said the evidence was inconclusive: too hot a fire. All of Mooreville was relieved that a disreputable young man nobody cared much for anyway might be the one who went to jail, and hoped nobody else would. How such a thing could happen, could explode out of the distant past they were all trying to live down, was something no one wanted to analyze too deeply. But it had to be ultimately Ransome Moore's fault: He'd let the rest of his crew go when he shut down the farm, and he'd never tried to do much for them, anyway; and, besides, there was that other stuff with the girl....

D and D talked. "Bet he's lawyering up."

"Yeah. Wonder *how*," Parten speculated. "He ain't got no money."

For a few days the two D's managed to be in places where Logan also happened to be. On one of those occasions, Clark began the conversation, abruptly and coldly, emerging from Lynne

Houston's notions shop as Logan ambled down the sidewalk.

"How you doin' today, *boy*?" he growled.

But Stephen actually had talked to a lawyer by then, off the record. "I'm just fine. You?" He wanted the deputy not to stroll along beside him—made him look like he was cooperating with him, in case anybody was watching—but there wasn't anything he could do about it.

"Been staying busy lately?" Clark went on. "Got a job yet? Guy like you needs a job. Always good to have an alibi."

"Look, man, I told you, I didn't do nothing. You know there was more than one person, to pull that off. That's your job to find out, not mine, you don't seem to be doing it. Just harassing me. By the way, this's my attorney." He handed over the business card of a lawyer in the next county, a young guy newly licensed, Parten found out later. Logan was happy to see the deputy grimace: *That* put him in his place.

After a while, when it looked as if that was the end of it, Ransome Moore hauled his bulldozer over to the churches to clean up the charred remains and laughed quietly, as David Burkes and Reginald Griffin sweated and in dismay watched their shoes get dusty.

10

"**WAS DON MAD** at *us*?" Cary wondered on the way home.

"He doesn't like Stephen Logan hanging around."

Seeing him enter Neil's office, nonchalantly, familiarly, had kept her from finishing her sorbet. She said it had made her cold, but Cary was disbelieving.

"That guy bothers people. Who is he?" she'd asked again, and Sara, remembering more than she wanted Cary to know, described him as somebody she'd gone to school with, who'd been in trouble through the years but had cleaned up a good deal just lately. "Well, he's creepy, I don't care how good he actually *looks*," Cary remarked. Sara agreed and drove on, plotting how to ask Don what the hell he'd meant by that remark of his, discarding the idea by the time she got home, because he was honest; he'd tell her.

—And so would Ransome Moore, she thought later, reading

the paper. Actually, Dominic and Ransome, never close friends, had respected each other—in weird ways, she mused, scanning Rheta's last installment before actually reading it. Dominic had hired Rheta when nobody in town would risk that, after her short-lived "boycott." And still Ransome had kept coming to Dom's restaurant, staging impromptu meetings with his business pals there. And tipping her well, Rheta had told Sara.

The top half of the paper was dominated by a color photo of him standing beside a fence, his hand resting against the cheek of a roan horse. He hadn't aged well—jowly, with a gut. Rheta asked if he kept up with things going on in his eponymous town these days. His indirect answer in a text block in the middle of the article: "You don't hold onto the past forever. When you try to, you hold onto *all* of it, the good but the bad, too, and the bad'll come back and bite you in the ass."

Sara chuckled and wondered how Rheta'd managed to get that into the piece.

Rheta asked if he was calling out anybody in particular. He advised her to look up all the old buzzards in town.

Sara could imagine David Burkes grimacing if he had the paper in front of him; the thought gave her pleasure.

Rheta'd also cornered Ron Matheson. He told about buying the Moore Farms lands seven years ago, after making a few quiet trips to look at it himself. The company'd been planning an expansion, but if word got out they were buying, prices would skyrocket. In a couple of magazines with national exposure he'd seen the ad offering Ransome's land for sale. It was one of several properties he'd looked at, but the most beautiful, and he wasn't interested in bulldozing trees and excavating enormous holes in the landscape. It was a part of his philosophy: Keep what's good and move into the future. So he'd encouraged the establishment of the historical district and had paid for the consult at the state level. Several company officers toured downtown after the land was purchased; and on the principal street (Sara realized he meant where Neil's office, the jewelry shop, Liberto's, Music Monster all were), they'd seen the core of a vibrant area not unlike some midsize villages in the Northeast, where people could walk and enjoy public spaces again. MTE had donated startup money for the outdoor seating, had even funded, with an outright grant, the cast-iron railing that ran along both sides of Main Street.

But when they'd offered grants to individual owners for the renovation or rehabbing of their buildings, something changed.

Were too many rules and stipulations attached to the grants? Rheta wondered; that was what a couple of people she spoke with had alluded to.

Matheson conceded there were rules about how the money could be spent and the required documentation, but he viewed that as a small price to pay. Somehow, instead, resistance had arisen. "You'd think there are bodies in the walls."

Rheta asked what he meant by that.

It was a joke, she quoted, "but this is not: You go ask the owners why they twist people's arms to turn down what we offered."

Did he want to elaborate on that comment about twisting arms?

He did not.

Like the earlier ones, this piece continued into the paper a few pages over, and Sara read the final paragraph before really looking at the photo at the top of that page. This was a posed picture, like the one on the front with Ransome and his horse. Here, Matheson wore a suit and tie and stood, arms crossed, leaning against a desk, a heavy, ornate desk with no clutter on top, only a letter opener, a nice wooden inbox tray, a couple of small items; it was too obviously cleared off, maybe for that picture. Then everything Rheta had written left Sara's head, as she saw the little sphere that Cary had a snap of on her phone.

SHE WAS READY for spring break, ready to be away from the college students for a few days, ready to bury for a little while the creeping disquiet that made her glance sometimes over her shoulder even as she went through her mundane routines, the things she'd done, unthinking, for years. It was anxiety she couldn't source, like a bad smell emanating from something spoiled that she couldn't find in the kitchen. It was a mix of Rheta's articles and fear of what might come of them, and looks Don gave her these days, and her own restlessness. She realized she'd needed that beach trip herself; and now Cary wasn't interested in going anywhere.

She talked out an email as she drove to MTE on Wednesday. The employees there had been kind, had taken care to see she had what she needed; but after she read those things in the paper, a strange sense of isolation had overcome the good vibes. Refining her message as she passed through the pine barren and approached the lake, she knew she hadn't connected with the employees at all. Their work had gone on while she was staring at their children and drawing versions of their activities to complete a book she'd have little to do with after its printing. She'd glimpsed Matthew once or twice as he'd arrived or left, but he only gave her a glance, and not a friendly one.

No, she had no relationship with any of them. But she was envious of the busyness of the office, and unhappy that for her it was over.

She parked, took the portfolio and her briefcase, went into Kid Kare. She had three drawings to finish today. They'd go fast.

She tapped out the email on her phone first: She'd enjoyed the project, appreciated the use of the room while working, and would send over to the main office the completed portfolio by the end of the day. She was about to start preliminary work on a new book herself (but *was* she?), so if they were happy with her art, it would be a good time to complete the financial details so they and she could move on.

Before hitting "send," she re-read the words, knew they were terse, maybe even truculent. She felt a rush of the same vague resentment she'd had the first time she'd talked to Ken Thomas, and that made her angry, because she knew again it was irrational. She sent the message anyway, feeling resigned instead of relieved. Why? She ought to be relieved; she'd made good money for such a small thing, and it was done. She remembered Thomas and Matheson weren't expected back till later that day. Perhaps by then she'd have left: all the better.

SHE STAYED MORE than usual that morning in her room: Why spend any more time with those women, when after this afternoon she wouldn't see them again? But, as always, the art soothed the emotions, and soon she was mildly ashamed of her bitterness and ambled over to speak to Kathy and Liz. By now, the children always leaned familiarly against her, pointing at things she'd sketched. She'd miss them.

She thought of something else, and snipped several sheets of watercolor stock into small rectangles.

"Can I get a list of the children's first names?"

Kathy pointed to the roll posted by the door.

In the main office she gave the portfolio to the receptionist. "Done. Please put this on Ken Thomas' desk."

"You're through? Wait a sec—" But Sara interrupted: "Yes, if you don't mind, just lay them on his desk. I have a little more work to finish, and I can't stay till he gets back this evening." She smiled in expiation for the firm words.

"All right." It was a grudging answer; and the woman headed down the long wide hall.

She'd stuck her phone in her pocket after snapping the class roll, and now she took a few pictures of the landscaping, the outside play areas, the lake that glittered off to her right. She might not return, not for a long while, maybe not ever. How things had changed since Ransome's years here! She wondered if he'd approve of how it looked now, and paused a moment, the cool breeze softening the effects of the bright early-March Southern sunshine; then she went in to work on the little rectangles.

In a few minutes she heard, "Centipede!" and the shuffling of feet as the kids went out. The noise died down a little as it had on other days, but didn't entirely stop this time. She stood at the plate-glass wall. All the older children were taking seats at the concrete tables to have their lunch. It was a pleasant, warm day, a good day to eat outside. She'd have been happy to have a sandwich with them, before she left. But she sighed and continued to sketch a child on each rectangle—a caricature, actually, with a flower, a toy, a book, *something*, and a name in a whimsical font. She glanced up to see Kathy and Liz tying cheap plastic squares down the front of the kids' T-shirts and, bemused, stopped to puzzle that out. In a moment or two someone appeared around the corner, pushing a cart with box containers and bottles of water and juice. When the children began eating the tomato rotini, she laughed, comprehending now the makeshift plastic aprons. She moved closer to watch.

"These are cute," someone said behind her. "This is a nice thing to do."

She turned to find Ron Matheson at the utility table, looking over the little rectangles. She'd almost made a sharp remark about how he liked sneaking up on people, but caught that one in time; he'd only find it funny. She wanted to snatch the cards and pack them away. Instead, she forced a tight smile on her face and stayed by the windows.

"I didn't think you'd be back this early," she said.

"We got through sooner than we expected." He gestured to a carton and a bottle of water on the table, as he examined the sketches. "I brought you some lunch. After your email, I figured you'd be out of here early afternoon, skip eating, but today was Italian day, and I know you like Italian food." His attention seemed entirely focused on the drawings.

She opened the carton. Inside was an adult-sized portion of Liberto's baked rotini, topped with grated mozzarella, a piece of toasted bread wrapped in foil. "Thank you. How would *you* know I like Italian food?"

"Don said so," he mumbled absent-mindedly, shuffling the pieces of paper. Then, as if aware of the insufficiency of that answer, he added, "He and I talk. We negotiate prices for these meals. He's tough. But he gives a break on delivery. Everybody in town knows you've been working here for a while, so today he sent a note with his delivery person: 'Tell Sara I made this batch with her in mind.' "

This made her feel guilty again. "How is it you get things like this for lunch?"

He laid down the sketches and took a stool across from her. "Eat while it's still warm. We pay Don's driver to get it here fresh. I've already eaten. I got back in time."

The aroma was irresistible, and she *was* hungry. She'd planned to have a sandwich at home, but the rotini was one of her favorites. She texted Louise—***Get lunch on your own, please***—opened the water, picked up the bag that held the plastic fork and a napkin.

"Yeah, they can't deliver the atmosphere, though," Matheson said dryly.

While she ate, he looked again at the rectangles. "So you did these for the kids to say thanks? So they'll remember you?"

"Some of all that." She took a sip of the water and gestured at the food. "But tell me what this's about."

"All right. Well, out here in the backwoods, just a little bit too far to drive into town for lunch, you gotta bring your own, and it gets old fast. We knew that in advance, planned for it. We started with a real cafeteria, not big, more a light-lunch, fast order place, hired our own staff...salads, lowfat things, 'eat healthy,' you know, because you Southerners do like that grease—" she started to object, realized he was baiting her again. "But then everybody liked the healthy stuff more."

She smiled a little. "Probably not. Grease *is* wonderful. You should try it sometime."

"I have. At my age, I don't need it, though. Then," he went on, "we heard grumbling. People who might've grabbed lunch downtown but now worked out here in the woods felt like we were taking the restaurant business, hurting the community places. A good point, so now we have deals with all the eateries in town, the ones willing to deliver, anyway, and we have variety and don't have to clean up a kitchen. There's the Styrofoam—" he indicated the rotini container— "but we'll figure that out. And today was Don's turn."

She took another bite. " 'Eat healthy,' huh. One of those decisions the newspaper says you make for the good of the town."

He rolled his eyes. "Holy shit, that, again."

"Did you plan this—" she motioned toward her brushes— "because it's good for the kids? Or to get people to like you?"

"Can't believe you're saying that, knowing it's costing me a mint. And, anyway, would it matter?" He looked coolly at her. "Judgy today, aren't you."

"Just seems paternalistic. The other branch, in Michigan, you run it this way, too?"

"There are several, it's not 'the' other one, and I know how that sounds. And, no, not yet. One day, though," he said grimly.

"What does this company actually do? I don't see anything being manufactured, so…"

"One branch does make things. Just not here. Not yet. What we do here's software, engineering projects—not what people call 'goods.' Some's classified, so don't ask. Is that everybody's problem: We don't grow corn and beans like Ransome did, they don't consider engineering a real commodity? We aren't farm boys?"

"Gimme a break," she scoffed.

"Matthew never said anything about what we do?"

The change in subject made her uncomfortable. "He came here long after we were divorced," she told him.

"But I'd think he would've mentioned it. Before it goes further, because I see you're getting agitated, he's a good accountant, and I don't get into my employees' lives. So no more about that. Please."

In a moment he added, "I can know their names, can't I?"

She finished eating in silence, and he seemed willing to wait her out as she kept her gaze challengingly on him. "Dessert?" she said at last. "If you're such a friend of Don's, he should've mentioned the tiramisu. Or an ice."

"Ices would melt on the way here, and tiramisu's too filling and would make everybody sleepy. We still have an afternoon of work."

"I don't," she said pointedly, cleaning up the table.

"No, and that's part of the reason I came with lunch. The artwork's very nice, and you did it in the time frame we needed, so, yeah, we can take care of the 'financial details,' as you put it, before you leave today, if that's what you want. I hope you did enjoy the work. There may be other times—"

"I enjoyed it, yes," she interrupted, to stop that line of conversation. "I'd have to decide on anything else as it came along. I'm independent, not a paid contractor. There's one more thing about this one: I don't know what you have in mind—we didn't talk about it—but I thought one of those last things I did would make a good cover. Is there a, like an artistic director I could discuss it with?"

"That would be me."

In spite of herself she raised her brows.

"I'm it. I reserve most final decisions for myself. You think that's funny, I guess."

"No, I expected that." If he could be blunt, so could she.

"I'll leave so you can finish these charming notes. I'm glad you got invested in what Ken still calls my 'wild scheme.' "

"Of course I'm invested. You brought that up several times. And so did he. What would you think? I mean, I live here," she told him.

He was passing through the doorless opening as she said this. Perhaps it wasn't quite what he'd expected, for he turned back. "So do I. I *know* what brought me here, what holds me here. Do you, or is it just easier to be here than not?" He glanced again at the rectangles of paper on the table. "I'll go, and let you finish those, if you haven't already, so you'll have time to come by Ken's office when you're done."

"Did you and Ransome really talk?" she blurted out. "When you bought the land. Did you actually talk about what was going to happen here, to the town?"

He shrugged. "We still talk about that, I guess, too much, and then he broadcasts far and wide what we've said. He forgets not everybody wants to be in the spotlight."

"Ransome always got attention," she agreed, remembering times, laughing a little as she gathered up the food containers to dispose of them.

"Well, not everybody wants it. He never lets that bother him, though."

"Never did. So what'd he do to *you*?"

"You saw the paper, I guess. Well, that reporter, just for one instance, she talked to him, and she must've told him I was next on her list, and he just handed over my private number to her. I try not to let just anybody have that. You probably understand. She called, I was wondering who it was and how they'd have that number, and she said she was at the front gate, ready to talk right then, just told me, didn't ask, more or less ordered me to have the guard let her in. Then she told the receptionist Ransome Moore sent her to interview me. So they just gave her a visitor's pass.

"She pulled that con on Ken one time several years ago. But I'd never met her. Anyway, Ransome owes me now, and I'm not going to let him forget it," he added. "And later I realized she and one of the P.R. guys are in some kind of relationship; I've seen her here once or twice with him. Maybe a fake relationship, for all I know—just a way to get in."

She felt she needed to interrupt: "Be careful: That's my sister." The moment she said it, she wished she hadn't. She'd listened with growing apprehension as he seemed on the verge of saying something worse. She saw he was confused now, and she thought about pretending it was a joke; but he'd find out, he was that type. "Rheta's my sister. 'R.C. Whitson.' She's my sister."

He rolled his eyes, wiped them shut. "Nobody told me *that*. You don't look like her. I'm glad you think that's funny, too," he went on edgily.

"No, just, the kids have an emoji for what you did."

"Yeah. I know. I told you, I have a grandson. I'll get your check fixed, so come pick it up before you leave. I guess you don't need to run any of *this* past your lawyer?"

"He doesn't look over every single thing I do."

"So maybe what I was told's just idle talk."

There was just something in those words. Had he said it as payback, because she surprised him about Rheta? "What were you 'told'?"

"I have to find out things, when I work with new people, especially here. I was told the two of you're engaged. This is a trustworthy person I'm talking about," he added. "And he didn't get it from Neil Griffin."

"If you paid that person anything, you got scammed."

"Don't worry; it wasn't Matthew," he said as he left, and gestured idly.

"You were just complaining about Ransome messing with *your* privacy!" she exclaimed; it was all she could manage right then, a stupid, childish thing to say.

"I don't have much anymore. Your lawyer spent a lot of time trying to dig dirt on me, I'm aware. But if you ever want to know what he found out, your sister's probably done research, too, and you could just ask her first. So much for my 'privacy.'"

SEVERAL MINUTES PASSED before she could make herself get back to work on the cards, and during that time the receptionist came in with a stack of cream-colored envelopes. "Mr. Matheson sent these. He said Caroline found them, they've been around a while, unused; they'll probably fit what you made." It seemed she'd only been told to deliver them, not what they were for. She left reluctantly when Sara offered no explanation.

She wanted to trash them, but the cards alone might not make it home. So she wrote each kid's name on the outside and slipped the cards in. It would've been nice to do the names the way she had on the notes, with a little flair, but she was still upset and it wouldn't be her best work.

So people figured she was engaged to Neil. It wasn't only Don, suspicious big-brother Don; or Rheta, trying to monitor her social life.

People thought they'd get married.

It was a thing she'd always known, somehow, she'd never do.

He'd helped; he'd been there for her. He'd drop in on her during those first few weeks after Cary was born, when she was on maternity leave, tired, lonely, wondering how she'd manage to raise a baby by herself and teach, too, because Louise wasn't in the picture yet, and there were days when Sara didn't change out of pajamas but only donned a different T-shirt at night. He came by one afternoon when she hadn't finished folding laundry and was rocking Cary, who wailed as Sara sat crying, herself. He took into the kitchen a bag with freshly-bought supper for the two of them, and found Sara's coffee cup from that morning spilled out near the sink, and unwashed dishes from two days. "Wow, I like how you've decorated my house," he told her with a laugh; then—she thought—*pretended* contrition at having let it slip that he owned the dwelling he'd "found" for her to rent while her divorce was finalized.

She told him he was only *acting* upset—this was just his way that afternoon to let her know she was in debt to him, and not just for lawyers' fees...an afternoon when she'd felt particularly inept and worthless; he should go before she started yelling. She shoved the bag of supper at him. He took Cary from her—"Get some plates"—and he'd sat in the rocker with Cary in the knee of his crossed leg, and Cary had quietened and watched him. "Leave the door open if you think I'll pinch her or something. She just needs somebody else to look at for a while."

"And you think that's you," she said, cleaning up the coffee, weeping quietly. She turned the dishwasher on and set out two dishes and glasses for them.

"You hear her crying anymore?" he'd countered.

"You really own this house?"

"Yes. I made you a good price on the rent, didn't I. But I could evict you if you're not nice to me."

"No, you can't," she'd said, laughing a little as tears fell down.

"You're right. Too much bad publicity. And, besides, there's a law."

And so she'd demanded all the keys from him, but how would she really know if he had extras? And, anyway, as he pointed out, it *was* his house, and he could keep keys to his own property, couldn't he? He cleaned up the kitchen for her that night, helped her bathe Cary, settled her into the bassinet; and then, seeing Sara stumbling over the full laundry basket in the living room, had led her back to the bedroom and tucked her into her own bed beside the bassinet, and he kissed her good night—only that, nothing else right then, that day. "I'm locking you in, don't worry," she'd heard him say as he'd left, and it wasn't until the next morning that she remembered those words. But it was a soft, padded cage, and she could've left if she'd tried.

Later, after another book was done, she'd told him he had to sell her the house, or she'd have to move. When he argued, she ran a con on him: She bought several moving boxes and set them around, one or two partly filled with stuff, and a few empty wine crates and some masking tape. He'd been convinced. She thought. Or maybe it was his way of taking a different sort of IOU from her.

But she had the house, and it was a comfortable little house; Cary could grow up in it, near her grandmother and her aunt, and eventually it was Louise and not Neil who shared space with her. She sometimes wondered if he'd wanted their rental agreement to just go on, so he had leverage to move in. She loved how he held her, his kisses when they slept together; but she caught him one time too many with a look she could only call "satisfied" on his face, and he reminded her a little too often that she had the divorce *and* the house because of him. He hadn't seemed surprised—Cary was not quite three—when she told him she was just too busy for right then, and Louise would be coming to live with her in a while, although there was a cold light in his eyes for a moment or two before he smiled and said, "Okay, because we'll still see each other."

IN THE OTHER room the kids were napping. She asked Liz and Kathy to put the envelopes into the proper little backpacks. She gave the women their own envelopes, too: she'd calmed herself by drawing a card for each of them, as well, which they now made a big deal of, hugging her, telling her to come back and visit. She said she would.

She wouldn't.

She stowed her supplies and took them to the car, went back to the main office, waved breezily at the receptionist. "Let Mr. Thomas know I'm coming," she said, reaching over to press the button she'd observed that unlocked the door to the long hall.

He was standing with that cup in hand as she came near him. "I was told to see you when I finished," she said, unnecessarily, as he was already nodding as she spoke. The open doors made her aware of listeners.

Thomas waved her ahead of him. "But he's got your paperwork himself. It's been busy."

She followed him to the elevators. "I assume everything's okay with the art."

"It's great!" He pressed the "3" button. "We knew it would be. It far exceeded what I had in mind, but, you know, I don't have much background in art in general, or art for children in particular. I think everybody involved with it'll be proud."

She'd never noticed from outside, but here on this level there was much more glass, and they were walking eastward. One side of this floor contained three enormous open spaces where men and woman hovered over large drafting tables, and oversized monitors hung from walls. Few noticed her and Thomas as they walked to the far end of the building, where the wide, open hallway ended in an array of ceiling-to-floor windows and two sets of exit doors. She blinked at the glare of light; but then they turned to the right, and Thomas nodded at someone guarding another door which, nevertheless, was open to Matheson's office, where he stood with his back to them as they entered; but she was sure he'd heard them.

"Nice day," he remarked, gesturing outside.

She saw then the deck that spanned this entire end of the building, a partly-covered deck with stairs coming up from the lower floors and down from the upper two. A door led from his office onto it, where tables and chairs were scattered around in cozy groupings. Matheson opened one side of the French door and motioned to the two of them. She knew her expression must be grim: What he'd said earlier rolled over, like heavy clouds, the calm she'd regained doing the envelopes. He plucked something from his desk and followed them outside. As if he knew what was going through her mind, he said, "I promise I'm not just showing off. Ken can vouch for it."

"It's true. He hides out here whenever he can. Which can be too often."

"Or not often enough. Take a chair. Enjoy the view for a minute. Pretty soon *somebody'll* need me for something. Will that make you happier?"

Thomas smirked. "Kind of intense, when we went by."

Sara gazed at the lake, blue as the clear sky, felt grateful they were on the east end of the building in the cool breeze, but she could not forget Matheson's last comments. Water glittered, overshadowed with deep-green pines. Thomas spoke now of having told her how pleased they were with her work, to which Matheson made an unconnected remark about some project giving someone trouble; he worked on the problem aloud, as if they weren't there. Eventually, his feet propped on another seat in front of him, he reached across to give her the thing he'd picked up in his office—a manila envelope, not sealed. Inside, a check and a smaller, sealed white envelope.

"I had them cut it after we talked."

"Thank you." She hesitated, not wishing to say too much in front of Thomas. Although, she thought grimly, whatever Ron Matheson knows, odds are Ken Thomas knows, too. Maybe he'd even done the snooping.

"But you just had to talk *your* business first," Thomas said sardonically. "He can't help it. He's an engineer. So pretend this is him, saying we're pleased you worked with us. We were happy to add the bonus."

"That." Matheson pointed to Thomas.

"I intended to use some of it on a few days at the beach." She smiled wryly.

"Enjoy!" Thomas said.

Matheson looked closely at her. " 'Intended'?"

"Now my daughter's decided she doesn't want to go."

"Waste of a good bribe."

"Go anyway. Go on your own. You earned it."

She smiled at Thomas' recommendation. "Yes, but if I did, I'd spend my time feeling guilty, and worrying about her, and when I got back, I'd find her and Louise—my aunt who lives with us—at each other's throats and mad at me for going. Even if they'd both said they didn't want to."

Thomas laughed. "That sounds about right."

Feeling the moment had grown awkward, she pretended to check her phone. "Speaking of Cary, I'd better leave now to get her from school."

"I've been wondering about that. In this little town, she'd be safe to walk, in good weather? If you don't live too far from school? None of my business, I guess," Matheson added.

Thomas glanced sideways at him—"Oh, my God, man, really?" he groaned, but this time Sara wasn't surprised, and had a nice check in hand and wouldn't splutter.

"No, it's not your business, *again*—" she liked that Thomas frowned at the word—"but I'll tell you anyway. There've been a few incidents—just 'off,' enough, to make me anxious. Louise calls it my 'famousness.' I mentioned that once, to Mr. Thomas."

"Ken," he interrupted.

"She's a little paranoid about us," she went on, ignoring him, "every time I do some public event. And, like I said, there *have* been a few things. One, just recently."

Matheson's expression changed, and his feet came down as he leaned toward her. "Should you bring it up with the police? I've had to deal with this kind of thing...."

"No, people just want to feel...connected to you, when you have a little repute, you could say. 'Famousness.' Not that I'm 'famous,' you know, but... They try to manufacture an acquaintance. Give you things."

"What?" Matheson continued. "Things that would get them arrested? Because, again, you should go to the police—"

"No. Little stuff. Trinkets. Cards. Like that." She grew more uncomfortable, realizing it sounded foolish, cursing herself for falling prey to Louise's imagination.

Matheson leaned back. "That doesn't sound too bad."

"It's not, I told you. It just keeps Louise all worked up, and so one of us gets Cary to and from school."

"She'll be driving all too soon, and this'll be a moot question," Thomas said, "and then your *real* worries will start, trust me."

"Damn straight," Matheson agreed.

At that moment one of the other doors opened, and two people stepped out. Matheson arose resignedly. "Yeah, Ken said things didn't seem to be going well. Okay. Let's have a look."

The two engineers left. Sara was relieved to follow Thomas and Matheson back inside. Passing the huge antique desk he'd been leaning against in the newspaper photo, she saw it: a much-smaller copy of the blue sphere, so much smaller that all the definition of the one she had was gone in this one.

"May I—?" In the palm of her hand it looked the way a miniature Statue of Liberty hanging on a keychain would look.

"I have one of these," she said. "Larger. It's big enough so I can see numbers on it. On this part." She gestured to the side where minuscule shapes fell out of the globe, held it up to the light and peered, but any details would have been lost in this copy.

"Really? Where'd you get it?" Thomas asked.

She shrugged and replaced the sphere on the desk. "It was one of those 'gifts' I was talking about, so I don't know where it came from."

"I ordered a lot of these for my officers," Matheson told her. "I see in it my philosophy, personal and work."

"Louise calls it glass half-empty, half-full."

Matheson laughed. "Never thought of that. Not my interpretation. Do you have a personal philosophy, Ms. Wells?"

" 'Personal philosophy'," Thomas scoffed.

The two people who'd approached them on the deck fidgeted silently now at the door of the office. She took another glance at the globe, disquieted by the offhand question he'd asked. But, unaware, he walked on, and Thomas herded her out ahead of himself.

"I have a few extras somewhere, I think, if you'd like one," Matheson added, striding on into the great room. "Just ask Caroline."

"I have one already, like I said."

Neither she nor Ken Thomas spoke until they reached the ground floor. He shook her hand and again told her the company would be happy to work with her on other things, if the opportunity arose. She thanked him, left, and, back in town, deposited the check at her bank. She actually *was* late, and she stuffed the signed agreement and bank receipt into the manila envelope deep down into her art bag, rushing on to school.

IN THE PICKUP line she sat stewing over what Matheson had said to her, what he'd asked, and cursed herself for obsessing over a cheap paperweight for so long. It wasn't until he'd passed on ahead of her, strolling on the other side of the street, that she noticed Stephen Logan.

11

THE SKIES TURNED lead grey and drizzled cold rain during spring break. "It always does," Louise griped.

They arose when they wanted to those days, looked out at the grim trickling rain and drank too much coffee.

Cary had friends over or went to their houses every day and didn't let the weather depress her, nor that she'd have to spend a couple of evenings at Matthew's. Sara didn't ask how she'd negotiated that, instead of a whole weekend at his house; but Cary told her in an offhand way, "Dad said he guessed it would be nice to have the week to myself. Plus, maybe he was a little tired of entertaining me two straight days." There was something else behind it, Sara figured; sooner or later she'd find out.

"See, it would've been lousy weather to be on the beach," she told Sara cheerfully.

Stephen Logan's case was moved up and brought before the judge. A bare twelve lines buried near the back of the first section of the paper said the case was advancing; Judge Williams had raised the original charges to "assault with special circumstances." Logan's attorney, Neil Griffin, had motioned for a dismissal.

What made Neil think Diandra Williams, a judge not known as a pushover, would give in to him and dismiss charges? Sara didn't think she would. The local rag had mentioned Logan's misdemeanors, petty crimes; the label "habitual criminal" had already floated around. And yet he had that new appearance of respectability and had gained support of a county group who felt disaffected by the changes in the community. They called themselves "MAP," for "Mooresville Associated Patriots."

Sara always cringed seeing Neil's name connected to unsavory cases, and had told him so, and he'd remind her that even the most horrible criminal got representation, and sometimes he had to defend one. That one tiny news item in the paper appeared deliberately, self-consciously insignificant, as if someone had pulled strings to get it buried. Compared to some of the new recent arrests listed on page three—the ones Louise avoided reading—this last one of Logan's did seem minor.

"Assault with special circumstances..." She read those words aloud, musing, and Cary looked up from her phone and turned a comically stern gaze at her: "You know that means hate speech, discriminatory acts."

Sara started saying, "Yes, I know—" But Cary went on, divulging other details she'd heard at school before the break. She realized these things mattered to Cary, mattered a lot. *You don't pay attention to what goes on around here*—Rheta's way of putting it. She tried to suppress that and listen to Cary.

No; she hadn't known about these other things. "...And that's what he said; he said that, those words. He said, 'Too many monkeys running this zoo,' before he left. So he gets extra charges. And he should. I told you last week, he's creepy. And Lynne Houston's making sure everybody remembers. Look it up yourself if you don't believe me." She went to the kitchen and passed back through to her bedroom, talking to someone on her phone, unmindful of Sara's disquiet.

For years—before Moore Farms closed down—the high-school wannabe rock bands hung out at Music Monster on Saturday afternoons, strumming guitars, trying out drum kits, breaking into riffs that drew people in to listen. That was really what the kids wanted and which Clay, and, then, later, Andy himself encouraged. It was good for business: I want one of those; I can play as well as they can. Or, I've always wanted to play that....

And that Saturday last month, Logan sauntered into the shop to nod his head along with the beat, like several other people finding a spot out of the cold wind. He took down a new mandolin hanging on the wall, tightened the pegs, loosened them; did the same to a guitar. Strings broke. "Oops, sorry, I'm sure you got insurance for that kind of thing, right?"

Kids playing music and bringing in potential customers...that was one thing; but damaging inventory was another, altogether. The manager that day didn't know anything about Logan and asked him if he was going to buy something—maybe he had in mind a beginner instrument. But he couldn't just loiter and handle the merchandise and break it.... She was polite about it. Seeing he had attention now, maybe not the sort he wanted, he brushed against her and headed out the door.

"Too many monkeys running this zoo."

Sara took her phone and looked at those online comments of Lynne Houston's. She didn't like doing it. People made too many remarks about Rheta's reporting, things that scared her, angered her. Sara remembered her predicting they would, when she wrote about something they didn't like. The Internet was anonymous. They could make up any fake name and say anything, if it wasn't bad enough to get them censored.

But Lynne wasn't the type to hide behind a pseudonym. No, there she was, over and over, line after line, asking Mooresville to remember everything Stephen Logan had done as a young man and the things he'd been suspected of doing. And now it seemed he was going to get by with this latest outrage. And she'd heard he might run for the vacant council seat later this year.

She shivered, put the phone face-down.

Before Moore Farms closed, when things were still bustling in town, she and Rheta would go by Lynne's notions and tailor shop to see if anything was on sale—Lynne always stocked the place with exotic fabrics, whimsical oddments like peacock feathers and metallic embroidery thread. Rheta rolled her eyes as Sara sorted through these things, looking for an unusual bit. But, later, Mooresville saw the forest springing up, and Lynne stopped stocking pieces of glitter and fantasy and survived on alterations her seamstresses made on clothing the wealthier women purchased in Charleston or Memphis and brought back to her for a better fit. Maybe Nora Burkes or Lindsay Mason grew condescending during those years, making it look like charity they were bestowing on Lynne. Maybe Lynne, like all of them in town, was grateful for business, even from women who nitpicked a better fit and had her redo seams. After MTE started construction of their facilities— after the razing of Sam Moore's comfortable farm house, after the barbed-wire fences up the highway were removed and more industrial ones added back—she filled her shop with locally handmade things, and it began to thrive. These days, if you wanted a unique gift, you went to her place. But she didn't do alterations anymore.

BY WEDNESDAY SARA started escaping the house two or three times a day, wearing sweaters and rain gear, hiking boots, light gloves. Cary was busy enough with her friends that, when Sara suggested a day or two in Memphis or New Orleans—really, anywhere—she turned an injured look on her and said, "You know I had to spend yesterday evening with Dad, and I'll have to go there Saturday night, too, so why're you trying to use up my time? If you want to go, it's okay with me." That was just the scenario she'd mentioned to Ken Thomas and Matheson, and one she wasn't going to get herself trapped in, so she put on the hooded coat and sloshed down the sidewalks.

She hadn't heard yet from MTE about the book project, probably wouldn't until they had proofs. She walked briskly downtown in the chill air, wondering if she should pop into Neil's office. She hadn't needed his legal opinion about anything lately, and ever since that morning when she'd started the work, he hadn't talked with her. Maybe other cases, and the Stephen Logan thing, were keeping him busy.

But he could be an ass, sarcastic and cutting when his feelings were hurt. She turned down the other side of the street, instead. She'd envisioned the restaurant, with its yeasty smell and warm, dim lighting, even as she'd left the house. Years ago Dominic liked saying everybody in Mooresville ate there sometime or other, and most people, twice a week; and he wasn't wrong. She stopped underneath the sodden awning, closed her eyes just for a moment, shivered, suddenly aware of how cold she'd gotten.

Inside, she tapped a message to Louise and Cary to let them know where she was. The place was pretty deserted. A couple of high-school kids snuggling in a corner booth were the only other people; and Don generally didn't show up until about five, for the evening-meal crowd. Sitting down at a small table by herself, she felt silly: What would she order at 3:00 on a cold, wet afternoon?

After the sole cameriera took her order, she noticed Chris sticking his head out the kitchen door. Dominic had died in the night years ago, a month before her father; and since that day, Chris had avoided the restaurant. Don had struggled to hold it together and get Dominic's affairs straightened out; at first nobody knew if it would stay open, if Don could do it by himself, him such a young, inexperienced man....

The server exchanged some kind of mute signal with Chris, and he went back into the kitchen without having seen Sara.

...It had been Chris who called her, his voice flat and so low-pitched she had to ask him to repeat things. Pop woke up with pains, and when he stood to go to the medicine cabinet, he just died. She said shocked, sympathetic half-sentences, not knowing *what* to say, wondering why he'd called her, and then knew, and said she would find Rheta and tell her.

The town squirmed self-consciously on the pews for the Requiem Mass, uncertain when to stand or kneel, or whether. Chris looked back as Sara took a seat with her parents behind him and Don and Giulia; his brows came up, then lowered in gloom. With every stir at the door, his head swiveled; and at last, not wanting to have to see that anymore, Sara gazed firmly down into her hands and occupied herself with the question she'd overheard already: Don was only twenty-three; and nobody was optimistic Chris would stick around any longer than it would take for him to find another job. She caught murmured words in worried discussion outside the cemetery fence later that day: "...really bad if it did close; what do you think?"

"Well, if giving Chris Liberto a job's going to shut down the restaurant, I'll go picket for everybody *not* to give him one, like that little smart-aleck gal—" David Burkes stopped as somebody nudged him and tilted a head toward Sara, who sneered a smile and turned away.

Chris held his hand out before leaving with Don and their mother; but Sara pulled him close, her cheek against his, and whispered: "I'm sorry," knowing he would understand what she meant. Because, on the phone, Rheta had been firm: She could not go, would not be going to that funeral. No.

A month later, the town felt it was a real shame, two friends laid to rest so close together, and both young men, really, not so old. Having been through the process four weeks earlier, they were less uneasy at the Catholic funeral this time, felt even experienced. Sara and Rheta gulped coffee those few days and made arrangements with, Rheta said, the same whirling rush of a girl on the eve of getting married: too many people around, no time to slow down to think or feel what they needed to think and feel, until it was done and too late.

It was a strange remark, and Sara was puzzled but forgot it in a moment; many things were said and forgotten then, shoved into a dark part of her mind until later when thoughts and feelings rushed back up and there was nothing to stop them.

It was the end of September, still hot enough to be lounging on the front steps in shorts, but with that thinness in the air that forebode autumn. They sat quietly, remembering the Moores' string of night lights that used to flicker off to the west in the orange sunset. The thank-you notes were finished, the casserole dishes returned. No more whirling rush now, but plenty of time to think and feel what they needed to. She remembered then what Rheta had said earlier in the week and started to ask about it, but Rheta broke the silence first: "Chris was bombed. Did you see?" Her mouth was grim. The now-lengthening shadows made crevasses of the lines around her lips. "I told Don to take him home, sober him up. Then get his ass back to the restaurant and make some money off a crowd that wouldn't want to go home after a funeral and fix for themselves. I noticed Lisa Evans hanging onto

Don today. I told you a long time ago you ought to do something about him."

"Don's my best friend, Rheta," she said, realizing it was true. "I never was interested in him any other way, and you know it. Did he tell you if he was going to try to run the restaurant himself? It sounds like that's all anybody in town cares about."

"He didn't say, but I'm sure he will. Chris didn't use to drink like this. Something's changed him, or he's just sick of trying to be a restauranteur. I think Don's going to free him, like a captive dolphin. To save him. How noble. Anyway, Don always did have Pop's touch, likes to talk with the customers, knows to change his recipes now and then. Chris always disliked all of that. So Don's going to release him into the wild." She laughed grimly. "I wonder how he intends to pay him back for it. You always owe something."

In a while it was too dark, and, as when they were girls, the mosquitoes too thirsty; and they had gone back inside to join their mother and Louise, who was staying there with them and Connie to grieve the loss of her brother....

CHRIS POKED HIS head out the door again, saw her that time and waved cheerlessly, stared past her as the main door opened and a cool blast of air swirled into the dining area. The kitchen door swung shut at the same time the front one closed, and the chilly breeze stopped. Still mystified by the look on Chris's face, she hadn't paid attention to who had walked in, but now a chair gently scraped up to a table right next to hers, and there was Stephen Logan sitting down, smiling pleasantly at her.

In high school she hadn't really known him. He was one of the rough-edged boys looking for a fight, looking for a joint, looking at the world under half-closed eyelids, because he thought that was tough. However it was that he'd learned to use his toothy smile and to wear nice-fitting clothing and keep his hair styled, the contrived air about it made that camouflage only seem menacing. He was— as Cary said—creepy, and in a worse way than he'd been when everybody could see him for what he was.

The smile made her nervous. When the server set down her caffè latte, she adjusted her chair to put slightly more of her back to him. She tapped a message on her phone and laid it next to her napkin, took the latte in both hands to make sure she didn't spill it on herself. Why was Logan here today, right after she'd arrived? And, she suddenly wondered, why had he been walking near the school last week?

The server brought him, too, a steaming mug, and a couple of biscotti on a plate. He cleared his throat and leaned slightly into her table. "It looks like we're the only people out on such a rotten day. Well, other than them—" he nodded at the teenagers. "Would you like one of these?" He gestured at his dish.

She gave him a quick smile. "Oh, no, thanks—that would defeat the point of walking. This—" she gestured toward her latte— "is fattening enough."

To her relief he just nodded and began dipping the biscotti and nibbling on it, crossed his leg, and gazed outward at the cold, damp sidewalk. She hadn't paid attention to the soft words he'd exchanged with the server when he'd come in; or did they just know what to bring him? Had he become a regular here? She was sure Don wouldn't like that. She was glad to see Chris was around...did Don want someone here when he wasn't, who could manage Logan, if it became necessary—had Stephen started routinely coming in?

Had he followed her?

She held onto the warm mug and sipped. Her phone buzzed: **B right there.**

She was vexed with herself for texting Neil—like a damsel in distress, she scoffed angrily inside, and he'd love that, he'd play it up. Not long ago she'd confronted the man in the park and had known she could deal with him. But the idea of confronting Stephen Logan felt different.

The door opened again; the young woman greeted him: "Mr. Griffin! So we'll have some business after all, this cold afternoon. I didn't think anybody'd get out in the weather. You want a latte?"

"No—coffee, please. Hey, kids. Leave some daylight there," he told the high-school couple as he strolled past them. They stared at him. "Sara!" he said, approaching her little table. "I saw you come in and wondered what the hell you were thinking, strolling around in this weather. Thought I should see if you need a 72. I could at least get *that* past Diandra."

She gazed uncomprehendingly at him—like those kids, she thought.

"A '72.' Seventy-two hours of involuntary evaluation. You

need it?"

Her hands steadied, and, dammit, that was the effect he had on her—it was something he knew, too, something he used. As if suddenly aware of the quiet chuckle from the table next to them, he nodded at Logan. "Stephen. Don give you a gift card you gotta use up? Is that biscotti? You going cultured on me?"

Logan made a little scoffing sound. The server brought the coffee and left.

"I offered to share them with this lady, but she says she's on a diet. I didn't think she needs to be, do you."

Sara glanced down at the phone. *Your creepy client may be following me around & I want you to get over to Liberto's right now & make him go away*, she'd written. She felt safer holding her latte one-handed now, and turned the phone face-down.

"Oh, she always looks good to me," Neil said, and if he thought that was a proper way to make the other man back off, she let him know with a scowl that he'd said the wrong thing. He tried again: "So how's the new job, Sara?"

Aware that Logan was listening, she chose her own words carefully: "It's done. I got paid well. Everything worked out."

"Need any legal advice about it?"

"It was pretty straightforward. Anyway, I think you have your hands full these days," and she smiled at Logan, who had inched forward so that he was almost sitting with them now.

"I remember you from school," Logan suddenly remarked. "Sara Collins. Wells now, right? You do books. I've seen you on TV, in the papers."

Neil's gaze would have frozen questions from other people—he was known for almost-but-not-quite intimidating witnesses by leaning slightly toward them and glaring coldly. But Logan seemed untouched. Sara tensed and looked into her latte, taking a sip before answering: "You guessed! We did go to high school together. Long ago. *Long* ago," she added.

He winked at her. "Couldn't be that long ago, if I remember you. Which class were you in?"

She paused, considering what to say next, but Neil saved her from the moment. "Women don't like to tell people that, Stephen—in fact, I might say I don't, always, myself."

"But we did go to high school together," she added, "you remember that right. Neil, I was out getting exercise because we've been shut up so much this week, and I was about half-crazy." It was an effort to steer the conversation into a bland path.

"Then maybe I should ask for that 72."

Logan broke the remaining biscotti and dipped half into his cup, ate a piece, patted his mouth with his napkin, crossed his legs again. "Let me ask your opinion about something, if you don't mind. You're a literate person. Hypothetically speaking, would there be any difference between saying 'monkeys running the zoo' and 'lunatics running the asylum'? People say that all the time."

"Stephen, don't discuss your case outside my office," Neil said coldly.

"C'mon, man, I'm serious. Lynne Houston, she's been here since I was a kid, she says whatever's on her mind. I have the same right. So, what's the difference between 'asylum' and 'zoo'? None. It's all the same. And I think my lawyer—" he winked at Sara again— "is going to get my case thrown out tomorrow on something like that. So what do you think? I'd like to know your opinion."

Neil's eyes told her: ***Don't go there.*** But she did. "Context, Mr. Logan," she started, when he interrupted: "Just call me Stephen, Sara. I mean, we went to school together! You don't have to get formal with me."

"Okay, well, I think it's about how you say something, and where, and who to, like, right now," she added, thinking to throw Neil a lifeline. "*He* threatened to commit me, but I knew he's joking, and I know *him*, so I know he wouldn't really."

"Oh, you know that?" Neil scoffed, raising his brows.

Her phone buzzed—Cary, asking if she and Louise should come to town to retrieve her, as it was pouring buckets at the house. Sara looked out the front windows and saw sheets of rain obscuring the other side of the street. "Well, I guess I do need a 72, because my daughter says I should come home, and look at *that*," she said.

"Didn't you check the weather? They say we'll have this system all week. You're making a strong case for yourself. So I guess I'll rescue you."

She frowned, hearing him say it.

"Excuse us, Stephen, I'm going to run Sara home, and if you'll stay right here, I'll be back in about twenty minutes and we'll go over to the office and do some prep for tomorrow. In the meantime, stay out of trouble if you can."

"Or I could come along, and we could talk on the way back," he suggested, starting to rise from his chair. Neil waved him off.

"No. Just wait. Jenny, hold my card—I'm buying Sara's coffee, and mine, after I return, and I may want more."

Sara turned to nod at Logan, who looked anything but a redneck country boy right now as he watched her leave with Neil. She forced herself to smile a little at the calculating, knowing face, took a last sip from her cup and pulled up her hood. Neil held the door for her. They dashed across the street and through the lower floor of his office building, to the parking lot behind it, and she sank into the front seat, shaking again.

"**DON'T REPEAT ANYTHING** you heard back there," he warned as they traveled the wet streets. She'd texted Cary to say she was on the way, then waited out the silence until he chose to speak first; it took a while, and she'd wondered why.

"I'm telling you, Neil, that man's a psychopath. Keep him away from me. He was walking down the street by the high school the other day, too. You find out this afternoon, today, what he wants. I don't like it. I don't know why you're trying to get him off for anything."

"Every man's guaranteed a lawyer."

"Yeah, you say that. It didn't have to be you this time. Let David Burkes do all the pro bono stuff. He claims to be retired. Let him do penance for having been horrible all his life."

He laughed loudly, reaching for her hand, but she pulled away. She hadn't thought of the rain getting worse, or she wouldn't have walked to town. Now she seemed to have trapped herself into arriving home, the two of them, in his car, after all this time. She didn't like Cary seeing him bring her home. She realized that as a revelation: She didn't want Cary to think they were connected romantically, although they had been; and, sitting to his right, she remembered other times when she'd been in a vehicle with him, a different destination ahead.

He stopped in the driveway, fumbled with his seat belt.

"No, don't come in, you'd better go back and deal with that awful case of yours, and Jenny has your card, anyway, but you tell him, you tell Stephen Logan, he'd better not be stalking *me*!"

He leaned back and smirked. "You want me to bring that up

with him? You want me to tell him that, really?"

"No. I do not. You figure it out. Get the point across. Doesn't he have a car?"

"Yes, and some sort of a job, consulting, he says, for some group of nuts here in the county. I don't ask questions. It's not my business who he hangs out with. But I'll impress on him he's being watched and doesn't need any more trouble. Maybe that'll do it."

"It wasn't funny, Neil." She warmed her hands at the heater vent. "I didn't want him sitting by me, and there he was, right after I went in."

"Probably just coincidence. He didn't look wet, like you," he reminded her. "And I noticed he wasn't wearing a bunch of winter stuff, either. No coat, no hat. He'd probably been in somebody's shop before he got to Don's. Just not the music store, if he knows what's good for him. So why are you so freaked-out lately?" he asked. "You've been acting scared of everything. It's not like you. I learned to my sorrow you're not scared of much of anything. Or you *weren't*. Maybe you've lived too long with that old woman who probably dreams somebody'll climb through her window and ravish her."

She gasped. "That was terrible. And it's not funny, I said. That man's creepy."

She saw the front door open just a little; Louise peered out and closed it back. He noticed and laughed.

"See? See what I mean? A person can't live well being scared all the time. By the way, that little knickknack—did you ever find out what it was?"

"It was nothing. It turns out, a lot of people have them. I don't know where they're made, but they seem to be pretty common."

"So you see. And you were upset about *that*. And I figured it was *nada*. And now this, now Stephen Logan, who walks around town, talking to everybody he sees, because he thinks he's a politician."

"That's actually true?"

"Yeah. Decided to run for city council. It's a dream of his, after this other thing blows over. And that will; really, the case's going away. Tomorrow, as he said. He'll pay that manager for her X-rays and visit to the doctor, and maybe a little more, and I'll make him say it was all a mistake, and might use that line he tried on you a while ago...and it'll go away."

"And you're happy with that."

He shrugged. "I don't think he purposely hurt her. I don't see putting somebody in jail for no more than he did. Whether I like him, whether you like him, that's not the point. He needs to shut up, I grant you, but so does Lynne. Everything could've already quieted down, if it weren't for her. Some things just need not to be said."

There was something about that she didn't like.

"But you, you need to relax. Why don't you come to my house tonight? Isn't Cary on break this week? She wouldn't miss you. Just tell the old lady you have a dinner invitation."

She looked at him, the way she hadn't for a long time. He'd truly been the other side of town—Most Handsome, and his looks hadn't suffered through the years; second in his law class; married for a while to a Chi Omega who'd been Miss Ole Miss years ago, with whom, the town gossiped, he'd had an open marriage until she left him finally to marry a Memphis doctor who traveled to places she hadn't seen yet but wanted to.

His returning gaze at her was meaningful, his lips slightly open; she knew that look— She shook her head. He knew she might do it, if not for Cary, if not for Louise.

"Not now; I'm too anxious. You're taking advantage of my emotions. I know your strategies."

He leaned over then and kissed her the way he had when Cary was little—a possessive, demanding kiss, the sort he'd used before to overpower her common sense, and she hoped Louise wasn't watching, because it felt good and she didn't care.

"When?"

She touched his mouth with her finger to silence any other question. "Send me a bill."

He grabbed her hand to hold her back, his face cool again.

"I mean it: Don't tell anybody anything about this afternoon."

12

SHE DIDN'T TAKE any more long walks the last four days of the week.

Thursday morning she got up even before Louise normally did, and made coffee for the three of them, opened the blinds in the living room for a view of the sidewalk, sat with her cup in hand.

"Expecting company?" Louise had quietly appeared in the doorway.

Sara knew what was behind that question. "No, and if you saw us while we were in the drive yesterday, if you mean Neil…no, he's not coming by. I didn't encourage that," she added. "He surprised me." It was too much information; Louise sniffed and looked mildly offended.

"Then you should've slapped him," and she left to bake biscuits.

That afternoon a slightly longer article in the paper reported that, as Neil had predicted, charges against Stephen Logan had been dropped. Logan was photographed outside the courthouse dressed in suit and tie, and, smiling, told reporters it had all been a blowup over nothing; he was more than happy to pay the lady's medical bills and hoped to do business at the music store again. Standing slightly behind him to the left, Neil glared stonily at the camera.

"Does this mean Mr. Logan will return as a customer to Music Monster?" a reporter asked.

"Stephen's just saying he's not holding grudges. He does not intend to provoke controversy, and he never did."

"When hell freezes," Sara said aloud. Cary, hovering nearby, overheard and laughed.

"What?"

"Just a comment about something I read."

Lynne had posted another philippic in the online forum, and Joe Sims duly published it in the sidebar of the editorial page: *Just another example of a white man with some connections getting off for something the rest of us wouldn't!* Sara laid the paper on the couch, folded away from where that story was displayed. But as Cary went to her room later, Sara noticed that—for the first time in many months, because Cary didn't like reading an actual newspaper—she picked it up and took it with her.

ALLIE ARRIVED, ALONG with Carson, on Friday. Earlier in the week they'd asked Sara to drop them at a movie playing downtown, but tonight they had a different plan: They'd stay at Cary's house instead and watch a DVD. She ordered them a pizza.

"And last night, somebody painted '1488,' the numbers, like, three feet tall on the front of that building next to Don's." Cary said it portentously.

One of Neil's buildings.

Allie explained to Sara what the numbers meant—explained with a casual familiarity that made Sara exclaim about intolerance until Cary cut her off: "Yeah, we know about those idiots; we see some of 'em at school, Mom." And she hurried the other two into the kitchen with a backwards, disapproving glare at Sara.

Carson had become a fixture at their house now, so much so that Sara asked Cary bluntly, because she knew Cary despised coyness, "Are you two a couple?"

Cary rolled her eyes: "No, Mom. You see it's always Allie around. We're the 'empty crowd.' "

" 'Empty crowd'?" Sara puzzled.

"You know: M-T-E. 'Empty.' Well, Mr. Matheson actually said it that night," she conceded, "and it was just Carson and me—you remember Allie didn't go, that time. He said 'M-T-E,' but we decided later ourselves to say it the other way."

"You didn't tell me that, before."

She shrugged. "He told us he was sorry we had to come to the picnics, that we could just call ourselves the 'M-T-E Crowd', like it was a particular group—guess he didn't get how lame that is— but he'd appreciate our help, that was when he had us get that stuff for the babies. And he said in a couple of years we can work there in the summers, an actual paid job, you know, helping the staff with the children.... I guess 'empty' is kind of extreme." She shrugged again.

"Okay, well, that's pretty important for you not to have told me."

"Geez. You expect me to tell you everything."

"No. But about working there, yes."

Later, while the teenagers were laughing at the movie they'd picked, she called Rheta; but it went straight to voice mail, which meant she probably wouldn't return Sara's call until sometime next day. On the Internet she found only one brief item about white supremacist graffiti on a local store—well, it wasn't a store, she thought, so much as an abandoned white elephant. She sought Louise to ask her about it, but Louise pursed her lips and offered the opinion that it was better not to give it any attention, as that was what those people wanted. Sara could always text Neil and get his thoughts. But his invitation to her on Wednesday, the assured look on his face after he kissed her, chilled that temptation. She was glad she had to stay home and chaperone.

After a while she heard Carson's father drive up. She saw the kid out the door and waved good night. Allie'd be there until Saturday afternoon, and the girls were likely to sleep in the den tonight; Sara had found them there several other mornings this week, sprawled on the two sofas. She double-checked the doors and went back to her own room.

ON SATURDAY MORNING Louise left the curtains drawn in the living room, but the smell of coffee woke the girls, and they fixed mugs to take to Cary's room, where Sara found them asleep again later. Louise gazed stolidly at them.

"So much for caffeine."

Later, Louise offered to buy groceries, a chore Sara was more than willing to cede to her, and left for downtown.

When Allie's mother showed up to collect her, Sara invited her in for coffee, but everybody was too busy these days, Michelle said apologetically, and so she just couldn't. They gathered up the items that had been pushed under Cary's bed, under the sofas, in the bathroom, and Allie and her mother left. Cary turned to straightening up her room and getting ready for the outing with Matthew and Jennifer. She put in earbuds and turned music on as she worked, sometimes dancing a little, flinging the sheets off and hauling them to the washer, and in a few moments Sara heard the machine start up.

"Would you please dry them before I get home tonight, Mom?"

Sara nodded, not sure what had brought about the outbreak of responsibility. She followed Cary back to her room and stood in the doorway as Cary repositioned a few misplaced things and then flopped down on the bed.

"Dad texted and says he wants me there by 4:30. We'll eat and then go to a movie. So I'll get to see the one we changed our minds about last night. Can you get me there by 4:30? It's already three, and I have to shower."

"Then you better get moving."

Cary gave her an intense, smiling look. "Why don't you ever have any plans? What're you gonna do with yourself after I go to college?"

—The question she'd been asking herself lately. She gestured flippantly. "Maybe I'll go to Mexico, like Louise did."

"If you do, you have to take me."

At Matthew's house, they stood outside for a few moments, uncomfortably, Matthew slightly apart, sullen and grim, and Jennifer, nervous. Sara wondered what he objected to now; Cary was showing signs of growing into amiability and tolerance for him, had done pretty much everything he'd expected of her. Just as she turned to leave, she found out.

"I hope you're not planning to work anymore at the company. It's awkward answering questions about you. If you need money, I'll send more child support."

She turned back, astonished, almost speechless. Angry. "I don't need your money, Matthew."

It was the wrong thing to say, or maybe the wrong way to say it. He jutted his chin forward. Jennifer fidgeted.

"Then don't work out there. It's just more problems for me."

"I'll work where I want to," she told him. "Deal with it."

Cary heaved a sigh. "Don't start anything up while I'm around!"

"We won't. I'm going now. We can talk about this later, Matthew. You guys have a good evening. Are you dropping her back at the house, or should I come get her?"

"I'll bring her home," Jennifer volunteered suddenly, nervously. Matthew grimaced but said nothing else, and Sara drove away.

NOBODY WANTED TO go with her to Mass the next day. Cary planned to luxuriate in one last morning of late-arising before school resumed, and Louise seemed to have something on her mind, and declined, too. Really, Sara just wanted to talk to Chris Liberto, if he was there, or, if he wasn't, then Don, and felt guilty about not going to church for proper reasons. After service she caught up with Don and Lisa as they lingered with their kids outside. "Can I buy coffee for us before you go home?"

"Where? McDonald's? My place? You hinting for me to give you a free lunch?"

Her laugh was forced. "I can afford it, thank you. And if I got lunch there, I'd have hell to pay back home. I just want to ask you something."

Sometimes Don's face fixed into expressions just like Dominic's, she realized. He paused on the sidewalk outside the church. "I don't want any coffee. But ask away. Last time a Collins asked a Liberto something after Mass, Pop gave Rheta a job. Cary wanting to work for us? She's a little young."

"It's not Cary."

"What a nice day," Lisa said. "We can sit right here for a while."

It felt wrong, bringing up outside the church what she wanted to talk about, but they retreated to the play area behind the building. Don kept that same disgruntled look turned on her. She sighed and began; there was no tactful way to do it.

"Is Chris working out front again? I'm just curious."

He shook his head. "Why? You see him there?"

It was a challenge; she could tell he already knew. "Look. This week Cary had all this stuff worked out to do with her friends. So we stayed home, and with the weather, I just about went nuts. So I walked downtown one afternoon. Wednesday. And I got a lot colder than I'd thought I'd be, so I got a latte at the restaurant and saw Chris there. I was surprised. I thought he was doing just the paperwork these days."

"He comes out when I ask him to. And I've had to start asking him to sometimes because I don't want to hire security right now."

"And that was another thing. Do you think Stephen Logan's hanging around too much? Because he came in and sat down right next to me, offered me his biscotti. It freaked me out a little, I'll be honest."

"He bother you?"

"No. I just—"

"He's trying to get under *my* skin. But I don't want a scene like in Andy's shop, so Chris's there on days I'm not."

"Chris didn't seem to *want* to be there. He ducked into the kitchen."

"I don't care if he wants to be, or not. He can still intimidate Stephen once in a while, and that's usually all it takes. Stephen remembers he's got a temper."

"But there he was, trying to get cozy, offering me his biscotti. And then he was wandering around by the school one afternoon when I was picking Cary up."

"The world doesn't revolve around you, dear. He walks a lot. You were just there when he went past."

She leaned back, disturbed at the tone in his voice. "I didn't say it was about us, or me. But you remember that day, when you asked him to leave, when I was there, and he—he just seemed *interested* in what I was doing."

"He says he's gonna run for city council, he might be interested in everything and everybody these days. Maybe, that day, he started thinking about asking you to endorse him. You do that sometimes." It was an actual sneer now. "Now, me, I'll do everything I can to help him *lose*, but he has the right to go where he wants, and somebody's trained the Cracker out of him. He's smooth. I don't find him any creepier than, say, Neil Griffin. Chris said *he* was there that day, too."

"Don," Lisa warned.

"Look, she wanted to talk, and I let her ask a couple of things, and now it's my turn."

He and Chris, children, had chased the streets with her and Rheta, the playgrounds, their own back yards—a mental picture of that went through Sara's mind, and the times years later when their fathers died, and they'd depended on each other; but she put that aside and made her face as grim as his. "I think two old middle-aged people shouldn't fight, Don," she told him.

"Why is it every time I see you lately, I see him? Y'all going out together again? It's a small town, but can't you find somebody better?"

" 'Again'? We weren't—"

"Gimme a break, if you weren't going together, you were awful close 'friends.' Any half-ass decent brother would ask you about it. So why'd he show up, why'd you go home with him?"

"First, it's not your business. But, since you asked: I had that psychopath sitting there next to me, offering to eat with me, and Chris ducked out. And I knew Neil was probably in his office, across the street, and I texted him to come get his creepy client. You want to see the text? I still got it here," and she fumbled in her purse.

"Don't show me your phone. I'd probably see all the other stuff you've sent him, or him, you. I'd rather not know."

"As for why I left with him—I didn't 'go home' with him, by the way—it was pouring rain and he offered to take me back so I didn't have to walk." She scrolled through the messages, arranged in order of time they'd come in, and there was the one from Neil, and above it, Cary's, asking if she wanted Louise to get her. She shoved it into his face—she realized that mistake as he grabbed it and thumbed down to read.

"Oh, Cary and Louise were gonna pick you up, but you went with him instead."

"Damn you to hell, I didn't tell you to go through all my messages," she told him, her face red. She yanked the phone back and pushed it into her purse. Lisa laughed as Don reflexively crossed himself.

"I knew we shouldn't've stopped here at church," Sara said. "Did Chris tell you about that day?"

"Of course he did. I told you he's been watching Stephen. He told me the whole damn thing that night. And, again, you could do better."

She ignored that. "Why do you think that stuff was painted on Neil's building?"

"Changing the subject will not help you. However: It looks to me like somebody got it in for him. You know what it means, right?" She nodded. "Well, Neil dissed Stephen the other day after court, so it's interesting when that pops up on his shack the next day. And then look who's connected with that group of Nazis here."

" 'Nazis', Don? Really?" Lisa objected.

"That's what they are!"

"Wait, you said Neil 'dissed' him—what do you mean?" Sara interrupted.

"You're kind of out of it these days, aren't you. Well, here's what happened. The paper printed some of it, but not everything. They don't. But I was there," he said grimly, "I was hoping to see that asshole have to do something more than hand over a few dollars his group gave him to get out of trouble. I wanted to see him go to jail. But Neil interrupted him every time he tried to go off on one of his rants, and you could tell Stephen was getting mad, but he just smiled his big ole grin. Paper didn't describe all that, did they. Bet you can find it on the Internet. But I was there. And before he left, he looked straight at me and said, 'Hope you enjoyed the show, Don.' "

"That's what I mean. He's causing trouble for you."

"No, you don't get it. For him, it was just another appearance, more publicity. He's not gonna bother you, and he won't bother me, either, not by actually doing anything. He's too smooth for that these days. That was a mistake, in Andy's shop, and whoever holds his leash probably's reminded him not to let it happen again. What I wonder's why they'd do such a stupid thing just to get back at your boyfriend."

"He's not—"

"Yeah, whatever you say." Don waved his hand, stood to leave. "Look, you obviously don't watch the news, do you. And I'm guessing you haven't seen the paper yet, either. So you go read today's rag, read the main story, then go to the editorial page, too. Rheta must have a connection over at MTE—she's always getting Ron to stick his neck out. He's as bad as Ransome was."

"Tactless," Lisa interrupted.

Don laughed. "That. But if you use the Internet, don't look at the comments today; they're really bad. He's probably pissed off about those. Should've expected it. I've warned him before, you say you're one of us, you take the bad with the good. Like old Ransome said in that article."

Lisa hugged Sara and told her to drop in when Don wasn't there, so they could drink wine. Don called the youngest child away from the swings.

"I'm just lookin' out for my sis, who doesn't have the sense to do it herself," he said. And they walked toward the church parking lot.

"YOU'RE ASKING ME what's the biggest negative about having a decrepit building on either side of my restaurant? Well, urban decay spreads."

That's not how Don talks, Sara thought to herself as she read his answer to the rhetorical question. Hang out with scum, it grows on *you*, too—that's what he would've said, was what he'd said to her. Rheta dressed it up. That was okay: it gave more weight to his words, perhaps.

"Another thing: vagrants. They use vacant buildings for shelter. Panhandlers hanging around when my customers leave at night. Some have mental issues. They're unstable. It's not their fault, but maybe we need an actual homeless shelter here."

Rheta asked if he'd brought this up with the owner of the

building.

"The owner's aware. Actually, if I were 'the owner,' I'd be a little worried about liability. But you should ask *him*."

Then Rheta had tracked Neil down, noting in the article that she'd tried twice, unsuccessfully, to get a comment from him, until she more or less ambushed him outside his office on Friday afternoon. Answering questions as he left, he told her, Yes, he knew there were issues with his property, and, no, he didn't believe his recent client had had anything to do with the graffiti, and then: "A few years ago I tried to sell the places to MTE, as a unit. No, I didn't have the restaurant building, there in the middle, which would've made the block, and Don Liberto didn't want to sell it, though I did make a good offer—and a good one to MTE, also. You might ask the CEO there how he justifies all that 'community improvement' he talks about, not even being *in* town. That's all I have to say."

She glanced at the lead piece on the editorial page: ***Mooresville Must Deal with Its Past to Have a Future***. A picture of Ron Matheson, sardonic expression and all.

The house was very quiet. Cary's door was open, but Sara knew already she had her earbuds in and was texting back and forth with someone. Dressed to the nines, Louise had gone for a ride with her friend. Something was up, there, but Sara put that thought out of her mind for the time being.

Music suddenly started from Cary's end of the house: Earbuds were out, and she was humming and moving around. She hadn't said anything last night when she returned from Matthew's; and Sara hadn't asked how it had gone. She and Louise were both hiding things from her, or at least holding things back. Did they not want to tell her because they thought she wouldn't like what she heard? Because they thought she'd flip out?

Don had said Logan's post-trial appearance was probably on the Internet.... On her laptop she searched for a video but stopped at one she found of Deborra Anderson interviewing Don in the restaurant. She watched the video a time or two, noted that Deborra hadn't been able to get comments from either Neil or Matheson.

Cary came down the hall with a handful of dirty clothing. "You been reading most of the afternoon. Anything new?"

Sara shrugged. In sock feet Cary padded to the washer and put the clothing in.

"I bet you've been looking at all that about Don and Mr. Matheson." She pulled her phone out of a pocket, glanced at it, put it back. "I already read it while you were at Mass. Mr. Matheson's right."

"People will think he's just preaching at them."

"You don't have to agree with every *thing* about a person you know. You can see their faults, and sometimes you think you can help *them* see..." she trailed off. "Anyway, he's right. People ought to realize everybody needs to come out against that kind of stuff...what was put on that building."

"I'm glad to see you take an interest. When did you start?" Sara didn't intend to sound sarcastic. "That came out wrong. I meant, I'm happy you care. I just didn't know."

Cary was watching her coolly now, mistrustingly.

"One time, we all did get along. We've been stuck here together for years, all of us, Black and white, poor, rich..."

"You just think everybody always got along. I've been out to MTE probably as many times as you did when you were doing that book for them. Dad made me go. He works there, he applied, nobody forced him to, and it's a good job. But whenever we go, he's all about how it used to be. It's always some remark or other. I get tired of hearing him." She held up one end of the earbuds. "So there are these."

"If you've been there so much, you've heard a lot of crap at those picnics."

"Yeah, you're saying Mr. Matheson shouldn't let people do that, and maybe he shouldn't."

"Did it scare you? Because I'll see to it you don't—"

"No, I hear it at school. You can't always keep me from hearing it. But, you, you stay all comfortable by pretending not to see it. I want to know people think that way, because then I know what they are. And I want things to be better. I think Mr. Matheson was saying it can't *be* better unless everybody sees what it was, so they can fix those parts."

"You evidently haven't seen the part of *him* that—"

"Oh, I know he can be a jerk. And clueless. That therapy session he calls open-mic at the picnics, for instance. But he's not wrong. People just say, he's not one of us. Like, outsiders don't have a right to say it; and the insiders *won't* say it. So it'd never be said. That piece-of-shit guy you went to school with—"

She interrupted: "You talk as if I chose—"

"—no, but you don't stop to think what he's bringing in here, into Mooresville, or maybe you do know but it's another one of those things you don't wanna think about, because it's unpleasant. Just turn those pages, like Aunt Louise does. Don't look."

She tried not to show her anger, found her voice getting loud, anyway. "You know, I do look. But people get mad being preached at, somebody that hasn't known them very long— You're young and idealistic, and I—"

"What the fuck! I thought we could talk! Don't patronize me!"

"Watch your smart mouth!" She knew that wouldn't help, but it was out, now, and she was mad; and, watching Cary's face grow severe, she braced for whatever was coming next.

"Nothing ever changes for you, and you don't really care. Everything just vegetates right in front of you, like those stupid old buildings your group talks about saving but never does."

They glared at each other. She was the parent; she should say something. "I apologize about yesterday afternoon. At your dad's."

Cary's chin thrust out; just like Matthew's.... "If you can't get along, at least don't fight around me."

"Yeah, I said I apologize. I'm sorry."

In the silence Cary gestured. "Nothing else?"

"Just sorry. What else would I say?"

"Like, how it wasn't your fault...it was his."

She didn't know if Cary was testing to see if she'd go off on that rant. "Nope. I had a part in it."

"Well, it *was* his fault," Cary burst out. "He has no right to tell you where to work or what to do. So I don't blame you for calling him out."

"I'll try not to involve you, though, okay?"

She shrugged and picked a granola bar from the bowl of snacks Sara had placed on the table. "And as for the things in the news, Mom, if I were you, I wouldn't look at the Internet today."

"Yeah. So Don told me after church."

"It's bad. Some people signed their names. It'll make you change your mind about them."

God, had *she* been this way when she was fourteen? Rheta had been....

"I'm not the only one who thinks like this," Cary went on.

"Why don't you call Aunt Rheta, get her to come over. Louise's not here right now, so she might—" She rolled her eyes; apparently that had got old with her, too. "She'd tell us about whatever didn't actually make print. Maybe you'd listen to her, if you won't to me."

"I listen to you."

"No, you hear me. You don't always listen."

They were an arm's length apart, and Sara remembered suddenly the battle over the purple streak, the battle she had fought until Rheta told her one day, "You gonna die on *that* hill? Really?" And in a few days, Cary still in the not-talking siege she'd launched, Rheta came over to visit, all her long hair tied back, except for an inch-wide band of light green; that, she let hang down her cheek and onto her shoulder. "Ruined my hair for you, you worthless rugrat," she said to Cary. "This had to be bleached, you understand, completely bleached, before I even got to the color. And it went baby-shit green on me. You should get on your knees in gratitude I'd do this for you. I can't even get it black again for a few weeks; it might break off."

Sara and Cary stared.

"And, you—" she'd shoved on Sara's shoulder—"just shut up and let her do her thing, because, really, you wanna lose sleep about it when you're seventy?" And just like that, she'd seen what it was really about, not the hair, and she'd gone to the salon with her....

...Cary, now, calmly: "I'll put out some snacks for us, if you'll ask her over." A big concession.

She: "I don't know if she'll come. Or can. She hasn't talked to me in a few days. Maybe she's busy."

"I'll call her."

"Send her a message."

But she'd already texted after reading the editorial page several times. She wouldn't let on—to either of them—that it was anything other than Cary's suggestion.

13

RHETA LOOKED AWFUL, wearing sweat pants and a ragged T-shirt, which she hardly ever did; and she'd had that long black hair cut in a choppy short style that Cary eyed.

"I don't stare at your purple thing, Missy, so just you don't make any remarks about me."

"What the hell'd you do that for?" Cary asked. Sara flinched a little.

"I don't know. When people break up, they do crazy shit. You'll find out one day."

Cary didn't answer that, and neither did Sara; it was Rheta's way of getting the bad news over with fast, like diving into a cold swimming pool all at once, not tiptoeing in. Sara silently pushed the snack bowl towards her and brought iced tea to the table.

"Nothing stronger? That would be you."

"A kid lives here."

"Don't fool yourself; she knows by now."

Sara glanced at Cary to see her shake her head just a little—whether to tell her not to go there, or to say she hadn't, or what, it didn't matter. Rheta gobbled a candy bar and poured herself some of the tea before slumping back. "Go ahead and say I can't keep a boyfriend, can't stay married. Whatever. Or just save it and throw it all at me sometime later. So I know you're dying to ask about the paper, and I'll tell you, I'll tell you *all* about it." She leaned on her elbows and glared at Sara. "But this is between the three of us. I mean it. I'd rather not have everybody in town knowing some of this. Just yet.

"Oh, and by the way, I remembered where I'd seen that little doodad of yours, that weird piece of crap that freak gave you. Because Michael had one in a drawer, and he left it when he moved out. Ron Matheson hands 'em out like candy. All the department heads and so on have one. But Michael Ivey doesn't anymore, because they smash to smithereens when you use a hammer." She took a breath. "That's done. So here's what you're dying to ask me about that shit last week."

ON FRIDAY, WHILE the town was driving or walking or biking to their destinations, she said, a couple of workers were scrubbing the numbers off the building façade. People who slowed long enough to notice what was going on, and then paused to understand what it meant, were mostly upset, but a few weren't, Rheta said: One or two beeped horns and went on their way, pleased about the whole thing. She knew; she'd talked to some of them.

She'd understood right away. She'd seen it in other places, written articles about it. She also assumed it was the work of some MAP goon, that group underwriting Stephen Logan's salary. Who else around here would do that kind of thing?

But she *didn't* understand why those people had gone after Neil Griffin. After all, he'd defended their guy. She'd been on another story the day of Logan's courthouse appearance; but she found and watched a video, she saw Neil interrupting his star turn. Like Don, she figured the graffiti was a warning to Neil to handle Logan more delicately. Opening her kiosk that morning, Don's niece had texted him about the graffiti scrawled close enough to the edge of the restaurant for some people to think maybe it was aimed at him. He'd called a couple of his own busboys to scrub and sand the numbers off—"and it not even really his problem. Neil Griffin never even came across the goddamned street!" Rheta complained.

So by the time she caught up with Don, he'd worked himself into a Latin rage as people wandered past, pointing and commenting. *She* didn't call Deborra Anderson; it was probably Matheson who did that, she said; Don and he were pretty thick friends. The hard person to get to was Neil. He'd told his paralegal—

"Jean," Sara interrupted: "that's her name."

Rheta looked disgusted. "I guess you'd know. Well, he told *Jean* not to let reporters into his office, and to filter the phone calls. People might email him, might even see him at the courthouse, but he wasn't going to talk to any of them."

So Rheta watched the assistant, *Jean*, leave on Friday evening, waited when Neil didn't walk out with her, and was standing by his car when he emerged into the back lot. He paused, gave her a cold look, and she asked him the things she'd prepared. He told her exactly what she'd put into the article.

She reached for another candy bar. "But there's more to it than what he told me. I went in thinking maybe, just maybe, it really *was* about the cost. Small-time lawyers don't do so well anymore. Bringing his real estate up to code might put him into a hole. Except, like I said before, agents will tell you stuff, and I found out he owns things all over the place, like Ransome and Wilburn do. He's not hurting for money. And he did try to buy Don out.

Wouldn't know shit about running a restaurant. So, why?"

"Chris might've told you."

"I don't talk to Chris. Don finally said the plan was to take on the debts—Don had a few, you may not know, from when Pop was alive and they were struggling, those bad years. And Neil'd leave the name up, but he'd own it, and he'd hire Don and Chris to run it for him."

"What the hell!" Cary exclaimed. "He'd be their boss?"

"I think when Don turned down Neil's offer, he just figured he could wait it out, those old eyesores'd keep falling apart on either side, and things weren't really improving here in town. Eventually, Don'd want to get out, would have to, maybe, and he'd offer again. He just didn't count on the new people coming in, things taking an upturn, foiling his schemes. Don doesn't need him anymore. Things are better now. You want my opinion—it's 'opinion,' because nobody'll say this out loud—right now Neil's just being a dick about it. Sorry, Cary."

"I've heard it."

"He's just sitting there letting it go to hell around Don, just to show he can. Nobody's gonna make him clean up, or rehab, or whatever. Because he doesn't have to. The council won't make him, most of them are in his pocket, or David Burkes's, or somebody's. And you get that asshole Stephen Logan on the council, it's a lock. Your sweet little preservation ladies—" this, to Sara, scornfully—"call off anybody that might have a little power over him, they're all in it together, anyway."

"Why'd he buy places if he didn't intend to do anything with them?" Cary wondered.

"Because he could. He just did it before somebody arrived with a different goal."

"Others besides him have done it," Sara told her lightly.

Rheta sucked down tea and gazed at Sara. "He made a couple of remarks about me trying to be the bigtime reporter and make up news here in my hometown, revive my career. No doubt you had the same thought. Own it. Didn't you. Asked me if Joe and the publishers were aware from the start that I was doing those articles that way. Said he'd suggest they employ some editorial control. He sneered—he did, really, he sneered at me. I asked him if he liked the company he was keeping these days."

"Somebody had to defend Stephen."

"You always defend *him*. You repeat whatever he says."

"Why would he expect Don to sell to him? I don't get it."

"Yes, you do, Cary. He'd still be the big guy in town, even after everything fell down around his ears. Just that simple. That's all some people want: Just be the boss. Just have the power." She leaned toward Sara's face. "People got different tastes when it comes to their love life. I guess when you're into somebody for a while, you have their back."

"I'm not 'into' Neil," and she gave Rheta a hard look.

"Say it for Cary's sake. But she's probably familiar with *that* story, too."

THEY HEARD LOUISE park—it was sooner than Sara'd expected. "Shit!" Rheta whispered, but she stayed and was pleasant, so pleasant that Louise loosened up and told them about her afternoon with Harvey. Rheta teased her: "I bet you two found a little deserted dirt road somewhere, didn't you?" Louise was a bit too vehement in denying that, and Sara had a thought come to her that she hadn't considered before. Louise laughed a little, told them all good night, and headed toward her part of the house. "Better start looking for another housemate," Rheta advised as she, too left. She checked her car for uninvited guests as usual and leaned back to hug Sara. Cary gagged, and Rheta shot her the bird.

Rheta's words came back to her the next morning when Louise met her in the kitchen, a fresh cup of coffee as offering after she returned from school. "I have to tell you something. You know I've been out with Harvey a lot lately. He's not happy at the home, and he owns a little house that's all shut up here in town. He's a couple of years older than me...."

"Why doesn't he live in his house?" she asked idly, half listening to another story about the old folks.

"He's nearly blind. He can't drive, and his wife died a few years ago. His son lives in Tennessee, and he gets down as often as he can, but he's got kids in school..."

"So you're thinking about seeing after him so he can live in his house again."

Louise sat down across the table from her, tapped Sara's cup rather sharply, and Sara glanced up, startled. Louise's face was lined from years of manual work, and years of family sorrows, but every day she put her makeup on. And the nice clothes! Sara looked at her own ragged shorts and T-shirt and felt embarrassed.

"You don't need me here anymore, not like you used to, and pretty soon Cary'll be driving. I'm not lookin' for another job. What I'm about to do is for me. And us."

"You mean, you and Harvey."

"Yes."

She tried to pick the right words. "If he's blind, you know you'll still have to take care of him. You sure you're not just trading jobs? You're not wrong; we *don't* need you the way we did, not that we don't need you at all, it's not just the work, but other things, emotional support sometimes—"

"You're really makin' a mess of this," Louise observed.

She laughed. "I am. But you know what I mean."

"I know what you mean. And you won't begrudge it. In the back of my mind I've always felt like other people, other women, they got things I didn't, family of their own, relationships. I didn't resent it. But this's just *before* me, and I feel like it's the right time. I'm comfortable with it, and so's Harvey. Somebody helped him at home when his wife died, but that wasn't what he needed, and it was why he moved to the old folks' place. He can see, some. I don't just lead him around," she added defensively. "His other senses are better. He makes me feel like he hears everything I say. Like it's all important to him."

For Sara there were no words more painful she could've said right then. For a long moment she didn't speak; it had been a while since Matthew or even Neil had made her feel that way. She knew Louise would misinterpret, and she did, coming around the table to hug Sara. "I don't want you sad. We're just down there on Stone Avenue, and I'll be coming around whenever I want to. And I'm sure he'll want to come along with me."

"I'm not sad. Just surprised. Of course you can visit anytime. When are you getting married?"

"Oh, we're not doin' that! I mean, we're old. We got his preacher to say a few words yesterday. Not to hurt your feelings, but we didn't want a production," she added. "We're just goin' to be living together. It'll be better for us with the money, that way."

Sara chuckled a little. "You better not tell Rheta. You been down on her about that kind of thing, you know."

"It wasn't because she was doing it—it was because she wasn't ever committed. It was always just a passing thing with her. I disapprove of *that*," she told Sara haughtily. "I didn't tell you, before, because you've been busy," she went on, addressing the thing Sara wondered about but wouldn't ask.

"You weren't afraid I'd object, or try to talk you out of it, I hope."

Louise gave her a stern look. "Wouldn't've done any good. We didn't need anybody's permission, you know." She took their cups. Though Sara's was only half-empty, she held back her objection, because, obviously, the coffee'd been just a convenient prop. "If you want to tell Cary, you can." She rinsed the cups. "Or I'll do it myself. We'll have to move his stuff back to his house, and mine there. His son's family's cleaning it for us; it's been shut up a while. I told them *we* could do that, but they said it'd be a housewarming present to us."

"Is his son okay with everything?" Sara asked cautiously.

"What is it to *him?*"

HAVING GOTTEN THAT off her mind, Louise put in a load of laundry and retreated to her room, from which Sara heard sounds of bureau drawers and closet doors opening and closing. "I'll have some things to take to the Salvation Army," Louise told her. "If you've got stuff, put it in one of these boxes."

Sara glanced into the room. It was plain she'd been planning for a while, for several cartons were already open on the floor, mostly filled.

She took her phone and sketch pad out back. The bad weather that had thwarted travel was gone now, and spring was here, not on the calendar, not by the date, but the spring of the South which arrived at the beginning of March. Louise had planted daffodils, snowdrops, crocuses years ago, and they'd been blooming through the chilly rain of the previous week. It was a pretty little garden. Sara hoped Louise could fix up Harvey's lot as she had this one, because it was so important to her.

She wondered if maybe it *wasn't* so important to Louise; maybe she'd just done it because she'd had nothing else to do after Cary got older.

Well, she could hold a little reception for them here herself, she thought, laying the sketch pad aside: no need pretending she was going to do any actual work today.

In a bit Louise came out the kitchen door with her bag. "I'm taking Harvey over to the house and the two of us can figure out what we need to do."

"Good idea."

"There's a lot to think about."

"You need help? You need me to do anything for you—you've been so helpful to me all these years, the least I could do."

"We've got it. And his son's there now."

THE HOUSE WAS eerily empty, as it was on the days Cary was away, when Louise used to visit the old folks. In a while she made another cup of coffee and took out the notes she'd prepared for the evening's class, read through them, did it again because they hadn't stuck with her the first time. Instead of doing it a third time—when she realized she still hadn't really read them—she laid the folder aside and opened up her computer. Don had told her not to look; she did it anyway, scrolling through the online comments:

Go back to MI if you don't like us.

What have you hidden in your file?

Who asked for your opinion? Heard about you already, just another rich guy finding another place to shove people around.

You come down here with your superior attitude to us, who asked you to? You need a bullet to the head.

Massa, come save us from ourselves! You our f***ing savior!

Don was right: it was better not to read that stuff, but she kept scrolling, sucked into the vitriol and dark threats—so mesmerized and at the same time repulsed that when her phone buzzed with a text, she jumped. She'd saved the number: "KT."

Ms. Wells, we have the page proofs back. Can you come out this morning and look over them?

She was on the road in fifteen minutes, unaccountably happy to have something different to occupy herself with. She'd texted back, *Sure, be glad to –30 minutes?* and received a single-word response: **Yes.**

She'd paused at that; something about it didn't seem right, that one terse word, as if there were problems Ken Thomas didn't want to mention in a text. She wondered if the drawings didn't fit the spaces just right, or maybe they were too dark—it didn't matter, she told herself, going through the pine barren, approaching the front entrance. It could be fixed. She was willing; she'd put that money in the bank, and it was a generous amount and she could give them some more of her time if she had to. And maybe he'd just been in a hurry, anyway, didn't want a long conversation with her right then.

She'd fastened her hair back into a ponytail, grimacing at the gray streak, and changed into nice slacks and a dark blue blouse; she felt good, thought how Cary would put it—"styling," she'd say—as she walked through the first set of glass doors. The office always appeared deceptively open, but then you had to get through that second set, and she wouldn't push the button this time, she'd wait like a proper businesswoman. She smiled at the receptionist as Thomas's voice broadcast through the speaker: "Sara, just come on to my office."

The doors on either side of the hall were open, as always; things seemed a little quieter. Well, it was a Monday, still early in the day. Thomas wasn't standing at his doorway this time, but seated behind his desk, eyeing her as she entered the room. It all felt off. She tried casual: "You doin' okay?"

"For a Monday. You may've noticed there's not a crisis right now. Give it time. Did you enjoy spring break with your daughter?"

Everything he said was reasonable and bland, but there was something in his face, a guarded, watchful look, that bothered her. "No, I have to tell you, with the weather, it was pretty lousy. Now Cary'd say *she* enjoyed it. She did things with her friends all the time, and they were all at my house, or theirs, and all the pizza and soft drinks..." She said the words lightly, but he listened in silence. "Well, so the galleys are here?" I can be as cold as you are, she thought.

"The page proofs, yeah, and they look great. You said you wanted input before it was printed. They're up in Ron's office."

Well, sure, he's got them—he could've just let you show me, but gotta pull that control-freak thing on me.... She followed him out the door. He headed for the elevators, but she decided to give him some of his own. "You know what, why don't we go up the stairs? After last week, I could use the exercise."

He glanced skeptically at her and turned aside into the stairwell, reaching ahead of her for the door, but she opened it first and held it for him instead. She scampered to the third floor and waited for him to catch up.

"You have a lot more energy than I do this morning," he

remarked, and she saw the eye roll. What had she thought she'd prove, using the stairs? Nothing, except that she was temperamental and, now, out of breath.

They panted along down the hallway to Matheson's office. "I hope everything's okay with the book. I got the feeling it's not. Sorry about the stairs. Impulsive moment. I guess I just wanted to pump myself up to prep for whatever's wrong."

She could see he was surprised by the confession; maybe he didn't get many apologies.

He nodded at the woman guarding Matheson's door. The east-facing bank of windows was shaded this morning by blinds partly closed, so the feeling she'd had of openness and fresh air the other time she'd been in this room was gone today. Matheson shook her hand, eyeing her the same way Thomas had, and gestured at the long conference table that stood against the wall opposite the windows. "They're laid out over there. It looks very good." There was no warmth in the words.

She stood over the table, shifting the materials around and examining them. Everything did look great: The sketches had been only minimally shrunk and maintained most of the quality she'd given them. And he'd decided to use the drawing she'd suggested for the cover; it had been slightly enlarged, which suited her. Maybe he did have good instincts about art. There was a page of instructions for parents and kids; it made her happy that they were easy to follow. She started smiling as she picked up the different sheets and laid them back down. Enthusiastic words on her tongue, she turned to the two men, who stood silently at a distance from her, near Matheson's ornate desk, and she realized they were quite somber.

"I mean, just looking over all this, I don't see any reason to be unhappy, and yet you two are; so what the hell's wrong? Don't make me feel like I've been sent to the principal's office."

Thomas cleared his throat. Matheson seemed to interpret that as a cue and said, "There's nothing wrong. It's perfect."

The few words didn't appear to be what Thomas had wanted. "It looks so good, we're gonna offer you an office and a title."

"Thanks for that, but no. I'm not job-hunting. —Oh, that was supposed to be a joke, I guess?"

Thomas glanced at Matheson, seeking input, but all he got was a scoffing sound as Matheson shook his head.

"So, when will the books be printed? Will you send me some copies?"

"Sure. How many?"

"Two will be just fine," she said with disdain, her glare locked on Matheson.

"Caroline and I will get everybody some coffee," Thomas said.

"None for me. I've had too much already," she told him as he departed. Of course, she hadn't. After her announcement, Louise had whisked that cup away. But again, it seemed, coffee was just a pretext.

As soon as Thomas was gone, Matheson said, "Would you step out with me to the deck."

"I came to look at those proofs, and I'm done. It appears we don't have anything else to talk about."

He grimaced. "Please."

"You thinking about pushing me over the railing?" she asked. "There'll be witnesses."

"Another joke, huh. No, I'd rather not broadcast through this whole floor."

She considered standing her ground, telling him he couldn't order her around, she didn't work for him. "It's your fault, you know, for having that open-door thing of yours."

"Well, they'll have to work harder to hear us, if we're outside."

When she didn't approach the door he held open for her, he looked back and made a soft derisive noise again, even smiled a little. "I'm not going to throw you off the deck. I told you a while back, being out here clears my head sometimes. And, besides, there're guidelines about…"

"Being by yourself with a woman, yeah, that would be Ken, right, his rules?"

"He's Baptist. Gotta be circumspect. Really: There's nothing wrong with the work. That's not what I wanted to discuss. Please," he said, gesturing again. She strode past him into the warm air, where he raised an umbrella against the sunshine, adjusted it a little, sat down, motioned for her to do the same. But she chose to stand, leaning against the waist-high railing with her back to the sun.

"It's not actually his fault, I'm sure, but tell me why you're both so pissed off this morning."

"Nobody's mad at you."

"Good to know. What, then?" She waited; but he seemed absorbed in watching the blue water of the lake. "Look, I came to see the galleys. I can tell they're fine. If I have to sign off on them, give me a paper. I have stuff to do. When he gets back, y'all enjoy your coffee."

"I don't need coffee, either. He's just giving me some privacy. You know that. I want to ask you about something else."

"I'm not doing any more work with the company," she said. "I told you, and I mean it. This was a one-off."

"Not what I was going to ask. Ken and I wondered what you thought about the things that happened, in town, in the area."

"Ah. All that blowback I read online, right? Did it shock you?"

He scowled at her. "You think it's a joke? Did you actually read it?"

"Yes, I read it. It's horrible."

"I bet it'll surprise you to know your sister asked me to do that piece. I wish I hadn't. One more thing she's talked somebody into. Yeah, there's been a lot of trolling. I want to know what you think about it. All of it. That crap on that building. What you read. All of it."

She wished Thomas would return. She realized she was squeezing the wooden railing, stopped before she got splinters. "Why me? What does it matter what I think about it?"

"You live here," he interrupted angrily, "as you've pointed out. You've done work for us. You're bound to have some opinion. So was what I said wrong?"

She'd thought about that yesterday, last evening, late into the night...what Cary'd said, what Rheta'd said. She conceded it: "You're not wrong."

She saw Thomas inside the office, trying to manage two cups in hand; she took a few steps towards the door. Matheson was suddenly on his feet. "Don't leave yet. I'm not done."

"Oh, *really*? You're gonna get in my way, physically try to keep me out here?" She saw Thomas turn and call to someone.

Matheson backed off, both hands out.

Caroline swung open the door, and Thomas stepped out with the mugs, setting one on the table near Matheson. At the quiet click of the lockset Matheson winced, a flash of understanding on his face. "I apologize. I didn't know he, I didn't understand— Are you sure you won't take the other cup?" he asked, suddenly quiet and

164

civil.

"I don't want coffee, I said."

Thomas sipped from the second mug. Enjoying himself, she thought.

"Ken, the engineers haven't found anything to ruin my morning yet; would you take care of that other issue I brought up earlier? Ms. Wells and I still have some things to hash out."

He gazed at Matheson. "I'd hoped that had already been done. Maybe I should stay."

In spite of her anger, she laughed. But Matheson didn't, and said grimly, "I'm a big boy. I'm fine."

"Not you I'm thinking about. It's not always about you."

They stared at each other, and Thomas left, scowling. Matheson went to the edge of the deck and gazed outward toward the pine forest, the landscaped road where azaleas were blooming already and trees leafing out. Sunlight slanted through the carefully-spaced pines and brought out hints of salmon-pink in the cypress decking. Halfway to the door, undecided whether to be enraged and leave—she thought she should —and wondering if that would be the easy way, and maybe she shouldn't let him off easy, should stay and give him a few of her own words, Sara paused.

"You could've told me, just let me know, just said, 'Let me help Ken'—" he paused. "I had no idea he was coming out."

"And keep you from making a jackass out of yourself? Not on your life."

"I wasn't trying to stop you from leaving; I just thought you were—"

"About to leave," she said flatly. "Told on yourself."

She heard the soft derisive sound even as he faced away. "This is what I wanted to ask: What do you think about your lawyer defending a white supremacist in court?"

"Everybody's got a right to a lawyer," she parroted Neil's words.

"Oh, yeah, *that* one."

"Did he troll you, too, and hurt your feelings?"

"Funny you should say that. You know what we found out about those posts? My IT people have diagnostics that suggest it may *have* come from an IP he owns. Some of it, anyway."

Massa, come save us…just another rich guy…who asked for

your opinion? She stared back at him, wondering if, in the long line of comments she'd seen earlier, some *had* been put up by Neil, risk-free in the anonymity of the Internet. Would he do that?

"I take it you're surprised. That helps, a little. I'm just trying to figure out who's on which team here. Something I gotta know. I always bragged about being able to figure things out. It's what we do here—computer stuff. We're good at it. I thought I had *you* figured out. You got on board with our project, put your name on it...."

She shifted uneasily, rested her hands on a chair back. "I had a pleasant drive out today. I was looking forward to seeing those galleys. My contract didn't include you demanding my attention whenever you want, making me listen because you're pissed off at somebody. I don't have to listen to you whine about all the blowback you get for things you said—which you should've expected."

"After last week somebody needed to say something. Your sister told me I should be the one. She made a good case. I thought it might help—I did," he insisted as she scoffed.

"Don't ask for forgiveness from me."

"It wasn't an apology. I'm not asking forgiveness from anybody."

"Good—I'm not responsible. It's on you and, maybe, Ken Thomas, your father figure who always seems to be trying to save your ass."

He'd dragged a chair to the edge of the deck, took off his jacket. "It's getting pretty warm." He laid the coat neatly, carefully, across the railing, took the coffee.

"He schooled you a little in symbolism, I see. 'Let's get past the stuffy coats and formalities.' Nice touch."

"In Michigan I'd still be shoveling snow. Spring in the South, already. But the summers here are hell." Ignoring her jibes. If his pause was to give her time to agree with him about something, *anything*, she refused that offer. He sipped, then went on: "Don't bring Ken into this."

"No, because, like I said, it's not his fault."

"Please sit down. I want to tell you a few things. Please. Just sit for a while."

She sank into one of the chairs by the umbrella. "Five minutes."

"Ten. I'll need ten."

"All I wanted to do—"

"Yeah, I know: look at the proofs. You did that. I'm taking advantage of your time. Can I? Can we just talk about a couple of other things a little?"

"You're using your minutes up."

He scoffed. "And you're probably counting. Thinking I'm a bully."

"Well, sure. We're just a new place to throw your weight around. Was it why you built here? Did you not have any luck with that kind of thing before?"

"Oh, yeah, we have our problems back home, where I belong. That's what you mean: that old trope...rich Yankee comes South, tries to run things. Well, I know something I bet you don't: Ransome told me to save this town, because he couldn't anymore." She laughed, and he stared coldly. "That's how he put it, his own words. When we bought his property."

"Do you hear yourself? You sound just like him! I grew up with that, don't forget. And *he* ended up leaving, didn't he? You earned every one of those online comments, every one."

"Including the ones your goddamned lawyer said?"

It had been there since he'd said it: the question, the wondering if he really would have done that. Part of her insisted, Neil was above doing things like that.

Part of her didn't know.

"And don't go clutching your pearls because I cursed. You've heard worse, I'm sure, from Rheta."

"And let's leave *her* out of it, too."

He shoved the mug away. "Too hot for coffee. You know, I *am* gonna tell you about Ken. Because he *has* saved my ass a lot, and he doesn't like doing it. My father—he still nominally runs the operations in Michigan, by the way—he hired Ken, maybe twenty, twenty-five years ago. Brought him to Michigan, from Atlanta. Ken took it as a compliment for a while—hired by this big corporation, young guy that he was, not much job experience.... He got promoted, and promoted again. One of the more talented people I employ. Did you ever think about that, how he's easy to get along with, but he knows a lot about all kinds of things? Even the engineers—you know, we're not a sociable sort—they all like him because he helps find whatever they've lost sight of. They see every goddamned tree in the woods, engineers. I know. I'm one of 'em. Ken has this ability to hone right in on the big scene, whether it's the money, which is really his 'thing,' or the big goal, or the balance in all of it. They get lost sometimes staring at each tree trunk, and he helps steer them back out to look at all of the woods. And that's not even his field."

"Yeah, he's a good guy. Better than a lot of people," she said pointedly.

He gazed at her in that assessing way he had. "How do you think he feels about all this 1488 shit, those Internet things you said you looked at? Or did you think about what was really going on in your preservation meeting when he showed up? Why Nora Burkes and Lindsay Mason, those people, why they just tuned him out?"

"You weren't there."

"He told me. Well, anyway, moving on—my father was wasting Ken. Once he'd hired him, the old man never really let him do what anybody else in his position would be doing."

"Your father's a racist?"

"No, a control freak. Ken wasn't the only talented person he was wasting. Don't get me started. Eventually, the good ones would all leave. He'd assign them to things they weren't interested in, or good at. It got worse as he got older. It was his loyalty test: Would they just do what he told them, or would they fight him?

"So when I was younger, Ken helped me, well, dragged me through some, let's say, *challenging* years. He's got that kind of real Southern ethic of trying to look out for stupid people, which is actually one of your more charming things. My father kind of 'assigned' him to monitor me, go through my division's accounts and blueprints, look over my shoulder. He thought that was a good use of his skills. I am serious. And after I—well, after I, let's say, grew up a little, realized what was going on, I complained, but by then the old man just thought it was funny. I finally acquired enough support to open the operation, here, in little old Mooresville. I told Ken he could move with us if he wanted to, or he could be rid of me, and stay in Michigan, and that was it—that day, he was ready to go."

"Or he could've gone and done his own thing. You just offered him a new place to do the same job" she interrupted. "How sad."

"No..." He took a slow breath before continuing: "I told him his days of looking after Daddy's irresponsible son were over. Not that I expected him to quit telling me when I was acting like an asshole, and he hasn't, by the way, as you just heard, but just it wasn't his *job* anymore. I mean, I'm older than he is, for God's sake. I asked him if he wanted to go home, South, to use more of that huge bank of things he knows about. And so he gets here and has to deal with the same kind of crap he did growing up. Do you realize how that hits him? And I don't want to lose him to another company somewhere else."

"You know that crap's everywhere, not just here."

"Oh, you're right about that. The thing that gets to me, he's dealing with it this time *because* of me, things I do. You all view him as an extension of me, so he gets the same shit I do. Leave him out of it. It's not on him."

She found herself clasping her hands the way Nora had in the last meeting, and jerked them apart. "Not everybody in Mooresville may be over that, but I am," she said grimly.

"Yeah, I know you are—but you may not have ever thought how much Don's father and his grandfather and, maybe, even Don, put up with, through the years. Italian immigrants in a redneck town. Lynne Houston. Her brother. They're successful, a part of your—*our* community now, but one time? I don't know."

"Because you weren't here. You just assume."

"That's what we do: We just assume. We don't think about it; we're not affected. Rheta says it's my 'time' to make everybody think about it. Regardless of whether people like me or not."

"Maybe people don't like you because you're an arrogant know-it-all."

"I haven't only talked to people. I've listened," he went on. "Everybody liked Lynne just fine when she ran the notions shop, and even after she got 'successful,' but now she raises hell, and people get all offended at her? I'm glad she's doing it. Anyway," he went on, "so I convinced my father that he needed to open a new division which I'd run, and here I am, thanks to Ken doing things a different way—yeah, some of those progressive little things were his touches, I tell you that now—and probably spending more money than the old man's happy about, doing those things, but, then—" his eyes narrowed a little—"it's not really just his company anymore, so I don't let that bother me."

"You ever read *Oedipus*?"

He laughed at her. "You could be right. If I'm arrogant, it's because I see my own time approaching when I have to figure out who I'll hand my part over to, and I'd hope it amounted to something besides just a dollar line in a column. That's why the book, you know. A lot of people who work for me have kids who don't have access to things I took for granted, growing up—" He paused.

"Rich and privileged," she supplied.

He shrugged. "That. I want to do what I can, so somebody's not sitting here on this deck in a few years, saying, 'I had to yank it away from the old sonofabitch, who never did anything good for anybody.'

"So, yes, I really do want the town to prosper. Sooner or later I think at least my son and his family'll be here, and I want them to like it. I want to eat at Don's greasy spoon for a long time, and I want my grandson to spend his Saturday afternoons hanging out at Andy's joint, where somebody else can enjoy that godawful guitar of his. And if I don't do my part to see it happens, then it won't."

"Your own little living museum."

"No, I want *some* things not to change, but you know, it'll all change. In time. Even Ransome knew that, and he's right. If you can't make it better, move over and let somebody else try. I'm trying, and your pal Neil attacks me for it."

She wanted to say something, to deny in ringing words what he was saying, but he continued: "Anytime you want to see what my guys dug up yesterday, I'll show you. Mr. Smooth Griffin isn't above some really dirty tricks. You Southerners all smile right before you stick the knife in. Save it," he added as she half-rose with angry words. "Do me a favor. Ask your sister to tell you who else really has it in for me, and at least give me some head's up. Please, seriously. I have to figure out who's running what, around here. Maybe I got it wrong this time, I hope so. But if my laid-back pal Don's worried, that's enough for *me*. I'm just trying to establish who's in bed with whom. *Figuratively*, you know."

She did stand up then. "I guess he filled you in on everything he said to me yesterday, or you wouldn't be bringing it up. The two of you have a sleepover last night? Mooresville's a little town, and everybody's connected, so of course I know Neil, and I know Don, and I even know Stephen Logan, him, too. Since y'all are so close, when I leave, you call Don and warn him to avoid me a few days.

170

Look, just send me those copies, don't summon me out here again. You write whatever you want, you pay the price for it yourself."

She went through his office and saw the little sphere on his desk. Rheta said it was easy to smash, and Matheson *had* told her he had some extras, and she could do that, except it would be on a par with running up two flights of stairs.

SHE THOUGHT SHE'D stop and have it out with Don before the lunch crowd arrived; but as she neared Main Street she saw Stephen Logan heading that way, and she changed her mind. He crossed the street in front of her at a light that turned red, forcing her to stop. When he scanned the street as he walked, he recognized her and waved, and she nodded unenthusiastically back at him, because she'd been raised to be polite, for God's sake; and she observed the nice collared shirt and his trim haircut. Somebody had definitely worked on him since his high-school days. She thought of other politicians who'd cleaned up pretty well, though inside they were the same people they'd always been—they were all alike.

The light changed. He continued down the sidewalk. She glanced at the rearview mirror and cursed him for spoiling her plan to yell at Don; maybe Logan ate there every other day or something, in which case she'd have to check the place out every time she wanted to go.

The next light also caught her, and she took one more look backwards to see him using a key to open the door of the building next to the restaurant—Neil's building—and go inside.

So *that* was why he hadn't been soaked to the skin in the restaurant over spring break.

14

AT HOME SHE locked the back door behind her—she'd have to start doing that herself, now that Louise wouldn't be on paranoia watch—and threw her bag onto the kitchen table.

She knew it was embarrassment, humiliation that her private life wasn't just not private but even open-source entertainment in Mooresville. Something everybody knew about and could debate.

Or, as Ken Thomas said about Scarlett: They owned her.

She stalked about the house, aimlessly going into different rooms, swearing. "Bastard. Son of a bitch. Damnation."

She wished she'd never signed a contract with them. The money wasn't worth it.

She stopped at last in the doorway of Louise's room, staring sightlessly at the boxes. Linens, mementos, documents, old letters. The things that defined your life. Move them from one place to another, even if their meaning was tied to the first place. She leaned against the facing, closed her eyes, breathed deeply several times.

Do you want to be losing sleep over this when you're seventy?

She reached down and gently pushed some items flatter into one of the moving boxes.

SHE WAS HUNGRY. And she knew better than to work on any new art right then; it would be like the macabre creatures she'd drawn at MTE when she first went there. Better to do some mindless, mundane housework. She threw away several pieces of junk mail that had lain on the kitchen counter for a couple of days, dragged the trash can over and with her hand swept some stray crumbs into it. Looked for something else. The bag that doubled as her purse had spilled out items where she'd slung it. She began shoving things back, throwing others away. Wallet, pens, a box of mints. Old lists. The envelope she'd pushed inside after she deposited that check. Maybe it *had* been worth it. She dwelt for a moment on the amount that went into her account, smiled grimly.

In any case, she needed to file that away for her tax returns. She cleaned out the random things, put a couple of pens aside, took the official-looking check stub out of the envelope, and stopped.

Another envelope, smaller and sealed—she'd forgotten about this one, hadn't even opened it, and picked it up with distaste. Two weeks it had been inside that other one; she hadn't even looked. It could've been something important. It was a familiar, cream-colored envelope—so, he'd kept one of those "unused" ones the day he sent the others to Kid Kare.

Thanks again for the excellent work you put into this "wild scheme." This is probably small payment compared to what you usually get. If we can work together again, it would be a pleasure. My apologies for offending you earlier today. Ron M

It was a typical note, and had no words, expressed no sentiments she hadn't seen at other times, but her pulse raced as she held it, unseeingly now, before her. Then she went to her closet, rummaged for the white carton she'd put on the shelf. She dug out the note that had come with the blue sphere, compared it to this other one. They were in the same handwriting.

"SONOFABITCH."

So over the past weeks he'd let her rattle on about her fear of people bringing her things, her anxiety about Cary; he'd let her wonder aloud about who'd given her that thing, theorize about what it meant—when he knew all along, because he was the giver.

She wondered if Ken Thomas knew. Hunger forgotten for now, she went back over what she could remember of that day, the day she'd finished the project, and she'd told them about the gift, when the three of them were outside on the deck. But she hadn't mentioned what the thing was, right then—not until they all left, and she saw the smaller one on his desk. *Then* she'd told them. And Matheson—no, it had been Ken Thomas who'd asked her where she'd got it. So maybe he hadn't known. And later Matheson said he'd distributed them to his company officers, and said he'd get one for her if she wanted it.

But he'd already given her the larger one, she reminded herself now, and he hadn't wanted her to know it was from him. So offering her another copy that day was just to throw her off. And Charlie, her old boyfriend Charlie: He was wrong. It wasn't carefully done, or unique. It was just a different-sized knockoff. As Cary suspected.

Matheson probably thought it was hilarious. She called him several other names, stared at the two notes lying on the table, started to tap a text on her phone, and erased it. No. She didn't have *his* number, just Thomas'. She'd deal with Matheson in person.

It wasn't quite 11:30 yet. All the business at MTE had taken very little time, she realized; it had seemed to go on much longer. She called the company, asked to be transferred to his office. She didn't want Thomas involved, especially not after everything Matheson had said about him; and, besides, this wasn't on him, and if he didn't know, she didn't want him to find out from her.

When Matheson answered, a surprised tone in his voice, she

said, "You know, we shouldn't leave everything the way we did. We lost our temper over stupid stuff. How about lunch around twelve?"

Silence. Then, "This morning you accused me of plotting to throw you off the deck."

"I'm superstitious. I don't like that kind of final words hanging around. So, Don's place? I'll buy."

"Maybe you'll have him do something to my food? Or, wait…you want us both there, light into us where we can't say anything back, don't you?"

She forced a laugh; it was fake, but better not tip her hand just yet. "No, I cooled down on the way home. So, yes or no? I said it'll be on me."

Still he hesitated. "Should I bring Caroline, or Ken?"

"What, you Baptist, too? You said earlier to leave him out of it, and I agree. Anyway, it's a public place. Everybody eats there. You'll be safe with me. Let's just make peace."

"Hang on. I'll see if she has anything on schedule." He returned in a moment. "I'll be there in twenty minutes. Will that do?"

"Close enough. Enjoy the drive," she added pointedly.

She took the ponytail down and parted her hair to show the gray streak: another silly gesture; why did she think she should look old right now—to assume gravitas she didn't feel? She packaged the sphere in the carton, looked at it a little regretfully: This larger copy was really pretty, a pleasure to stare into, like a gazing ball. Part of her was sad to give it up; but that was the plan, and she'd have to be willing. She put the carton inside the art bag, disguised it with a scarf dropped on top. She checked the back door again, locked the front one behind her, and drove downtown.

She was there just before twelve, and sat under an umbrella near the sidewalk, along with a crowd of lunch-goers who'd decided this was a nice day to eat outdoors. Good thing she'd left the house when she did, for only two tables were available. She kept the bag at her side on the concrete.

Don came out and spoke to several other customers and then to her: "Come to apologize?"

"Yeah, right," she snapped. "I'll talk to you later, and we'll see who apologizes. Today I have a date." Might as well give him a preview, she thought as she ad-libbed.

"We reserve the right to refuse service."

"Don't bother. He'll be wearing shoes and a shirt. Is he already here?" She saw Matheson approaching from the next block, striding fast through the crosswalk.

Don was puzzled. "Here?"

"Yeah, my date. Is Stephen here already?"

Appreciating the alarm on his face, she turned away and said, "Oh, no, here he comes," as Matheson drew nearer. "By the way, Don," she added softly, grimly, "I'd appreciate it if you didn't tell people everything you think you know about me. Now say hello to my employer." She smiled at Matheson.

"Employer? You just turned down Ken's offer," he retorted, sitting opposite her.

She was delighted that Don seemed utterly confounded, standing silently beside the table, glancing back and forth at them. "But I did work for you for a while. Don, get one of your servers to bring me a weak lime margarita." He stared at her, knowing she rarely ordered a drink even at night. "And a salad. Whatever you have lots of today—house, Caesar, I don't care. Mr. Matheson, what'll you have? It's on me, I told you. First dates, it's good for the woman to pay, right? It sets a tone. Assertive, but generous. Besides, I'm definitely not a broke teenager."

Now both of them gazed at her.

"Well, go on," she urged. "I'm hungry, and I want some food, and it looks like he doesn't know what he wants yet, so just double my order."

"No margarita for me," Matheson interrupted. "Water, please."

Don scoffed and disappeared into his restaurant. Matheson sighed heavily. "This isn't gonna end well, is it. I should probably leave now. But I'll let it play out, since we're here. Will it help if I just proactively apologize for this morning?"

"Let's enjoy the food. Then we can talk."

Of the two available tables she'd sat at the one slightly away from most of the others, one closer to the sidewalk railing. She caught bits of the talk around them that seemed to float, punctuated with street sounds, in and out of the budding branches of the river birches that swayed overhead. Matheson watched the traffic and tilted a salt shaker back and forth, back and forth, on the tablecloth.

A young college student who'd been in her fall semester class brought them napkins, silverware, vinegar and oil, a small plate with hot bread slices. "Ms. Wells! I'll be your server. You enjoying your classes this term?"

"Well, you know how it is…" She tried to recall his first name but couldn't. "No class seems as good as the one right before it. Did you do something fun over the break?"

"I had to work." He made a sad face, then put the smile back on. "If you need anything, I'll be out again in a while. Don gave me your order. We're fixing it just right for you."

And he left.

"I bet you're a good teacher."

She shrugged, not wanting the conversation to go there, not wanting to feel guilt for compliments given before she dropped the bomb. "He was flirting; he's after a nice tip."

He smiled. "I'll take care of the tip."

She started to object, then realized he hadn't argued about her buying lunch, which Matthew had always done, and it wasn't just about a meal—he found it insulting if she paid for things when he was with her; and Neil wouldn't have allowed it under any circumstances, because paying gave him power. The fake smile left her face as she recalled the afternoon she'd hiked here in the rain, and Neil had left his card with the cashier to pay for her latte. He hadn't even asked. Suddenly the pleasant anticipation of revenge left her, and she only wanted to get the ambush over with. And she too sighed.

"What?" he asked. And the server arrived with the salads and her margarita and his water.

She shook her head and began to pick around on the salad; he took that as his cue. They ate for a few minutes, dipping the fresh bread into oil she poured out on the saucer. She sipped the margarita, held it away and made a face.

"What?" he asked.

"It's not quite right…." Don had mixed it virgin; she'd roast him about that later, and he'd better not have put alcohol on her bill. Matheson said nothing, keeping his eyes on the salad or the sidewalk, waiting for her, and she made herself finish some of the food before she spoke.

"So, guess what my sister told us she did."

"There's no telling."

She sipped the juice. "Well, first, she and her boyfriend broke up."

"Michael." He paused. "I know who works for me."

"Oh, yes, you would. Michael, yes."

"Look," he interrupted, "before *this* goes any further, I told you she's been out there with him a few times. Till the other week I just didn't know she's your sister. I do talk to my employees," he added reasonably, "even when we're just doing social things. Maybe especially then."

"For practice," she needled. "Whatever, but anyway, they broke up. Did you know?"

"No. That's too bad, I assume, or is it? Maybe not?"

"Don't ask me; I never met him. So a while back I showed her that gift I told you about, the one delivered to me anonymously, the large version of those little small ones, like the one in your office. The ones you give everybody. You know."

He stopped eating.

"When I showed her, a while back, she couldn't think where she'd seen it. But when she rearranged her apartment after Michael left, she told us, she found his own little one, in a bureau drawer. I guess he didn't think much of it, since he left it there? Do you usually make people have them on the desks?"

He put his fork down. " 'Us' being you and Cary? You and your aunt?"

"Cary and me. So she took a hammer or something, I don't remember that part, and smashed it."

"I'll have to give him another one," he remarked. "Or maybe not."

She liked the nervousness in his words. "So here's what I invited you to lunch to ask." She lifted the bag into her lap and opened the carton, brought the sculpture out and set it between them, gently touched the smooth side, keeping her eyes on him. "This one's nicer than the little ones, don't you agree? But on the other hand, she said it felt good breaking Michael's. So maybe I ought to do the same. Put it out of my mind that way, quit worrying about it. I bet if I dropped it on the concrete—" She lifted it a bit off the table, and he quickly put his hands over hers and forced it back down.

"So who told you?"

"You did, you jerk. You wrote the note when you paid me for the artwork, and you wrote the note you put in with this thing. I compared them. So I'm guessing you've had some good laughs with your friend Don about pranking me."

He leaned back. "Don knows nothing about it, and it wasn't a prank."

"Didn't you think I'd eventually find out, since you got them all over the place? Do you think I'm stupid?"

He grimaced.

"And, by the way," she continued, "that's called 'stalking'."

"Stalking?"

"My aunt asked me, I remember, and I just shrugged it off— she asked how anybody'd know where we were that day unless they'd been watching us. So it was, what, kind of an early bribe to get me to sign onto the book project?"

He was staring downward, shaking his head. "What good would an anonymous bribe be? You knew about this when you came out to the company this morning, didn't you. You were already pissed."

"I didn't know, and I wasn't pissed, no…if you recall, that was you! I only found out a while ago, cleaning up random stuff. The note," she explained. "I found it in that big envelope you put everything in. I hadn't thought about it till today."

"The note where I apologized to you."

She waved dismissively.

"I wrote that note in a hurry that day, not thinking of the other one, or I wouldn't have written it myself, I wouldn't have done one at all, I would've got somebody else to do it, printed it on the computer, something. I'd had no idea you'd agree to do the art, and when you did, after you started working, I always had Caroline or Ken do the notes, instructions, you know. You remember hell was breaking loose that day, we'd just got back, I was distracted. You went past my desk, and made a comment about the one there, and I thought, Oh, shit, but I couldn't take the note away from you, could I. You hadn't said anything about it all this time, so I thought probably you hadn't put them side by side. Maybe you'd thrown the other one away, I didn't know."

The server returned and asked if they needed anything else. "The check, please," she told him, because she had done what she intended to do; she just wanted to leave.

"No dessert?"

She shook her head. "Not today." He departed.

"Like I said in that note, the first one," Matheson continued, "I watched your TV interview, I was impressed with how you give time to things, even things that seem to make you uncomfortable. I told you earlier today how I have to feel like I'm doing my part in the world. I just wanted to let you know, if you think nobody notices it, well, some people do. I figured you wouldn't accept anything valuable—"

She broke in with a scornful laugh. "But you did order an extra-large one for me."

"It's not that."

The server returned with her bill, and she immediately gave it back with her card. "I'm in a hurry; could you run it now?"

"You got it." He scurried off.

She shoved the remains of the salad away and rested her chin on her fist. "Would you take this—" she gestured at the sphere— "back to the office with you? If I keep it, it'll always creep me out, knowing you had somebody watching me, knowing where I'd be."

"You told, yourself!" he broke in fiercely. "Anybody could've found you. I didn't have to 'stalk' you. Maybe you oughta think of that next time you do an interview. *I* have to; you bet I've learned some things this weekend!"

She winced, remembering. "Fine, you're right. Look. If you won't take it back, I'll just donate it to Goodwill with my aunt's things. She's moving out, and there's stuff we'll have to dispose of."

"Moving out? *Y'all* have a fight, too?"

"Smartass."

"Anyway, no, I don't want it back, because it was a gift. Even though it didn't turn out the way I expected it to—it was still a gift, and I meant well by it…you don't believe that now, I guess. Just keep it."

"I'd rather not," she told him vaguely, her attention distracted by Neil's sudden appearance from his office across the street. Following her gaze, Matheson made the scornful noise he'd made earlier. Neil glanced left and right as if to jaywalk again and stopped, his eyes on her table. She turned away quickly.

"I appreciated lunch," Matheson said coldly. "Thank you. And as for the sculpture, whatever you do, just don't go Rheta on me and break it. There isn't a replacement."

"You could always order the large size again," she jeered, and lifted it.

He reached across the table and bumped into her forehead, hard, and seized the blue globe, set it on his plate amid the scraps of lettuce. She recoiled—"What the hell!"

"Sorry. Really. Didn't mean to— I'm just packing it down." He took the box and bag from her lap, his hand brushing the fabric over her knee as she leaned away from him, rubbing her forehead. "I can't just order the 'large size,' because there isn't a 'large size.' This is the original. The others are the copies."

He stowed it back into the carton, and then the bag, and pushed it gently toward her, stuffing the scarf in around the edges.

"Thank you and come back," the server told her as he handed over her card and receipt.

"You said you found the numbers, Roman numerals, right? XVIII and XIII? Letters of the alphabet. My initials: 'R' and 'M.' I made it, and I'd rather you didn't smash it. Keep it for Cary, because I bet she'd like it, if you don't; and who knows, it might be worth something sometime."

"You're an artist?"

He shrugged, arising from the table. "I do things. For myself, mostly."

"You understand what narcissism is, right? Making copies of your own work and forcing them on your employees?"

"They don't know I made this, and I'd rather you didn't tell anybody. Another reason I don't need it at the office. Somebody'd figure it out. At a certain time, not long ago, it was therapy. Another of Ken's sermons: 'Do something creative. It'll help you get focus in your life.' Anyway, it's my philosophy. Like I told you. Every corporation has a vision. I want them to think about it every day."

"You want them to think about your vision."

"It is *my* vision for my business." He glanced across the street, but Neil was no longer on the sidewalk. "My lunch is disagreeing with me, but, thanks, and, you know," he patted his pockets, "I left my wallet at the office. You don't mind picking up the tip after all, do you? I don't want to run a tab with Don. See you around." He turned and left.

She shook her head, signed the receipt and shouldered the bag, walking away in the opposite direction. As she passed the building to the left, she glanced at the front window and saw the poster: "Stephen Logan for City Councilman!"

15

THERE WAS THE evening class: She was grateful to have that, grateful to have something to focus on, because the afternoon had been a waste after she'd stormed into the house, a waste, no planning, no grading papers. And then it was time to pick up Cary, and time to hide her emotion from Louise until she could credibly claim she had to leave early to do something at the college, couldn't talk much right then. Later, driving home, she let the crazy thoughts rush back from the different parts of her brain she'd shoved them into. She thought about the sculpture, and that brought today's meeting to her mind, and Neil, and then she pictured him coming out of his office across the street, staring at her, and that made her remember Matheson's comments about wanting to figure out which side she was on, whose bed she was in—

She turned the radio on loud and finished the drive. When she walked into the kitchen, the sullen look on Cary's face meant Louise had spilled her own news. Great: More drama to deal with.

"Well, how'd it go?" Louise said brightly, and Cary side-eyed the glaring gaze of the betrayed.

"It was fine, and I see you know," she said to Cary, "and like me I hope you're really glad for Louise. Since she's moving so far away—what is it, eight whole blocks?—we might see her only, maybe, once a...week. So I can understand you'd be upset." She patted Cary's back to show the words were meant to be consolingly sardonic. Cary shrugged her hand away.

"Besides," Sara added, "now we have another room for ourselves! So, guest bedroom, office, retreat for you or me, when we have company? It's not every day you get rid of a relative who's overstayed her welcome."

Louise nodded slightly to her, approvingly.

"So tell me, first day back and all that..." Cary gagged and left the table.

Eventually they went to bed, and the house grew quiet: They were all tired or consumed by their separate problems tonight, Sara thought. Coming home earlier from the restaurant, she'd slung the art bag onto her dresser, walked away from it hoping the orb had broken; and it seemed now like a reproach sitting there, shrouded in fabric, hidden from sight as if she were trying to cover up a sin. She sat on the bed for a few minutes, staring at it, then put it back on her night stand where she'd been keeping it. Now she envisioned Matheson building it by whatever method he'd used, shaping it with his hands, then sculpting it with tools, carving out the cubes and the ripples in the places where water appeared to solidify. She picked it up, held it close to her face, found the numerals. She and Susan hadn't even considered they stood for letters of the alphabet.

How many other pieces had Matheson done?

She turned the light off and lay in bed, gazing at the ceiling.

LOUISE HAD DISPOSED of most of her household goods years ago when she'd moved to Golden Acres. What remained was her bedroom furniture and personal items, and she liked Sara's suggestion of renting a van to move all that. They packed down the photographs, the knickknacks, linens, bedspreads, pillows; but more than once Louise had to repeat something to her, asking rather sharply where her mind was. She apologized and said she'd just make the van arrangements, leave Louise to do the sorting.

She picked up her phone, saw she had three messages: one from her mother, one from Cary wishing her a good day, one from Neil.

I want you to get in touch with me ASAP.

Oh, and missed calls, too. Ever since that cold Wednesday afternoon when he'd brought her home in the rain, he hadn't tried to contact her. The graffiti and interviews and newspaper stories had all happened since then, so maybe he'd been occupied with that. But now he had some *thing* to tell her. She stood for a moment, phone in hand, and dialed the nearest U-Haul store. She didn't have time for him right now.

That afternoon they had boxed up all the items that could be boxed, and disassembled the bed. They put Louise's clothes, hangers and all, into the back seat, the better to rehang them after the fifteen-minute drive across town. Sara left to get the rental van and saw she'd missed two more calls from Neil. She texted her mother that she was busy with Louise and wondered how much to say, and felt relieved when her mother answered, **Good. I was**

worried she'd try to do it herself.

So Connie knew already. Louise had done a good job of keeping it from *her*, though. Or, as Rheta said, had she just not noticed?

With Cary's help they made short work of loading the van. Stone Avenue was in a quieter, older part of town, and Harvey's house looked to be about fifty years old, trying hard, but not shabby. Sara unconsciously evaluated it as if for a historical determination.

Harvey followed Louise around a lot, and Louise was a little bossy, Sara thought sourly as they worked. And Harvey's son and his family appeared happy, maybe even grateful that someone was going to be looking after him now.

That was her cynical take on it, which she kept to herself.

Gradually the van was emptied and ready to be returned.

"Should we leave yet?" Cary fretted. "Everything's still a mess in there."

"Look, they must've already told his family what they want done in each room. We *don't* know. We're in the way. They don't need us."

Cary turned sideways and considered this. "Are you jealous?"

An angry answer was right there, hanging on her tongue; but she held it in, because the question was mild and reasonable. She parked the van in the store lot. "I guess I am. Maybe, a little."

"So get yourself somebody," Cary suggested.

She tried to laugh. "Really. You say that, but you'd pitch a fit."

"You might be surprised. Especially if you went to Mexico with him." She gave Sara a sly grin and hopped out.

They were silent on the way home. Cary tapped on her phone; Sara felt her insides tightening at the thought of having one less person around, and how she'd get accustomed to that. Through the years whenever she and Louise started getting on each other's nerves, sometimes she'd go outside and swear, or turn her back and stalk away to keep from saying too much; but, really, what would she do now?

You know she's going to be here another day or two, at least, sleeping on that couch, she reminded herself. But it was obvious they'd planned this for a while and weren't wasting time. She turned at the last light before the street her house was on and chuckled a little, prompting Cary to look up quizzically. "They're anxious, like a couple of teenagers, aren't they?" she said. Cary shrugged and went back to texting.

Then Sara said something else as they neared the house in the twilight.

"You raised hell when *I* said that!"

Sara parked and waited for the trim man in the expensive suit to get out of the car sitting in front of her house. He carried a sheaf of papers in his hand.

"Hi, Cary! You okay these days? Mind if I visit a while?" And then Neil walked behind them into what had once been his little rental house, the house he'd sold her, the one he'd held over her head for years. Walked in as if he just belonged there.

"**IF THIS IS** business stuff, y'all don't mind if I get a sandwich and do homework in my room, do you?"

Cary had always seemed indifferent to Neil. Sara had tried to keep her unaware of their past relationship; she thought, hoped, Cary considered Neil only the person who tended to legal things for her mother. A friend. Maybe closer than some friends, but not much more.

He laid the stack of papers on the table and watched Cary prepare a tray. "I'd have brought a pizza if I'd known you hadn't eaten."

"Yeah, it's okay," Cary told him absent-mindedly, reaching for a package of cookies, oblivious to Sara's silence. "We've been helping Aunt Louise and her boyfriend move into their house." She stopped suddenly and laughed. "Weird! 'Aunt Louise and her boyfriend'! Too funny. 'Move in,' together," and she picked up the tray and left, shaking her head.

"So her guy finally got in through the window," Neil murmured. "Or she climbed through his. Why didn't you answer earlier?"

"You just heard her: We've been busy all afternoon helping Louise. Who'll be coming in, herself, before long." —She hoped.

Neil leaned over the table toward her, and took her hands in his. His hazel eyes held her gaze; but she pulled back from him.

"What's the matter—you didn't seem to mind Ron Matheson doing this yesterday." He didn't release his grip, so she stopped pulling. Years ago, she'd learned that staring him down when he tried that on her brought up whatever sense of fairness he had, and he'd retreat. It worked now, as then. He took his hands away.

"I don't know what you're talking about." She drew back against her chair.

"Yes, you do know what I'm talking about. The two of you, all cozied up at that table, you leaned together, and he kissed you, and then you both left." He crowded her again. "I thought he'd only paid you for artwork."

She stumbled to her feet. "Get out of my kitchen and get out of my house," she said, her voice shaking with fury. —And she remembered heads crashing together as he'd reached across the table to get the carton to pack down the sculpture.

"You two didn't care who saw, or you wouldn't have been there at lunch on a busy day," he continued.

She walked to the door and held it open. "I made Ron Matheson hear me out about something, and he grabbed for something I'd brought, he was mad, and I was mad, and we kind of bumped into each other." She didn't want to tell him anything about the sphere, but she'd just set her own trap and she knew that before he left, he'd ask; it was the way his mind worked.

"Shut the door. I'll be good."

"And why'd you come in that suit? It doesn't intimidate me, in case you thought that would work. You've used those tricks on too many witnesses. And on me a few times."

Very casually he rose and strolled toward her, closed the door, set the chain. She moved to lean against the sink and motioned him back to the table. He made a production of taking off his jacket and carefully laid it over a chair back—just like Matheson had done yesterday, she thought bitterly...but he was mocking her; Matheson seemed to have been trying out courtesies he didn't understand. She remembered scoffing at him about it....

"So you say you were arguing about something and he bumped into you, trying to get, what did you say it was? From my side of the street—and I have a direct view, and the street's not that wide—to me it looked—"

"I don't care what you think it looked like," she told him coldly. "He grabbed for a box I'd brought, he hit his head against my forehead. I may even still have a knot—" She realized she'd been too preoccupied to think about that, but the blow had hurt a little. She rubbed her hairline.

"Why'd he want the box?"

There was that prosecutorial stare that usually worked on nervous witnesses: I know you're hiding something. You may as well just give it up now....

"Beats me. Maybe he needed it for the rest of his meal. Which he didn't eat. But if everybody in town thought we were having a romantic moment, oh, my God, I need to buy an ad and straighten that out, because it's as far from reality as you could get."

He was puzzled; he recognized the evasion and watched her face for signs of uncertainty, ways to poke holes in the story. "Don would've given him a box."

"It was just a clumsy move—we'd had words, I told you there was something serious I had to get him straight about, and he just reached over..."

"He was being aggressive about your personal space?"

And she knew that stratagem, too, the one where he gaslighted, put possibilities into someone's head, things they didn't remember happening exactly that way, but which, now, seemed reasonable. "No, he wasn't. —I don't have to explain this to you. He was no more aggressive about my personal space than you are."

He blinked once. "That little sculpture was in the box, and he was the person who gave it to you." She knew she'd squinted a little and that he'd seen. "So how'd you find out? Did he tell you? Why'd he give it to you in the first place? Did it have anything to do with hiring you for that thing he's going to plaster all over the county? Everybody's heard all about that by now." He did an eye roll; his voice was sarcastic.

"So let me tell you some things. I found out on my own, comparing handwriting, since I had other stuff he'd written, instructions. I was through with the project anyway, and I just had him meet me and was going to return it to him. It was that. Only that. And as for all that other crap you're bringing up— I'm guessing it's a 'man' thing, where any kind of relationship with any woman gives you rights..." She'd tried to keep her voice low, but now it wasn't, and she remembered Cary was in the house, and why hadn't Louise showed up; that would put a stop to it.

He smiled. "So you were telling him off, like you're telling me off. Well, he probably thought that was exciting, and he leaned in, right? We may be more alike than I thought."

"Oh, my God, didn't you listen to me? There was no kiss. I was furious, and he's got a temper, too, so he was mad, and that's all it was."

The words had no effect; he approached the sink and stood close, very close, and she felt she ought to move, but that would look as if she was scared or nervous, but it wasn't that which held her there, it was that yielding that happened, or could happen, when a relationship had been intense, no matter how long ago, and those old attractions were aroused—it's like divorced people hooking back up, she thought as he leaned over her, it's the same sort of thing: You know what sea you're navigating, you don't have to maneuver the shoals of the unfamiliar. He kissed her very lightly, turned and picked up the papers he'd put on the table, came back as she leaned against the countertop. She saw smugness on his face, the triumph when he put his back to a witness who'd just been made to doubt himself, the triumph he'd let her get a glimpse of when they'd signed the final papers for the house: Did you win? Or did I?

This time he leaned against her, and she closed her eyes as his body molded against hers. "I don't want you to feel like I'm pushing you, too. So I'll leave. Do me a favor. Read these papers. I did a background search on him, and just if you wonder what sort of person he is, gifts or jobs notwithstanding, you might be interested. I'll get out of here before Cary comes and finds us like this, or Louise, you know?" Still pressing against her, he laid the papers on the counter behind her. "I mean, this'll complete the set: You know all about me, and I'm assuming he knows about you, and so now you'll know about him."

"I don't know all about you."

He gave her a sly smile. "You know what matters."

She shook her head and turned her cheek to him, and he laughed and pecked her there and retrieved his coat, smiling knowingly as he let himself out.

EYES CLOSED, TOO many mental pictures surfacing, breathing too fast... She must look like she'd had a seizure. She had to calm herself before Cary saw her. She'd like to blame him. And he would've backed off if she'd made him: This, she knew. But she hadn't.

"Mom..." Cary called from her room. "Has Aunt Louise got here? I heard a car..."

"No. It was Neil leaving."

Now Cary would come and ask her what was wrong, if she'd heard any of the exchange, and she should be honest with her. But Cary just said, "Oh, I thought it was her," and in a bit Sara heard the bathroom door close and the hum of the water in the pipes as Cary turned on the shower. The pipes were as old as the house; when she'd bought it, she hadn't had money to redo the plumbing, so when anyone turned on a faucet in any room that had one, you knew it, no matter where you were. She could afford to renovate it all now, and maybe should.... She thought about this fleetingly as she sat down and looked at the papers, clipped into a folder, looking official and important; distracted, she got up and wet a paper towel under the faucet to pat on her hot face.

Matheson had said Neil had hired somebody to chase down the history of MTE, the history of Ron Matheson. She riffled through the papers. He must have done this some time ago, not just since she did the book project—some papers were dated from months past. Years ago, even. He'd been investigating Matheson since before the company'd physically moved.

Matheson said he'd dug a lot of dirt on Neil, too....

She pulled the clip off and looked at the documents distastefully, warily.

Rheta wouldn't wait; she'd be reading already.

The water wasn't rushing through the old pipes anymore. Cary'd finished her shower; she never took very long ones. Sara reclipped the pages and turned them face-down, waiting for Cary to appear at the door—she did that occasionally, when Sara taught late, and would sit down in the kitchen to grab a snack before bed. She'd amble in, hair wrapped in a towel, or not, flop into a chair opposite her and unload about something.

"Where's your tray and plate?" She tried for normalcy.

"Oh...I haven't even eaten yet. It's just a sandwich and cookies; they're in a plastic bag," she added. "I can eat them anytime before I go to bed. I wanted to shower first. So...what did Mr. Griffin bring? Something about that project you did?"

"A lot of documents. I'll look over them later. I'm going to bed—tired from the moving. I hope Louise is happy...she's really eager to get there."

Cary looked wisely at her and smirked. "Don't change the subject; you already used that line on me once tonight. And I heard just a little, I couldn't help it, because the doors were all open. I didn't think at first it would be private, so I didn't get up and shut them…so did he do something that made you uncomfortable? Like when he brought you back in the rain?"

So she had seen. In spite of herself, Sara felt her face reddening. "About that——"

"Oh, I don't care about it," Cary interrupted, "I mean, I know you can handle it. And I didn't actually see it, I just heard you and Aunt Louise talking about it. But, tonight…" At another time, Sara would have found the whole thing laughable: Cary, like a tactful girlfriend, trying to find out how she'd dealt with a handsy boyfriend… Mothers were supposed to be in that role, not daughters, she mused wryly.

She went for some honesty: "Neil thought he saw something when I was in town, something he believed was going on with me and Mr. Matheson. Yeah, I know that's kid-level stuff. And I had to tell him. He and I aren't——" Steadying breath… "We, he hasn't got rights to say some things."

"I think we have it easier these days, people my age." Cary spoke slowly, choosing words. "I think we just stop crap more than y'all did when you were this age. That's what Allie thinks. And we talk about all kinds of things…I mean, *all kinds of things*," she added. "Like, Allie got her period last week while she was here, you didn't know, did you, and she just *told* Carson she had cramps and didn't want to go to the movies, and he was, like, 'Oh, well, sorry you don't feel good, we can watch something here.' I mean, we just tell each other things. Allie's mom says they didn't do that when she was a teenager."

Sara wanted desperately for the innocence never to be betrayed—wanted her always to believe honesty and guilelessness were all it took for relationships to work. And she knew you didn't tell your romantic partners everything, not for a while; not till it was safe. And that was just wrong. "It was a different time. I didn't have boys hanging out like 'friends'——"

"Like Carson. He's just one of the family here." She snickered.

"Well, there were Don and Chris…" She wanted to be careful, because Cary was only on the cusp of fifteen, after all, and there was a lot to find out before she was eighteen. "I don't know whether it's easier for you or not. But don't worry about Neil. He's always thought he has some rights with me, because he's known me for so long. I have to push back with him. Sort of like Don."

"No, not like that," Cary said, "not Don. When I told you earlier you should find somebody yourself, I wasn't thinking about Mr. Griffin. But, whatever: I'm sure you can deal.

"But if you can't," she continued, smirking, "just use that word you had me use when I was little, when I felt uncomfortable in somebody's house I was visiting, and I'd call you, or when I was ready to leave a birthday party or something. You remember?" She snorted. Sara did remember, and tried to laugh along.

"You remember? I'd talk about my stuffed elephants, and you'd know. So I guess you could just say, 'elephant', and I'd know to rescue you."

She made herself laugh with Cary about it, about relying on a code word to warn her teenaged daughter to hang around to chaperone her.

About that word "rescue" again.

"Or," Cary added, giving her one last knowing glance, "you could just tell him he can't come here if he's going to make you uncomfortable. Or I'll tell him, if you want me to."

She left the kitchen. Sara dropped her head into her hands and shut her eyes.

16

RANSOME MOORE SLIPPED into town without letting any of his old friends know. That wasn't how he'd done it, years ago, when he'd leave for a week or two, checking on one of the other business concerns he and Wilburn owned, and on his way home—weary of feeling like a nomad—would stop somewhere to call and ask Regina to get "the circle" together that evening at Dominic's. And she'd phone Lynne Houston and William Sykes and Clay McGowan, Andy's father; and sometimes he'd tell her to invite David Burkes, who was never rude to Regina but always said he'd try his best but couldn't promise. David would fume for a few minutes about the whole thing every time: Ransome *knew* he wasn't about to walk into that restaurant, sit down at a table and subject himself to jokes at his expense—he suspected (and was right) that the invitation itself was a joke, one that, if he turned it down (and he was always going to turn it down, dammit), would make him look scared; and, if he accepted it, would paint a quick target on his back. And of course he'd never be able to give as good as he'd have to receive, or get into a shouting match with Ransome in a public place like that; he'd have to just sit and take it, grit his teeth, pretend to be in on the joke.

But what if Ransome, this time—any particular time—didn't actually intend to do that, meant instead to patch things up between them and just share a nice dinner with friends? Then, of course, his refusal of the invitation would only make him look like a petty fool. —So went David Burkes's ten-minute inner soliloquies after each of those phone calls; and in the end he wouldn't go.

And, meeting the others and enjoying the good wine, the hand-prepared pastries, the company of the old friends and the Libertos (even Dominic might join in, and, later, Don and Lisa), Ransome would ask Regina: "Shouldn't you have invited David?" Everybody would wait for the punchline, knowing it well, but enjoying it nonetheless, and she'd smile and shrug: "I did, Ransome. I guess he couldn't make it this time." And the boisterous laughter that followed would make the other diners wish they'd heard that particular joke.

But of course Regina wasn't there to do phone calls for Ransome anymore; and, anyway, texting had replaced spoken invitations since those days. So he himself could've let people know he was visiting; but he didn't. He had things, not friendly, funny things, to discuss with the people, and not all of them friends; and he wouldn't risk going to Liberto's to say them—not because he mistrusted Don, but because right across the street was the office of someone he did mistrust, and that second-story suite looked out on the heart of town where most people found themselves several times a week. More than once in the past he'd hosted a dinner one of the "circle" hadn't been able to attend, and the next day maybe David would ask him why Clay hadn't been invited—was he mad at *him*, too, now? And if David hadn't done the spying the previous evening, his law partner Reg Griffin would've done it for him. But either way, they knew all about Ransome's gatherings, and he didn't want them to know just yet about this one.

So he'd texted those three people to meet him out in the country at Sooie Hog Bar-be-cue. Ransome grimaced every time he thought of that place: he didn't much care for their barbecue pork. It was just okay, once in a while, to his way of thinking, when you were needing a quick sandwich—and that name! He wondered if the Razorback machine had ever threatened a trademark lawsuit, and he hoped they would, one day. But at least the place wasn't across the street from the Burkes Griffin Law Firm, and he couldn't imagine anybody really thinking he'd be out that way, not after all these years.

He chuckled a little as he drove along the country highways back toward *his* town, taking different turns than he would've before, to arrive at the establishment with the huge pink concrete pig out front. A few cars were lined up in the bright afternoon sun. He knew one of them—the shiny, lovingly-detailed old red Thunderbird. As he parked his own tan SUV, he rolled his eyes: That guy didn't have any sense of discretion, and he must not appreciate the risk in driving a valuable antique, either. As for the other three vehicles, he didn't recognize them, but one of them was probably what the two newspaper people had come in. He didn't see the car with that ostentatious vanity plate that had been renewed over and over through the long years, the one everybody in Mooresville had always known: L3GAL1.

So at least word hadn't leaked out about Ransome's meeting this afternoon.

THEY SETTLED IN at a small rectangular table in the back, near the restrooms.

"If anybody that knows you comes in, Ransome, you jump up and dash into a stall in the bathroom and stay for a few minutes, and then come back out and pretend like you just saw the three of us here, sit down with us like you're renewing acquaintance."

The three men, including the one who made the suggestion, laughed. Pretty lame plan, Rheta objected, because it might work on the first person who walked in, but anybody else, later, would've seen the group together and arrived at their own conclusion, and it was stupid to go to the bathroom and redo the whole damn drama for every arrival at Sooie Hog.

Considering the time of day, it wasn't likely many people from Mooresville would be dropping in, anyway, Matheson pointed out, as some worked at MTE, and they'd already *had* their lunch. The four of them shrugged fatalistically and ordered the pulled pork sandwiches, and beer for Matheson and the editor, and water for

Ransome and Rheta. Ransome kept his back to the front entrance. It had been a while since he'd been in town, and there was a good chance nobody'd recognize him from that angle. He was balder now, for one thing, he told the other three. And they could just keep their mouths shut about anything else.

Rheta and Joe didn't bring out their phones. Neither intended to take notes today.On the way out they'd agreed this whole thing would be a waste of time. "But just give him his moment," Rheta said.

Matheson had removed his tie and left it and his suit jacket in his car, unbuttoning his shirt to affect a sort of disguise, your Everyman who stumbled into the joint from a drive out in the country. Ransome pointed out, when they settled in at the table, how that "common guy" disguise would vanish the minute anybody saw him get into his red car; but Matheson had laughed and said, "All this hide-and-seek stuff today's us just pissing in the wind, right? But we don't have to draw attention to ourselves *inside* the place, anyway."

Rheta fidgeted with her napkin until the sandwiches arrived. Matheson, watching her fold and unfold it, knew better than to ask if she was all right. He didn't think much of that new hairdo; made her face thin and hard, no softness to give a lie to her years. Rheta knew he was glancing at her now and then, figured it had to be the hair, and looked right back, coldly, daring him to say something. But he was a lot like her and wouldn't, she knew, would just keep shifting his gaze, and sit there. Hell, she told herself, she knew she looked like shit today.

When the waiter left, they all took a bite of their food and stared at each other. Matheson spoke first: "Why're we here, really?", and three pairs of eyes turned toward Ransome, who gestured for them to wait and carefully, deliberately, chewed and swallowed another bite of his sandwich, wiped his mouth, had a sip of water. So they waited, Joe smiling at little. He'd seen Ransome do this, long ago.

"I been keeping up with what goes on around here." He set the glass down and leaned forward.

"You always do," Rheta groaned.

"And, to my way of thinking, y'all got a problem you better solve before it gets out of hand and all kinda shit breaks loose."

Joe leaned in, too. "Which of the two or three problems I know of you talking about?"

"That smoothed-out redneck asshole Stephen Logan." The name seemed to cause discomfort to his taste buds as he said it. "Why'd y'all let him run for councilman, this election just two months out? Considerin' his past, and the people supporting him, you'd think it was a joke; but he may get elected if people don't wake up, and there you're gonna be, and if it happens, I'm gonna file suit, make you change this town's name, goddammit, I won't be owning *that*."

They all laughed.

"He's got the right to run," Joe reminded Ransome.

"Yeah, and you got the *obligation* to report on people who're running."

"Nobody else's come out. He's running independent, so he didn't even have to file papers with a party."

"Shit, man, neither would anybody else, then!" Ransome said, a little too loudly, Matheson thought; he made a "calm down" motion with the palm of his hand. "What, Ron, you want your company associated with a place where you got a neo-Nazi on the city council? You want that in your quarterly reports? —You got to get another candidate." Ransome dropped his voice. "Lynne'd make a good one, and I might say, it's her time. She's already out there, raisin' hell, got a followin'."

They were all silent for a moment.

"Or you." He turned to Rheta. "You could do it."

"But then I couldn't tattle on everybody. I like tattling," she said.

"That's all you do these days—sweet little things about the grannies? You used to be a hell-raiser."

"Don't give her the idea, Ransome; she's already got me in trouble, sneaking in pieces I didn't okay."

Rheta side-eyed Joe.

"No, don't blame him!" Ransome talked, loudly, over whatever she'd started to say. "I had things to do, myself, years ago. I ran an operation that supported the town. You know it's true—call me an old fool if you want, but it's true. I was a busy man. But all that time I did what I had to do, I was a voice of reason on the board of supervisors." Joe snickered. "May not've been a very high bar. Go on and laugh. But y'all about to let the town go to hell because nobody wants to step up. You—" he turned to Matheson, who had been expressionless the whole time, watching him. "Why don't you run?"

"I'm doing things, the best I can, in my own way."

"The hell. You'd be like me—you'd give 'em hell like I did, not a bad thing."

The edge of Matheson's mouth lifted wryly. "In your time it wasn't. There's the problem of getting elected in the first place. All my Internet friends've recently said nobody likes me."

Ransome looked at them, an expression of incredulity, disgust, on his face, the frustration of an old man who'd always been able to get things done and now couldn't. "So none of you gonna do anything? Fine, let me tell you what Logan's gonna bring in here— well, it's already here, the Griffin building now his headquarters, and that group that's backing him, right in there with 'im, and you're gonna just sit back and let it happen? And then I guess the town'll be in the news again, won't it"—he turned on Matheson— "what'll that mean for your company, but I guess you two'll be happy for a controversial story, South and its old ways, never changing—" this, directed at Joe and Rheta.

Joe held back things he'd always wanted to tell the old man. Rheta drummed fingers on the table. "Nobody wants that, Ransome. None of us want to go down that road again."

"Then you better figure something out."

Matheson sipped his beer. "I'll talk to Lynne. I agree, she, if anybody, ought to run."

"She's the only one raising hell, speaking up, the only one with any guts. But prepare yourselves. I don't have to remind you, she's a woman and she's Black," Ransome went on.

"What the hell!"

"You just hang on a minute, Missy. *I* suggested her, but I'm just reminding you to deal with your realities. Some folks get a choice between a Black businesswoman and a white redneck man with a bad past, they're gonna go for the white redneck. Maybe even against a white businesswoman. No matter how long she's been here, no matter how long they've known her, none of that'll count in the voting booth. Don't ask me to explain it. But there it is. You—" he leaned across the table and pointed a finger at Rheta— "you know it's true. It's not pretty, it's not right, but it's true. That's the reality."

"Then why even bring her into it?" Matheson asked.

"Because the town needs *her*. It'll be good *for* the town. People that came through the bad times, held on without selling their souls, those are the ones you want runnin' the place now."

"Hell of a thing to say. You caused the 'bad times,' Ransome. You sell your soul?" Joe was still mad.

"Did *you*?" They glared at each other. Ransome shifted his gaze and paused, finally to continue, "But you gotta even the field out. You gotta show what an asshole the guy is."

"You gonna give me anything to work with, after all these years?"

Matheson glanced around at the others. He was the odd man out, as always, here in this tight little group that had history among them, everybody knowing what was in each other's mind without saying it.

Joe went on, "You gonna tell who they were? I'm sure you know."

"You could've done your job and figured it out!"

"I don't own the paper, you know very well who does!"

"Hell, he doesn't own it all—the one with controlling interest would've let you! And *you* know *that* very well!"

Matheson looked to Rheta for a clue; but under the choppy fringe of bangs, under the frowning brows, her eyes flickered from Ransome to Joe.

"What the hell, fine," Ransome continued. "You know one of 'em already, the one that actually did it, because he's running for councilman, am I right? Those others...you know they were prominent boys, I guess you'd say; there were a couple of 'em, and they made sure they could say they didn't *actually* do it. Not with their own hands: It was *his* matches. That was why they always had him along with 'em anyway. Say they were drunk and out for the ride, they were kids, they were immature, they wouldn't have done it, ever, on their own. *He* did it. And he may have. Or maybe he didn't. They'd all probably lie, now. Don't people do that—lie, generally? And there could've been another boy or two, hanger-ons, kids tryin' to run in that crowd."

"You just shooting your mouth off?"

"I imagine a good many kids wanted to hang out with the big dogs. That's human nature, till you grow up. Maybe even then. Am I wrong, Ron? Ain't that really why our 'big dogs' stay mad at you: They expect you to join the club with the other rich boys? And you won't."

Even after all the time he'd spent with Ransome, all their late-night gut-spilling talks, Matheson hadn't heard that one before. Ransome was relentless: "Probably didn't know how, did you," he laughed, and Matheson grimaced.

"So, anyway, you're a kid, you got your run-of-the-mill summer job, after-school job, you wanna do exciting stuff when you're done. Not be just another boy punching the time card. Don't I recall Dom firing Logan some time pretty soon after that happened?"

"He hired me right after he fired *him*," Rheta remarked, "when none of your friends would hire me." She made a face at Ransome. "But Pop didn't fire Stephen because he'd found out anything about him. It was because he smarted off in the restaurant, and Pop got tired of it. So I was told." She found memories from that time mostly unpleasant, found herself fidgeting now.

"I appreciate everybody filling me in, helping me feel like one of you," Matheson complained. "Here's what I have: arson, a while back, right?"

"Black churches, two of 'em." Ransome spoke quietly, watching for Matheson's face to register whatever emotion he felt on hearing the words. "It was about what, Miss Rheta—thirty years ago?"

"Little more, yes."

"Boys, out joyriding, I imagine, hitting the bottle, and the big dogs most likely'd brought the bottles along, 'cause they could just swipe it out of Daddy's bar out by the pool—" Ransome's grimaced. "Maybe Logan eggin' 'em on... And once they had one blaze going, they worked on the next one, but by then at least some of 'em were having second thoughts, because *that* fire wasn't set just right, fire marshal said so later. Only way it burned was, the church was about to do an addition and there was extra lumber stacked close, and it caught up in that."

"Shit. Shit. Nobody ever charged?" Matheson asked.

"Nobody saw it, it was the middle of the night, nobody confessed, nobody implicated anybody else," Joe told him.

Ransome took the conversation back: "Yeah, Ron, four or five boys here in town did that, all those years ago. One of 'em most likely your fine candidate for city council."

Rheta had been considering names, and now added quietly,

"I'm thinking one's died."

Joe looked at her, tapped the table. "Jonathan Ingram."

"Colon cancer—young man, early forties." Ransome nodded. "He did go around with that bunch. Who knows if he regretted it; he took that to his grave. Well, you know about Logan—you knew all along about him, and I could name the others, but I'm not; that's your job. You do your work. They might tell on themselves. I'd like to think at least one of 'em still has a conscience."

Deep silence followed this narrative. The Ransome of other days would have leaned back in satisfaction, as if after a very pleasing dinner, as if it had been an interesting story, or a long joke with a good punchline. Today his shoulders were hunched over the table.

"Frank?" Rheta asked softly.

He shook his head. "You know he had no use for that crowd, and, besides, he was home that night. Oh, I did ask him," he added, to her, "yep, I did, 'cause you never know. Old men like to think they understand their sons, but most times they don't. But I can vouch for where he was. Y'all remember Colbie Jones?"

Joe and Rheta again nodded.

"That summer he was still working for me, it was before all that happened, you know. I was shutting things down. He was mad about losing his job, just mad at the world..." Rheta thought she might be the only one of them who noticed that pause. "He said all that shit to the papers, to y'all—" he pointed an accusing finger at Joe—"which you didn't have to print, 'cause he was just shootin' off his mouth, and you knew it, just kid stuff, like you prancing around with that sign of yours...so I sent him off to Baton Rouge to keep 'im out of trouble. That kind of talk could've got him killed."

"Wait! Sent him off?" Rheta interrupted.

"Please do tell me you weren't one of those fools thinkin' he was fed to the bayou," Ransome jeered. "You're too smart for that."

She jabbed his shoulder. "You got him out of town? His mother, too, I guess."

"Somebody had to look out for him down there in Louisiana. He wasn't but eighteen. Been on the farm all his life. I wasn't about to turn him loose down there."

"Well, he had *plenty* of reasons to have it in for you, didn't he!"

"After a while," Ransome mused, waving his hand vaguely as if to banish it all, "we worked out our differences, and one day he told me what *he* knew about that night."

Joe slapped the palm of his hand down, angrily.

"Nobody made *you* not ask him," Ransome went on. "You just didn't do it."

"Why'd I ask a Black kid about a thing like that? That wouldn't even make sense."

"But you also didn't even talk to Stephen Logan, did you?"

"He lawyered up fast. Pro bono, and the man played on sympathy. 'Just because he's poor, doesn't make him guilty.' And I was a kid myself. What could I do?"

Rheta turned a contemplative glance on Joe.

"You sound defensive, Joe," Ransome needled.

"*Nobody* could talk to him, after a while, dammit. Darrell Parten tried, you know—"

"—Sheriff at that time, pretty good guy," Rheta interrupted to tell Matheson.

"Yeah, and they got tired of seein' his face. He'd figured out he could get attention that way, played that card for a while, didn't he. And all of you finally told yourselves he really must not know anything—just shootin' his mouth off." Ransome looked disgusted, "something you should've considered with Colbie, because it was true, with him."

"I was a kid. You blaming me? No responsible paper would've assigned that story."

"Who would've held you back from some decent reportin'? David Burkes? We already covered that."

"Hey," Rheta interrupted. "Stop going for each other's throats. Like a couple of old curs."

Ransome settled back in his chair, his eyes still on Joe. "Y'all at least know what he's been up to all these years? Need me to tell you that, too? Well, for a while he worked a job over the line in Franklin."

"County next door," Rheta told Matheson helpfully.

"I know *that*," he snapped.

"I've kept up with him, Ransome." Joe stared at him balefully. "It may make you happy telling yourself I let it go, but I know things. Married a quiet little Pentecostal lady. Got to be manager of that hardware store, went to another one then, bought it out, made it profitable. Give the boy points for being scrappy. Then he sold it, more profit. Everybody in town knows all this."

"Where'd he get the money to buy it in the first place?"

"Robbed a bank? Saved up his salary? How the hell would I know?"

"Ask?"

Joe sneered. Rheta eyed him and then said, "What we *don't* know is how he's supporting himself right now."

"Proceeds off that sale," Matheson suggested. "Some kind of annuity from it."

"Well, that 'MAP' group has him listed as a consultant." Ransome once more looked as if he'd tasted something bad in his sandwich, which he'd picked up and nibbled again during Joe's summary.

"*Them.*"

"But did *you* know that? I guess not," he went on. "Scoff all you want, Joe Sims, but you ain't done your job. Who are they, who helped *them* get started? How can they afford to pay our boy anything, and for consultin' *what*? How'd they have money to do it?" He shook his head emphatically. "Makes no sense. Is it one of those other guys doin' it?"

The other three had forgotten their own appetites. "Okay, so we failed."

"No, *you* did," Ransome shot back. "Miss Rheta wasn't here again till a few years ago."

Joe scoffed: "About Colbie, who you say is alive, and knows things, I guess you mean he could incriminate Logan. But where's he, and why should anybody believe him now? That summer he had a grudge against everybody in town, maybe especially *you*, with some reason, I might add. I don't fault him for it, and you shouldn't, either. But if I were a lawyer, I'd be a damned sorry one if I even thought about putting him up on the stand by himself. And he wouldn't have run with that crowd. They wouldn't have let him."

Matheson wondered if the old man was just trying to con them because he wanted to be a player again. "Why didn't you tell me any of this when I bought your farm?"

"Why the hell should I? Just like Joe could've found out things if *he'd* tried, you could've found out if you'd just looked into it, it was in the archives—you found out other stuff. Would you've changed your mind about coming here?"

"I might've!"

"It had nothing to do with relocating a business."

"And you really wanted me to buy your property, didn't you."

"And you did."

Matheson smiled. "You sorry bastard."

"You talked big about making things happen here, all your high-flyin' plans to improve my poor old town—well, here's an opportunity. That was one of the main reasons I sold to you!"

"Oh, you had other offers, did you?"

"Yes, in fact, I did. You don't know so much as you think you do."

"Why didn't you tell *us* some of this back then?" Joe said, only slightly less angry. "We might've pushed harder—now it's probably too late. People close up over the years, they get good at hiding things, even from themselves. As time passes, some may forget what actually happened, as they get old," he added pointedly.

"You're full of shit! You had as much of a chance as anybody else to find out about it. You go take a long, hard look in the mirror." He turned to Matheson. "Everybody was scared about who might end up in jail, which of our local boys, nice kids, might've got sucked in, about to face charges." He scowled at the editor. "I bet you were even a little worried, yourself; you knew some boys the right age. At the time I had my own guilt to bear, as you keep pointing out." His voice wavered, the tone of an old, unsure man. "But I always believed in doing what you can."

"He went out with one of his bulldozers and cleared the ground and started rebuilding," Rheta explained to Matheson.

Ransome's eyes gleamed. "And there they were, David and Reg, looking damned uncomfortable in those suits and ties, 95-degree weather, standing beside that Mercedes and David's Caddy, looking as out-of-place as an Ole Miss homecoming maid butcherin' a hog." His waggled his finger. "Don't tell anybody I said that. The Ole Miss folks'll be jumping all over me."

"And he fronted money for rebuilding," Rheta added. Ransome softly cursed. "Shut up; I have *my* sources."

"But again, why'd you believe Colbie?" Joe said. "Why should *we*?"

Ransome stared at the back wall. "After he got down to Baton

Rouge, I was in touch with them again…you know how it is, you can say things from a distance. When you cool off, both of you, and you don't have to look at each other. It wasn't all at once….We talked, that's all, and I told him I was sorry. He took a while, but, me telling him *I* was sorry…that helped. We've kept up, through the years. Off and on."

They waited for him to continue, but Ransome had drawn a line, and he was thinking now, careful not to let his mouth get ahead of him the way it used to. "He was close friends with one of those boys."

Rheta leaned in, frowning in concentration, and something started bothering her. "How could he've been? A Black kid, friends with a guy that burned down Black churches in his community, that's not reasonable, I don't believe that, Ransome."

"You *know* how it is sometimes—you write about it yourselves: People'll do awful things, even against their friends, just to be brought up a little in the world. Colbie knew this friend of his was involved. He told me he knew. I never asked him any more about it. And you won't get it out of him, either, Joe. Colbie's friend—that person's gotta do it himself. He's the only reason I didn't say nothin' all these years.

"But we're not talking about him today. He don't matter right now. One day maybe he'll do the right thing on his own."

"If I start guessing all the boys from that time, your old face'll tell me which one it was."

"So, then, you *won't*! Don't go there, Joe."

"And you can find anything on the Internet, so I'll just Google him."

The old man laughed. "You go on and do that. He don't go by that anymore. And try looking up 'Jones'."

"Maybe you did him in yourself. You had good reason, and no self-control—"

Ransome's deep belly-laugh drew the attention of the teenager behind the register.

"After so many years, does justice just not matter anymore?" Joe asked loudly.

"Does it? You tell *me*."

"I'd say it always matters."

"Back then, it didn't matter so much to you! You're a fine one to be askin' me that question."

"I was just a kid myself, goddammit!"

"I must've *forgot* what you said, before: Why *are* we here today?" Matheson demanded sourly.

"That fake accent needs work," Ransome advised. The other two laughed, and Matheson sipped from his bottle.

"But he's right. We're gettin' sidetracked. We need to think about the here and now." Then Ransome leaned over the table, serious again, and they huddled in as well. Sooie Hog had almost cleared out; it was the middle of the afternoon, and, as Matheson had said earlier, who'd be coming here at that time of day? But the moment felt too significant, required them to huddle in.

"Maybe it'll come now, if it didn't then. Justice, that is. But maybe not in a courtroom. Maybe another way. Just like back then, he's lawyered up again, somebody gettin' him off for things. But, regardless, you gotta keep pushing what people remember about him, if they're a certain age."

"The churches," Rheta said. "What happened in Andy's place." Joe cut his eyes at her, but she went on, thinking it out loud. "Remind people, tie it around his neck. He did do a lot of talking for a few days, till somebody convinced him to shut up. Somebody important enough to pay him off, maybe. Somebody that could still be payin' him off."

"If you don't have proof, that's libel," Joe interrupted. "I'm not going there, Ransome. I don't need that."

"One domino falls, another one does. You just gotta line 'em up. Just offer Mooresville a choice. That's all we do—that's our job. *That's* why I drove down, Ron, *that's* why we're here. Doesn't matter who was in the car, and who brought the matches, and who stood by. If you're goin' along for the ride, you all did it. Right? Talk all you want about 'justice' maybe in a month or two, after the elections, hell, whenever.

"But right *now*, here's what you got: Logan was, what do they call it, a 'person of interest', and now he's renting, or—" he waggled his brows at them—"*is* he renting, or is it provided free? And why *would* it be? Why don't you ask them both—it's a legitimate question. Tackle those two, give people another choice—Lynne Houston, that they've known forever, a smart woman, a member of the community—"

"Wait, wait," Matheson objected, catching on a little behind the other two, who were eyeing Ransome. "You're saying Neil Griffin was one of those boys?"

A WHILE LATER they left, not separately but at the same time, as there was no one else in the restaurant, and secrecy felt silly. Joe and Rheta had driven out together. She intended to talk on the way back to town about the last thing Matheson had said to the group before Ransome—mindful of the penance he'd always owe—picked up the bill for them and they hung around outside a few more minutes.

"I couldn't get elected dog catcher in Mooresville," Matheson had begun.

"Sanitation chief?" Joe offered. "A few might enjoy seeing you cleaning up their shit."

Matheson's eyes narrowed, his mouth grim, not liking Joe much at the moment. "But since people hate me anyway, I *could* say I just recently learned about this guy's past, which is not really wrong, is it. I could ask if people remember what he did—"

"Allegedly," Joe interjected. Softly, Ransome swore.

"—or *maybe* did. And I can by God get Neil Griffin's name in there, too, since he owns his campaign headquarters."

"So what you're saying is, you contacted me today to find out why Stephen Logan's background hasn't been brought up," Rheta hinted. "I heard you say it. I was taking notes, you all saw me."

"Well, it wasn't me, I'm old and irrelevant." Ransome chortled and he slapped Matheson's back—passing a baton to another runner, Rheta thought—as the four paused near their cars. "But here'd be my plan: Ron, first, talk to Lynne. She's so mad right now, she'll likely agree to do it. And if she doesn't, the rest won't matter."

"Y'all were big pals back in the day. Ask her yourself," Joe taunted.

Ransome didn't answer that but continued to address Ron: "Endorse her if Joe here'll let you do it in that paper. You'll take some more heat for it. You good with that?"

"Couldn't get worse than the last time Rheta roped me in."

Ransome then said he'd come out to MTE sometime and visit; but Matheson figured he probably wouldn't, and he understood: It would be painful to see a place he'd known from childhood so changed, a place his family had owned for generations. Ransome climbed up into his SUV and headed back toward the northeast, an hour-and-a-half drive to the town where he and Wilburn lived now, though Regina had died last year, and neither brother had ties to anybody but themselves there. He could've stayed in Mooresville at one of the new chain hotels, but staying in a hotel, unnoticed, in a town your family had founded? He wasn't in the mood for that.

17

MATHESON RETURNED TO the office and parked the Tbird in its special garage, near the visitors' house, and walked back to the main building. "Sorry, Ken—later," and he waved Thomas off. The pork didn't suit him, and the beer had been run-of-the-mill. He went straight to the deck with a bottle of water.

He'd learned a long time ago to make decisions and move on. He wasn't someone who often felt uneasy, not at his age, not in his position. But an unease fell over him as he sat and looked at the glimmering lake, the pines that had started putting out new growth.

He sipped the water. Actually, several things were bothering him. Why hadn't anybody ever mentioned there was something weird between Logan and Griffin—not in all the time Logan'd done well financially, secured a convenient place for whatever business he claimed to run, got off the hook for assaulting somebody? Now that they'd told him about the churches—now that he was alone with his own thoughts—it felt obvious. Joe Sims and Rheta had been surprised—but then, no, not really. *He* seemed to be the only one really surprised.

He changed his mind: Possibly Ken would see it from another angle. He texted him to come out; no response. Maybe he was pissed about having been blown off, earlier. Irritably, he texted Caroline: **Pls find Ken. Thx.** Shit, won't even go to your own desk, he reflected. In a while, he heard footsteps on the stairs, and presently Thomas' head rose above the handrail.

"Look at *you*," Matheson jeered.

"Sara Wells sets a good example."

"Yeah, and she's a judgy nag, too."

Thomas was panting a little in the heat and adjusted an umbrella to shade himself as he sat down. "Two flights, eighty-five degrees. There you sit, resting your butt after all that hard work, eating lunch in the country. So, *now* you wanna talk to me?"

Sometimes it was hard to tell when the man was kidding and when he was truly and well pissed. And the older they both got, the more those times happened. He couldn't blame him much for that…. He told him, watching his face when he went over the parts about the churches, asking what *he* thought about Griffin and Logan, whether *he* had insight about why nobody'd talked about it, whether *he* thought it could be true. Because, even knowing Ransome as well as he did, he still had doubts. It was just hard to believe, he told Ken—that a whole town would suspect, but would cover for those men, all those years.

Thomas gazed at him the way he did when something was so transparent, so straightforward, that Matheson was wasting his time by asking. A sarcastic, disgusted look.

"Nobody said anything because those fine, upstanding white men wouldn't have a bad side, would they. Now, other people, poor people, what they call white trash, brown people… They might; so what would they have to lose? Yeah, Logan pulled it off by himself."

Matheson slammed the bottle down. "You know that? You hear it somewhere?"

"And what'd *you* just do? Exactly what I said. Yeah, I know all about it."

He left the deck, ignoring Matheson's, "Wait, I meant—"

So there he was by himself again, thinking about the spoiled rich boys. What did Ransome say: Everybody was scared about who might end up in jail?

One of them being Neil Griffin.

He sipped the water, which wasn't helping, because it wasn't indigestion.

And he told himself it wasn't schadenfreude—it was that wrongs could be righted. It was that he might get things moving, finally.

Ransome had warned him several weeks ago, before the newspaper stories had come out—had leaned close into his face as they talked in Don's living room, had glared at him: "Watch yourself. There's a difference between influencing things, or just enjoying the power."

Matheson had tried to be funny and cool: "Power corrupts. Absolute power—"

"Oh, my God, a philosopher!" Don had snickered.

Ransome went on: "This is the question: You want power just for the sake of having it—that what you want, for people to know you got it? Or you one of those that does things with it, and sometimes people find out, or sometimes you don't get credit, and you'd be cool with that?"

"You did both! How many times did you knife David Burkes in the back? And get credit for it?" Matheson had retorted.

"Go to hell," Ransome told him jovially.

"You threw your weight around for years, and owned it! Had *your* cake and ate the whole goddamned thing!"

Ransome had thought that was hilarious, and agreed....

Matheson took another swig. For sure he'd felt a rush when he'd outmaneuvered his father, and, today, when he'd told Joe and Rheta to go on and quote him. Griffin deserved it in spades, even more so if Ransome was right.

That was adrenalin rush. He knew it.

And they wanted him to talk to Lynne Houston, get her into the race. More power plays; more exhilaration.

But the warm air, the heavy food in him—that wasn't making him squirm. All those online comments had got to him. He'd always been able to hold his own with people like Ransome, could give it back as well as anybody. But those random, anonymous people—he couldn't respond to them, because they chose to stay unknowns, like all the bugs swarming here most of the year. You couldn't get a lock on where they were, or what they were, you were reduced to flailing impotently at them.

"A new place to throw your weight around"—funny he'd used the same words on Ransome that Sara'd used on *him*. There was truth there, but from her, it felt harsher than when he'd said it. Every time he passed Liberto's, going to work, walking down the street on the weekend after buying things in town, mental pictures of that day returned to his mind: the wind blowing through budded branches of the river birches; a hum of pleasant conversation; a gift shoved back at him. Their heads bumping as he reached into her lap for the carton.

What would happen next? If she learned what they'd learned today, would she—this was it, he had to own it—would she rush to Griffin's defense? He wasn't sure what she and Neil Griffin had had, or now had, but some people were funny about their former lovers. She didn't seem to be that way about Matthew Wells, but he didn't know what it was about Griffin…. And he couldn't even tell her now what he knew. If he did, she'd take it as just another attack on the man.

The whole thing made him angry, and he didn't want to think why.

RHETA AND JOE were silent for a couple of miles as he drove back into town. Joe spoke first. "You believe him?"

She stared unseeingly at the edge of the road a few car lengths ahead as it flew by. "I don't know. Maybe not all of it."

"You dated Frank. Do any good to talk to him?"

"Ransome's probably already warned him not to say anything to us, and he may never have told Frank, anyway."

"You could be right." Joe was taking the curves pretty fast, not paying enough attention as he considered the problem. "You think Frank was involved?"

"Ransome knew everything that went on, back in the day, had his fingers in most of it. He would've known about Frank, and he would've probably made him confess. Slow your ass down, Joe. I don't wanna end up upside down in a ditch today. I'd rather not be the headline."

He eased off the accelerator. Neither of them spoke for two or three minutes.

Again Joe broke the silence: "Well, he talks saltier these days."

She laughed, then sighed. "Regina's not around to censor him anymore…. When we did those stories on the district," she began.

"When *you* did them," he corrected.

"I sold a lot of newsprint for you that week, you know. Anyway, one thing Ransome kept saying, one way or another, was like today: 'My time's over,' that sort of thing. I think he just wants to fix this election, *so to speak*"—Joe snickered—"and be done with everything here, with that last big thing. And if I were him— thinking like he would, I'd…" She paused. "I think he's setting things up so it all just goes down on its own. We're just gonna be the facilitators."

"Matheson stepped in it."

"Maybe. I think he's got his own agenda now."

They thought about that as Joe drove through the narrow alley into the back lot. "Some people'll say we're going past reporting. And are we?" Joe pondered. "Is Ransome jerking us around like he always did? And you know we can't afford to defend a legal action. People don't read us like they used to, they go to the Internet. We're hanging on, but just."

"Ransome got press back in the day, and things got done. Good things, bad things. Anyway, it'll be on Ron, not us. And he seems willing to take the blame. I don't know why. I wouldn't go there, if I was running a big company. I'd get a proxy for this fight. So do we go with it or not?"

"I say yes, but carefully. I don't want Neil Griffin filing anything. We can't pay it."

"You and your 'careful.' Gotta take a stand," she said. "And, Joe, I gotta ask this: Why didn't you try harder, back then, to find Colbie, or go after Logan, or something?"

Joe had parked, and it was a warm day, but they sat in the car another few moments while she waited for him to answer.

"David Burkes owns forty-five percent of the paper," he said at last. "Has for years. —It's a thing," he told her defensively, as she swore.

"I've dug, and I didn't find that!"

"He uses another family member as front. Hard to trace. It's how it is with the big rags, too. And they tell you to handle some situations carefully, don't rock boats."

"You gave in to him, while I was working my butt off in college and then in Atlanta? Really? You did that? So everything Ransome tried to shame you about's actually true?" They'd worked together several years now, and from the grim set of his mouth she knew it was a punch he hadn't expected from her.

"Mooresville's not Atlanta, Rheta."

"Yeah, those are true words." She grabbed her bag; he looked away from her sneer.

"And, by the way," she added, staying two paces ahead of him, so all the rest was thrown backwards like small, heavy missiles, "since you didn't try to find it out yourself: I assure you, Ransome knows good and well who was involved, everybody who was in that car that night. I guarantee it. Every last one of 'em," she said, and as they went back into the newspaper building, she added, "And you are aware Emily and Colbie were going out together, right? Or did that not occur to you?"

Joe stopped as if a wall sprang up in front of him. She headed to her desk. "Boom."

18

RANSOME ALTERED HIS route and headed out west. So what if he got back thirty or forty minutes later than he'd intended. He'd just call Wilburn to let him know. They'd got to be as bad as two old women—keeping up with where the other was supposed to be, and when. Turning onto the back roads he still remembered, he said aloud, "Shit, get weak and sissy when you get old...."

He came back to the highway a little west of the company, just past the line where his old soybean fields had usually been planted. Now he'd make his way back towards town, tying that loop, and retrace the road up northeast. He figured Matheson'd had enough time to get back to the office himself, so he wouldn't cross paths with him, wouldn't have to answer questions later, deal with pity or compassion....

He drove more slowly as he passed the complex on his right, noting happily that they didn't fill in his lake. He felt sad that Regina wasn't along with him, but he wouldn't have recognized the place as ever having been his, now, and so it didn't mean much anymore. Everything was changed, not just the land, but him as well.

"And damn good!" he said aloud, lifting his chin as he passed the main entrance and entered the pine forest he'd planted long ago. "Damn good, about time."

He'd put this trip off for several years. It was like a visit to the dentist: Now it was done, and everything felt better, and clean. That was what he knew: Pull off the bandage fast, and move on. Deal with pain as you had to.

MOORE FARMS WAS a three-generation enterprise, farmed almost a century, modernized as the years went by, until finally they didn't need field workers anymore. It was the way of the South. By the time Ransome had been elected supervisor of his district, he had just the crop manager and a handful of young guys working for him, more to give them jobs than anything else...very different from his father Sam's time.

Fifty years ago the field workers displaced by technology had lived in weatherboard houses scattered along the highway out to the Moores' home. Sam Moore, son of Ben, had watched the same path roll out in front of him that had, all over the South: The big farms required less manual labor; the men and women who for decades had labored for him had no skills and hadn't been encouraged to get any...nowhere to go, no nothing. Eleven-year-old Ransome saw Sam brooding over fields on hot, dusty evenings in mid-summer, after the tractors had rumbled back into the shop and he'd locked them up. Back in the day, after the second war, Ben had personally traveled up North to buy them—combines, lumbering, Rube-Goldberg-looking contraptions that he knew the second he saw them would change Moore Farms forever. But these machines weren't cartoons dropping marbles onto a sluice, generating far-fetched reactions; they did things fast, faster than his horses and his field workers could ever manage; and the workers knew it too.

Ben wasn't religious—and Sam and his boy Ransome were like him, there—but in some part deep inside him was a belief that when you asked people to give you their sweat, their toil, all of you were bound together in a transcendental way, and you owed atonement if you broke that bond. It was an eccentric idea in a Southern landowner, but he was an eccentric. He needed the new machines, and having them meant he had to let go the workers he hadn't prepared for any other work, or encouraged to be prepared for any other work, and he was responsible for it—he felt it, without knowing that he felt it. But he didn't know what to do, so he did nothing; and then he died.

Sam took over. Occasional expiation was allowed *him*. Sometimes he helped their sons and daughters go to college. Not many people knew about his charity, and they wouldn't have believed it if they'd been told, and would've disapproved of it if they did believe. The farm workers had been phased out by machines; they approved of the machines. They didn't approve of the families who remained in the beat-up old houses. The beat-up houses were eyesores, and made the whole area look bad, contrasting poorly with the shiny, brutal combines and pickers Sam and, then, Ransome bought.

Getting older and heavier, smoking too much, Sam watched his land become cleaner, the furrowed lines straighter, more regimentally correct, and he *also* felt it—keenly felt more and more as if something were stretching and tearing, ripping away. Ransome knew that Sam, if he'd lived long enough, would've loved GPS farming, would've also felt the emptiness stretching out not just in front of him but in the universe of that anonymous signal. But one day the shredding became a real thing, and he died of a massive coronary out by the shop he'd had built to house a new piece of equipment.

Ransome and his brother inherited that farm, and a couple of other ones in other parts of the state, and followed Sam's example of improvements, always shrinking the number of people they had on the land, always seeking penance for an inexorable process they wanted to control and never would.

SAM ACCEPTED HIS part of the burden of guilt. He saw the change in Mooresville with all that new field equipment he bought, automated stackers, the things that made his farm better. He was willing to take some of the blame, figured he had it coming. Like Ben, he didn't know how to fix it, didn't know if it *could* be fixed. He died that day by the door of that new building, glaring sightlessly out at the fields.

Wilburn opened up the Fresh Grab Go store in town and stocked it with things Ransome sent from the farm: local oats; peanuts; sunflower seeds from the enormous patch Ransome planted out next to the highway, as much to make folks notice his farm as anything. But people were going crazy over sunflower seeds by then, the health-food movement, hippies grown into middle age trying to stave off heart disease. They were running a health food store before it was in style, Wilburn would chuckle in later years: Everybody went to Fresh Grab Go to buy ingredients for their trail mixes and homemade breads. It turned into a thing, and folks showed up from a hundred miles away, like it was another damned Rock City, he told Ransome.

They were young men raised in the South, raised not to show weakness or tender emotion. They knew Sam had believed he ought to do *something*, he just didn't know what. But Ransome did. In the back of his mind he felt sorry for the men and women whose parents had toiled for Sam so long. There was an opening on the board of supervisors, and Ransome ran, a job he'd win because everybody in the county knew him. Not necessarily liked him; but, then, he'd always considered diplomacy a waste of time with many people. He could just as easily get his way as a bully.

Mooresville's local TV station, WREM, offered to broadcast the supervisors' weekly meetings, something most areas had begun doing, transparency, and all that, they urged. Ransome thought it a silly thing, until a moment of epiphany came to him—about water, dirty water, he'd tell himself, laughing quietly years later as he thought of it: He'd found clarity in dirty water. Dirty water, the thing that let him see the light.

His family was familiar with his inner dialogues; they paid no attention when he chuckled aloud without explanation.

Even Sam had known the water utility in the county wasn't much to brag on, but Sam was a tinkerer and installed filters to purify what flowed through the pipes at his house. Ransome saw Colbie Jones and his cousin—kids he hired to do odd jobs— drinking from the hose after a long day prepping his cotton field, but in his mind he saw that filter system. He ran some of the hose water into his own bottle he'd been sipping from, thought about his kitchen faucet, felt some of Sam's self-loathing.

Next meeting, he passed out glasses of muddy water—no explanation, just a visual aid. He'd planned it out, to illustrate the need for a utility upgrade out in his district. East and north of town the community college and wealthy subdivision had newer systems; his mostly agricultural area didn't, he pointed out. The other supervisors stared down at their cups. "What you got there," he said, "is what comes out of everybody's taps out my way—" And he dared them to drink it. But the cups remained on the long table, untouched, and the reporter assigned to that meeting scribbled on his little notepad.

David Burkes called his bluff. "How do we know you didn't scoop this out of a ditch on your way here tonight?"

"You don't," Ransome told him.

In reality, earlier that afternoon he *had* scooped the water from a creek that trickled through the south edge of the farm; it wasn't too dirty, actually, but it *was* creek water.

"But we can go out and run the taps at some of my constituents' houses, see for yourself, we can do that, bring a camera along—" There he halted, thinking, ***Dammit, should've taken that offer the TV folks made last month. Well, next time…***

Things changed for the supervisors from that moment on.

David Burkes knew how that image of him standing outside

those houses in Ransome's district would play. "You're just grandstanding," he scoffed. "We aren't going to caravan out anywhere," he added to the reporter.

Ransome motioned they fund a real study of water quality, not just the routine thing they ran for *E. coli*; and the other supervisors were impressed by this skillful manipulation of a damned tough trial lawyer, and seconded and passed the motion. Ransome's constituents got better water.

David Burkes considered that night the point at which things started downhill. From then on, Ransome would enter the meeting room, slap David on the back before the broadcast started and ask him how things were going, ask if he'd sued anybody important lately. Ransome liked seeing David's face get red and his cheek muscles twitch.

"When you gonna quit asking me that every week, you sorry bastard," David Burkes would mutter, with a tight smile, noting where the TV camera was stationed, keeping an eye on the print reporter who liked to hang around altogether too much, he thought, before actual business was even going on; he needed to tighten the reins on *that* one. Now, somehow or other, the media was there for every meeting. David liked it just fine the old way, where he could stall things he considered ill-advised—things Ransome initiated more times than not—with just a hooded glance at one or two of the other supervisors, and few of the residents ever saw his subtle maneuvers unless they'd gone to the meetings.

But with the TV there, it was all different. Ransome would check the time, slap David on the back once more, and work his way around the room to take his seat at the other side of the long conference table. Ransome would grin at him before the cameras turned on, and then he'd get serious. David thought it likely that Ransome was passing judgment on David's whole life. And why'd he think he was more righteous than the rest of them? But every week it was the same, Ransome commenting about responsibility for all the community, not just some, looking straight at David when he said it; Ransome needling him about pouring more resources into county services instead of a study of traffic flow in the upscale neighborhood of Mooresville, where, coincidentally, David and several of his cohorts lived.

Ransome proposed a bond issue, the revenues to be spent on improvements at the public high school. He threw that word "underprivileged" around whenever he got an opening. The vote was called, the bond issue passed, and even David Burkes said, "Aye," through tight lips.

Ransome enjoyed the hell out of it. He sat back in his upholstered claw-footed chair at those meetings and smiled cheerfully, made them grit their teeth and smile back: The cameras were on now. Cameras were a good investment, he decided. He basked.

When they became teenagers, his children were embarrassed and turned the TV off when the supervisors' meetings were broadcast.

ONE DAY HE learned about karma. It was a dark moment in his own life that he never told anyone about, not even Regina, especially not Regina, as he still yearned for her to believe in some good in him. It returned to him frequently through the rest of his life, a mental screenshot reappearing, unbidden, from nothing, the bright glare of it forcing him to close his eyes, as if a spasm had suddenly afflicted him. He'd always remember how it occurred, because the memory brought exquisite pain like a tooth extraction gone very wrong, like waking up in the middle of your own surgery, and he knew about *that*, because it had happened to him once.

It was about Emily and the boy—he saw him all the time, why *wouldn't* he just ask him! But he never did…fear, maybe, of finding something dark and alive in himself, slowly and certainly devouring a vital part. A cancer he'd never thought *he'd* have.

When he was elected supervisor, he'd started arranging a meal every week with the small businessmen he knew; no lawyers like Burkes or Reg Griffin, no bankers like Mark Mason, but the people that ran the shops up and down the street and highway. They'd eat salads and rant about the economy, and he, a supervisor with more power than a state senator, listened, and he picked up the tab, because that was the right thing to do. And he'd bring those complaints to the supervisors' meeting, now televised so that all who wanted to know what went on, could. And one night after he'd listed several complaints, and Burkes had gritted his teeth as he listened, Ransome exited the supervisors' meeting in the dark and heard Burkes talking with a few people from his neighborhood.

"They tell me you shutting everything down." David smiled

maliciously at him.

"Time to stop," he said, not wanting to explain to that asshole.

David went on: "Letting everybody go? Rumor is you're gonna keep one of 'em on as a son-in-law. That right?"

His mind wrestled a moment, sorting that out, trying to think up a smart answer. David's group was utterly quiet, eyeing him, waiting to see who won this time.

"You angling for an invite to the wedding?" It was all he managed.

David scoffed. "Me? Not hardly."

He knew it was true: he'd paid no attention to the joking friendliness between the two of them, taken it for granted as an extension of his own feeling for the boy.

The better part of him said: so what? Nice kid; she could do worse.

But it was too much, too much of a change. The dark empty fields alongside the highway closed in on him, and he drove home.

Then for a while, whenever his mind went there, which was often, he was given to jerky, sudden gestures that his family ignored, as they ignored those unexplained chuckles. The gestures came from nothing and looked like a man swatting insects away, or boxing himself...which was about right.

He'd grunt aloud. *Ask Emily. Or ask Colbie.*

He shook his head. Regina found it odd. She didn't understand he was hearing a voice that bellowed: *Stop. Stop complicating it. Ask.*

He and Wilburn had desultorily talked for a decade about how tough farming was, how old they were getting. They'd gone over last year's tax statement, the balance sheets the accountants gave them. Wilburn started dropping by the big farm some afternoons, watching the sun set as they grew somber and quiet.

One day, Wilburn had said it: "Time, Ranse."

So early that year, they'd done it. Quietly. He hadn't realized anybody'd found out yet.

They owned thousands of acres in other places. They were silent partners in other businesses in other states—most people in Mooresville had no idea. They didn't need to farm for a living anymore.

Irreligious, Ransome still knew what a confessional was for. And he knew that somehow and someday he'd be held to account.

He closed his eyes and grimaced. He'd keep the two workers on for the summer, send them off to college in the fall, college out of state, maybe LSU. *She'd* go to one in Tennessee, she'd said she might like to; and during the remaining summer months as he closed everything down, did the paperwork, he'd see to it Colbie stayed busy. If they still managed to find a way to pass time together, he'd take that as a sign it was meant to be, he wouldn't interfere anymore.

He swatted at the invisible thing. Regina took notice and shrugged and didn't ask.

Emily might never forgive him, and later on he could despise himself for that; and he figured he probably would. Maybe he was no better than David Burkes.

Ransome had known for years Frank never wanted to farm, never intended to yield to family destiny. Frank was happy. He laughed: "Do you know what Tourette's Syndrome is, Dad?"

HE SUMMONED A youngster named Joe Sims to his farm, one of the junior reporters, because he wanted it done his way, wanted to be the one who said it publicly first, and he had the power to demand the stage.

"Don't need the money," he told him, "it's risky now, if you don't have to. I've farmed long enough, don't have time to be with my family and be a supervisor too. We'll all just have to focus on attracting businesses and bring more opportunities to the area, for everybody, not just one group of people, and not just me, and I'll help with that."

It was a shock. People had observed the fields weren't being prepped this year, but no one really wanted to know why. They said he had to be losing money. They wondered if his business savvy had finally left him. They said he probably had cancer.

A local TV reporter spoke her melancholy epitaph closing the piece she broadcast: "An era ended, along with the last four jobs of the generations-long Moore Farms." She emphasized dolefully the number "four," as if it were forty instead.

The newspaper guy found one of the kids he'd had working part-time on the farm, a local youth, Colbie Jones, and asked for his reaction. Colbie'd worked for Moore Farms every summer since he was fourteen, repairing stuff, driving a combine when it was required, and he personally thought Ransome *wanted* to keep people poor and ignorant; that way he could always say he was better than them. Men like him did that. Joe the reporter wrote it all down. He wasn't sure about printing it; but his boss was.

David Burkes laughed out loud when he read it, a gut laugh bursting out of him, prompting Reg to walk to his door and say, "What's funny?" It delighted David to see Ransome accused of a thing he wasn't guilty of, might never be guilty of. It was for him delicious payback. He quietly slipped that new kid Joe a raise.

Seeing those words in print, Ransome had been very angry, then swatted at the air and figured he deserved it, and maybe more, and he remembered to be grateful Colbie hadn't brought Emily's name into it.

Though of course people knew. He thought of David's malevolent questions, and he grunted.

THE EVENING AFTER the churches burned, later that year, eating supper with Connie and the girls, Hal asked if they knew any boys who'd do such a thing. Rheta flicked her long black hair over her shoulder and pointed out that it was Colbie's mama's church, one of them was, anyway, and somebody just didn't like him shooting his mouth off back in the spring and, then, all summer. Oh, and Emily'd gone out with Colbie most of last year, or hung out with him at school, anyway; they were sort of a couple. Rheta thought Ransome Moore might've got somebody to burn those churches. A warning not to date his daughter unless you're white. Maybe Frank helped.

Hal told her not to slander Ransome. "He's done a lot of things, but he wouldn't do that."

She shrugged. "Who knows. Would he?"

RANSOME HAD HEARD people blaming Colbie—"stirring up trouble, like back in the sixties," was how they put it.

Ransome and Wilburn understood, by *feeling* it, why people were stirred up: It was desperation born of facing years of not knowing where you'd make your living. Somebody had to be blamed. Somebody was at fault. Otherwise, the world was a random place of undeserved cruelties. They wanted it to be the others' fault. It had been many years, Wilburn said, since he'd seen people line up like that against each other.

Ransome handed the Amtrak tickets to Colbie's mother and

spoke gruffly: "They know you're on the way, they're holding that job for you." He tried to shake the kid's hand. "I know people that can get you a job, too, part-time, when you're not in classes." Colbie, agitated, pulled away—"Man! Leave me alone! You don't have nothing to do with me now!" His mother told him to hush up. He pulled away, swearing at both of them.

Ransome stayed more at the farm for a few weeks, a hangdog look on his face; but Emily avoided him, regarded him with veiled, resentful eyes when she couldn't find excuses not to be in a room with him. And then she'd glance away first, and the cold truth would freeze his gaze on whatever object he'd turned to: *You sent him away, you. For his own safety; that's what you said.* It was well and truly digging a knife into your own back, and twisting it.

The TV reporter *could* have claimed forty or even fifty jobs and got away with it, for the grain company in town closed by the next year, and then the farm chemical reps quit visiting Mooresville and frequenting the two motels and the hamburger joints and Dominic's restaurant, and eventually even the trucking firms cut back on schedules. So far as Ransome knew, Colbie and Emily never saw each other again, and so it showed they really hadn't cared so much, and he'd been justified, didn't it?

Living in the big house at the end of the string of night lights, he performed his own solitary expiation....

WHEN HE WENT into town, he was quieter. The talk about cancer came back up. One day, he overheard another thing: "You think he got rid of him?"

Overhearing was, after all, how he'd learned people knew about Emily and Colbie.

All his life he'd known that when you overlook a rusty spot long enough, it turns into a hole, and things fall apart. He was surprised people thought he'd be fool enough to do something so crude and unproductive. And everybody knew he was a loudmouth—he owned that. Never in his life had he done things underhandedly, in the middle of the night. Never had he been mad enough to want to kill somebody. But, they were wondering, where was Colbie, and his mother?

Despite the money and power he had, and Sam had had— despite being elected over and over, and people up and down the streets greeting him heartily, he'd always been a loudmouth farmer dabbling in politics. No matter the decades his family had been here, no matter how many acres he owned, no matter that his name was the town's name.

He could laugh off most of that.

But he couldn't laugh off being thought a murderer. He told everybody, told that newspaper kid, Joe, told the anchor of WREM-TV, held court at Liberto's with his pals and told them. They all said if he knew where Colbie was, where *was* that? and he answered, just, "Well, all I'll say is, he's not in a bayou..."

Frank pointed out he was denying it too much. He listened to that. Frank said he should get some people to go with him and rebuild those churches, show by doing instead of talking. It would help the church members, Frank said, and it would be good for his image, and it would bring the county and town together for a day or two. Ransome gazed at Frank, trying to see, until Frank, grasping for a translation, told him, "You'd be the healer. Besides, every guy around here's a suspect, if he's over sixteen, and that includes me."

Ransome wouldn't tell them that Colbie was safe and sound in Baton Rouge—a fact that would've taken heat off him; but he didn't want Emly knowing where the kid was. If they really cared so much, Ransome reasoned, they'd find each other on their own. He grunted and swatted the air.

He got in touch with the TV people and ordered them to interview him. You never knew exactly what kind of thing Ransome might say or do. He'd called one of the other supervisors a sonofabitch during an official meeting—not as a joke, either, and the TV crew'd had to bleep it out for the late news—and there was that dirty water stunt. So they'd give him some air time.

David Burkes and his partner discussed Ransome's call for unity and decided it would be in their interests, as the more prominent of the town's two legal firms, to sign on. They'd both send checks to the churches, too, and they'd even make an appearance out there in the sticks. Rebuilding seemed like a stunt to them, but a stunt they could profit from, and there were obvious benefits in this one: It was a good photo op, and elections were coming up in another year. It would be useful, then.

They arrived at the first church—left a heap of blackened rubble for two months—and worked their way through the small crowd, shaking hands, patting backs. It was August, and hotter than hell. They shucked their suit jackets, spreading them carefully over the back seat of their cars. Ransome watched with a laconic smile when they loosened ties a little and awkwardly took places next to him for a photograph with the minister of the church and several congregants.

"So how do we help?" Griffin leaned in to whisper.

"Get out of the way," Ransome said, motioning to the driver of the idling small bulldozer he'd brought over on a flatbed—one of Colbie's cousins he'd hired just for this job today, a cousin whom last summer he'd regularly employed on the farm...until he didn't. Ransome wore a short-sleeved tan cotton shirt, no tie, and a broad-brimmed, light-colored farmer's straw hat—owning it, after all those years. Burkes and Griffin, loitering awkwardly in the dust thrown up by the bulldozer, knew no matter how many pictures with Ransome they were in, there'd be no doubt who was really behind the cleanup. They knew at election time he'd be voted back in by a wide margin. And he was. But it was his last election. He didn't run again, and they were gleeful.

19

WITH ONE FINAL cold spell, winter gave up; and though the calendar said it was spring, when the month changed into April, early summer had arrived. Louise moved permanently into the house on Stone Avenue. Cary asked if she wanted a party, and Louise sniffed. "We aren't social butterflies, no, thank you."

Sara then saw more of Cary's friends, and since Louise did visit on the evenings Sara taught her night classes, so Cary wouldn't be alone, the house seemed about as occupied as it ever had, until Cary had to spend the first weekend of April with Matthew.

Jennifer came by the house to get Cary and stood uneasily in the living room while they waited for her to bring out her backpack. "I like this room," Jennifer offered, a thing she'd said before, as if, Sara thought, it had been shuffled around from the back of the house somehow and was new or different.

"Well, anytime you want to come and sit in it, you're welcome."

Cary appeared with her stuff and gave her a **Really, Mom?** look. She hadn't griped much about the weekend visit this time, had been almost comically stoic. Matthew had no particular plans for them, she'd told Sara, and so she intended to ask him and Jennifer to leave her alone by saying she had homework. "Which I do, by the way," she added.

"But not much," Sara guessed.

"He won't know, and he won't ask, anyway, he never does. And I'll get them to let me meet Allie and Carson at the park or somewhere, so it'll be fine."

When they left, she started grading papers and, in a while, hauled out the ingredients for homemade pizza. Louise had invited her to drop by the house on Stone, as if out of pity, as if she didn't think Sara would function on her own. She could do that—go there and have a chat with Harvey and Louise, go out with them somewhere. And maybe she would, soon. But not tonight, not this weekend. She told herself sturdily she wouldn't be at a loss for things to do. This weekend she was getting used to the new normal; and she mixed the dough.

It was nine-o'clock when she finally ate, and that was too late for pizza. She should've had a salad.

Going to bed, she gave the blue sphere a sideways glance, as she always did at night, still wondering what to do with it, and at the clipped stack of papers Neil had left on her kitchen table. She'd read them finally, though not for a day or two, but, at last, several times, so she knew by memory the information they contained. Neil had once or twice texted her since that day. She hadn't responded to those messages; but the last one he'd sent was a little too condescending for her to ignore: **Well, sweetie, when you're over your hissy fit, let me know what you think.**

I already knew this stuff, she'd answered. *It's a yawner.*

She expected, and got, an immediate call back. She watched her phone light up as it buzzed, and as she pressed "Ignore," she sniffed scornfully. He was too predictable.

Tonight she turned on her side and dimmed the lamp, looking into the darkened hallway for a moment. Tomorrow she'd vacuum the carpet in Louise's room and think about *that* space....

NOTHING NEIL HAD given her mentioned Matheson's community involvement efforts. There was a statement about MTE's financial health—good, no surprise, though with more outlays than historical trends had shown. But, again, no surprise: Matheson himself had said he was spending in ways his father didn't approve.

There was a page detailing what the company had paid Ransome Moore for his land. She'd laughed aloud: Ransome might want people to think everything he did was for Mooresville's benefit, but he'd raked in a fair haul. Good for him, she thought.

Halfway through she'd found what she knew Neil must've wanted to her to find: a list of Matheson's transgressions, as he wanted her to see them. The two marriages, both of which ended in acrimonious divorces—well, so what? she thought. Mine wasn't Suzy Homemaker, either, at the last; and neither was Neil's. And somehow, from somebody, she'd already known about them. The second marriage ended amid demands for settlements and a house, and accusations of emotional cruelty. Then there were pages detailing other relationships—complete with photographs—one ending right before the company had opened its facility in Mooresville; and that liaison had made the papers in Michigan, she read, when it ended, because of the socially prominent woman he'd been with.

She smirked at the thought of Neil's spending so much effort on that part of his report: Neil himself wasn't a saint, and she wasn't, either; and yet he thought that would shock her...and the photos of Matheson with attractive women at social events... She laughed out loud again.

He'd done a stint in rehab for medication addiction—that, after the second divorce. About that, he'd been "transparent"—she snickered at the word, imagining him saying it. It was in an interview: "It always comes out, anyway. Just tell it up front."

Other papers documented his takeover of the company, but she dismissed all that. His father must be elderly by now; and what one person would call a "takeover," another might call the passing of the reins. Or maybe the wrenching away of the reins: That's the way Matheson had framed it.

She'd reclipped the papers all together and left them on her bedside table, weighted down by the sphere, thinking wryly that was perhaps symbolic: Did the art compensate for the sins, cover them, expiate them? In the past weeks she hadn't decided, and, alone in the house tonight, she wasn't going to gift herself a bad dream thinking about them again.

Tomorrow she'd start on that room. She made her thoughts turn that way. Cary said it would be nice to have a place to work on her computer, read, have her friends over without putting them into the living room every time. So she'd go to town and find a small sofa, put in a lamp or two, move a table…. She made plans, deliberately keeping her mind on them…and she must've slept some, for daylight awoke her in the morning.

FOOT TRAFFIC HAD picked up at the building next door to Liberto's, and Don didn't like it. He'd told Stephen Logan to keep his campaign literature on his side of the narrow alley—he called it "litter," not "literature," and Stephen tried to correct him, condescendingly, before realizing it was a deliberate mistake. Then some of the customers were unhappy with him, because they supported Logan. He had plenty of business, and one thing Dom had taught him was you had to stand on principle sometimes. But then Logan's volunteers started hanging around out front, passing campaign cards to passers-by, and he didn't like that next to where the spring lunch crowd usually sat and ate. He searched city ordinances for a rule that would prohibit politicking in certain locations, but there wasn't any such law, except on election days when you couldn't do it close to a polling place.

"You could build a wall." Lisa shrugged, hiding her face, so that when he stared in outrage, she thumped his earlobe. "C'mon, I'm joking. Go next door and ask him to hold off during lunch or something."

"He'd say that's when he needs to do it, when people are around. And he'd be right!"

"I'll just do it myself. He won't be rude to me."

"No, you won't!"

No, Logan wouldn't disrespect Lisa, not to her face, but it would delight him to realize he was annoying Don. He considered the irony in the truth that, when they were all young, they'd handle this kind of thing with words, get in each other's faces; and now that they were old, it wasn't acceptable to do that, unless you were Ransome Moore and had got by with it all his life.

Lynne Houston announced she was running against Logan. It

had taken him by surprise. In a brief interview Logan had smiled his wide, bleached smile and claimed to be thrilled at having an actual contest, one that would display important differences between candidates. Lisa took that personally, as a woman, and doubled down on her threat to have words with him.

Don strolled down Main to Lynne's store a day or two later and picked up a few signs. If Logan could plaster his own stuff right up to the restaurant wall, *he* could put some signs up, too. God knows, he wasn't ashamed of politicking for Lynne. But he wondered who'd talked her into it. He asked Lisa, he asked Chris, he even asked Alison. They got tired of hearing the question.

SUNDAY TURNED RAINY. A couple of the church-goers complained about not being able to eat outside, as if *he* could adjust the weather. His regular guy was sick, too, so today he had to forgo the quiet Sunday at home he scheduled every week. He moved a couple of his inside tables to the sidewalk, close to the store front and under the broad awning, for it was typical muggy spring rain, and nobody'd be cold. But the drizzle dampened moods as well as feet, and those people apologized for the trouble they'd caused and straggled back in. He grumbled as he helped the busboys move the tables back—not because of the work, but because one of his "Lynne Houston for City Council" signs lay on the sidewalk again. Somehow, mysteriously, they kept being knocked over. He knew the only way to catch whoever did it would be to station somebody to watch, and he couldn't spare an employee just to stand around. Every time he had to reset the sign, he imagined Logan peering out a window and snickering. —Which he'd do himself, if he'd been the one trashing Logan's signs.

So the tables inside, the placard back up, he dried his shoulders and hair with a towel and inspected the clientele today.

It had been a while since he'd had to cover on a Sunday. Maybe things had changed, but he thought he heard an undertone today different from the usual Sunday-afternoon atmosphere. And he didn't have any close acquaintances in this bunch to ask.

He shook his head at the sound of the low-pitched conversations. Pop had been the best at reading the customers' moods. He could bring somebody just what they were about to order. —Or so they'd swear, he remembered, chuckling a little; maybe it had all been only an act they played out, Pop and the diners.

Alison was there most Sundays, waiting tables for extra cash. He detained her when she came back for pitchers of tea for refills. "Listen—find out what's going on. Nobody looks happy."

"Sure, Don, but, like, it's raining," she pointed out. "Everybody wanted to be outside, and they can't, and that's why they're pissed."

"Seems like it's something else…something wrong with the bread, or the sauce…"

She rolled her eyes at him. "You just forgot what they're like on Sundays." And that was true, maybe; each day's crowd was unique. Mondays had a different feel from, say, Thursdays. She could see she'd made him feel dumb, and she relented: "I'll ask, but, really, Don, chill. It's nothing."

He stepped into the alcove where he liked to discreetly observe his clients' reactions to a change in recipe, a new spice in a breading. Alison made the rounds of her tables and spoke to people. She paused to ask an elderly couple from the county— Ransome's old neighborhood, he thought, out there at the edge of the pines—if they needed anything. She listened to the woman's words, as the old man nodded. The old woman reached into her lap and passed her something. Alison brought it to Don, tossing it into his hand as she nudged past him, on the way to retrieve a pitcher.

"Here. I asked if they knew any good news, and she says you can have her paper and read it for yourself." And she returned to refill glasses, smiling and chatting them up. Don edged into the kitchen where he unfolded the sheets of newsprint.

"MTE's Matheson Calls for Investigation of Candidate's Past."

And, beneath the fold: "Local Businesswoman Cites MTE Support in Campaign."

20

SARA *SURVIVED* THE first weekend alone in her house— *survived*: She ridiculed herself with that word, but it was what she'd done. She'd been alone. It had taken almost fifty years of her life. By Sunday afternoon she wondered how many other women had gone from college to marriage to children without knowing if they could *survive*, alone.

On Monday Lynne Houston called to ask for an endorsement and campaign help.

"More volunteer work?" Louise would've scoffed; but the truth was, the plan for a book wouldn't come, and the classes were wrapping up for the semester. She'd intended to travel a little bit in the summer, but that was before Louise had moved out and Cary acquired new friends who kept her busy.

She hesitated. Lynne was quick to read that as reluctance. "I guess you get bothered a lot with stuff like that, so just say if you can't!"

Sara broke in with an ad-libbed line about only being afraid Lynne would never ask.

She was sure Neil wouldn't approve of her getting political. She could hear him now: *You'll lose readers if you do this for one candidate.* And she'd tell him: *Don's managing!*

"Some people told me you'd be able to help with the statements I'll have to put out, you teaching at the college, you know. But, one thing..." Her tone changed, and Sara envisioned her leaning towards her, the way she had long ago when Sara wandered through the shop and picked up something shiny and unusual and asked about it. "Nobody's gonna tell me to chill out. Not that I don't know I'll have to do that, but if it comes to it, sometime, I'm gonna say what I gotta say. I guess you know that about me."

"Be you. I won't be writing your speeches, don't worry."

Lynne didn't answer; Sara noted that.

Mooresville always held city council elections around the first of June. The seven different positions were term-staggered so no more than two elections at a time came up in any given year. It made for a feeling of never-ending politics, but some people thought that wasn't a bad thing, as it reminded people of their civic duties. When she was shopping downtown, it had always annoyed Sara to be accosted by earnest people offering buttons and cards outside the businesses. This year she took more of an interest.

The Parks Authority granted permission for the two candidates to hold a meet-and-greet the second weekend in April at the big old pavilion near where she used to sketch. —"Used to," she mused unhappily. She hadn't done that in months, not since Ron Matheson had sent his little gift to her. She'd gaze at the sphere, contemplating how everything had blown apart since that day. She'd thought about packing it up, sending it to him by FedEx, maybe, but hadn't. It sat on top of those damned papers, held them down. Every night she thumped it irritably before turning off the light, wishing there was actual science behind voodoo.

All the nights she'd pondered the documents and tapped the ball made her think of the man, the box, the cool breeze, the note— She'd grimace about that, and remember confronting him at the restaurant; and how childish now she felt, reacting the way she had. She tried to stop those memories by thinking of other times she'd sketched in the park. Those were better recollections.

So it was her notion to have the event there.

She presented the idea to Philip, director of the Authority. He gazed unhappily at her, wanting to please the local celebrity, she thought wryly, but perhaps also mulling over things Lynne had said for months now, and maybe a little anxious about whether Logan's supporters would show up. He arranged a meeting with her and Lynne and Logan and made the offer, ordered them to limit themselves to ten minutes, after which, he warned, "Speech-makin'll be over, and everybody'll have to go somewhere else." Philip tried to look stern in his tiny office. Lynne nodded solemnly; Logan maintained his flashy smile.

"After that, you want to politic any more, you can; but you'll be minglin' in the crowd, not up in the old gazebo like it's a stage," Philip added.

And as they left the meeting, Lynne did ask Sara's help with her speech. "Lord knows, I know how to gab," she said, "and Joe puts everything I send him in the paper; but you may need to tone me down in front of that crowd. Otherwise, I'll go off like I do online."

"That might not be a bad thing, going off."

Lynne glared her down. "Really. You think we're all just gonna be fine with each other? Then why's there a redneck white guy ahead of me, or so they tell me, and Ransome Moore's bugging me about it? I don't think he believes we'll be fine with each other. Or maybe he's still the same old Ransome and just likes a fight?" She scoffed and laughed. "Lord, I miss him."

"He asked you to do this?"

She looked at Sara, and there were years of knowing, maybe centuries, on her face, and Sara realized in a moment Lynne wasn't the shop owner anymore who'd put up with kids roaming around shelves and rummaging through bins. She was almost of Connie's generation. And Sara didn't really know her; what Matheson had said to her that day popped up in her head, another unpleasant memory to suppress. *We don't think about it because we're not affected.*

"No, that was Ron Matheson," Lynne said.

"Good of him to put you out there while he hides in his office."

But Lynne gave her a certain look. "He's taking a lot of flak."

"Anyway, don't bring up the stuff in Stephen's past. Make him attack *you*, if he dares, and leave the rest to the media." Then she felt remorse, thinking of Rheta, and how some of her stories had brought vilification and threats to her personally. Well, it was her job, and she didn't seem to shrink from it. She must have grown thick skin over the years, thick enough so it didn't bother her.

"That's about what Ransome and Ron told me."

Sara with effort kept her face immobile, emotionless. She might've known he'd be throwing his influence around.

"They both said don't bring up his past. I didn't agree with that. I *don't* agree with that. We had an argument about it."

"I bet you did."

"Yeah, Ransome's the same as ever. Then Ron got another man that works there, Ken Thomas, to weigh in. Guess they figured him being Black, too, he'd remind me to be calm." She rolled her eyes. "I told him I'd only go so far. And I think people need to be told what Stephen Logan's been and done. It does matter. All my ideas and plans don't count for anything if you don't bring that up. I think it's a big mistake."

"They want you to be yourself, but tell what you know about business, community improvement—your ideas, let those be your message."

"Oh, I know what you mean, you don't have to say it. I know what *they* meant, too." Lynne gave her an expressive glance before continuing: "Hold your temper. Shut up."

"You feel like they're pushing you around?"

Lynne threw her hands into the air. "Am I a woman? Are they men?"

Sara remembered Neil in her kitchen.

"But I'd like to find out who got that man cleaned up and slicked down. I'd give that person a corner in my shop and take a cut and make a load of money."

They'd pulled together the remarks Lynne was delivering now. In an effusive, Southern-gentleman way, Philip had scheduled her to speak at the beginning of the program—"Ladies first!"—but she'd startled him, and Sara, "No!" and a big smile turned on Logan: "I'll go second," and, later, just to Sara, "Uh-uh, no, I am not going to let him have the last word! Honey, in high school we read *Julius Caesar*."

SOMEHOW, TODAY, THE role of campaign manager had been pinned on her like a badge, Sara realized. It was flattering, but she didn't like being out there, prominently, up in the old pavilion standing behind Lynne, feeling exposed.

And, suddenly, she remembered again Matheson's words: "...You give time to things, even things that seem to make you uncomfortable." Well, he'd probably have a different take on that today. She took a small step backwards and made herself look over the crowd.

People with families, people holding hands, teenagers, middle-aged folks, a fair representation of the whole county and town, because that was the first time a Black woman had run for city council, and everybody was curious. Many were assembling slowly in the area of the old pavilion. Sidewalks cleaned and edged now, additional benches added here and there; signage updated with a historical look about them...and in the center of the pedestal where Nate had stood, a sturdy concrete planter full of impatiens and periwinkle. So Nate was gone. She observed people commenting on the flowers; others shaking their heads. All of a sudden, why, she didn't know, she wished the speeches were happening somewhere else.

When it was time, earlier, Logan had stepped forward acknowledged her and Lynne: "Good morning, citizens, voters, and my opponent Lynne Houston, and everybody knows Sara Wells," with a broad smile at them, a gesture in their direction from a lectern Philip had got his crew to haul into the gazebo. Lynne nodded back, but Sara stared at him, unwilling to give even that. She thought she saw a second of understanding in his glance before he'd turned away to begin his presentation:

He was just a regular guy from the community; his background was plain. He'd been poor, he didn't have a fancy education. He'd seen all the economic downturns through the past two decades, he wanted better for Mooresville. But spending money on all these public works wasn't the right way to do it. Raising taxes on businesses in Mooresville wasn't right, either, and there were people who wanted to take that money and put it into programs specified only for particular groups; did they deserve that?... He came close, she realized, to that line, but never quite crossed it. He was loud, but not too loud, and watching him from the side, she was chilled at how skillfully he wove in phrases and ideas that seemed to resonate in this crowd.

There was a pattern—she started counting: Yes. Fourteen times, "guy." He wanted to make sure everybody remembered Lynne was a woman.

Right before he stopped—early, at eight or so minutes—he pointed to the empty pedestal. She sat straighter as he gestured at it: "Right here's an example of what's wrong: people getting offended by a piece of rock, and it's pulled down, cost money to do that, whose money? Yours. It's just history, that's all. That's *not* 'progress', 'progress' doesn't stomp on people's rights, and if you vote for me you'll see me putting a stop to those kinds of things as we move ahead to brighter times." Some in the crowd clapped. When he turned another brilliant smile on her and Lynne as he stepped away from the lectern, she stared defiantly at him. She turned to Lynne, shook her head ever so slightly.

Lynne frowned at her; but only she saw it.

Sara'd offered to introduce her. "I'd like to talk about my friend Lynne Houston," and she recited facts about Lynne, her family, her years in business, her community work. When she finished, Logan half-stood and laughingly remarked, "They didn't tell me I was supposed to get somebody to brag about me!" A rippling murmur and, on the other hand, some chuckles drifted in up from the crowd. She turned a cold smile at him and retorted, "And I guess they didn't tell you not to cut into your opponent's speaking time!" That drew a few more laughs as she sat down.

The words she'd given to Lynne told of her life in Mooresville, how she and her brother survived the lean years after Moore Farms shut down, how she'd done it with good business practices and budgetary responsibility. As the speech went on, in her mind Sara repeated the things she'd written for Lynne to close with: A minority member of the community, she'd benefited from acceptance and wanted to extend that to other people who deserved opportunities but needed help; there wasn't really much difference between the goals she and Logan professed.

She turned slightly toward Sara and almost eye-rolled halfway through that line. Of *course* there was difference between Lynne and Stephen Logan.

Sara froze. Why'd she written that?

Lynne ad-libbed: "But the differences matter. Think about them. Remember what you know."

She stepped away from the lectern and came out of the gazebo, still talking: about change, about the dreams of young people, about the future of the town. She laid her speech notes on one of the steps. She didn't need the microphone, she said, and didn't they all know that about her…. Chuckles. She mentioned MTE and how the company had brought in positive things, new citizens, and Sara noticed a few faces become less friendly at that. She appealed for a mandate to bring other good things to Mooresville. Polite applause, a few wolf whistles, and she walked out onto the grass below the pavilion to shake supporters' hands. Stephen Logan followed and did the same.

Sara noticed Don and Lisa in the crowd, greeting Lynne, introducing her to other people, and there was Cary with a few of her friends, all of them sporting "Lynne Houston for City Council" buttons on their T-shirts, on their jeans, on their baseball caps. You can't even vote, she wanted to say, but that would be discouraging, and she watched them work their way into the group surrounding Lynne. Logan's supporters circled him as well; and as she gathered up some campaign materials in the gazebo, Sara knew Lynne was going to need more help from somewhere else. She left the pavilion, headed to the Houston circle and turned at the sound of a certain strong voice behind her.

"You want to respond to Matheson's call for an investigation into your background?"

Rheta. She stood near Logan, her spiky black haircut marking her in that group of sedate bobs and plaid shirts. A murmur rose, almost like a hum, a low rumble in the throat of an old dog being made to move from a sunny spot on the rug.

"Didn't you listen? I told everybody a few minutes ago, I'm just a plain man." The smile stayed on his face. "As a younger one I did get into stuff, I've owned it."

"Yeah, others did, too, but about the more recent court appearance—"

"You do know those charges were dismissed? You do keep up with the news?"

Logan's group of supporters laughed.

"It wasn't dismissal, but a settlement where you paid off the manager's medical expenses and something else, maybe emotional damages? Who provided funds for that payoff?"

"You also know the judge found insufficient cause to continue the case."

"It was a settlement," she interrupted, "and with that, both of you got the case dropped. Now I'm just asking where the funds came from for the payoff—"

"It wasn't a 'payoff'," he said, the smile gone.

"Why'd your lawyer have the records sealed? Was it to keep people from finding out who paid?"

He smiled tightly. "The funds came from my account. I'd hate to have to pull that up right now and let you see, you'd probably dox me. But you want me to do it?" He brought his phone out of a pocket.

"Can you give a statement disowning the organization that calls itself 'MAP'? Did they furnish you funds to pay off the plaintiff who filed the charges against you?"

"It wasn't a 'payoff'," he insisted again, "and by the way, I get contributions from a lot of organizations, people concerned about the future of our town, the state, hell, the country—"

"Do you want to comment about Matheson asking for an investigation?"

"He has his agenda. You should ask about *that*."

"Who's paying your rent in the Griffin building?"

"That would be a contribution in kind."

"So is it included in your campaign statement? Is Neil Griffin giving you that contribution, is he a supporter? Are you up-to-date on your campaign statement? I won't have to bother you with these questions, if you are. I'll just look it up."

Sara drew near the group of people edging closer to Rheta. She'd never seen Rheta actually doing a public interview, and it came to her this must be a common response to tough questions, but it was scary. Rheta kept her eyes on Logan.

"You aren't giving me time to answer. You gonna ask her the

same things?" He nodded at Lynne, whose circle had quietened down as the impromptu interview continued.

"Her reports are filed," Rheta remarked. "She didn't have to pay anybody off. Nobody's called for an investigation about her past."

"Well, Matheson can say or do whatever he pleases, and I guess he pretty much does; he's been trying to run things ever since he moved here, and you and your media pals can kiss up to him as much as you want—you got to get *somebody* to read your paper, right?"

A hand holding a cell phone came up in the crowd, as Deborra Anderson also pushed forward, her cameraman behind her; the group parted to either side of them.

"Yeah, you want to put this on the evening news. Well, like I said, Matheson can spout off all he wants to, there's nothing much in my past that people don't already know about, and I have a lot of support—" he gestured around him— "so nobody must care about things from years ago, that a lot of other boys did. We got drunk. We raised hell. All in the past."

One of the men who had moved towards her earlier reached out toward Rheta's phone; she threw off his hand—"Hey, buster!" Anderson's cameraman had turned to film that, too. Logan seemed to consider something and waved the man back. "Don't. They all gotta earn their living somehow, they don't work like the rest of us," he scoffed.

"Where? Where do you work?" Sara burst in, and Rheta turned a ferocious, wide-eyed look on her. She thought, later, it wasn't fear for herself, but for Sara, and this kept her from sleeping that night. But that was later.

"I just see you walking around town all the time, nobody knows who even buys your food, because it seems like you never pay for anything," she went on. Rheta shook her head just a bit and frowned intensely.

"Well, Sara," Logan scoffed, "as I remember, the last time we were together in a restaurant, somebody paid for you, too; I think it was Mr. Griffin, my lawyer, wasn't it? Did you tell your candidate here about that? So maybe she should ask *you* about some things."

She saw no sympathy in Deborra Anderson's face as her camera guy continued to record, and Rheta turned and snapped another question: "You don't have any other comment?"

Logan waved dismissively at her and made his way through the crowd. "I'm sure you planned this ambush to make me look bad, but it may backfire on you. People know who they wanna vote for, and it won't be *her*—" he jerked a thumb scornfully at the other group. "It'll be for a man who stands up for the rights of regular people like them. It'll be Stephen Logan." Some "Yeahs!" erupted near him, and he walked away, followed by a few people. And the low grumble went on, and people glanced back at Deborra and Rheta and the camera guy.

LATER THAT NIGHT, lying on her side and staring toward the window of her bedroom, she felt sick. They'd been outmaneuvered, and it was their fault. She knew both speeches were filmed; but Logan's would be the one everybody remembered. And for all the wrong reasons—because of what had happened afterwards, because of Nate being gone, because of Logan's using some words over and over. Coverage was coverage, even if it was negative. And there'd probably been people in that crowd who didn't think Logan *had* sounded bad...just strong, righteously upset.

And she'd failed. She should've told Lynne to let him have it. She'd really believed these people whom she'd grown up with would in the end be reasonable. Not emotional. Look at facts. Admit the truth of the facts. Yet why would they? For both of them it was supposed to have been a day to bring out emotions. Support. Patriotism.

Where'd Matheson been? He should've come. He could've done something, intervened, when Rheta was asking her questions. But even as that angry thought came to her mind, she knew his input would've made everything worse, and he'd been wise to stay away. Maybe he was financing the campaign literature for Lynne. She hoped so, then wondered about that, knowing it would have to be disclosed as a contribution, and how would that look?

Even before they left the park, she'd pulled Lynne aside to explain Logan's sarcastic comments about the restaurant.

"It's all good, girl," Lynne told her. "I figured it was something he made up."

"Well, he didn't entirely make it up," Sara conceded. "I *was* at the restaurant, and I do pay Neil to look over my legal stuff. And, that day, he did buy me a latte. So there was some truth. But it isn't..." But what *was* it? She stopped.

"You know, Sara, if we win this, we win, and if we don't, we don't. Sooner or later, that man's gonna get taken down by something, you know."

"I'd like to have that attitude."

"You haven't put up with those people as long as I have. So we'll do what we have to do."

It was only later that she remembered the "we" and groaned.

Cary was all wound up as if she'd been to a concert, going on and on about how great Ms. Houston looked and sounded, how stupid anybody would be to vote for that other creep. She'd tapped on her phone, texting with Allie at supper; Sara, absorbed in her own thoughts, didn't fuss about that.

They cleaned up the kitchen. "Mom, I'm really proud of you. You're doing something important."

"Like nothing else I do? Really?"

"You know what I mean. I'm going to bed now." Not true, Sara was aware, because her phone had continued buzzing even as she left the kitchen.

The election would be around the first of June, about six weeks away.

21

BY NOW SHE recognized some of MTE's phone extensions, so when the call came on Monday morning, she pressed "Ignore" and sent it to voicemail: She didn't want to talk to Ken Thomas today. Or perhaps any day.

She'd dropped Cary at school, where Carson waited for her by the door, and came home to drink more coffee and measure the space where she'd thought about putting a small desk in Louise's old bedroom. She resolutely kept her phone in the pocket of her sweatpants and stood in the doorway of the room...it could be repainted, but she'd already cleaned the carpet and had that new couch moved in. Thinking about that problem, she absent-mindedly answered the phone when it buzzed, answered without looking at it.

"Ms. Wells, I was afraid we might miss you today."

Damn! How did Thomas have her cell number? But she knew that: She'd given it to him back in February, of course, when she'd called him after the preservation meeting, and he'd used it at least once since then. She hadn't had reason to communicate with any of them over there for several weeks.

"How are you?" she said pleasantly: It wasn't on him, she remembered, just on his boss.

"I left a voicemail earlier, and then I had to step—out to Kid Kare for a moment, and I happened to have my cell with me and decided to try again." It was almost smooth enough to be believable, but she'd heard the pause as he grasped for an excuse.

"I guess everything's all right, with the project."

"Yes, and we have a print run going."

"Already?"

"It seemed wise to get it moving along. School *will* be over before we know it. We want distribution happening the first week after that."

That was true. Her night courses met three more times, and the last of those would be for the final exam. Cary would have another week or two in school after that, and then, summer vacation.

"You said you'd like a few copies, and we have some here. I thought you might drop over?"

Why not just mail them? "I could," she said. "Or you could send them by Cary. She tells me she's going to be at the cookout this Friday."

A silence that wasn't quite silent lasted for a few seconds before Thomas spoke again. "I could do that. If that's your preference, I'll have a package made up. Or I could courier them. I just thought you'd enjoy the drive today. And honest: I wanted to see your expression when you look at them. I'll know if you're happy or not."

"I'm that easy to read?"

"Most people are. I don't mean that in a snide way—I just, well, it occurred to me we could enjoy looking at them together...."

Yeah, *sure*... Another, longer pause filled an awkward moment, and she sighed. "All right, Mr. Thomas, I'll come over and pick up my copies. See you in fifteen."

She resented changing out of the comfortable sloppy clothes; she hadn't had to do that in a while now. She yanked a brush through her hair…needs trimming, she remembered, and by the way, why hasn't there been a preservation meeting since the end of February—since Ken Thomas had got her number…. She threw on a respectably boring blouse and pair of jeans as the question simmered in her mind, something that had occurred to her, she realized, when he'd called a few minutes ago. The group met every month; why not in March? And she hadn't heard about a meeting this month, either. She'd call Nora or Lindsay on the way over. They'd probably gone out of town during spring break in March and hadn't convened.

Though why would they have, she wondered, driving through the acres of pine trees: They didn't have children in school…. She was puzzled, and, rather than fret about the meeting fast approaching as the trees thinned out, she dialed Lindsay's number.

Lindsay answered too cheerfully: "Oh, we just did an executive session last month. There wasn't anything new going on, so we just had a dinner, us officers, and called it done."

Sara drove through the entrance gates at MTE.

"I mean…if you'd like me to email you the minutes, I'll do it. But there weren't many minutes. We just had dinner and talked a little." She was on the defensive now, Sara could tell, and something wasn't just right about it, but she was parking and put that into another file of her mind. She'd work through it later on in the afternoon, after she got home.

"Sure, that'd be good," she said. "I'm going to a meeting myself, so just send them. Did the couple redoing that house on Windsor get back with the group?"

"Um. I don't think so. I'll ask Nora and let you know when I send you the minutes." They disconnected, and Sara was sure she heard relief in her voice. She locked the car and walked into the reception area.

Lillie was in the front; she beamed in recognition. "Ms. Wells! Are you visiting today or back to work for us?"

"No, not that—Mr. Thomas asked me to drive out, he has something to give me." She shut up, already having said more than she intended, and smiled again, instead.

"I'll just walk with her to Ken," Lillie told the receptionist, and Sara followed her through the security doorway and into the long hall. Lillie was chattering as she had that first time: Her kids were so excited about the book, they remembered seeing Sara drawing things, maybe even drawing *them*, and they'd talked about it all the time. Sara made obligatory answers but felt her stomach tightening as they drew near Thomas' office. Since Lillie hadn't warned him they were on the way, he was sitting behind his desk, tapping on a computer, but he stood quickly when they came into the office. She shook hands with him, sensed no aggrievement in those brown eyes behind his wire-rims.

It's not on him, she reminded herself.

He reached for his phone, but she forestalled that. "If you don't mind, let's keep this simple, just us, today."

He sat down and gestured for her to do the same. She took a comfortable armchair, dragged it closer to his desk as he watched.

"How have you been?" he asked.

She sighed—wondered why that came out, made herself smile again. "We're fine, thank you. Cary's looking forward to school being out. I'm redoing a room in my house—my aunt's moved to another place—close by, at least, so we see her all the time, you know, but she's not under my roof anymore. So we had that adjustment to make...." She stopped: talking too much again. Had she missed adult company so much she'd even resort to chatter with Ken Thomas?

"Are you doing all the work yourself?" he asked politely.

"It's not much work—I made that sound like a big job, didn't I. I just cleaned the carpet, bought a couple of pieces of furniture, moved some others. Anyway, yes, we're fine. You and your family?"

He shrugged. "Everybody's well. Mary and I are signed up for a cruise, end of June. She's all excited about it."

"She'll enjoy it."

The conversation was going nowhere, and she sighed again, glanced toward his windows. "You have some copies?"

He tapped his fingers on the desk. "I should've— Well, truth is, I don't have them here, in my office. I was about to call Caroline to bring them down, and then you asked me not to. I understand you two have had words—that's not my business—" he added quickly as she scowled— "and he didn't explain, so I'm not going there, don't worry. But to get the books sent down, I have to make this call, all right?"

She nodded, feeling childish and unreasonable. He spoke to Matheson's secretary on the intercom and turned back to Sara.

"It was a quarrel. It's not your fault," she told him stiffly.

He shrugged. "He can be a horse's ass sometimes. Oops, inappropriate again, huh. I see you're helping with Lynne's campaign."

"I got into that accidentally." She seized on the change of subject. "I've known her a long time, so when she asked, of course I was glad to."

He kept tapping. "Good help."

"Gotta do what you can."

He leaned in, his expression intense. "You think she'll pull it off? You've been here all your life, I guess. You know the people. Is it possible?"

"Not unless something changes. We kind of screwed up letting Stephen Logan get that press last weekend. She, wisely, I think, didn't want to speak first; she wanted to follow him and have the last word. And then he ended up getting the publicity anyway."

"But it was negative."

"Doesn't matter. It was publicity." She repeated her belief to him: "Coverage is coverage. And I screwed up. I told her not to go after him."

"So did I. It seemed..." He hesitated. "Safe. It seemed safe, at the time."

"It was. So she came off mild-mannered. Easy to push around. Lynne," she added, shook her head.

"And then he's a white male."

"That too." She nodded sadly. "Ought not to matter. Looks like it still does. It wouldn't have made any difference if CBS had been shoving a microphone at him. Or nobody. It's all the same."

He turned a cool, almost appraising look on her. "You grew up friends with Lynne?"

With anybody else she wasn't any more familiar with than she was with him, she'd have dissimulated, covered both sides, but she recalled Matheson's words about him and decided to say the truth: "No. I went to her shop. I knew her. The way I know you. Business. And her brother, William."

Ten beats, as he looked at her.

"I mean, she *is* older than I..." she began, but that wasn't enough. "No, I don't know her as well as I should, for our small little town. You're wondering if I know anybody else in her community. Honestly, I don't have many people of *any* color I'd

240

call actual friends. That's sad, huh."

His eyes became less cold. "Don Liberto," he suggested. "Lisa."

"Yeah, them, maybe. But he's more of a brother."

"Neil Griffin."

She knew he was waiting for her to betray how she felt. "My lawyer. Are lawyers your friends?"

"Hm." He glanced toward the window now, and then at the wall behind her.

"I don't know if my help's gonna be real 'help' after all. I mean, with Mr. Matheson, he's the outsider—I know, he's not, *really*, but to them he is—and so he has to be careful what he does. And me..."

"You're the eccentric artist. The intellectual."

Something was rising inside her, a slow, sad tide of despair, and her voice was less steady by the moment. "I guess so. Apparently. No matter how long I've been here. Well, for what it's worth...tell him, tell Mr. Matheson, his help's appreciated." She stopped to recall the words he'd said at the restaurant. "Tell him people notice he's helping. But he may have to do more than that, for us to pull this off."

There was a soft rustle behind her. "Glad you approve of *something* I've done."

Thomas sucked in a deep breath, closed his eyes, shook his head.

How long had he been silent, at the doorway, and why couldn't he have just kept his mouth shut? She watched Thomas, her back to Matheson. "Do you always sneak up on people?"

Thomas' eyes were narrowed, his lips hardly moving: "You could've put it on that table, left without saying anything."

"You find out things this way."

He came into the room and offered her the books. She felt she should examine them but her thoughts strayed to the campaign, to the meal at the restaurant, to the sphere that sat beside her every night, weighing down a stack of documents describing this man's life. When she didn't reach out, he set the books down, perched against the edge of Thomas' desk, his feet planted on the floor. "So what do I need to do?"

It would have seemed a safe topic now, but she found herself breathing harder, her throat getting tight: "I wouldn't have said that before last Saturday. But I think we're in trouble. And I don't *know* how you can help. You can't change people's minds, like with a TV remote." She spoke passionately, realized her eyes were watering. She leaned back in the chair, knew it was lost, and she'd have to ask: "Dammit, you have any tissue?"

Thomas, alarmed, began opening drawers and pawing around in them.

"Bathroom," Matheson said, nodding toward the hall.

Thomas moved around his desk as if that suggestion were for him. She held up her hand and left, grabbed a handful of tissues from the restroom.

They were waiting in the office when she returned—waiting and silent. "Well," she said crossly, "I'm kind of emotional about this election."

"I am too," Thomas said.

She dabbed at her eyes.

"So, then, what *can* I do?" Matheson asked her, leaning closer.

"I would've thought, with his past, people wouldn't even consider him, but, here we are. I would've thought, what he did in Andy's shop earlier this year, that would've been enough. But he's got everything figured out, looks like. And that group that's supporting him seems to have money to give him, whatever he wants.

"But it's not going to be about money," she added quickly as Matheson arose and started to say something. "And you can't change the community, not that way. They have to see it themselves. You can't do a coloring book for this."

He settled back onto the edge of the desk and stared at the floor. "What if there was something he absolutely couldn't defend."

"Oh, you mean those churches. You found out about that. You know what: Nobody ever proved anything. He never admitted to anything, either, and there wasn't anything to tie him to it. I think he was trying to get attention, with the paper and the sheriff; he wanted it, then, he still does: attention. –Is that what you're talking about?"

He gave her a strangely intense look. "More or less. What if something did tie those things to him?"

"I mean, that would make folks remember…"

"What if it brought other people down with him, though? You

know there had to be other people involved. What if they were implicated? Would you feel different about it, then?"

Thomas remained very still, as both he and Matheson gazed at her.

"You mean Frank Moore. Frank didn't do it." She was confused by the intensity of their faces. "But if he did, then, yes, he should bear responsibility, too. Or anybody. Do you know something?"

"I don't. Ask your sister that. She's doing the investigating."

She shook her head, frustrated. "Then I'll never find out. She won't tell me."

"I suppose not. By the way, tell her *I* said for her to be careful. She's messing with people that have lots of strong opinions, pushing their agenda. But they have no self-control."

The alarm she felt at the first words was mitigated by a sudden thought. She smirked and raised her brows.

"Yeah, well, I don't do things *they'd* do," he scolded. Thomas laughed, and the moment felt less ominous. She looked for the books, found them on the other side of where Matheson was propped.

"They look nice," she told them.

" 'Nice'?" Matheson scoffed.

Leafing through the one on top, she held back a grin. "They look great. What's the plan for distributing them?"

"First, they go to the employees' kids, and we'll do that here." He walked to the window and opened the blinds.

Thomas closed his eyes again. "Can't leave anything mechanical alone," he murmured.

"You like it dark in your cave. I always forget. Then," he continued, "we'll have an event at the library, maybe the park. Not everybody wants to drive out here to the woods. So we'll bring these books into town."

"What about the country kids?"

"I think we'll have to deliver them to mailboxes. Like phone directories."

Thomas shook his head. "Dollars flying out the window."

"So we'll get some of the employees' teenagers to do it, pay them for a little work." He gestured irritably. "It'll be okay. It'll get done. Just think *tax write-offs*, Ken."

Sara thumbed through the pages, admiring.

"Your name's on the front, you see," Matheson remarked. "It wasn't meant to be about you, but..."

"But it will be, and that'll get more attention for the project. Take attention off you."

"I assume you don't mind."

She glanced up, and a moment of agreement passed between them. "I approve."

"Good. They're running now, so if you didn't approve, it'd be too bad. Sorry. I had to make that decision." He glanced at his watch. "Let me know if Lynne needs more campaign stuff. Tell her to stay positive. The negative'll get taken care of."

That's an odd way of saying it, she thought. "But will it?"

"I have to get to work."

She took that as a cue to leave, and picked up the soft-bound books and her purse. She reached out to shake Thomas' hand, saw those tissues on his desk and disposed of them. Matheson followed her to the front reception area, and she turned to take leave of him, but he reached ahead and opened the door, gesturing outward. Her discomfort returned; she walked uneasily to the parking lot, aware of his presence at her side, but he said nothing until she unlocked the car and started to open the door. Then he put a hand against it.

"I meant what I said: Don't forget to pass that on to Rheta."

His eyes were somber enough to make a shiver crawl up her back. "What do you know?"

It was as if he were counting numbers silently, to make sure he said only what he intended to. "Nothing. Really. I don't *know* anything. Ken tells me stuff's been said around here in the building, on break—no threats or anything—" he added quickly. "Just discontented talk. These are grownups; they're entitled to their opinions, so what can I say. But the election may get ugly. Tell her to be careful. That's all."

"I will. Thank you."

"Wait. Something else."

She paused, and realized he felt as awkward as she. He glanced back at the main office, hesitated. Then, "I hope you've forgiven my poorly-thought-out attempt of a gift. I shouldn't have done it that way. I'm sorry. We have to work together on this election, and I don't want you mad at me."

"I'm not mad anymore," she said, knowing that was true. "I was embarrassed, when I figured it out. It felt like you'd played a joke on me. I overreacted about it. I wasn't…expecting it."

"I understand. Look." His hand was still against the car door. "Why don't you bring Cary on Friday and stay for a while yourself? We're having pulled pork." He grimaced.

"I don't work here. And I don't eat pulled pork."

"Good. I don't care for it myself. There'll be other stuff, too. But, do come. She enjoys being here with her friends now, and the weather'll be good, I think. It might be fun. I feel like I owe you," he added off-handedly.

"Cary may resent it."

"No, she won't. What's the difference between her coming with you or with Matthew and his—are they married? Are they a couple?"

"They're together. –Oh, you don't know? How can you not know?" she mocked lightly. "I thought you knew everything."

"Go on. I guess I asked for it. Can't they just let *you* bring her, and then you could stay for a while?"

"I'll need to ask her, Cary, I mean," she told him.

"Well, do that." Suddenly he took his hand off the door and opened it for her. Bemused by the abruptness, she laid the books in the back and climbed in, cranked the car. He leaned over and kissed her forehead. "Making up for the bump I gave you at Liberto's, maybe."

The engine hummed as she sat with her mouth open, hearing the last words: "I'll just tell people you're my date."

22

HE WALKED VERY fast through the hall toward the elevators, changed his mind when Thomas called his name and left his office to hurry after him: "What is it about you and her and stairs?"

"Good for your health. You said so yourself. Said she was a good influence."

Thomas, breathing heavily, followed him up the steps and into the office that had full, strong sunlight streaming in from the deck.

"I guess I have to close my shades for you." He fumbled with the adjusting wand.

Thomas laid a few papers on top of the antique desk and said as he left, "She always have trouble with the main door, man? Like you're having with those blinds?"

"Too many damn windows in this place." He grimaced at the sound of quiet laughter fading out down the hallway.

TREES, SIGNS, FIELDS flew past Sara. She drove in the daze from which you awake to realize you just finished a long part of a journey without really remembering it, or even having done it.

She parked on the street. Texted Rheta to ask whether she was there or out on assignment. Told her she needed to talk *right then*. Headed to Rheta's office, anyway, knowing why her mind had sent her there.

The answer was laconic but, at least, immediate: **Come on up.**

She fidgeted beside a chair in the minuscule, grubby space.

"What's wrong? You look like crap."

She blurted the thing that had been gnawing quietly away in a dark section of her mind, down below the other thoughts flying around: "Ron Matheson wants you to be careful. He says you're messing with people who think self-control is weakness."

Rheta's brows lowered in a scowl. "So he told you about the meeting. I thought we could trust him to keep his mouth shut more than we could Ransome, but apparently we were wrong."

"What? Meeting?"

"Well, *crap...*" Rheta comprehended her mistake. "Okay, scratch that. Let's start over."

"Meeting?" Sara repeated.

"Hush. Forget it. Let's leave that, okay? Why'd Ron tell you to warn me? When'd you see him last, when'd he say that?" She grabbed Sara's arm. "Let's get a soda."

She hurried Sara down the stairs to a room where a few vending machines stood against one wall and a couple of laminate tables took up the tiny space left. She dragged up two chairs to the one positioned near the side wall.

"I'd rather not have everybody hear this right now. So be quiet," and she leaned across the cheap table. "When did he say that?"

"I drove out there this morning. Something about the book project. And we, that is, he and Ken Thomas and I, we were talking about Lynne. And he brought it up."

Rheta stared past Sara, her gaze focused on the narrow

entrance to the break room and the hallway past that. "I guess he's heard something that bothered him. Well, so have I, but I've heard worse."

"You've had threats, other stuff?"

Rheta shrugged. "Nothing worse than usual, I said. But maybe he *has*. And by the way, you need to stay out of it when you're around and I'm working on Stephen Logan! That'll get *you* on a list, yourself, one of his!"

"Those people were getting in *my sister's* face!"

"They didn't know that, then. But there're plenty of people in town who do. So just, let me handle him, okay?"

"Stop it. I'm anxious about you."

"You want a soft drink? Coffee? No, forget that; nobody's made a new pot."

"I'm good."

Rheta's eyes came back to meet hers. "Okay, so maybe this'll make you feel better: Nobody's letting me leave alone in the evening. And I have to text Joe when I get home at night. We've started letting somebody know where we are, being a little more careful, till this election's done."

"So you *have*— Does Mother know?"

The scowl returned. "Hell, no, and you aren't going to tell her. She's got enough sense to know what I do."

"Why can't they do something with Stephen Logan?"

"I'm not sure he's behind this, not him, not actually doing it, not even telling somebody to do it for him. It seems like he's just talking it up, empowering his lunatic fans. So he can say, 'My hands are clean, I didn't tell them to.'"

"Same thing."

"Inciting to riot's more specific."

At the same moment, as if a memory of long ago returned, they reached for each other's hand on the plastic laminate top. "If you see him, tell Ron I *am* taking care, to the best of my ability. Tell him I'll let him know if I need help. He's probably got some goons around he can spare."

Startled, Sara laughed.

"Well, you know he's gotta have security, big company like that, contracts with the government. I mean, he looks like he might be able to handle it himself, but somebody's gotta be shadowing him most of the time."

"Never thought of it."

"So pass that on to him. When will you see him?" she asked, absent-mindedly.

"He invited me to the picnic on Friday, bring Cary instead of her going with Matthew and Jennifer."

"Don't guess I'll be doing those again," Rheta interrupted, still engaged in some inner reflection, her eyes focused on the doorway. "Well, if you go, mention it if you see him."

Sara patted her hand and left without unloading about the other.

IT WOULD BE something she'd have to figure out on her own.

She and Cary were eating supper, a quiet one—they'd all been quieter meals since Louise and Harvey moved to Stone Avenue. Louise had been a stickler for decorum, Sara reflected, and she spooned *flan* into her mouth. Louise would have fumed at the sight of Cary with her phone beside her plate; Sara was too preoccupied these days to pay attention to it. Cary'd asked Sara about the *flan*, which Sara admitted was a throwback to Louise—and *of* Louise's, she thought, wondering suddenly if her aunt had prepared it those times as a reminder to herself of her adventure in Mexico.

Cary finished and glanced at the phone again. "I miss Aunt Louise." In a moment she added, "Sometimes."

"I think she stayed with us about as long as she should've. As much for her sake as ours."

"Probably."

Cary took both their plates to the dishwasher, Sara again silently noting that willingness. They went to the living room— well, it was still the routine.

"Would you stick around for a little bit?"

"Sure…" She glanced about as if expecting someone to pop up. "Actually, I wanted to talk anyway."

"Well, me first." Sara wasn't sure how to start, and plowed in: "I had to run out to MTE again today. You wanna see what the books look like?"

"I guess…"

Sara handed her one of the copies she'd stacked on the bookshelf earlier. While Cary leafed through it, she continued, "It turned out well. They invited me to the cookout on Friday, at least for a while. They said, Why didn't I bring *you*, and then you could leave with your dad and Jennifer."

"Yeah, that's fine…" Cary's voice was a little too unemotional, and she laid down the book and said, "It's nice, Mom."

"But would you mind if I did stay for a while?"

"Why would I? *You'll* be hanging with the old folks, anyway," and it was a reminder to Sara that she *would* have to hang with the old folks and not own Cary.

"That's true. So then you could leave from there with them."

Cary flopped down dramatically on the sofa. "That's what I was gonna ask you."

"I'm sorry, but you know—"

"No, I'm not asking to get out of it, I know I have to go over there. And, well, I'll enjoy the cookout. It's not that. It's just… Lately, they look like they're getting on each other's nerves." She hesitated, started again, louder and faster: "Like, he'll want her to do something, cook a particular thing, or maybe just watch something with him on TV, and she won't want to, or not right then, and he—well. it's like he sulks, and then he remembers and digs it in later. There's lots of that lately, and it makes me uncomfortable, and—and it makes me sad, too." She sighed. "Would somebody just decide they've had enough—do people do that all of a sudden, just say, 'This is it, I'm outta here,' or is it a long thing over a long time?"

In her mind she finished the implicit P.S.: ***Because you did it, just had enough and left***. She picked out careful words: "I don't speak for everybody. For me, it was after a long time. It wasn't a last-minute, sudden thing. You know that; you've asked how long we were together. I just…after a while, it was just something I couldn't do anymore. Are you worried about him and Jennifer?"

"Yeah, because, you know, they're not married, just planning on it—'sometime', they keep saying, and it'd be easy for that to turn into 'never.' "

"They won't," she said, and as an epiphany she knew it was true: Matthew and Jennifer would figure it out, whereas she and he hadn't. Maybe they'd both been too unwilling to compromise, maybe they'd just become too unhappy, maybe neither of them had thought of failure as an unacceptable thing but only another alternative…but he wouldn't let it happen again, she knew somehow with an assurance that made her tone firm: "They aren't going to break up. They'll probably have a big fight before long, and they'll make up and then they'll get married one day in private, and you'll go over there and they'll tell you it's done. Will you be upset at not being in the wedding?"

Cary put her finger on her tongue. "Gag. But what makes you believe that?"

"Because he's too committed to her. And he knows what it's like to be alone, and he doesn't want it to happen again."

Cary glanced up at her and held back another question—she could see her change her mind about saying it—and flung herself off the couch. "Well, I hope you're right, because I kind of like Jennifer, and, actually, I guess she's better than he deserves—he'd better figure that out!" she added fiercely as she headed back to her room.

"HE KNOWS WHAT it's like to be alone, and he doesn't want it to happen again."

Ann Landers had said one time it was better to be alone than to wish you were.

The line went around in her mind for a long time after she lay down, giving the sphere its routine thump. She'd moved it to pick up the documents, then replaced them: She didn't have to read them again to know the words.

She'd just returned from getting Cary to school next morning when a knock at the front door interrupted her sorting laundry. After talking to Rheta, she'd resolved to be more cautious, and looked through the blinds. A florist-shop van idled in the drive, and, as she swung the door wide, a young woman offered her two arrangements. "I guess he likes both of you." She smiled mischievously and scampered back to the van before Sara collected herself enough to ask anything. "He said I was just to leave them, even if you weren't here. He said you might object, but, me, I'd keep 'em." In a moment she drove the van on down the street.

One was a mug with a couple of daisies and baby's-breath tied with a bright ribbon, the other a white rosebud framed in cut ferns in a small glass vase. She plucked out the cards, took the flowers to the kitchen table, feeling as nervous as if she were seventeen—as if she were younger, even, Cary's age, getting her corsage for prom.

She knew who they were from, but she read the cards anyway: *I signed this time. I can be taught. Coming or not? Text me—* and a number. The note with the rose read, *Make your mom bring you so she's not such a hermit.*

She laughed softly every time she walked through the kitchen that morning, glancing at them, sometimes touching the flower petals. She took her art supplies out back to the little garden Louise had cultivated through the years, laid them on the patio table. All that work, all that time, when Louise had probably had other things on her mind.... She knelt down on the flagstones and weeded the flower beds which had become small jungles during the rain over spring break. She texted a photo of the results to Louise: *I'm not gonna let your garden go to waste!* In a moment there was a pointed reply: **I wouldn't be spending all my time on that. Get out and have some fun.**

I don't know how to start, she wanted to answer, but instead she cleaned her hands took the supplies back inside.

SHE HANDED OUT campaign literature and bumper stickers that week to people in front of Liberto's, some of whom, she noticed, took the materials to the nearest trash bin and tossed them, sometimes with an arch look backwards at her, as casually as if they were throwing away paper napkins. After a while, on the first afternoon this had happened, she was triggered into calling, "I got plenty more," and one guy looked at her and said, "But you don't have *this* one." After that she learned to ask if people wanted the things, and if they said no, she assumed it didn't always mean they weren't going to vote for Lynne.

She hadn't heard back from Lindsay, and something in her knew they were cutting her out of the loop, whether because she'd become involved with MTE or with Lynne, she didn't know and didn't care. And she hadn't answered Matheson, though the mug with its sprightly daisies like wide eyes reproached her: You're enjoying the flowers; you should at least let him know *that*. Cary had looked askance at the rose. "Is he a pedophile or something? That's weird," and shrugged when Sara explained what white roses meant. "Whatever. If you wanna go, like I said, go. I texted Jennifer yesterday and told her you'd bring me, and she was cool with it."

She'd asked Don if it was okay to distribute cards and flyers in front of his restaurant, asked coldly, unsmiling, as he stared at her.

"I got signs up. Why'd I mind you doin' it?"

She didn't like his tone. "Go on, pinch me," she urged, "and I'll hit your arm, like when we were kids. Just do it. Get it out of your system." She crowded him until he backed off a pace or two.

"Are you dating Ron?" he asked belligerently.

"Oh, my God. If I were, would I tell you? And what—you didn't like me hanging with Neil, now you gotta complain about somebody else? I might've let Pop do that, but you don't get the right."

"But are you?" he insisted.

She leaned over the wrought-iron fence by the sidewalk as the warm breeze blew through the river-birch branches. "No, I'm not, Don, but it's not your business." There she stopped, her own recent words coming back to her.

"But when you were having lunch here, you kissed—"

"No, he was mad, I was mad, and he leaned over to grab something I'd brought to return to him, and when he did, he bumped into me. Wait, who've you told that story to? Lisa, I bet," she guessed, raising her voice, gesticulating at him. "Did you tell Lisa that? I bet she set you down, didn't she." She could see by the slight flinch she'd guessed right. "You're the best brother I never had, but it's all good. I'm not dating Ron Matheson, and, by the way, I haven't heard from Neil in—" she paused, realizing it— "in ages. Now back off, jerk."

It was inevitable that one day shortly after that, Stephen Logan would pass by. She glared at him, but he was unaffected: "You want me to take a flyer?"

"I'm not giving you any."

"Be nice—there're people watching." Which was true: Don's business was flourishing again in its cyclical way, now that the weather was fair and not yet too hot, and customers had paused, forks loaded with pasta, to observe the two of them. Logan reached over and touched her arm lightly. She wanted to recoil but kept very still, returning his gaze. "When the election's over, I may want to hire you as a consultant for the city. It's about time you got paid for supporting local things. I know these organizations you sign onto don't give you a dime."

"How would you know that."

"Public record. Plus, I ask sources. So after the election you'd have a chance to recoup some losses."

"Ugh. You assume you'll win? Really?"

"You know I'll win," he told her softly, the flashing smile belying his cold eyes.

She shook her head, forced calmness on her face. "I'm not one of your crowd, Stephen. I'm not interested in working with you."

"Not even for the good of the town? Where's your spirit of bipartisanship?" he goaded.

She scoffed. "Like that group you associate with. And you need to tell your hired help to quit harassing people. Including the press, by the way." There, she'd done what Rheta'd told her not to. Thank goodness for that name, "R. C. Whitson."

"I guess you mean at the park the other week. They show up, they're fair game. They're used to it. Even your friend the news anchor."

"Move on to your burrow, Stephen." Don approached with a coffee in a disposable cup. "Here. Take a bribe. We're in public, so it's okay." The nearest customers laughed a little at this. "Quit bothering my sister."

Logan's smile never wavered as he glanced at both of them. "Sister? Not hardly." He took the cup, held it up as if toasting them in victory and ambled to the building next door. The handful of people who'd heard the exchange clapped lightly.

"And, shit, there's the troll's twin," Don griped, eyeing Neil, who had stepped out the streetside door of his office. "I'm going back inside. This upsets my digestion. I'd advise you to quit for the day, Sis," he headed for the door, "and I'm not giving *him* any coffee. And I bet Stephen doesn't like his, either." She didn't ask what he'd done to it.

She'd actually seen Neil before Don had, noticed him opening the door, and he, too, had flashed her a brilliant white smile and held up one finger and motioned, as if to say, "Don't leave; come here." And hemmed in by Logan and Don, she'd stayed put. Then came the texts—she'd felt her phone buzzing in her pocket as Don walked away: **I wonder which rat poison he used.**

??! she texted back now.

From across the street, she saw him laugh. **Find a way to escape the mafia and step in for a minute. I need to tell you something.**

She began gathering the stickers and buttons into a bag, turning to the tables behind her: "Y'all want one of these?" A woman held out her hand and asked for a button and pinned it to her dress, but no one else appeared interested, shaking their heads politely at her. Sara gave them a smile, picked up the bag, dashed across the street, aware that Don was probably watching.

"I WAS ON the way out, dear, changed my mind when I saw it, like everybody else on the street did. It's part of his game," he told her.

She sank into the comfortable armchair close to his desk, the one she'd used so many times in the past, and looked out on Main the way *he* did, when he claimed he was thinking out a problem. People down below wandered along the sidewalks, going in and out of the five or six shops on this block, and the restaurant across the street. She found herself in that moment wondering about this person or that one, why they were in town in the middle of the day, why they appeared hurried or, on the other hand, despondent; what was Lisa Liberto in such a rush about—

Abruptly she twisted the chair away from the view. "God, Neil, you're a voyeur!"

"It's how I get my head together sometimes. You've seen me do it."

"What 'game' of Don's are you talking about?"

"One-upmanship. He's good at it. Stephen probably thought he won that round running you off, getting a free java out of the restaurant, but he didn't taste that coffee before he left. Although," he mused, "maybe he just threw it away. I would've. He wouldn't have spiked it with anything really bad. Probably too much sugar, or watered it down so it's hardly coffee. Or it was all dregs. I don't care." He rolled his chair nearer to hers and touched the "Lynne Houston" pin attached to her shirt. "So. All relevant and progressive... You don't like the view anymore?"

"I figure you use it these days to keep track of what your guy's up to down there. He's a piece of work. So what do you need to tell me?"

"Not a thing. I played my own game and got you to come over."

She remembered: the kitchen counter at her back; a stack of papers he wanted her to read. "You didn't have anything to say?"

"Nothing. Just wanted you here. And," he went on, "it was fun watching Don's face as you crossed the street. —Stop frowning at me. I did give him points about the coffee."

The chat was becoming disconcertingly uncomfortable, an edge creeping into their words. "I have things to do, if you haven't…" She stopped, unsure of what she'd intended to finish that with.

"Oh, don't go yet. I hardly ever see you these days. And if it's the campaigning you think you should be doing, trust me, dear, that can wait."

"Meaning, you think it's insignificant," she said. He leaned forward, rubbed gently between her brows.

"Frown lines," he said.

She jerked her head. "Neil, do you know why your building was vandalized in March? Why did whoever it was choose *your* place?"

His eyes narrowed a little. "What a weird thing for you to bring up now."

"But didn't you wonder, didn't it ever bother you? I mean, you were representing somebody in court who they, I guess, support, you were defending him in an action—why would they go after you?"

"Intense lately, aren't you." He watched her carefully for a moment: She'd seen this look before. "I tell you, I don't know…it could've been aimed at Don, you know that, right? He's a minority, it's widely known we aren't friends, he was there at the courthouse, openly gloating, when Stephen and I came outside, after Diandra handed down her decision."

"That doesn't make me feel better…to think we have somebody around who'd do that sort of thing. To you, or Don, either. Are you actually helping your awful guy down there? I mean, you're giving him space…why would you do that?"

"Ah," he said coolly. "Now that bothers me. You been listening to that big guy on campus."

"What an ironic comment. *You* were always the big guy on campus."

She'd enjoyed the dark, mysterious serenity of the office in the past; today, it felt more and more claustrophobic, the shelves looming with their old volumes, the rich flocked wallpaper closing in…. She pushed herself out of the chair that was always so easy to sink into like a soft nest, and stood with her back to the window.

"So did you actually read what I gave you, or were you seduced by another margarita? If you read it, you see he's ended up in court several times with his little romances."

" 'Little romances'? I told you about that the other week. And I paid for my own drink that day. And I didn't have a margarita."

"Sure looked like one to me."

"Well, you do actually spy, don't you! You get a pair of binoculars for Christmas?"

"I know what a margarita looks like. I've bought 'em for you before."

"Don left out the alcohol."

He laughed. "Sneaky; I like it. Guess he didn't want you drinking with Big Boss Man that day. Did he charge you full price? That would be even better."

"He didn't do that. He knew that'd be one bridge too far."

"You're trying so hard to keep from laughing. Go on: It's funny. And sit down." He gestured at her chair. "I mean, if you want to, sit down. Gotta be careful about that these days, with you. By the way, I'll vote for Lynne, of course. Who'd vote for *that*?" He gestured dismissively downward.

"And yet you're renting campaign space to him."

"Actually, no." He interrupted her objection, "It started out as just office room. He's been there longer than anybody's realized, because would I advertise that he's the tenant? Not hardly. Up till lately, he'd just come and go quietly, sometimes out the back, I think. That day over spring break, when you needed me to rescue you at the restaurant? He'd probably ducked out and taken the, what, five steps to the right, to get away from his place for a while. When he first approached me about it, he said he needed it for, well, something or other entrepreneurial thing he wanted to try, and I didn't think he'd stay there long. Figured he'd get tired of whatever it was. Or it would fail. I wasn't specific enough with the lease, so I'm stuck with him."

"Why didn't you tell me that then? Why'd you leave it hanging that day, that he was dry—but the rain was so fierce… It's almost like you felt sorry for him. And I never knew you to take pity on anybody." She said it jokingly, aware he was inching closer in his chair, and it was dangerous, dangerous, like how it used to be, years back, when she was a new mother and lonely. She thought she should walk toward the door; but the office was cozy and backlit, all heavy wooden bookshelves and tables and nice brocade upholstering, just what lawyers do to present a caring, warm persona to a client. And, then, the feeling of being secretly above the world here, the memory of him in bed with her…

She should leave.

"No, I didn't feel pity—maybe one of those moments you say are rare, for me, when I just felt like doing something to help a person who had a hard start in life. Like your pal Matheson. I'm a do-gooder, like him."

"Yeah, sure," she scoffed, pushing his chair backwards.

She'd said it lightly, as a sort of joke, but his face changed, and the teasing uplift of his mouth left as he grasped her hands. "You don't believe me, but I guess you believe him? That he's doing things out of the goodness of his heart? Anyway, Stephen's there, and I can't get rid of him right now, so take it for what you will. So how'd you get roped into Lynne's campaign?"

"She asked. I might've offered anyway."

"She's gonna lose, you know."

"She wouldn't, if people like you'd support her."

"I said I'll vote for her."

"I mean, publicly…actually coming out and saying it, not just to me."

"You want me to? You haven't asked yet."

Suddenly she wanted out of the warmly pleasant room. He'd rolled closer again until their faces were just inches apart, her knees at the edge of his upholstered chair between his thighs, and a memory of a similar thing flashed over her mind: Her asking him to sell her the house instead of renting it to her, the unstated tradeoff…*Would you like for me to do that? Just ask me, and I might….*

His intercom squawked at that moment. "Mark Mason's here. Can you see him?"

He grimaced: "Just a minute." Then, "Can we go to a nice place out of town and just have a glass of wine tonight and make up?"

"Cary's got friends coming over," she lied. "I'll text you tomorrow sometime."

"You probably won't, you're unreliable, but I'll wait and see. Now, do me a favor and show Mark in, because I can't actually get up right now; I have to cool down—" He leered at her, and she shook her head and laughed as she departed, waving at Mark. "He says for you to go in."

Jean's face was vaguely hostile, she noticed. Had it always been, when she came to Neil's office?

23

I HAD TO make Ken give me your #. You coming or not, dammit?

She snickered at the text, not knowing, of course, how Thomas had delighted in putting Matheson off a day or two before giving in to his demand, made him ask several times as he got madder about it, finally told him, "Man, you're worse than my grandson," and scribbled the number down in an excruciatingly slow manner while Matheson hovered by his desk.

"All you had to do was forward me that contact card," Matheson muttered, snatching the sticky note, thinking that he hated Ken's laugh.

It was Thursday, and the week had been discouraging. She still had lots of Lynne's campaign stuff to give away, but there were only so many people in Mooresville to hand them to, and everybody who wanted them probably had them by now. She'd tried not to let Neil's and Logan's self-confidence get her down, but there it was: She'd seen as much on the faces of citizens that week.

Since Cary'd already told Matthew Sara was taking her to MTE on Friday night, she'd be heading there anyway, or be made a liar, she thought; so after a few moments' reflection she tapped back: *Why? Gotta know if to buy 2 or 3 pkgs of buns?* Let him think about that; and she awaited the response, which came pretty fast.

Nope, Pepto-Bismol. U in?

She chuckled, typed, *Sure. Get me a whole bottle.*

She hadn't thought too much about Ron Matheson in the past days. A brotherly kiss on the forehead, in expiation for the sin of bumping it, wasn't noteworthy, and, meanwhile, the gnawing creature in the back of her mind fretted more about Rheta, anyway. She'd made it a habit this week to text her every day, asking how things were going, and Rheta was always truculent—**Still here, worrywart**—but at least she did answer. But Sara had seen evasion, reluctance, suspicion in some faces on the street this week. She was sensing what Don had, some weeks earlier on a rainy Sunday afternoon, but she hadn't talked to him—if she had, the two of them might have decided there was more than just free-floating, ill-defined anxiety worrying them, and Don might have called Matheson to ask him what he knew, what he'd heard. As it was, handing out her buttons and cards in front of the restaurant had only depressed her, and maybe the picnic would do her good.

She dressed in jeans and a long-sleeved blouse. Cary took a look and said, "You're gonna burn up in that, but, hey, whatever." She herself wore a huge T-shirt over leggings.

"You think I should put on something like what you're wearing?"

Cary surveyed her from head to tennis shoes and scoffed, "Probably not. But if you want to, if you feel like doing it, sure, go for it. I mean, whatever." She picked up the backpack with her stuff and they left. On the way, as Cary tapped on her phone, Sara softly cursed. Had she locked the back door? She couldn't remember—she grimaced, thinking of Louise's mild paranoia: She would *not* go back and check.

CARY GAVE HER a solemn glance. "Have fun." She walked off, leaving her backpack in the car. From that Sara took it they probably wouldn't see each other much the rest of the evening. She let her get a fair distance away before heading towards the group of people gathered around a long row of the tables she'd last seen in the art room closets. An aroma of burning hickory and barbecue filled the air as she approached, looking for some face she recognized, but not Matthew's, please, she reminded herself, although of course she would have to see him tonight. Roaming around the outer edge of the group, she spoke to and smiled at a few people who saw and knew her. She picked up a soft drink and ambled towards the source of the rich smoke wafting through the air. There, holding drinks, lounging against another row of tables, were some of the engineers she'd seen in the main office, and with them, Ken Thomas and Matheson. They all seemed intense, as always—are they talking programming again? she wondered—but as she neared, she discovered it was the election they were discussing, with some in the group stone-faced and grim, and others, animatedly waving arms around. Thomas stood near the cooks who dished out pork from a large pan. The two guys worked with giant forks and spatulas as the spicy steam arose; Thomas almost seemed to be protecting the servers, and they looked nervous, she could tell from their glances at the crowd as they worked. Matheson's words returned to her mind: *We just don't think about it, because we're not affected.*

"...on the other hand, just because she *is* Black?" one voice said firmly. "That's racism in reverse. Also not using your right to vote the way it was intended. Also—"

"Nobody said to vote for Lynne because she's Black, Wilma," Thomas told the woman who'd spoken, a person Sara'd noticed in the large engineering room. She froze where she was when Matheson recognized her and jerked his head once in a sort of warning.

"But that's what I hear everywhere. 'She's different, she's a new direction'—well, that's just fine, Ken, but I don't go and buy bikinis because they're different and a new direction. I know what works on my old fat white body."

Everybody snickered; then he said, solemnly, "Lynne knows how to run a business, how to balance the books; surely you want somebody who can do that? Has Stephen Logan ever done anything like it?"

"He had that business over in Franklin. And anyway—Lynne, her clientele here in Mooresville that knows her," a man standing next to Wilma remarked, "well, they gave her business, because they felt sorry for her, and so she's never really had to *worry* about her books balancing. Anyway," he added coolly as Thomas glared at him, "I doubt she does that herself. She's not an accountant. She's hired somebody to do it. I'm not sure she's smart enough to do that herself."

A clamor arose then, and other people began to disagree, and the man and Wilma were joined by a couple more Logan fans. Thomas turned and looked pointedly at Matheson, who put fingers to his mouth and blew an ear-splitting whistle. "Okay, enough politics for tonight. You guys talk about it on your own time from this point on."

He told people to fetch some more chairs, to work on the bonfire, which Sara now noticed at a distance from the rows of tables; that had definitely contributed to the fragrance in the air. The crowd dispersed, and she stood still, watching Matheson and

Thomas exchange quiet words near the two guys with the forks. In a moment, Matheson nodded and went into the child-care facility, returning with a megaphone. Neither of them had spoken to her, but, then, things had been happening. Matheson climbed upon one of the concrete tables and shouted through the megaphone, "*Hey!*" Then he whistled again, and an appalled silence fell upon everyone. "The food's done and hot! Let the kids get theirs first. Where I am is pulled pork. Over there, chicken strips. Desserts, next to Kid Kare. Salads in between the meats. Beverages in the coolers beside the desserts."

The crowd moved toward the serving tables. Thomas said more quiet words to the guys arranging the pork, turned and blocked Matheson from moving, waved his arms energetically, shook his finger at Matheson, said something like, "...how many times? You can't depend on..." and recoiled coldly as Matheson told him, "You need to calm down!" She could see those were the words, could even faintly hear them. She wondered which of them would yield first; it was Thomas, and Matheson remained where he'd been for a moment, his face flushed with displeasure. He looked up, noticed her, trotted around the end of the long row of tables, took her hand to pull her aside.

"You won't see him for a while," he said quietly. "He's gone to cool off."

"Why should he?"

"Because it won't help right now. There's already been enough said."

"He should've had the chance to say what he wanted to; *they* did."

"You're right, and he'll kick my ass about it later, and probably should. But I can't have any more hell breaking loose."

THEY SAT NEAR the bonfire, which he told her he'd had built to drive away mosquitoes, not for the heat, as heat wasn't an issue now in late May.

Already there'd been tension before she'd arrived. The open gripe session he allowed before they ate had gone to hell fast this time. Some employees wanted to know why he was getting involved in local politics—"I think the term was, 'Stay in your lane,' " he said sardonically. "They said I've been meddling, when I can't possibly understand the people and the area yet. I think I heard that before," he added meaningfully. Through it all, Ken Thomas had stood by, getting madder and madder, and it showed; and it looked as if they might have been *trying* to get to him. "He's always yelled at me about this, said you can't trust a lot of people to do the right thing, so why do I let them vent."

She told him he should've made everybody stop—he was the boss, he could do that; and he agreed he could: "I did, finally, didn't I?" But they already thought he imposed his will on them too much, he reminded her. He didn't want that hanging around his neck: that he'd stopped a discussion because he only allowed ideas that agreed with his. "When the election's over, maybe things'll calm down. Anyway, I just redirected everybody to the food. They'll drop everything else when it comes to food."

Knowing he was baiting her again, she jabbed at him with a fork. He was picking around on the chicken, glancing back occasionally in the direction where Thomas had walked off.

"Go talk to him."

"You serious? Don't you remember what I said? He's seen worse, lived worse. Go treat him like he's sulking? You kidding me? Plus, he's probably right, again. Excuse me, but I have to mingle for a while."

He left her to walk around the groups, making random comments, moving on. He spoke with some of the employees who'd stood with Wilma and the man Sara had heard when she'd arrived—in fact, she noticed, puzzled, he seemed to share a huge joke with them and eventually returned to where she sat.

"They went right back to their mumbling after you left, picked up their phones to put it on social media," she told him softly.

"Yeah, I figured they would. But it's not my place to force everybody to be buddies on the playground. No matter what you might think about that."

"You let it get going, you have to control it."

He ate another bite, frowning. "By the way, the flowers—"

"—were nice, and I guess I should've told you before now."

"You were being assertive with me. I understand."

"Yeah, okay, sure. That. Cary asked if you were a pedophile," she added casually.

Matheson's loud guffaws made several people stare in their direction; Matthew was one of them. Curious about what his boss's demeanor would be with Sara, he'd positioned himself and

Jennifer not too far away. Sara nibbled on her chicken. She felt sorry for Jennifer, who, judging by her expression, had been unhappy all evening, probably about Matthew's maneuvering. Taking pity on her, Sara dug her phone out of her pocket as Matheson shook his head, his laughter subsiding.

Cary's backpack is in my car. You want to get it?

Jennifer read the text and met her eyes and nodded, rising and saying something to Matthew as she did. Sara handed her plate to Ron: "Would you dispose of this for me? I'm going to walk with Jennifer for a minute."

She'd learned he had that trick of assessing things with a careful glance, and now he stood and ambled around, headed indirectly toward Matthew. "You enjoying yourself tonight?" she asked the younger woman as they strode from the fire, away to where the cooler dusk seemed to gather thickly around the vehicles whose owners had used the front lot, the one where employees regularly parked in the daytime.

"Oh, you know. It's a cookout—" But she struggled with the words and stopped there.

"Cary's worried about you and Matthew." She decided to be direct. "She's afraid you'll break up. She told me this week."

Jennifer looked straight ahead and didn't speak.

"She says she hopes Matthew knows he doesn't deserve you." She heard a quavering sigh. "I told her I didn't think breaking up was in the picture."

"I wish I was that confident—" And that did it, and Sara let her cry for a while as she patted her back. *I know what a jerk he can be*, she wanted to say, but that wouldn't be helpful.

"And I'm pregnant," Jennifer sobbed.

Sara froze—it felt as if she'd come to a solid but invisible wall there under the trees. It had been so hard for her, and then Cary was raised without her father in the house, and she wanted to shake Jennifer now, tell her to shut up...but she listened instead, motionless in the dark with the breeze moving pine needles gently around over her head.

"I didn't mean it to happen—or I *guess* I didn't mean to, maybe I was hoping, but, yep, and I feel like it doesn't help, now."

"Have you told him?"

"No, as much as we've been fighting, I didn't want...but he'll figure it out soon enough. I can't eat, and *that* hit fast—"

"Sometimes it does."

"—so he'll know pretty soon."

"Tell him tonight. Tell him and Cary both, tonight, when you get home. Bring her into it, it'll make her feel less alienated from him, and don't be tentative. Be joyous. I was," she remembered, "even though—"

"You wouldn't be together," she finished.

She retrieved Cary's backpack, forcing herself to sound cheerful, to say Cary would be excited…but walking back to the fire, with the younger woman holding the bag tightly as if it were a life preserver, listening to the nervous chatter as they went, she just felt old. And she didn't know Cary'd be excited or happy or anything—but, she reminded herself, it wasn't Cary's job to feel anything in particular, she was nearly an adult herself, so what *could* she be expected to feel?

She stopped Jennifer on the edge of the cookout area and gave her face a quick inspection.

"Well, I guess you wear waterproof mascara," she said laconically. "Looks like a bug bit you and your face puffed up a little." That was mean and unnecessary. "But you look okay."

Jennifer patted her cheeks "And I've been crying lately. He's been annoyed about that."

"Yeah, well, tell him to get over it. Just, just give him the news tonight; it'll be better."

They separated, and Jennifer returned to where she and Matthew had been, glancing every once in a while in Sara's direction. Matheson had accumulated a group around him a few steps away from her, along with Thomas; he had them all discussing baseball now, a safer topic, maybe. Matthew, Sara observed, had joined them and was feigning keen interest. She remembered he'd never liked baseball much; but his attention, she hoped, was diverted from wondering about his boss and his former wife. Cary sat with her friends, poking marshmallows onto sticks and holding them as near the fire as they could, catching them ablaze with no intention of eating them, watching them slide off into the embers, laughing hilariously. Sara leaned against a pine, staring into the flames. She was alone, her evening changed, colder.

THE TEXTS ARRIVED one after another; she was trying to get

the phone out of her jeans pocket, but several messages had buzzed in before she could unlock the keypad and start reading.

There is someone outside my apartment right now, doing something to the wall.

called police they're not here yet, tell Matheson

are you there? Answer

get some of MTE security here NOW window broken

She leaped away from the tree and stumbled, staring at the messages, turned and hurled herself blindly toward the parking lot, tapping out *K on way* as she took a few jogging steps. Matheson had kept her in sight after she'd come back with Jennifer, and left his group of baseball fans.

"Where you goin'—what's wrong?"

She thrust the phone at him; he took it and held her wrist to keep her from running on as he read, then met her eyes. "Don't leave." She grabbed for the phone and read the latest text.

No stay there ur names here too

He yanked his own cell from his pocket and talked fast to someone, using words and letters that meant nothing to her.

"You can't go. I've got somebody on the way right now. *Right now*, Sara." She heard the screeching of tires in the distance. "It'll be all right."

"You say that...!" She tapped into the phone. ***Ron sending ppl now you OK?***

"They'll be there in five minutes, I promise—I sent them to the address Michael Ivey had in the files, is that right? Is that the right address?" he repeated as she stared at the phone.

OK but need somebody NOW

"Yes or no, right address?"

She nodded.

"They'll be there in five minutes. I called a couple of my guards who weren't on duty tonight, and the ones you heard—"

"How'd they get away so fast?"

"They were at the main gate. They always are. Listen: They're always around; you know what we do here, I can't have my employees in danger, so after everybody arrives—"

"Okay. Okay." She shuddered, typed again. ***Ron says 5 min.***

K. They've left. I'm all right. Stay where you are.

It was the most coherent and easiest to understand so far. She dialed Rheta, but the voicemail picked up.

Matheson heard the recording. "She's probably got somebody else on the line. If she's answering, she's okay. Right? Think about it."

He had grasped her shoulders, she realized—when had that happened, she didn't know, but she shook off his hands and read another text: **Stay at MTE. Don't come out here. I'm all right**.

"Does she own a gun?" he asked.

"No idea."

"Well, she's telling you what I'm telling you. I don't know what that means, 'Your name's here, too,' but she's telling you you might be in danger if you get on the road to her apartment, so don't." His phone rang, and he stepped aside and talked quietly into it.

"Okay, my guys have the police following them; they were going pretty fast, probably blew through a speed trap at city limits, but that's good—more help on the way, huh? So pretty soon your sister'll have a giant block party in her yard." He looked back toward the tables, the people gathered with food on plates on their laps, many of them turned toward him and Sara. "We're attracting attention. I don't want any more crap starting up. Would you turn and kind of hold your hands up and shrug, try to look as if, I don't know, somebody played a prank—like you just got a big old round ceramic thing from a crazy man, maybe."

She performed the skit as he asked—shrugged, pulled her mouth into a thin sort of smile, and started walking back. "Please call those guys again."

"I will in a minute. But, first, you aren't going to like it, probably, but you should go to the guest quarters. When everybody sees your face, they're gonna know something's wrong. I don't want Matthew batshit crazy. Or anybody else. I know you have to talk to Rheta. You can make all the calls you need to from there, nobody'll hear you, you won't have to explain anything, and you won't be on the road with whoever was at her house. Is your stuff in your car?"

"My purse."

"Then drive your car over to the guest house."

"I don't know where—"

"I'll get somebody to go with you," he interrupted. "Soon as I can, I'll find out what happened, but if she says it's dangerous for you to be there, then you don't need to leave. So we're going to tell people your aunt called—does Matthew know she's moved?"

"Yes."

"Good. He and Jennifer'll have Cary with them later, so she'll be all right. So we're going to say your aunt called and heard something outside her new place, and it turned out to be, what, raccoons knocking garbage cans over? I've heard that's a thing in town. But you have to check on her because she's elderly. Believable?"

She nodded numbly.

"I'm going to get someone you know—Eliot—he'll go with you to the guest house. Drive over there and he'll let you in. Lock the door and stay there for now. We'll get you home later. Okay?"

The phone buzzed. **Ron's goons here arguing with cops. Neighbors writing a petition about me.** He took it from her and laughed softly. "She's fine. But where can she go?"

"She won't leave—she's tough."

"Windows broken and who knows what done to her apartment, police'll put up tape, start rummaging around, collecting evidence. She can't stay there overnight. You have other relatives?"

"Mother—but, no, Mother can't get mixed up in this. My house. Can we send her to my house with one or two of your people?"

"Yeah, that'll do. She wouldn't sleep at her apartment, even if things got boarded up, even if the police would let her, which they won't."

"She won't be able to sleep anywhere."

"Probably not. Tell her I'll take care of boarding up the windows."

She sent that comment on.

"But I don't like this crap about 'your name'... How's your house registered? Could somebody find you on the Internet?"

She scoffed.

"Yeah. But then, my guards'll be there.... Did you hear what I said for you to do? You don't look like you're paying attention."

"I'm worried about her!"

"Yeah, well, I am, too, but right now, as much about you as her. So tell me what you're gonna do. Say it."

They had stopped away from the people still glancing at them once in a while. She felt exposed, wanted to leave. "You're going to get this guy, this Eliot, that you say I know—"

"You've met him."

"I don't think so, but, anyway: He'll drive with me to the guest house, and I'm locking myself in and talking with Rheta, and Cary's going with Matthew, and somebody'll bring Rheta to my house?"

"One of the guys'll get her there. They were obviously targeting her, her apartment. But maybe she'll rest, or feel safe, or something, at your place. And somebody will get you home later."

His phone rang again. He turned his back to her and spoke brusquely into it, held it out then, looked at it in disgust. "And the cops want to know if my guards are really my guards. They have my private number, so now it'll be all over town. So I get another phone." He tapped a message and looked hard at her. "Are you okay? You know I'm trying to get it worked out for everybody's safety, for tonight, and if you're good with everything I've said, we have to put on a show, right now, because even more people are watching us."

"I guess so," but she really wasn't. The adrenalin was wearing off, now that Rheta was safe. She gasped, stumbled. He took her arm. "I left the back door open, I think. Didn't mean to, but since she doesn't have a key to my house…"

"Always lock your doors," he preached solemnly.

She walked beside him back to the tables, where expectant, curious faces gazed at them, and they told the fiction, people laughed at Louise's expense, Matheson and Thomas shared one quick, meaningful, grim look, and she smiled wanly and left.

"Ms. Wells, I'm sorry this's happened. Let's hope it's as close as you ever get to something really blowin' up on you," Eliot said as he slid into the passenger side of her car.

She took a closer look. "Sorry I was rude to you at the park earlier this year," she told him.

24

RHETA HAD TEXTED Joe after the first rock hit her front door: **Get the cops over to my place.** She told Sara they'd been more or less expecting something for a while and had agreed they were each other's first call. "And this is much, much worse than anything when Ransome shut down his farm. I never knew there was anybody around here who really despised, I mean really had it in for me, but there are, and something set 'em off tonight. Or maybe they been planning for a while, who knows. Joe and I believe it's those 'MAP' thugs, but there're other people who don't seem to mind hanging out with them sometimes. It's kind of shocking," she chattered on in a weak voice.

She'd crouched down behind her triple-locked door, but the glass shattering in the entryway windows had terrified her. Then there were torches—"Those goddamned things people use at parties, and they stuck 'em in the grass all blazing, and a sign next to 'em with those numbers and my name, and yours, too. That's when I knew you'd have to get Ron involved. You said you'd be over there tonight, I knew he'd have his security. Cops weren't in any big hurry. They had their Friday-night speed traps to monitor," she continued bitterly. "The two D's wouldn't've ever let that slide." Sara didn't know who she was babbling about. Then she chortled, rather shrilly: "But Ron's guys gave 'em hell when they all got here."

The guest house was a shed-type building, with a loft and one full-height glass wall that showcased a view of the lake, a large sofa situated to take in that view. She wondered if the sofa made into a bed—probably, if it was actually a guest house. A tiny bathroom filled the dead space under steep steps that ascended to a loft, and next to the bathroom a stacked washer and dryer; and the little leftover space downstairs housed a kitchenette with fridge, microwave, coffeemaker, stove, café-style table with several high stools. Talking to Rheta, she paced back and forth, even going up to the loft and observing the night view of the lake, though in her state the landscape didn't register on her. A security light glittered on the water; she turned from it and crept down the stairs.

Rheta told her she'd be fine at Sara's house with one of the security guys. Sara told her to go through the back door.

"You left it open, you idiot? Louise really was your guardian angel, you never appreciated it. But I'm glad you left it open, tonight, because Ron's man won't have to break in."

She was gathering a few things as they talked—her computer, some clothing. Sara told her to eat whatever she found, use Sara's toiletries, watch a good movie.... Rheta guffawed at that, then suddenly stopped and kept listing what she was bringing. Sara checked the lock of the guest house again. You *are* an idiot, she scoffed: Ron's people are probably around, here and there, at the gatehouse, in places you'd never think of.

She'd already texted Cary to say everything was okay; Cary'd accepted that without question, maybe buying into the drama she and Ron had acted out...probably not; probably she'd already seen things on her phone. She'd even texted Louise, since she'd lied on her: *I'll explain, but if anybody calls with questions, just to let you know, it's fine.*

They both fell silent after Rheta said to someone else, "Okay, I have what I need," and she realized they'd been chattering for a while. The guard's answer was that Matheson had someone coming tonight to cover the windows. Sara heard a deep sigh, then, "Okay, I guess we can go. You riding with me?" and another brief exchange between two other voices as one finally said, "I'll stay here." Then a subdued Rheta asked her: "You good? You gonna be okay?"

"Are *you*? Nothing happened to me."

"Oh, something happened to you. You just don't have the sign in your yard. But something definitely happened to you." Sara heard another ragged breath, then, "I'll text when we get there. I know you don't have any booze, so I'll guess I'll have to make do with juice."

"Yes, you will. Love you." She pressed the disconnect button and sat down on the bottom rung of the steps, shaking.

IN A BIT she decided to look into the cabinets and fridge and found some cheese and, in the freezer, half a loaf of bread. She'd been too nervous to eat much, earlier, but the trembling had to stop, and maybe a sandwich would help. There were utensils in cabinet drawers, and soon she'd thawed the bread and was perched on a stool, eating. Rheta texted her: **Here. We're partying and wrecking your house**. Sara sent a smiley. When the keypad beeped and the lock slid back on the door, she leaped up, grabbed the knife she'd just used.

Wide-eyed, Matheson laid half a lemon pie on the table. "Should've knocked. Sorry."

She put the knife down, flexed her shaking hands. "Or texted, or just called your name, or something. Geez."

"You found things to eat, that's good. I saw you didn't enjoy the food. Didn't think there'd be much here. I brought this pie, what was left of it." He eyed her sandwich, dragged one of the stools up to the table and propped his chin on his hands. With the knife she gestured toward the cheese.

"Nope." He stared down at the table, something like despondence on his face, an expression she'd never seen on him before. She knew he wasn't a young man, but right now he looked old, exhausted. "One of my IT guys thinks an employee probably got the whole thing going. One of those people that were all agitated earlier—you were right, Ken was right, they told some of their friends what Ken said earlier, and some of those people put it on social media, and before you know it, there you are: The snakes crawled out of their holes, had their fun for the evening. They might be on the sidewalk next to you tomorrow, and you'd never know it, because they only do this when they think nobody's gonna catch 'em."

"Oh, God, the other day I had a moment like that." —In Neil's office...

"The police don't know who was at Rheta's, because folks stayed in while all that shit was going on. So, no ID. And then they left, and all anybody knows is the usual: dark sedan, older make. It was night. Torches look better at night, you know.

"My guy says there was chatter on some websites, and it started after the uproar, before we ate. Don't say it—" he interrupted her. "I can't fire people for what I've let them do, encouraged them to do, all this time. Know what I did, when we were cleaning up? I made a statement."

"Did you whistle again?"

"No, the megaphone that time. And I thanked everybody for their work, and hoped they'd all had a good evening, and appreciated the help putting things back in order, and then I asked them please to get along. Just get along. They're all in it together."

"My high-school gym teacher: C'mon, guys, show respect. How'd they take that?"

"They were quiet, clapped a little. Sort of embarrassed. Like you said, I got it going, and they didn't want it to stop. It's energy in the air, when people gang up together and know they've got each other's back. People'll say anything when they're not accountable. I didn't hold anybody accountable. Know what your sister told me it was?"

She did: She remembered what Rheta'd said; but she didn't really want to repeat it now. Matheson didn't see her hesitate, went on: "She called it free speech—but, just, on my terms."

She tried to think of a way to contradict that, or at least ameliorate it...gave up. Nothing.

He left the stool and stared out the glass wall into the night, his hands braced on the windows as if he were pushing against a barricade. "Also, Joe Sims texted me. Seemed to be really mad, at least, what he calls mad. About damn time; he's been well told off just lately, by several people. He said he might have to endorse Lynne, might go after Logan."

" 'Might.' "

" 'Might.' Maybe he thought he couldn't, in the past—small readership area, can't afford to lose your audience. Interference from the publishers that own it... This wasn't my idea of how I'd like for things to change."

She finished the sandwich, put the pie into the refrigerator, gazed at his back. "Ken told me something a long time ago."

"Hey, look what you just called him." There was no humor in his words. She went on:

"When I first talked with him. He said he owned Scarlett O'Hara, he said all Atlanta had to own her. You realize now you own *us*? Maybe you didn't intend to, but you do. So, about Joe?"

"I offered anything he wanted, or needed, but he told me to stay the hell out of it. He has a few regrets." He turned, put his back to the glass wall. "Some bad stuff's coming out before long. You ready for it?"

"You mean, about you? Neil did that research, just like you said he would, and gave me a copy." She shrugged.

"I don't care about that. There's other stuff. I don't think you know."

"What're you talking about?"

He gestured distractedly. "Let's not go there tonight. This's bad enough. I've been worried about your sister. Told you I was, last week. I'm glad you were here, and not at home, or at her place. I'm responsible for what happened."

"You're not responsible. People do things, they make their own decisions, they don't have to. They could *not* do something just as easily as do it."

"I am responsible. Time for me to admit it."

"But nothing terrible happened. Anyway..." She dreaded bringing it up, but better now from her, if he hadn't thought of it himself: "Anyway, you're gonna have plenty on your own to deal with. It'll be on the news, and you're a big company, and you're here where it happened. You may change your mind about locating in Mooresville."

He stared at her; she saw the same obstinance she'd seen weeks ago one morning on the deck at MTE. "I don't give in to that kind of shit. That's not who I am. Would *you*?"

Nobody knows what they'd do until they have to decide, she started to remind him, but he'd see that facile comment for what it was. She asked instead, "Why didn't Rheta want me to go to her apartment?"

"After those thugs left, who knew where they were? They'd found out you're her sister, so maybe they even know what car you drive. They could've been waiting for you to show up. Maybe they knew where you were." He paused, swore. "Which somebody might've passed on tonight."

"I don't think any of your employees expected this to happen."

"No, they just got mad, but they helped it along. They kept it going. You said that, earlier tonight—tonight!—I could've played the boss and put a stop to it, but I didn't." He closed his eyes and leaned wearily against the glass. "I don't want you to go home."

"Have one of your security people follow me or something. I'll be okay."

She'd been pacing again, nearer and nearer the door, and he moved towards her and drew her against him. "I don't want you to go home tonight. It's not just your safety. You know?"

SHE DID KNOW, when she'd driven over to the guest house. It was a decision, her decision. In a part of her mind she heard Rheta saying, *Just about any human being is better than none.*

But when his arms tightened, his hands moved on her back, she pulled away, and he sighed. "You know I'm the least of your problems right now. All right. I'll follow you home myself. I'd rather you stay and not risk anything. You know Cary's fine, and Rheta's got more protection around her than she probably even wants. I'd like you to stay here, and me to stay here. But let's go. I'll take one of the company cars."

Her phone rang. Startled, her nerves shattered from all that had happened, she scampered to pick it up from the table. It was a number she didn't have in her contacts, and she stared, and the ringing continued. Matheson took it from her, answered angrily: "Hello? Who's calling? Who is this?"

A hesitation, and then, even with Matheson holding the phone at his ear, she could hear shrill words coming from the speaker.

"Wait a minute, would you, here she is." Ron passed it to her.

"Sara. Chris. Chris Liberto. I got your number from Lisa. Where's Rheta? Is she all right?"

"She's okay. She's shook-up. But one of Ron's security people's staying with her, so—"

"Where is she? I went over to her place when I heard, and there're policemen, and tape all over, and lights—" He stopped.

"Everybody knows already?"

"There were sirens, and a car chase, so, sure, everybody knows. Lisa gave me your number. So is she in ER, where is she?"

She interrupted him: "Calm down. I said she's okay. There's tape and all that because windows were broken, but she's not there, she's at my house."

"With you?"

"No." She looked briefly at Matheson, who seemed to be interpreting the conversation. "I was at MTE with Cary, one of their picnics, when it happened, and I'm here for right now; they don't want me out on the road yet, because they don't know—"

"Where the bastards are, yeah. So she's not hurt."

"She wants a drink, and you know there's none in my house." She had a sudden thought: "Now, that's something—"

But he interrupted again, and words poured out, and she held the phone away from her ear as he said, "You don't know what went through me when I heard about it. I know what she does, it's always scared me to death, but not like tonight, I thought I wouldn't see her again, when I heard, and I didn't know—"

She glanced at Matheson and saw a grin appearing on his face. "Chris!" she yelled. "Shut up! I know what you should do, okay? You through?"

The voice stopped, and he said, "Yes."

"Run by somewhere and get a bottle of wine. Just wine, and take it to my house. I'll tell her to let you in. She'll be glad to see you, and, well... 'Bye, Chris. Get the wine."

She tapped a brief message to Rheta: *Chris is coming with*

booze; wait for him, and laid the phone down, and a strange hysterical laughter burst out of her. She sat on the bottom step and put her face in her hands, looked up and saw Matheson watching, waiting for her to become herself again.

"Please don't go home. And I don't want to go home either. Okay?"

25

THE SUN COMING through the glass woke her up. Light streamed through the windows, heating up the loft.

She stirred, twisted to look out and winced at the unexpectedly glittering water of the lake, dazzling her eyes like tinsel flashing, the strobe of an emergency vehicle.

And there was a warm body next to her in the bed. She looked at that salt-and-pepper, too-long hair above his shoulders. He was on his side; the soft breath of deep sleep was regular and, in a way, soothing as a white noise machine.

She lay flat on her back, now wide awake, staring up at the heavy, low beams overhead in the loft, and tugged the oversized T-shirt down on her thighs. He'd rummaged around to find her something to put on after she'd awakened about four o'clock, shivering, but, as she told him, not from cold, but because she never slept naked. He'd thrown drawers open, grumbling until he came upon the enormous old Red Sox jersey and gave it to her. "See if that works. I'd like to sleep," he told her. Then he'd laughed: "God, we sound like an old married couple." And he dozed off again.

She sucked in a gasp now, thinking of those words, and he rolled over suddenly, staring at her. "Do you ever sleep? It can't be seven yet."

She looked at the phone. "Six-thirty," she told him.

"Gotta wonder if Rheta's doing this to Chris," he griped.

She gasped again and stared upward, her thoughts turned now to last night.

"Well, again I said the wrong thing," he remarked softly, "but it was going to come back up in a while."

He threw himself off his side of the mattress, pulled on his shorts, clambered down the steep stairs—really just a ladder, she thought, remembering having navigated it several times last night. In a few moments he had coffee brewing and music going on some kind of player.

She picked up the phone again, called down: "You have a charger?"

"Nope. Left it in the main building," he said, raising his voice from below. "Yours dead? Use mine."

That was too comfortable and familiar right now. She couldn't do it. She squinted at the screen, saw it was about twenty percent, and tapped to ask Rheta if she was all right. Then, when no response immediately came back, but her battery bar slid over to eighteen, she left the bed herself and headed downstairs.

"Where's a landline?"

He'd made toast and was pulling out a few half-full jars of assorted jams from the fridge, lining them up meticulously with the labels outward for her to read. "There's not one."

"Inconvenient guest house," she remarked.

He turned one of those looks her way, as when it seemed he was trying to figure something out. "There's a direct line to my office. Upstairs. You can call from there and get the answering service and they'll forward your call."

And then it'll show up on Rheta's phone where I am, she thought. "Why don't you keep a regular line here?"

"Don't preach at me. Everybody's got a cell phone. It's not my fault if people don't bring their chargers with them."

"It's not *my* fault having to share company with an inconsiderate host," she smarted back. She nudged him aside and looked over the regimentally-ordered collection he'd spread out. "OCD a little?"

"I don't keep it stocked, and I haven't stayed, myself, in, oh, a couple of months. So, not much to eat."

Then she remembered Thomas mentioning to her one time when Matheson had spent the night here. She sat on one of the stools, pulled the T-shirt under her thighs. "Did you have company then, too?"

He leaned over the table and met her gaze. "I did not. I haven't had 'company' in some time. A long time," he added, reaching now for spoons. "You're asking if I sleep around. I do not. I'm too old for that. You are, too. I'm sure Neil Griffin's papers filled in the gaps you didn't know already. If he did it right, that material petered out at a few years ago." He found plates and gave her one. "Lighten up. It's just us. Nobody else. Nobody from the past."

They decided to eat outside at a table installed near the building. By then it was on towards seven, and pine warblers and towhees were calling and hopping around in the trees. The coffee was quite good, she told him, and the toast was, well, filling.

"Be glad we have anything at all. I haven't brought groceries here in a while."

She heard the faint sound of a car passing down the road, but it was far away: He'd sited the cabin so that it felt isolated, all by itself out in a pine forest.

"When did you build this?"

His eyes roamed up the high glass wall. "Four years ago. Not long after we opened."

"Did you stay here a lot yourself then?"

"Not as much as I'd have liked. I'd bought a house outside of town—you know that development, high-end, close to the college." She drove past it every evening she taught. It was where Neil lived, and David and Nora Burkes—most of the people who'd run the town all their lives. "A good investment, but I sold it, anonymously; you wouldn't have heard about it," he went on. "I have some acres west of here, too, and I had a small house built there after I got rid of the other one." He tossed a piece of crust out underneath the pines. "Sign I'm getting old: I like small now. I'd stay here more, if people weren't able to figure out when I did, and start hanging around late and coming over here with problems for me to look at after regular hours. Damn engineers, never leave stuff at work."

A soft mocking noise escaped her.

"I know. But see where it got me?"

"People would say, 'Pretty far.' "

"Yeah, they would. They'd say that." He watched the glittering water.

"So you like the woods," she said in a moment. "Aren't you afraid somebody'll come along and cut down all the pines between here and town some day?"

"Not at all."

This rankled in her somehow. Everybody'd been shocked when Ransome had planted all those trees, but now they were there, a welcome green space in the landscape where there had been nothing but rows of different sorts of crops pointing to the horizon. "Really? You don't worry about getting here some morning, and skidders hauling out everything on that little rise, all the trees gone, to make room for a development?" She gestured to the east, where the pine barren stood thick at the edge of the trimmed lawn around the cabin.

"I own it. Well," he amended as she took a sharp breath, "the company owns it. I didn't want the whole road between us and town to turn into another strip mall, you know? It happens. You get a big-box business somewhere, the whole area fills up with crap. Ransome put the trees there to let you know he was detaching from Mooresville—"

"He what?"

He gave her a bemused, intense look. "None of you thought that? Well, he did; there was a lot more of the poet in Ransome, one time. He understood symbols. But, besides not wanting title-loan places and cheap motels all the way to town, I thought, that wasn't a bad idea of his. So I recommended buying all his land holdings."

She gazed at the trees. "All the way?"

"Well, it's not that far…what, five or six miles? People project their own motives onto other folks," he went on, "so the board of directors figured I wanted it all because of the timber, that one day I intended to sell it off—and I might not object to that, but not now; and it wasn't why I wanted it at the time. And if we do cut it, it'll be replanted right away. Our type of business…it's better having a buffer around us. You're looking at me like I'm insane."

"Just finding out things."

"Don't think I'm all that complicated. I keep my cards close. Can't afford not to. People know what you're doing, they throw up roadblocks. I like the trees, more as I get older; I'd like being here, in this house, except it didn't work out."

"Your engineers coming over all the time."

"Yeah. That. So, you gonna slop around in that shirt?"

"Who's sitting outside on lawn furniture in his drawers?" she retorted. "I'm covered, more or less."

A house sparrow flitted down to pick at the crusts; soon two others were there.

"I need to check on Rheta, really," she told him. "Do you mind fetching me that charger?"

"You won't use *my* phone? Everybody else in town probably knows the number by now, so why not her too? Actually, she's got it," he added. "Ransome gave it to her."

"Yeah, you told me."

"Stop smirking. Those interviews she did, she'd text me questions she hadn't thought of when we were together. Yeah, so just use it. If it bothers you, tell her you're using mine because yours's dead, and, by the way, that wouldn't be a lie, would it."

She didn't say, but Rheta'd ask why she even had Matheson's phone…she didn't want to go there; it would be worse than the company number showing up. "I probably ought to be with her."

"She's safe, she's got somebody, two somebodies, actually: my guard and another guy who'd lie down in front of a train for her. Yeah, go on and call her, say you're on the way. You wanna spoil it for them? You want me to text her and say your phone's not working? Or you could do it yourself and pretend to be me." He picked up his mug, frowned, put it back down. "You don't want her placing us together. That's it, isn't it."

She glared at him. "I could make up any story to explain that. She knows where I am."

"Does she know where *I* am, though?" he asked.

"Would you go get that damned charger, or I will, and if I trip the alarm, you'll be the one explaining to your guys why I'm wearing a Red Sox t-shirt and stealing the boss's device."

"I don't *want* to go to the office right now. Rheta's safe. Cary's safe. I'm enjoying being with you. After last night, I want a little peace for a while, and it's a nice morning, and you're being unreasonable!"

They laughed suddenly at each other. She finished the cup of coffee and the last piece of toast and watched the glittering reflection of the sun on the lake. He reached over and put his hand on top of hers on the table, and they said nothing for another few moments.

"I have to wash my clothes," she told him at last, "and get a shower, and you may as well bring me your things from yesterday, so we'll have a full washer." He followed her inside, took her mug and laid it next to his in the sink, and put his arms around her waist. "No reason to get up so early. Since our clothes'll be in the machine anyway, let's just lie down. We won't do anything; we'll just sleep. You do that sometimes, right?" He pressed a button beside the door and she saw that at one side of the glass wall there was a very tall curtain hanging that began moving on its mechanical track to cover the window.

"That cost you an arm and a leg, didn't it."

BUT THEY DIDN'T just sleep.

The washer was chugging away below the stairs later that morning. There had been a friendly quiet after they got out of bed again. She gathered his jeans and shirt and socks, and hers, from the night before, and he cleaned up in the kitchen, washing the plates and knives and coffee cups. They took turns in the tiny shower—"The one thing I regret about this place," he'd said—"this minuscule bathroom." He was rummaging around in the kitchen when she emerged wearing the Red Sox shirt again.

"There's not much for lunch, so we'll have to go into town. I believe we should show up together at Don's, surprise him...what do you think?" He raised his brows, and she said, "You like causing uproar."

She heard his phone ring, saw him step outside to talk, assumed it was business-related, but he was somber when he returned. She was shifting the clothing into the dryer when she realized he was standing near her, waiting. He set the timer himself; then, a quizzical expression on his face, said, "You okay with a speech along with lunch? I warn you, it might kill your appetite."

She shrugged. "What're you talking about?"

"That was Joe. Deborra Anderson called him a couple of hours ago." He gestured around in the cabin. "You don't see a TV, do you, because I won't have one here. If I'm here, I want peace and quiet."

"And so you enforce that on your out-of-town guests, too?" she asked pointedly.

"Not how I would've put it, but, yes, I guess so. Anyway, no TV. But Deborra and Joe've been 'invited'—" he sneered —"to a 'press conference', that's what it was called, in front of the Griffin building. Appropriate venue."

She didn't understand that, but her stomach tightened, her pulse sped up. "Who..."

"Oh, you know; I don't have to tell you. And we won't be able to watch from here because of my discourtesy to my guests, as you put it. Turns out there was a lot more chatter on social media last night than we, you and I, would've thought, and most of it's people saying Stephen Logan's responsible for what happened; and some actually *were* pissed and started picketing in front of his campaign place." He gave her another odd look and grasped her hand, tightly. "Including your daughter and her friends—"

She sucked in her breath. "Oh, hell, no, she *didn't*—"

"In one way you oughta be proud of her—"

"She's fourteen years old! She's grounded *forever*!" She pulled her hand away and paced back and forth between the kitchen and the door, the long curtains swirling around in the wake of her passage. "When was this going on? Who's with her?"

Matheson perched on one of the stools. "Chill, Sara. She's doing what she thinks is right, and remember, she probably found out what happened was aimed at you as much as at her aunt, so of course she's mad. Do you blame her?"

"How'd she get out of Matthew's house?"

He laughed incredulously. "Does he lock her in? He may not have known what she was going to do, but surely he doesn't run herd on her like that!"

That was true: Matthew didn't. She wondered if Jennifer had shared her news last night with them, wondered if Matthew had been so distracted by that news that he didn't think to ask where Cary was going with her friends. "I *told* you I needed my phone charged! I'm going to find out what the hell she thinks she's doing."

"You do what you believe you should; she's your daughter. But if anything'd happened to her, you know you'd've been told—your phone's not totally dead, a message would've been sent, or a phone call. People have my number, too. Rheta knows you're here. And, by the way, I said we'd be hearing a speech. Aren't you going to ask what that's about?"

"I don't care about that, when Cary—"

"She's not by herself; she and her *friends* aren't by themselves. There're people, twenty, twenty-five, out in front of Logan's office, or were when Joe called me, and Don's seeing to it they have all the iced tea they want." He stopped her frenetic patrolling by taking both her hands and standing in front of her. "She's well protected, trust me, and she's probably learning things—several things, some she doesn't like, but that's the way it is. I know Rheta did something similar a long time ago—"

"Yeah, and I don't want Cary to go through what she did!"

He pulled her to his chest and held her. "Your blood pressure's sky-high. Last night—that was another thing, that was real danger. But today this's different. Look, the clothes'll be dry in a few minutes. We'll leave, we'll go to town, we'll listen to whatever Stephen Logan's going to say. He called Deborra to make sure he had coverage, but Joe's already dropped by to take a few pictures. And if you want to say something to Cary, you can do it, but for God's sake, don't do it in front of her friends."

She knew his words were sensible. "I'm telling you, she's not getting by with this."

He fiddled with the dryer settings and turned the heat up, then climbed the steep stairs to the bedroom.

"I let everybody down," she went on, "I stayed here, with you, instead of being with Rheta, after what she'd gone through, and Cary's out, parading around town—"

"That sounds like streetwalking!" he protested from upstairs, as he ransacked the bureau and minuscule closet for another set of clothes for himself. He leaned over the loft's railing to glare down at her. "You think you have to watch her every minute of her life, you can't do anything on your own without worrying about her?"

"I should've been at home with her. I'm scared for her, for both of them! I should've taken her home and stayed with her and Rheta. But I stayed here with you!"

"You'd do better being scared if nobody in town *did* what they're doing. *That* would scare me." He descended several steps, clutching a pair of pants in one hand. "Wait a minute. You're guilting yourself about being with me, about going to bed with me?"

She didn't answer, and he seemed on the edge of saying something else, but didn't. He went back upstairs, and she stood for a moment, thinking about what he'd asked. She decided to search the bathroom cabinet for makeup someone might have left behind, stopped to consider what it would mean if she found any, then shrugged and used the half-empty bottle of light-colored foundation that turned up. It would have to do.

UNLOCKING HER CAR, she gave him an unhappy look.

"The sensible thing is not to have two cars in town."

She hesitated, because that was true, but it was another small concession she felt, somewhere inside, was leading her into commitments she didn't want to make.

"If you don't want me showing up with you, drive me to where we keep the company cars." He rolled his eyes. "This's ridiculous."

"Just get in or I'll take you up on that," she'd said.

She drove in silence, aware of his glances at her, as if he wanted to say or ask something but knew better, right then. He was on his phone some of the way, and she was fine with it, being desperately in need of a few moments' peace in which to think; but her thoughts flew around too much in her head, and before long they were near Main Street, and her heart was pounding again. There was a state-fair feel to the scene on the sidewalk as they strolled past Morris Jewelers, crossed the street, headed toward the nexus of the uproar. They waited for the light to change and stood on that corner watching the twenty or so people milling around in front of Neil's building down the next block. Matheson took a look at her face and grasped her hand. Startled, she tried to extract it— "We're not going to walk up holding hands like children!" she snapped at him.

"A little quieter, please? I'm only holding your hand to keep you from leaping in and gouging out eyes or yanking hair. Geez," he told her softly as the light changed and they stepped into the street, "I thought *I* had self-control issues."

"You have no idea what a scared mother is capable of."

"I *had* children, you know," he said. It was the first time he'd said the word. Neil's dossier hadn't mentioned offspring at all, she remembered, and Matheson himself had only talked about a son.

She spotted Cary in the group who shifted from foot to foot and then sometimes paced a wobbly circle in front of Logan's office on the broad sidewalk—broader there than the available area outside Liberto's, because there'd been no reason for anyone to socialize in the other place, and so there were no tables, umbrellas, railing to crowd the walking room. If Cary saw her, she didn't show it. Sara felt Ron's pace slowing, and with his hand firmly grasping hers, she was forced to slow down, too, until he pulled her to a halt at the right side of the restaurant. The protesters included a few older people, she saw, a minister, some college students, an instructor she recognized, and there were Cary and several of her pals. There was Lisa Liberto, in sweat pants and a Jerry Garcia T-shirt. And Charlie and Susan; she waved at them. They were all a polite bunch. When they weren't milling around, they kept their backs to the masonry wall to stay out of the way of the passers-by; when their occasional oval revolved in its cycle, it was mostly in silence, and they held up hand-lettered signs but didn't talk.

MAP=Mooresville Anti Progress
Stop Hate

After a while, on Cary's second revolution since they'd been there, Cary refusing to meet her eyes, she twisted Matheson's hand. He leaned into her face: "Hang on. Look—" and he nodded at one of the sidewalk tables where Rheta sat, dressed in jeans and an old plaid shirt of Sara's, her face obscured by an Auburn baseball cap with the bill tipped. In the clothing, with her short haircut, she looked like a man. Maybe that was her plan today.

"Told you," Ron continued. "She's probably been keeping an eye on her since she got here."

Rheta didn't see her and Matheson, and Sara had only a view of her back and hands…her hands were fidgeting with a tall glass of iced tea, her foot tapping at nothing, in the air. Sara thought it a well-earned karma that Rheta should be there, guarding her niece as she did her part to protest injustice.

"Let's sit down," Matheson said quietly. "Joe said Stephen wanted some press here about 1:00. That's in a while, and I'm hungry, anyway, so let's order something. Deborra'll be showing up first with her camera guy, I'm guessing. Look—" he gestured vaguely at the milling group— "there she is, and Joe'll probably just wander up the way he always seems to, as if he's just covering a crafts fair. So what do you want to eat?"

"Got your wallet today?" she asked.

His chin dropped for a few seconds before he laughed, and she took advantage of his surprise and yanked her hand away. There was a table toward the middle of the sidewalk area, not so close to Rheta. In a moment, a server appeared from the restaurant, menus in hand, and they asked for water.

The protesters had stopped their shambling walk and were once again leaning against the wall, or almost leaning. Cary steadfastly kept her eyes outward; and Rheta scrutinized the crowd, when she wasn't watching Cary.

"Why're they *here*? Why not go to the MAP people?"

"Funny thing. They don't seem to have a physical address. People assume whoever messed up Rheta's apartment last night wouldn't've done it without Logan's guidance, so these folks"— he gestured—"chose this place."

She played with her water glass, reached for her phone to glance through those messages again, but it was nearly dead now.

"Don't," Matheson said quietly. "It'll stay with you if you keep looking." She shoved it back into her purse.

One side of the heavy old doors opened to their left, and Don bustled out pulling a cart loaded with paper cups of water and tea. Breezing past Rheta, whom he didn't acknowledge beyond a nudge with his elbow as he passed her, he handed the cups to whoever called for them in the group of sign-holders. A few of the clientele hanging around the edge of the sidewalk clapped when he yelled, "Stephen, you thirsty?" Finished with the distribution, he was barreling back toward the front entrance when he saw Sara. "What are you two doing here—together, again?"

She grimaced at him as Rheta's head now turned away from the group who sipped their water, and toward their table. She lifted the brim of the Auburn hat, winked once, and went back to her monitoring.

"There was performance art last night, Don, I'm sure you heard," Matheson told him. "A fire show. So I've been told there'll be a speech today, too. More street performance. Can you get us some of whatever you got a lot of in there? We're hungry."

"I'll find something. I'd really just as soon not have this right in front of my place. Whatever they film, whatever pictures they take, there'll be my awnings, and my sign, and my customers. Like I arranged it all."

"Good crowd, though," Matheson reminded him.

Don sent out a couple of subs with sausage and provolone and salami. The number of people hanging out on any fine spring Saturday would have been pretty large, but today the crowd was growing by the minute in an atmosphere like a long line for an amusement park ride. Sara took a bite of her sandwich. "Let me have your phone. Please."

If he heard the resigned tone in her voice, he didn't gloat, but only handed it over. She texted Rheta, *Is everybody here because of S L?*, and got an immediate answer: **Yep. Your boyfriend there made sure folks knew.**

Boyfriend???

There was no response; she stared at the back of the Auburn cap. Before handing Ron his phone, she deleted those messages.

"I didn't have that much to do with it," he mumbled. "And I was reading over your shoulder."

She didn't look at him, fearing what she might see on his face. Was that what he was now, her boyfriend? She felt removed from the whole place, removed from him: How, in less than twenty-four hours, could things have changed so, become so dangerous with entanglements and connections? The sunlight felt too bright, the people shuffling around in front of her looked jerky and machinelike. She wondered if it was a type of PTSD, wondered what dissociation felt like, if she had that because her brain had decided it was just too much to cope with.

They ate in silence, watching people approach the restaurant and linger as a quiet chatter pervaded the area. She wanted to tell them to go home, they were only giving Logan what he wanted— free publicity—to continue his momentum. Lynne! She hadn't even thought of Lynne since yesterday and now wondered if her candidate was at the shop, or was canvassing, or at home, or what. She snatched Matheson's phone again, found he had Lynne's number, and tapped a note, explaining why it wasn't her phone, and asking if she knew about what was happening.

When a reply came, Matheson read the screen.

"I'll be back," he said, and he dashed away.

She started to protest, *Why? What's up now?* but resumed observing the protesters, seeing that a few new people had joined them, and that some Logan supporters were arguing with the others. She picked up on the words now and then: *He didn't have anything to do with that... You're just losing, and you want to make it controversial... This is free speech, and you can't do a thing about us...*

Two policemen showed up, alert but for now only watchful, and accepted cups of tea that hadn't been claimed.

In a few moments Matheson eased back into his chair, speaking in a very low voice. "There were some people in front of Lynne's place, too. Kind of the opposite from what's here. You can use your imagination about *their* signs. She wasn't there. Shop was closed.

She said she was out ringing doorbells. I told her to keep doing that. Better than being here, seeming to *listen* to him, to be worried about him..." He shoved his phone at Sara, gave her a quizzical look. "Did I do right?"

She nodded, shivering though it was a warm afternoon.

"I told Joe. He's on his way, but he and one of the reporters are going to detour by her shop and snap a few photos. He said if they were people he knew—and he figured some of 'em would be—that'd probably be enough to send 'em home. They wouldn't want their pictures on the front page of the paper tomorrow."

In another moment, she noticed Jared Brown and Joe on the other side of the street, near the entrance to the Griffin Burkes Law Firm; maybe they'd come down that side to avoid the crowd in front of Don's. Last night Ron had said Joe was finally mad, but she didn't see that on his face this afternoon, but only a kind of blank watchfulness.

Suddenly she remembered and looked up at the second floor. There she noticed an occasional movement behind one of the windows where blinds had been raised.

MATHESON TAPPED HER hand and pointed.

The front door of Logan's campaign office had opened, and Logan emerged. Crisp light-blue button-down shirt, nice slacks, casual loafers, hair brushed away from his forehead and probably gelled, she thought. In any place, he'd be regarded as a nice-looking guy with a pleasant smile. Joe and Jared had crossed the street and shouldered their way into the group of protesters that now faced Logan in a semicircle, waving their handmade signs in the air; Cary stood behind the first row, and Allie next to her.

"Everybody here contribute to my campaign? If you haven't, I've got receipts handy." Some people laughed.

She almost gasped: He was so smooth, so trained, she thought. She glanced at Matheson, as always doing his analyzing, assessing.

Deborra Anderson and her guy were already recording; she stepped forward. "Mr. Logan, you let the newspaper and us at the station know you wanted to make a statement about last night's events, where a group of people, not apprehended as of yet, vandalized the home of a local journalist, apparently in an effort at intimidation."

"Whoa, Deborra." Still smiling, he shook his finger. "Let me get a word in. I know what happened, and I came out here to say I deplore this kind of thing. Like everybody else in town. Mooresville can't tolerate things like this. But not just by one group, but all of them—" He gestured at the protesters in front of the building.

Her expression stayed the same. "This seems like a peaceful protest. *That* group, last night, planted torches and signs with white-supremacist symbols on the journalist's lawn, and windows were broken. One of the signs also had a sticker your campaign's distributed."

Joe, Sara noticed, was scribbling on a notepad; Jared, holding out his phone and recording.

"If you'd let me talk," Logan complained. "I said, was going to say, we don't condone stuff like that, and I assure you in no way is my campaign connected with it. Any materials of mine that turned up on the signs weren't handed out by me—"

"Nobody's suggesting you gave them anything directly, but that is your campaign literature. You've seen the pictures?"

He frowned. "I don't deny somebody took those things and used them, but I had nothing to do with it."

"People have said by accepting endorsements and contributions from hate groups, you're encouraging their actions, like last night. Could you disavow those groups today?"

In Stephen Logan's mind a picture flashed up, a momentary glimpse from his past of an overweight, tired old sheriff and a sarcastic young deputy keeping him in an off-balance chair and trying to get him to talk too much.... "I've reached out to all people in Mooresville. The other side wants you to believe we're divided, but that's not because of me. They think that, they want you to buy into this idea, that if you aren't with them, you're going backwards. I remind you, the people who built this community did it without tearing down things we love about our town."

Deborra was persistent: "So will you disavow those groups that promote messages of division and racism, like MAP, will you return their contributions and separate your campaign from those groups?"

"Some very patriotic people belong to—you do know what the letters stand for, right?"

"I do," she managed to say, before he went on: "It's 'Mooresville Associated Patriots.' They're patriots. You don't want them to have free speech, but this group"—waving again at the people who stood near his door—"can? And I'm to understand you think there's something wrong with that kind of person, a patriotic group, a group that wants the best for their country, you think there's something wrong with the name?" he railed. The crowd murmured, but—Sara noticed—listened. He waved dismissively at Anderson. "You're like the other media, all of you biased, always taking that other side. I've just come to expect it of *you*."

Sara remembered Ron's words again: ***You never gave it any thought.*** Deborra' father had been the first Black man to serve the community college as president. One thing Ron had penned in the op-ed back in March was that some people's voices weren't always heard, and the community should come to terms with that. She noticed Deborra still didn't react, but she felt rather than saw it when Ron stood up. Deborra turned at the movement, and so did Logan.

"And I wondered if Mr. Matheson would show up today, getting involved as he will do. The town did okay without you, Sir, or we would've figured it out eventually on our own, in spite of all your helpful suggestions. In fact, I hope you've noticed nothing violent happened before you got here. Maybe your type of 'help' causes division."

"What I want to know is why've you always had a free pass about your police record? I think a good look's overdue. And there definitely *was* stuff before I got here. You know what it was."

"Yeah, a while back, Miss Deborra said the same thing, and just like I told her then, we've all done things when we were young—you too, Mr. Matheson, and I'm sure yours wouldn't stand inspection, either."

"I'm not running for office."

"Oh, that's right, you're exempt from that, media won't touch you, which is fine, because by now people know you anyway."

"What I want out of the media," Ron interrupted, "is for them to find out what you're getting from those groups, find out what you paid to get out of that legal mess a few months ago, or who paid it for you, find out what you're hiding."

Rheta suddenly adjusted the Auburn hat again. Logan looked past her, didn't see her, but answered Ron: "Go on and throw your money around, put it into Lynne Houston's campaign, a woman who doesn't represent the town any more than you do, a woman who spent the last several months raising hell just to keep people stirred up—that's about the only thing she's good at, raising hell, but you're gonna lose this one. You got your newest girlfriend here today, I notice, local lady; she'd benefit from some investigation into *your* past," and Sara shrank into her chair, saw Cary edge backwards in the semicircle.

Matheson twitched but didn't answer that. He turned to Joe, scowling. In all the uproar, Sara realized Joe'd stayed discreetly behind a couple of people, silently scribbling in that old-school notepad he carried, and now he turned away from Matheson and lifted his hand. "I'd like for all of you who still read my rag—"

"Have no choice, Joe, no other paper here!" someone yelled good-naturedly.

"You who read it will want to pick up a copy tomorrow morning as we make an announcement we haven't done in many long years. It's a good buy, two dollars," he added in his Southern drawl, "there're some good ads in it. And," he held up a forefinger, "remember, we're running all the graduates tomorrow, so you'll want, really, three copies! Maybe four!"

A general aura of relief washed through the crowd, people laughed and began to straggle away; but to Sara it didn't seem the right thing for Joe to have done. It seemed a distraction to entertain them. Logan and Matheson locked eyes. A couple more steps brought Ron almost face-to-face with him; a few protesters edged forward as if in support, or, Sara wondered, as if they were kids in high school about to see a good fight. The tense smile stayed on Ron's face. "Don't mess with people I care about, and don't encourage any of your thugs to, either."

"You care so much about some media person who does hit pieces on you like she does everybody else? This has-been?" He glanced at Rheta. "Or just her sister that's more famous now than she is?"

So he'd found out, since the day of the speeches. She figured he would; and, after all, those signs at Rheta's apartment…she'd told Sara both their names were on them last night. Or maybe he'd remembered, from long ago, himself.

Matheson loomed one step nearer. Deborra motioned toward the camera guy; Logan noticed and, Sara realized, thought of publicity. "You threatening me?"

The two stared each other down. Matheson scoffed as he

turned away. "That's all I have to say. For now. For now."

Sara sat down, trembling—when had she jumped up? she didn't even know. The remains of the sub in front of her seemed greasy and withering, her water glass sweating in long rivulets on the table, and at first she didn't notice Cary standing beside her.

"Mom? You okay?" She patted Sara's hand. "You all right?" And they grabbed at each other in a shaking, squeezing hug, and she swung Cary down partly onto her lap, teenager though she was, and she looked over Cary's shoulder and saw Rheta's cup overturn as she came to her feet, grabbed Matheson's arm, her face blotched, questioning. Rivulets of iced tea streamed across the table and onto her sneakers. He shook off her grip, grimaced, looked away from her. Sara heard his words, though they weren't directed at her: "Well, that didn't work."

26

CARY TOLD HER she was going to Allie's house for a while. "Because I think Dad and Jennifer want the afternoon alone," she said, and Sara couldn't tell if there was sarcasm or relief in the words. And she didn't ask if Jennifer had told her news.

"Hi, Mr. Matheson," she added, eyeing him with curiosity.

And Sara didn't pull away this time from Ron's hand as they walked back to her car—it steadied her, gave her a firm thing to hang onto. She hadn't eaten enough since Friday afternoon—but it wasn't just that. He asked if she wanted him to drive, and without thinking, "No!"...and then she said, "Yes," and handed him the keys: It wasn't any different from Lisa taking the wheel sometimes, if Sara'd had that other glass of wine, no different.... She stared out the window as the fields and, then, trees disappeared behind her shoulder as he navigated the streets, heading back to the country and the pine forest.

"You're really quiet. I won't ask if something's wrong, because, obviously, everything's wrong," he remarked, "or, lots is wrong."

"I feel like I've been hijacked. Like I don't have any control over what's going on in my own life. A windstorm's come up and

I'm in the funnel, being dragged along."

After that, the rest of the way, he drove without saying anything, without looking at her. At the gatehouse he sent a code over his phone and eased through when the bar raised, then took a left onto the narrow drive to the cabin.

"Aren't you going to get a company vehicle, like you said?" she asked. "You're going to stay here without a car?"

He sucked in a deep breath and killed the engine, turned in the driver's seat to face her. "If I need a car, I can walk over. But I thought *we* would stay here, and *we* would have your car if we needed one. I assumed since you handed me the keys... I should've asked."

"I'm going home." She knew what she'd see in his face even before his expression changed. "I'm going to make sure Rheta's okay, and I'm going to my own house. I'm guessing your guys are out of there by now."

"You just saw Rheta. You know she's okay." His voice was still very quiet.

"I just saw Rheta, so I know she's *not* okay. And I'm not okay."

"And neither am I. Things happened, and I have no control over them, either, couldn't do a damned thing about it—I had to just stand and watch." He stopped.

"You didn't go through what Rheta did."

"Don't judge me. I know I didn't. I know I didn't go through what you did. But I'm not okay. I started something—or let it blow up without trying to stop it, like you warned me, and so I'm responsible. You got it? You know? Let me wallow in a little self-pity."

She smiled a little.

"I'll drive over to the office and get that charger, and you can talk to her all you want."

"I'm going home, and I'll take you wherever you need to go, the main building, to get a car, even to your house, but I'm going to *mine*."

"You'll be there by yourself."

"No, I won't. She'll be there, and maybe Chris, and possibly even your security person. I won't be by myself."

"But I *will*!" he blurted, then closed his eyes and took another deep, slow breath.

The lake glittered in the broad of day, making her blink and squint.

"So, this with us, it's just, that's all it was for you?"

"I don't really know what it was, for me or you."

"Either of us, we could find somebody else—wouldn't be hard, I've done it, so have you. But I don't wanna do it anymore. I'm tired of it." Another pause, another count to five. "I don't do one-night stands. I can't do that now."

"I have to go home, Ron. I have stuff to figure out."

He played with the steering wheel, then executed a neat three-point turnaround, opened the driver's-side door, stepped out. "I'll walk the rest of the way. Be careful on the road, don't stop if it looks like somebody's crowding you, and let me know when you get there. –Please. And thank you."

"I'll take you wherever—" she protested.

"No, I guess I need to figure it out, too." He held the door open, motioned for her to get behind the wheel. She walked around the rear of the car and slid onto the still-warm seat. "At the front gate just wait till the sensors pick up the car, then go out pretty fast—don't waste time, or you'll end up with a dent on your trunk. Just...just let me know you're there. Okay?" He leaned in and kissed her, a soft peck on the forehead again, then turned to walk across the landscape toward the main building, and he didn't look back.

SHE USED UP the last of the battery with a text to Rheta: *In the driveway. I'm back*.

The door was locked, which she'd expected, hoped for, actually. Rheta's car wasn't there, so she probably wasn't, either; but Sara didn't want to be met at the kitchen door by somebody holding a weapon.

Her house was silent. She turned the dead bolt behind her and crept through to the living room where the security chain hung across the front door.

So nobody left that way. They used the back one, the way she'd come in.

It felt strange being in her own house, where different people had spent the night, at least one of them someone she didn't even know. Rheta seemed to have slept on Cary's bed; the coverlet was rumpled. She looked into her own room and saw the bedding there also disarranged. Had the security guy slept here? She started to strip the beds, changed her mind. Better to wait for Rheta's explanation about that. If she was going to stay here another day or two, Sara wouldn't go to the bother of changing linen on whichever bed she'd used.

She decided to make herself a cup of hot chocolate. But, the phone!—she retrieved the charger from her bedside table, where the blue sphere and the clipped-together documents underneath it silently warned. She backed away, as if from a stray animal that wandered up, retreated to the kitchen with the charger, waited there for the microwave to heat the mug of water.

In a few moments the battery revived enough for several texts to buzz in: Two from Neil. One from Matheson. Two from Cary. The last was from Rheta: **K, not there, coming soon.**

That was ten or so minutes ago. She was stirring one spoonful of hot chocolate powder into the mug, wondering how long it would take Rheta to return, when she heard the lock slide open. She gasped and whirled around.

Rheta entered warily. "Didn't mean to startle you. Here's your key. I got it off that keyholder thing there, which is way too obvious a place for you to keep your extra ones."

"Everything's going to startle me for a while."

"Yeah." Rheta took off the Auburn cap and slung it onto the table. She fastened all the available locking devices on the door, hung the key back, and sank down in one of the kitchen chairs, closing her eyes, leaning back.

"I was about to have hot chocolate. I can fix you some."

"It's summer, you know. But sure." While she rubbed her eyes with the heels of her hands, Sara turned away and shoved another cup of water into the microwave.

"We told each other we expected it. Joe and I. We made plans, thought we were pretty cool. You just don't know how it feels till it happens."

"Did anybody get anything—description, car tag, anything?"

"Only a few people were home. Hell, it was a Friday night, people out doing things. The ones that *were* home were as scared as I was, I guess, and then it was over, and, no, no tag numbers. Joe talked with the police. No clues. Too much chatter on social media to sort out who really did it. Low priority—nobody hurt, no damage to speak of—"

" 'Nobody hurt'?" Sara yelled. She hadn't meant to.

"Yeah…"

She brought their mugs to the table along with the canister of hot cocoa mix and added another spoonful, and they each put more into the steamy water until, giggling as tears fell, they'd wasted enough.

"I used to like hot chocolate." Rheta shoved the cup away, sloshing it.

"Comfort food. Good after walking home from school in the winter. Does Mother know you're all right?"

"I called her last night, told her it was minor—she'll see the paper tomorrow, she'll find out then, but thank goodness she doesn't use the Internet much, because it's all on there."

"So where's Chris?" Sara asked.

"Chris? I guess at home."

She sipped the hot, rich drink, keeping her eyes down. "Didn't he come by, last night?"

"Yep, and he wouldn't leave. Slept on Cary's bed. I didn't smooth it up…sorry…"

"He stayed in Cary's room?"

Rheta's brows lowered. "No, we didn't go to bed together. We did drink up most of that bottle he brought—and I thank you for that, by the way, and we stayed up until it started getting light this morning. And then, when it wasn't dark anymore, I thought maybe I could sleep, so I went to your bed, and he went to Cary's room, and he slept a little, I guess. I wouldn't know. He came to your bedroom door when he was about to leave…sonofabitch woke me up at eight-thirty just to tell me that. I said get the hell out, let me sleep, but lock the door behind you. Ran off that other guy last night when Chris brought me that bottle. Don't need two extra Louises hanging over me." She glared at Sara. "Why're you asking?"

"I just… He's always loved you." Boom, the words were out.

"Yeah, so he said." It was offhand, dismissive, and she swore and jumped up to pull a paper towel off the roll. "He always wanted to believe that. I told him it was not happening. Tried to be sweet, take it on myself: I'm the last person he needs, I'd be terrible, all that crap. I'm too old to try now, and you know it. And I know it. And I guess now he knows it: I told him enough times last night." She dabbed at her face and threw the paper towel down like a gauntlet in front of Sara. "So, where'd *you* hide yesterday?"

she asked, and Sara's phone buzzed.

YOU SAID YOU'D let me know you were safe.

The battery was still low, and her back was toward Rheta, when she picked up the phone to look at that message.

Sorry. Phone had to charge first. Rheta's here.

She OK?

She answered with a thumb's up, hesitated—not wishing to get involved in a long chat right then—finally added, *Did you get home?*

There was a rustle behind her. She glanced up to find Rheta dumping the cocoa down the drain, giving her a knowing leer the way Cary would. Matheson didn't answer that question immediately. She'd decided he wasn't going to at all and had laid the phone down, when another text arrived: I feel at home HERE because I remember you being here. So I'm home, yes.

"Oh, let me look." Rheta smirked.

"Just a friend checking on me…"

"Yeah, I *know* that smile, I've done it myself. And not just me but everybody saw that hand-holding today. So you can tell me or I'll just find out by asking him. He *will* tell me, too. He can't stop himself."

"No, I'm going to ask *you* something. What was that all about, you and him, when we were leaving downtown?"

From eight feet away Sara could see Rheta's expression go blank. "No." Just the one word, and she flexed her hands and glared fiercely at Sara. Her phone buzzed several more times with messages coming in—and she hadn't answered Cary yet. Or were those from the time when her phone was dead? She hadn't checked. The two of them watched each other in silence.

"I have to go," Rheta told her. "I'll be back, if it's okay with you, but I have to go to the apartment and get in. For some things I need."

"Can I drive you?"

Rheta stared at her, not saying anything but just looking her fear, the way she always had, still trying to pull off that "I'm older and stronger" shit. And she could've gone before she came back here, to Sara's house, but she didn't—she'd returned and announced her intentions, and *that* was why she must go, Hal would've said. She could almost hear it from him, and he'd be right. She held up her hand, grabbed her purse and the partly-charged phone, and said firmly, "I'm driving. You aren't going by yourself yet. We'll go together."

SHE THOUGHT THE daylight would make things more mundane—tiki torches left over from a late-evening party, maybe, broken glass from somebody stumbling around after too many beers.

But there was the police tape strung haphazardly around, wriggling sinuously now on the ground where it had fallen or been taken down.

"Joe said the cops were through. Ron's got my windows boarded up pretty tight, looks like." She sat and stared at the front of her apartment, making no move to get out of Sara's car.

"Let's go through the back." Sara maneuvered around the street to a rear drive and parked, waiting for Rheta to decide. But still she sat frozen in the car. Sara began casually, "Well, tell me about that getup you have on. Where'd the shirt come from? I think it's mine, isn't it."

"You don't know everything I have in my closet." She pulled a set of keys from her pants pocket. "I guess we have to do this. Let's go. Yes, they're your clothes." She strode to the back entrance, unlocked the door and went in. Sara followed a few steps behind, nervously turned the deadbolt, ready for—for what? To take her arm if she wobbled? To fight off somebody hiding inside? But of course there was nobody inside, and Rheta turned on all the lights in the darker places, like the windowless spare bedroom, and closets, and under the stairwell, to make sure.

Are we going to be doing this from now on? Sara wondered. "New normal," Rheta murmured, as if thinking the same thing.

"What did you need to pick up?"

"Not much…I have the computer already, some clothes. I just wanted to come look…"

They glanced sidelong at the broken glass still lying on the floor of the front entrance, turned away, then took second, fast looks as if at a used condom somebody'd dropped. Rheta scampered upstairs and in a moment called back, "Everything's all right up here."

"Let's clean up the glass."

They spent another quarter-hour sweeping and throwing away

the shards from the two panes that had been shattered inward. Rheta hammered her fists on the boards screwed into the walls— "Guess I'll have to get all this spackled," she grumbled—and at last seemed content with the strength of the barrier. "I'll have the manager fix it on Monday. I *ought* to stay here tonight."

Her eyes were just wide enough again for Sara to know what the answer should be, and she said it firmly: "I wouldn't, until the glass is replaced. You'll be anxious about the boards, whether they're secure. All the noise, when they're redoing the glass...you probably wouldn't rest at all. Grab what you need, and come back to my place."

Rheta offered no objection. She descended the steps the second time with a light bag in her hand. "Just something to wear tomorrow, and some makeup, and a book I was reading," she muttered without meeting Sara's gaze. She checked the front door locks and made certain the back ones were all fastened, and they left. "All those years in Atlanta, nothing. You do what I do, as long as I have, you think you know, you think you're tough." Sara heard quiet gasps all the way home.

ON THE WAY she'd intended to tell Rheta everything that had happened with *her*; yet hearing the gulps, she changed her mind. Rheta stood in the kitchen with her bag. "Cary coming back today?"

"I don't think so. Wow, I haven't even looked at her messages."

"Yeah, what kind of mother are you," Rheta scoffed. "It's been a whole hour and a half since you saw her."

She smiled a little at that. "I think she's going to stay at Matthew's. So take her bed. Unless you want to share mine. You'll want fresh sheets, I guess."

"Nope. I think Chris slept on the comforter. It's good."

There were now three messages from Cary: **U need me to come back today?** That one had been followed by, **I will if you want. Dad says OK.** And the third one: **Can u answer pls**.

She tapped out her reply—*Here with Rheta. You decide. If you're having fun, stay*—and awaited a response, which was a vomit emoji and **Ugh.** Then, **But I'll stay. Got news for u tomorrow!**

So Jennifer had told her. She debated, decided to play dumb, to let Cary's announcement be more dramatic. So, *Can't wait!*

She heard the ancient pipes begin their hum as Rheta turned on the shower. She reread the texts from Matheson, her face warming, and stopped at Neil's messages, wondering if she should just delete them. The time stamps were from today, but that was all she could tell unless she did open them. The afternoon was creeping on, the leafed-out trees shading the back door, making patterns on the tile floor, while she waited with her phone in her hand, undecided.

Rheta would probably have said it was typical of her to put this off. She steeled herself.

The first one, from the small hours of the morning: **Just heard. You & R all right?**

That was anticlimactic. The second text, from later, right after Logan's speech, was long, long and cold and—she saw—ever more agitated and ungrammatical as it continued.

In spite of everything I've told you, I see you appear to be getting cozy with RM. Yes, I did watch from my window, and what I saw was more than business relationship or just bumping heads. Wish I hadnt sold the house to you, Id now have a way to get your attention. I will call you TONIGHT. Answer the phone so we can talk. N

The softly moaning pipes shut off, and presently Rheta padded into the kitchen with water dripping down her shoulders and onto the towel she'd wrapped around herself. "One thing I did forget, pajamas."

"You know it's just four o'clock."

"I'm not going to bed—I'm gonna wear something that'll keep me from going out again tonight."

"Some people go out in pajamas."

"God, you know I just went over there to make myself go, I knew I had to…. Didn't even get stuff I could've actually used. So, pajamas, please. Or something. Got some sweat pants?" She assessed Sara's clothing and sneered: "Probably. Just anything'll do." She started back down the hallway, then took another look at Sara. "What's up? Look like you've been slapped."

She'd sat down at the table with the phone in front of her, trying to decide whether to be furious or insulted or, possibly, just careful. The phone had gone dark, suggesting to her no answer, as she sat thinking. She went now to her bedroom to get something that might hang on Rheta's lanky frame, silently handed it to her, returned to the kitchen, where once more she plugged the phone in and stood beside it in deep contemplation.

"Good, you don't have to be nice to me, like those guys last night were. Shit. So just tell me, do we order in tonight? Do you have things to cook? And what's the hell's wrong?"

"Somebody's going to call in a while. Not likely to be a fun conversation. Just warning you. So I may take it outside, or maybe in Louise's old room."

"Nice sofa in there. What're you gonna do with that room?"

"Cary wants it to be a hideaway where she and her friends can go when they want privacy. What d'you think?"

"Sure, why not. But I've wondered for a while why you're still holding onto this little house. You could've bought a bigger one a long time ago. What's the attraction—that one time it belonged to Neil Griffin? You're not that big a fool over him, are you? So why've you stayed here?"

"I didn't want anything larger. This was our home, Louise's and Cary's and mine. I didn't *need* anything larger. You and I, we grew up and lived in the same house for years, you know. Cary'd probably flip out if I decided to move."

"D'you ask her? Just because that was the way we lived doesn't mean it has to be that way for her. One damn thing after another, you pile up all those reasons like bricks in front of a door, everything you try to get out of doing. Somebody's gonna come along sometime and knock 'em down." She rolled her eyes. "Anyway, so Neil Griffin's gonna call, right? I guess he was sitting up in his little pillbox spying everybody out, looking down on everybody, the way David Burkes used to, in fact from that same place before he retired. Well, you go on and chat with him, but if I had him on the phone, I'd ask why he sent people to torchlight my lawn and break my windows. That's what *I'd* wanna know. And I'd like you to ask *for* me, because I'm your sister."

"He didn't 'send' anybody to do it, you don't really believe that."

"I don't know. Did he?" She scoffed. "You know what? Joe felt like what happened last night should've happened to him; he owes me for some things I learned, just recently, about him, so he tries to atone for them. But I don't count on him for much anymore. Deborra's outgrown him, and he knows it. You heard your boyfriend talk about how Stephen Logan oughta have his past dissected? It'll happen tomorrow. That's Joe's way of growing a set of tiny little balls, at last: allowing it in his paper." She paused dramatically. "So when your other boyfriend calls in a while, you could ask him what I told you to, unless of course you also repeat what I just said, to him, to give him a head's-up. Which I'd rather you didn't, as I'd like it to be a surprise."

"Neil's not my 'boyfriend' any more than Ron Matheson is. And he's not mixed up with that group."

"Nobody said he was. He's too damned concerned about his reputation to get involved with them. But he provides space for Stephen, gets him out of that mess in Andy's shop, and who paid for the medical stuff, who pays for his campaign stuff, who pays that group to let him 'consult'? Betcha a dollar it turns out to be Neil Griffin. And why would he do that?"

"He told me he was giving him an opportunity because of his upbringing."

"Oh, God, drink that koolaid. Neil Griffin, a philanthropist? Geez, he's only always been looking out for himself. You know that. But you're so blind about him. You gotta figure out some day who he is, really, and decide if you like that person. Instead of just being comfortable not knowing."

"Why don't you tell me, if you know something I don't? That's what Ron always says: 'Ask Rheta.' "

"Like you'd listen? You aren't, now! Right now!" She turned away, a fierce look on her face, took a box of crackers from the cabinet and stalked down the hallway to Cary's room, calling back, "When you're ready to start supper, I'll help. Okay?" She held the door partly open, glared back at Sara: "Okay?"

"Sure, yeah."

NEIL WASN'T A racist, nor a neo-Nazi—neither of those; she knew he wasn't. He could be manipulative, secretive, devious; he'd say all those were good things, in lawyers. But he wasn't involved with MAP or any other group Logan would've been mixed up with; she was sure. In the early years after Cary was born, she'd known him as intimately as a woman could know a man, and she would've known, surely, if he were any of those things. And he'd always mocked the politicos in town, and, of late, been scornful of what he called Matheson's plan to reform Mooresville. Maybe that was what Matheson, Don, Rheta all held against him…that he mocked them.

She forced herself to go outside to the garden Louise used to nurture, and pulled more weeds for a while; but every time a car slowed down on the street, she stiffened and waited tensely for it to pass. You can't live like this, she told herself. She recalled suddenly that whatever signs had been planted at Rheta's apartment had been removed, probably as evidence, and she didn't know exactly where her name had been on them, or in what context, but it wasn't as bad as what Rheta had been through, was it? She'd been safe at MTE while Rheta was crouching behind her front door…. A car honked—she reminded herself it was probably because the driver avoided a cat or a dog on the street, or maybe recognized someone. She shivered convulsively and sat down at the little table, facing outward, and decided to get it over with.

He picked up on the second ring: "Babe, you okay?"

It was too familiar. She squeezed her eyes closed for a second the way she still did whenever she had to get an injection. "Yep. Fine. No thanks to Stephen Logan and his thugs."

"No matter what you, or I, may think about him, he's not the one who did that."

"But some of his people think it's what he wants. And people are crazy, you know."

"Your sister all right?"

"Yes. She's with me. Neil, what the hell was that text for?" Saying it loudly felt good. She'd read the words in his message; they'd burned into her; but she hadn't allowed herself to really, really think what they'd meant. Until now. "I own this house, and that was too far."

"Slow down, don't say things you'll be sorry for later. I'm kind of mad, too, you know. Nobody knew where you were last night. I found out around midnight what happened—"

"How? How'd *you* find out?"

"It was on the scanner—"

"You *listen* to police calls, for what purpose exactly?"

"Slow down!" he warned again, his voice colder. "I'm not an ambulance-chaser, as you know, and I don't listen to calls. But I know people who do. I've kept up lately with some rumors, and I found out, and nobody knew where you were. Don't you realize I was concerned?"

"Did you even try to find me?" she challenged.

"I did text you. It was the middle of the night! I wasn't going to call. I figured you'd be on the phone with Rheta. Check your messages." And she remembered the brief one he'd sent much earlier. "I actually drove over to your place, and there was a car I didn't recognize, and one of Matheson's vehicles from *his* fleet—" he said it scornfully— "and lights on everywhere, so I assumed you were all right. Was *he* there with you?"

"I'd been at the company cookout with Cary," she began wearily, then stopped: "And, no, he wasn't here. He'd sent some of his security people to Rheta's to get her out of her place and bring her here."

"Well, where—" he began, and she stopped that:

"Don't ask me anything else with that tone, like you're interrogating somebody. Rheta and I've been through stuff you haven't, stuff I wish didn't happen to anybody, and we're all right, but not really. I'd been sent to a safe place. My phone died. So why'd you say you were going to call me? What do you have to say? Because she and I are going to have a quiet evening, just us, in *my* house, and I don't want this to go on any more. I'm tired of it."

She stopped. What did that mean—those particular words right now? She remembered years ago, when Charlie had been her occasional date, when they were both in college, and Matthew had been Charlie's friend, and then at some point she realized she and Charlie were only clinging to each other for the same reason—the *same* reason, she saw it now—that Rheta'd told Connie she'd been hanging onto her first husband: ***Just about any human connection is better than none.*** And she and Charlie had sidled away from each other, and Matthew had been there instead....

Was it that with Neil? He'd been with her when she needed a human connection, and now she didn't need that anymore, at least not with him? And so what about her night with Ron? She heard Neil say something to her but thought instead of Cary's question: "Do people just say, 'This is it, I'm outta here'?" She'd had only three serious, really serious, relationships in her whole life— Charlie, tender and childish though that one was; and Matthew; and Neil; and she was just tired of feeling owned, obligated....

"Sara? Did you hear me? Are you okay?"

"No, I didn't—my mind's like a squirrel in a cage right now, you know. What'd you say? It's been a long twenty-four hours."

"I'm sure. I just asked if you wanted to eat with me, and, if she'd come, which I doubt, but if she would, bring Rheta, and we'll get away from here and go to Jackson, or even the coast, make an overnight trip—I still have that condo there with room for all of us—"

And that was it—the smothering incestuousness of having grown up together, all of them, her, Rheta, Neil, Stephen, Lisa, the Libertos—so it could be a natural thing for them to hide each other, close out the foreign, shut eyes to the wrongs.

"No," she said firmly.

"It might be good for you not to be in town till everything—"

"Neil, why've you stayed so tight with Stephen Logan? What is it with him?" The words came out suddenly, she didn't wish to take them back; she'd been trying to say them for a long time.

The silence, and then his voice, quiet, very cool: "I'm trying to help you, and that's all you think of? Some shit Ron Matheson's put into your head?"

"You didn't answer."

"Where *were* you last night?" he asked, and it was the one thing he shouldn't have.

"You tell me what I want to know, and I'll tell *you*," she said. "And I really can't talk to you anymore right now. So I'm hanging up. Not hanging up *on* you—just getting off the phone."

When Rheta came looking for her later, she was tearing out all the leggy old plants that had hung on through the years, all of Louise's long-tended landscaping—lantanas, mondo grass, vinca, all of it—and piling them into a trash bag, regardless of whether there were half-formed buds beginning to set or new leaves opening. "What the hell!" she said before she squatted down next to Sara and began ripping up vegetation herself, with ferocious pleasure.

27

JOE'S BANNER WAS the same size as usual. Nothing special. *Lynne Houston: Better Choice for Mooresville. Page 3.*

As prosaic and understated as a headline could be, and it looked weird in the space where Joe usually put things like "Local Family Collects Supplies for Teachers," or "Local Student Going to Yale."

" 'Lynne Houston: Better Choice for Mooresville'," Sara mumbled out loud over coffee the next morning.

Last night she and Rheta had rummaged around in the cabinet and found cans of soup for dinner—soup, and tuna, for sandwiches—instead of ordering a pizza. Neither of them had to tell the other why they didn't want anybody ringing the doorbell after dark; Rheta just used the opener on the tins while Sara boiled an egg. They'd said very little to each other as they ate; and sometime around nine they realized they were exhausted, ready for bed. Rheta stumbled into Cary's room, but presently Sara was startled to see her standing at her own door, holding a pillow.

"This is weird. Can't rest. Can I please sleep with you?" And they'd shared the bed the way they'd done as little girls, and when Sara had woke up early to make the coffee, Rheta was clutching the pillow to her chest as if it were a doll. Or a person. She gave Sara a look, took the pillow, went back to Cary's room, "For just a little more rest," she said.

Sara had closed Cary's bedroom door and slipped out the front to retrieve the newspaper. The delivery man always stuck it in the plastic receptacle next to her mailbox; and, yanking it out quickly, she'd looked up and down the street, paranoia sweeping over her again. Back inside the house, she'd locked the door and breathed slower.

You can't live like this.

Joe's lead under the banner was a summary of what had happened at Rheta's house on Friday night, with photographs of the torches—extinguished by the time Joe's photographer had snapped the shots—the windows broken out and closeups of the signs. Sara stared at those for a long time: bumper stickers with "Stephen Logan For Councilman" on them—Lynne's said, "For City Council"—and then "1488" and underneath that, "Whitson and Wells Fuck You!" So that was what Rheta'd meant in her text on Friday: **ur names here too**.

Journalist's Residence Vandalized by Unknown Hate Groups.

On the right side below the fold was a smaller article about a business indicating interest in moving to Mooresville. She turned to the editorial section. Then waited for Rheta to get up.

"YOU'LL SCALD YOUR mouth."

"But that'll wake me up. I should pour it down Joe's."

She'd expected Rheta to swear, to fling the pages around, snatch up her phone and start texting.

"I thought he was going to do more. Something."

Rheta sneered. "For him, this is more. I told you not to expect much."

She'd thought he'd say that people had to see that men like Logan were dangerous, re-energizing hate groups like those that had attacked a journalist's home, that they had no place in the government of the town, of the county, of the state, that it was time for Mooresville to understand that the kind of publicity the town had got wouldn't attract business. But he hadn't. "Why didn't he bring up the churches? Or remind everybody about what Stephen did when he was young? He just talked about Andy's shop this year and how it was settled out of court." Sara jabbed at the paper. "He did put that other thing, about the business prospect, right under that banner about your house."

" 'Do you want corporations to shy away because of this kind of shit?' Well, that's a point." Rheta put an ice cube into her coffee. "It's something. I knew he wouldn't do anything else, much. 'Lynne's a better choice.' "

"But everybody still does have the other choice."

"Joe's on the safe side of truth. That's what he wants—the safe side. Well, everybody's visual these days. They want that news in fifteen seconds, with a colorful graphic. Nobody reads. Deborra does more news now than Joe does. And I bet he ran it past David Burkes first."

"Why would he do that?"

She blew the melting ice to the other side of her mug. "David's owned a lot of the paper for years. So whatever's controversial goes through him first. It's not in the employee handbook," she added. "But everybody knows."

"I didn't."

Rheta sipped again. "Yeah, well, I didn't, either, till just recently. I feel for him, kind of, Joe," she added. "He was in a foot race with Deborra, and she's way ahead of him now. It wasn't just that people went to television and video; he did make choices. And he didn't adapt. He turned the paper into the place you go to read about your neighbor's ice-cream party last night. Funny: He's social media now, entertainment, and she's news. That's got to bother him sometimes."

"Why would David Burkes pull a story?"

"Oh, he doesn't pull them—he's not that heavy-handed. He tweaks them, or tells Joe to. Joe's long since stopped bucking him about it. Sometimes he does try to do a real thing."

"Your series back in the spring. Surprised he let..." She stopped.

"Let me have a go at Neil? Yeah. That one was out of his hands." She narrowed her eyes and smiled. "People got interested in the history, that first part, and so they wanted to read what else I'd say. He was okay with all that. I went back and added things he didn't know I was going to, in the other two parts. ...It could be worse. The other major owner'd be on David all the time, if he knew what he does. He's thinks it's all Joe's doing, that Joe's gone soft. Joe used to appeal to *him* once in a while, if David really interfered; but I think maybe he, Joe, was ashamed to keep begging for help. Or maybe he just got to where he didn't care so much. So this is it. This's all he's gonna do. Don't throw out my coffee; gotta let it cool some more. I'm getting my phone."

Sara had to ask: "Who's the other owner?"

Rheta snorted, looked pityingly at her. "You know that. Even you aren't that oblivious."

And she realized she did: the man who'd walked away.

SIPPING THE COOLED coffee, Rheta tapped out some messages, and her phone buzzed with answers several times. Sara didn't ask about it, and Rheta didn't volunteer information. After a while, she took another cup of coffee with her to Cary's room and shut the door.

It seemed that morning more people had Sara's number than she remembered. Some of the texts, she expected: Cary, demanding if she was attending Mass, and if Cary could come home with her afterwards. She closed her eyes at that message. She didn't want to get out.

Matthew, attempting to be nice: **I guess your all right. Cary wants to go there this afternoon OK?**

Lisa, asking if there was something she'd like Don to send her and Rheta for lunch about noonish.

Chris, wanting to know how Rheta was. She closed her eyes again.

Neil, sorry she was mad at him. She read that one twice, the second time aloud, derisively.

There was nothing from Ron. She wondered if he was testing her, holding away until she caved—but that was Neil's style. And she had caved. Many times.

Rheta'd been using her own phone a lot, too. Sara heard low murmurs from Cary's room, an occasional laugh.

She called her mother and told the story as calmly as she could. "See you in a bit," she told Connie, and that hard conversation over, she started answering the questions.

To Cary: *I'll go, but we come straight home then. Tell your dad*.

To Lisa: *He knows my fav. Thanks a million.*

To Chris: *She's here.* That seemed cold, indifferent, but there wasn't anything else she could say to him.

She didn't respond to Matthew or to Neil.

Well, if she was going to Mass, she'd better pick up the pace: It was almost nine o'clock. She knocked on the door and told Rheta her plans, asked if she wanted to come along.

"Are you insane?"

"I'm just trying to accommodate Mother and Cary. Maybe I'll find some peace there, too. You sure?"

"I haven't been to church in years. Not starting again now."

"Okay." She turned away, added, "Cary's coming home with me, and she may want her room. Sorry. That new couch in Louise's old bedroom makes into a bed, so…"

The door opened suddenly. Rheta stood glaring at her, the loose clothing falling around her arms and chest like a sheet hung on a scarecrow. "All right, I'll move my stuff in there, and I'll run a load of laundry while you're gone. And why don't you start calling it something like, 'the den,' or 'the office,' whatever. Louise's happy, and that's done. It's yours again, you own it."

"Point taken." She laughed. "Need help with the bed?"

"Nope."

Sara watched her strip away the comforter, yank the sheets off and pile them on the floor. She took the pillowcase from one pillow but saved the other one and hauled it into what she'd called the den, where she laid it on the new sofa. Sara watched.

"I think Chris slept *on* the bed, not in it, like I said. But I'm washing the sheets because I was there, too, at least for a while last night and today."

Sara began to remove the pillowcase from the pillow on the couch.

"No, I've already used that one, I'll wash it later. You got more laundry than just these things, right?"

She hauled the linen to the laundry room. In an immediate moment of clarity Sara understood why she didn't want the pillowcase washed, and let it go. There were rustling sounds, the din of the lid being slammed down—Sara winced—and then the machine started up. Rheta followed her to her own bedroom and stood in the doorway as she dressed for church.

"So why're you going, really?"

She explained about Cary's text. "And, by the way, Lisa told me Don's sending us something for lunch, which is sweet of them, so don't be startled when his person shows up." Sara hesitated. "You know Chris doesn't go to Mass much anymore."

"You think I'm avoiding Chris? I just don't want to get out today. And not there. Everybody'll feel sorry for us. Pat our little heads."

"Sympathy's not a bad thing. Doesn't make you weak."

"I can't stand it today."

Sara sat on the bed and buckled a pair of sandals. Rheta's eyes were drawn suddenly to the blue globe on the table, near the lamp. She picked it up and turned it around and around. "You ever find out who it was from?"

"Yeah. I know who gave it to me." And she told Rheta about the notes and the restaurant lunch.

"Ah. So how're you gonna deal with him?"

"What?" It was all she managed to say before Rheta interrupted, "You slept with him Friday night, didn't you. I would've. I know where you were, after all, and I doubt he'd've left you...." She shrugged. "When you feel like there's nobody there for you, and suddenly there is, you cling to that person. So what're you gonna do about 'im?"

In the hanging silence, Rheta set the globe down and started out of the room. "Go seek your forgiveness. But I'll tell you this. Being really, really close to somebody—being physically close—you just can't meet them anymore on a daily basis, look 'im in the eye, shrug it off. Either it means something, or it never meant anything at all, to anybody, and we're all just stray dogs hooking up, moving on. You can't have it both ways."

"Yeah, you said all that before. Which has it been with you?" Sara demanded angrily. "How many times've *you* walked away from somebody you slept with, you just walked, and that was that?"

"Too many. Go to church."

"JENNIFER'S PREGNANT," CARY said when they left for home.

"Really?" Sara tried to sound amazed but failed, and Cary gave her a disgusted look.

"You knew already!"

"Sorry, yes, she told me Friday night, just before all that other stuff happened. I said she should tell *you* later, herself. So how do you feel about it?"

Cary scoffed, keeping her gaze on the streetscape on her side of the car. "I guess it's okay for them. What am I supposed to 'feel' about it? It's nothing to me. If they think I'm gonna babysit all the time, they're wrong," she warned, "but, really… If they want a baby, fine. You know, Mom, it'll be more than fifteen years younger than me. And I don't really have much of a relationship with Dad, so I doubt I'll have one with it."

"Wow."

She twisted in her seat. "Please. Get real. It's just the way it is. What I figure'll happen is, they'll be raising it, and pretty soon I'll be in college, and we'll be kind of like cousins." She shrugged again, turned to stare out the window. "I'm not crying over it. Or ecstatic either. It is what it is."

The rotini was sitting on the table, hot, when they arrived, along with a fair amount of crisp bread and even a salad. And there was Chris, who'd brought it. Actually, he told Sara, Lisa sent him, said they'd feel more comfortable when somebody they knew knocked on the door, carrying a package. Although, maybe that was wrong, he added: Rheta was barely tolerating him for the moment, keeping an eye on him and being sarcastic with him.

"Yes, just barely! So why are you still here?" she said.

"Is there enough for all four of us?" Cary asked.

"If it's not, I'll just be the waiter and let the three of you have it. I haven't been the waiter in a long time. I'll just lean over you and make you feel guilty."

The meal was almost normal, even if Rheta did stay on her feet and ate from the counter top, avoiding the kitchen table where the other three sat; but it didn't seem to bother Chris or Cary that she chose to keep away from them. Nobody mentioned the news, or Stephen Logan, or what had happened on Friday night, until after they'd finished eating. Then Chris asked what Sara thought about Joe's endorsement.

"Not much."

"Let's not talk about that," Rheta burst in. "Some of us've lived it just lately, you know."

The three at the table glanced at each other. Chris tried again: "Lynne came in today as I was fixing up this food. Don told me she was emotional. She felt guilty you two had the worst of it."

"She shouldn't feel guilty."

"Easy to say. But she does. Have you talked to her yet?"

The question made her uncomfortable. "No. Ron checked out her shop yesterday while all that was going on in front of the restaurant—she had no idea—"

"Yeah, but I don't think anybody did anything to *her* house—"

"I said, can we talk about something else?" Rheta yelled. The room grew very quiet.

"You still have any of that wine?" Chris asked.

"Not gonna do it. Gotta work through it without *that* crutch," Cary warned. She leaped ahead of Rheta to snatch the mostly-empty bottle and scurry with it out the back door, and they heard the thump of the garbage-can lid, and she returned with a triumphant look on her face.

"You little shit!" Rheta stood with arms akimbo, and for once Sara knew the two weren't joking.

"Not gonna start that, Aunt Rheta." She pointed to one of the chairs. "Sit down over here with us. And you, *you* know better than to encourage her," she solemnly scolded Chris.

Chris grimaced and dragged Rheta to the table and into a chair. She flung off his arm. "Yeah, do remind him he's an alcoholic!"

"He can't handle himself so well, but he can handle you," Cary smirked.

He leaned over and pecked Rheta on her cheek, and she elbowed him away: "Stop, jerk!"

"I'm not worried," he told her. "You wanna slug me? Go for it."

HE DEPARTED IN in a couple of hours, offered to haul off the trash bag of dead plants they'd left by the backyard gate. "I'll put it into the bin out back of the restaurant."

Rheta disappeared too for a while, returning to the kitchen in full makeup, a dressy summer sweater and pants, her hair styled.

Cary looked up. "Date?" She'd been hanging around Sara more than usual tonight, almost shadowing her. There were times lately when Sara missed Louise's strategies; Louise had always been able to get Cary to talk—and her, too, for that matter, sometimes just by annoying them. It seemed Cary had disposed of Jennifer's pregnancy in her mind, and she couldn't imagine what else would hold her here. She'd read the newspaper, thrown it aside, then tackled a binder full of notes she'd been working her way through for a final exam, her feet on a chair opposite where she sat.

"Date?" Rheta scoffed. "You could say that. Or, 'Plan B.' "

Cary put down the binder. "Well, you look great, so you two have fun, and don't let him get you drunk. And tell him we said thanks again."

"Well, it's not Chris, it's *her* boyfriend, one of them, anyway," and Rheta walked out the door. In a moment they heard her car start as she drove off.

"What'd she mean by that, Mom?"

CHRIS DIDN'T THINK of Sara's oversized bag of weeds and plants that afternoon and left it in his car until dark, when the evening crew emptied into the huge bins out back the trash cans that had filled up in the restaurant. The three people working that Sunday night had started accumulating the garbage when Chris slapped his forehead: "Give me a minute and keep the lid open." And he went out through the side door into the dark narrow alley into which he and Don always inched their vehicles: Don didn't believe in taking up parking spaces his customers could use.

Chris discovered someone else there, a man moving around silently in the tight space between the restaurant and Griffin's building, a man with a backpack, though it wasn't actually on his back. Another vagrant; he'd moved them on, before, and they were peaceful, usually; but this guy peered at him in the gloom before swinging the backpack at him and punching him in the chest. Chris fell against the brick wall of the restaurant, temporarily stunned, and the man ran around the back of the building and into the alley.

And then he was gone.

Chris had left the side door open a little, and the light from inside leaked out and gave him something to focus his blurry eyes on. In a moment he heard two of the evening crew—Devin and Owen—push the back door open and prop it with the cinder block they usually shoved against it to keep from being locked out. He heard them: "Said he'd be here, I don't see him"; and then, "What's that smell?" and a shout: "Hey!" He shook his head and called in a croak, and Devin peeped around the end of the building and found him trying to get to his feet by bracing against the brick wall and inching upwards. Owen in the meantime had thought fast and turned on the water hose to spray the pile of papers smoldering underneath the ancient wooden stoop at the back that Don had said many times he was going to have demolished.

They called the fire department, just to be sure, and Don because he should know. He parked down the street and jogged to the restaurant, thinking about another time of fire, and stood silently, watching. One of the pumpers parked out front, with two hoses snaking through the narrow alleyway on the other side. The small crowd of Sunday-night customers were mildly interested at first; but Don feigned yawning indifference and explained there was a trash bin fire and the pumpers were there only from an overabundance of caution. He himself was waiting tables by then, having excused Devin to run Chris to the ER.

"Your head's like your pop's was: too hard to dent," the doctor on call told him—an old friend of Ransome's and Dom's, he did an X-ray and shaved off a patch of Chris's hair and slapped a dressing over the bleeding knot that had formed. Chris eventually returned to the restaurant and waved at people as he entered through the rear door so the back of his head wasn't visible.

After everybody went home and he and Don made sure the firemen had destroyed and shoved away the old wooden porch, they sat upstairs in the office and decided not to hire anybody to keep watch that evening. "Don't know where he went," Chris said.

"You hear a door shut, close by?"

Chris had a wrenching headache now—Dr. Brown had told him he would—and the implication escaped him. "Man, I was out. He could've come into the *kitchen*, and I wouldn't't've known."

"Or even next door, I guess."

But the pain was ratcheting up, and he only nodded, very

carefully. "We could put up walls to close off the alleys."

"City wouldn't let us, I think. You can't protect against everything."

"Mean dog." Chris snapped his finger. "Two of 'em. Keep 'em in the alley. That'd do it."

"That was a pretty good hit on that head, wasn't it. We were lucky tonight. I should tell Sara to give you her garbage every day." Don faked a laugh belying his narrowed eyes.

They locked up and decided to leave the back lights on.

RHETA RETURNED AFTER seven, scrubbed her face, and slouched into the living room in the same loose clothing Sara'd found for her to sleep in. Cary sat poring over the binder, Sara pretending to look at the paper. But Rheta could tell she wasn't really reading it, as she picked it up and laid it back down over and over, different parts; and Cary was frowning, but not, Rheta thought, at the notes.

They'd had a fight. Glad she hadn't been there to see it. "Any leftovers?"

"We just ate the rest of the salad. Look for something in the fridge." Cary made a moue of scorn.

Sara shrugged: "What she said."

Peeved, Rheta stomped into the kitchen. They heard her opening and closing cabinets and the refrigerator door with more force than she really had to.

Sara had answered Cary's earlier question with the response she'd been giving everybody: *I don't have a "boyfriend."* Cary asked about her holding Matheson's hand, and she told the explanation he'd used: He was trying to restrain her, because he thought she might leap into the group of protesters and make a scene. "Sure," Cary scoffed. "Well, whenever you want to say the truth, you should hope I want to listen."

So after that she'd conceded that she and Ron were trying to figure out if they wanted a relationship, trying to see if they wanted to be together.... And that provoked Cary: "Geez, either you do or you don't. Wow, I mean, even teenagers can figure that out."

Sara had held back a retort, and Cary had picked up the study materials again; and Rheta had returned, washed her makeup off, started scrounging for food in the kitchen.

And then, as they heard Rheta clattering about, Sara's phone began buzzing. Cary glanced up sullenly when the first two messages arrived.

Sara, Joe here. If Rheta's there, just keep looking at the phone. Don't show emotion. There was an incident at Don's.

Her heart started to race—my God, how many things are going to happen? she thought. She scrolled down:

A minor fire out back. Chris interrupted the guy trying to set it. He's gone to the hospital.

She asked if Chris was okay.

I think he's all right, just banged up some. Restaurant's okay too. They were hauling out the trash and Chris went to get something from his car and bumped into the guy. I assume it was a guy.

Her legs began to tremble; she forced calmness on her face. "Get something out of his car"? That would've been the bag he'd taken away from her back yard—she'd caused him to be hurt! She typed something like that, and Joe immediately responded:

Thank you, because you probably saved the place and maybe some people, who knows. He happened outside at a good time. Don't tell Rheta right now.

Cary sighed deeply, dramatically, disgustedly, but didn't look up.

Sara asked if it wouldn't be on the news, the Internet.

Joe didn't answer for a moment, then agreed she was right: It was probably already on social media, would be on the TV's website, if not the late news. He told her to think of something to keep Rheta busy, and she reminded him Rheta had other contacts who'd tell her, surely....

But that was too late, and they heard Rheta cry out, "What the hell!" from the kitchen, and a chair screeched protestingly across the floor: Of course she *would* have her phone with her. She appeared suddenly in the doorway of the living room. Cary, eyes wide, tossed aside the binder.

"Do you *know*?" Rheta demanded.

"Joe just told me."

Rheta slid down the wall and hunched with her face against her knees.

SHE AND CARY sat on the floor beside her for a while, Cary reminding her over and over everybody was okay, Chris was okay, the building was okay. "But why would anybody do something to Don's place?"

"He made it pretty clear how he feels about Stephen Logan, didn't he?"

"He always *has*, though."

Rheta groaned, "Oh, my God, oh, my God…" After a while, Sara hauled her into her own bedroom again and brought the pillow from the office sofa.

She checked the doors, tried to ease Cary's apprehension by turning on the backyard light, told her not to stay up too late studying because it wouldn't help to cram at the last minute.

Later, long into the night, she saw a glow from Cary's room, knew that advice was wasted. Then it came to her that Cary's door was open. She didn't usually leave the door open.

But then, so was her own…so that she'd be able to hear sounds, things she heard every night. She lay back-to-back with Rheta, who had actually gone to sleep. A dog yipping in a back yard down the street…a creak from the kitchen after the air conditioner turned off…a mockingbird rustling in shrubbery next to the back door… Sara gazed at the blue sphere so close to her face on the night table. It had an odd trick of picking up stray light, even dim light, on the tumbling cubes Ron had fashioned somehow, and now a slight shimmer seemed to emanate from the side facing the hallway. She felt her sister's breath coming evenly—it hadn't been even and steady at first when Sara had ordered her to lie down, but eventually she'd drifted off into a doze and then a regular sleep. Sara remembered waking up on Saturday morning—only yesterday—with another body pressed close to hers, and she thought now that he and Rheta were both lost searchers, and maybe she, and everyone else, too.

28

THERE HADN'T BEEN so much tension, anxiety, anticipation in Mooresville since the time of Ransome Moore, and on Monday *he* was watching from his home in the northeast part of the state, growling and swearing at the news as Deborra reported it. None of them knew how to manage a town; he was going to have to drive back down and preach it. He read the news online, he watched the videos the local TV station posted, he was computer-savvy; he'd had to keep up with innovations, or he'd have gone bankrupt long ago.... **Sonsabitches!** He shoved his rolling chair away from the desk in the downsized little house he lived in now. Regina used to fuss at him back in the day whenever he swore out loud. She'd ignored the random swats at the air. But it startled her to hear obscenities yelled in the stillness of a house, and she had enough Baptist in her to disapprove anyway. But Regina was gone, and these days if Ransome felt like swearing, he swore.

Today, Monday, it was all about that asshole Stephen Logan who ought to have been run out of town thirty years ago—he should've offered him a ticket instead of Colbie, he knew that now, he'd known it then. Should've rid the town of that riffraff by sending *him* away, and not to college.... He guessed he'd be paying his penance for the rest of his life—and he was resolute enough to do it. He wasn't a man given to much introspection, but he knew some things you just paid for in one way or another for a long time, if they were bad enough.

He pulled himself back up to the computer desk again, softly said, "Shit," and read the story. Seemed Logan had taken offense to Joe Sims's editorial yesterday, thought the man owed him equal time now. Said he was consulting with his lawyer—"Goddamned sonabitch," Ransome swore again—to sue the daily rag, and maybe the TV station, too. Ransome had always enjoyed his takedowns of Reg Griffin's partner, David Burkes, had felt a keen, surly pleasure in watching the man seethe, unable to answer Ransome's barbs. But he didn't know much about Reg's son, beyond what he *knew* about him.... He didn't know whether Neil Griffin would cave if somebody stronger challenged him. He didn't know whether Logan had a fair complaint or not. All lawyers would interrupt, "Can you be sued—?" with, "Yes," without even waiting for the rest of the question; but was Neil Griffin one of those lawyers who practiced that way, filing first, discovering later?

There was a video posted to the TV station's website—a clip of Stephen Logan standing outside his office—dammit, *why the hell* did the man give him that space, was it for old time's sake?, Ransome wondered sourly. For all those months he'd been watching this dog-and-pony show, harboring a growing apprehension at how much smoother and slicked-down Logan'd become. It was why he'd invited everybody out to Sooie Hog, try to get them to see what they were dealing with in his town.... Now, on the video, Logan showed just enough anger to seem reasonable as he said he was tired of the media in Mooresville trying to run the election themselves and interfere with the citizens' right to choose, to choose him, in fact, as he was clearly the better candidate; he was tired of them trying to link him to what some extremists had done; and he was therefore preparing a petition against the paper's owner and the TV station, that his lawyer would be handing to the judge shortly, perhaps on the next day or the one after that.

Ransome pushed himself away again with another strong word about the lawyer and stood up, glancing around the small, nicely-appointed room. On the farm long ago, he'd just go out and ride one of the horses, drive a piece of farm equipment around, get in the small bulldozer and knock down a few mounds of dirt, and he'd feel better and would have a plan figured out when he came back in. There wasn't anything like that around this pleasant, cozy house. He turned back to the computer to shut it down when another headline on the website caught his eye: *Deborra Anderson Interviews Businessman and Journalist about Recent Vandalism. Watch at 5!*

Ransome glanced at the time. That would give him an hour or two at the business he and Wilburn still ran together, though they usually only showed up after lunch, and then didn't really need to—they were only getting out and about, trying to make themselves feel relevant; the store ran just fine under the management they'd put in. He'd get home early enough to have that chat Matheson invited himself up to have today; and after Ron left, he'd decide what he'd do about supper, maybe get a sandwich. Or maybe he and Wilburn and his wife would go out for a meal, and he'd have something interesting to talk about as they ate.

He didn't have to be told who'd been interviewed. Before he and Matheson got down to business, later, he'd razz him about wanting the spotlight all the time.

RHETA SHUFFLED INTO the kitchen when Sara and Cary were eating breakfast that morning. "You always get up at this time?" she grumbled, pouring herself some coffee.

Sara raised her brows at Cary to warn against a mouthy retort. "Usually," she said, "because she has school, you know."

Rheta glared at Cary: "You not driving yet? What's wrong with you? You must be at least, what, eighteen? Did you fail a few grades? Old enough to be bossy with me. Old enough to throw out my wine."

"Just keepin' you straight, Aunt Rheta." Cary ate the toast Sara had spread with peanut butter for her, drank a long gulp of juice. "Mom always forces food on me. It'll be her fault if I have eating disorders when I turn into a teenager."

Rheta laughed. "Smartass. All right, when will you be getting that permit? I know you're counting down."

Cary thought. "Three months and two weeks."

"You don't have it to the day?"

"That would be OCD, wouldn't it. By the way, you could brush your hair, what's left of it, anyway. You looked pretty good yesterday when you went on your date…you one of those people that put on the dog for a man but not for your family? I hate that kind of woman."

Rheta, in the process of getting out a bowl for cereal, halted and squinted at her. "You need to learn manners."

Cary shrugged, hid her smile by stuffing the last piece of toast into her mouth. Sara silently poured herself another mug of coffee and capped it to go.

"How long before you get back?" Rheta asked.

Sara shot her a look, wondering if she didn't want to be at the house by herself…or if she wanted Sara to do something with her…it was impossible to guess, as Rheta had turned to gaze out the window over the sink.

"Twenty minutes, there and back," she said. "Depends on traffic."

"Okay. Well, I'm gonna get dressed. Have a good day, you smart-mouthed urchin," she told Cary. "Y'all yell when you leave, all right?"

She headed back to the bedroom; Sara and Cary exchanged quizzical glances. In a moment Cary decided it was later than she'd realized, and she ran off to brush her teeth, her hair, grab her much-lightened backpack—"Just two days left!" she exulted when she returned. They dashed out the back door, making sure it was locked behind them.

Rheta's car was gone when Sara arrived home, something that made her heart beat fast at first, and then she knew. Inside the kitchen on the table she found Rheta's note: "Thanks for putting me up, the food, the wine, NO thanks to Cary, and I'm gone to reclaim my life. Told the manager to get the window fixed TODAY, and I intend to supervise while that's being done. You know where I'll be, and I WILL answer texts if you send them. Love."

She turned all the locks—all of them: new normal, she told herself wryly—and wandered back to her own bedroom. She really hadn't felt it was necessary to wash the sheets, but there they were, stripped into a pile on the floor. She hauled the linen to the washing machine. Cary's pillowcase was in the load.

RHETA HAD ASKED her what she was going to do about Ron. While Chris was there, Cary was home, Rheta was staying with her, she'd been able to put off thinking about it.

She hadn't wanted to think about it.

But sometime or other she had to—had to put him into a slot somewhere so that her life could go down the comfortable back road she'd intended it would from now on: getting Cary grown and through college, walking towards retirement herself, puttering around in later years. After Matthew, she'd deliberately avoided getting involved with anybody...Neil being the exception, but Neil had been a diversion, someone she'd never really thought she'd commit to. Sitting at the table with Rheta's scrawled note in front of her, she knew that now. Neil had been convenient to have around for a long time, and, once, they'd been friends, then lovers...but she'd never even considered being with him, always.

She'd got some counseling after the divorce. There she was, raising a baby on her own after being married over a decade— married contentedly, anybody would've assumed; and she thought she ought to figure out why she'd chosen this difficult thing to do by herself when she didn't have to. The counselor told her to picture one thing that crystallized her feelings about the time with Matthew. And what instantly came to her was a trip. They'd gone west, to some conference he was to attend, and she'd wanted to drive through the mountains on the way back, and he'd given her a disdainful glance and flown on down the interstate and said she'd better look out the window because that was as close as she was going to get.

The counselor's eyes had flickered a little, though she'd kept a blank expression on her face.

From the moment she'd told Matthew about Cary, when she was about five months pregnant and people were watching her waistline and she knew she *had* to tell him, he'd demanded to know why she'd filed for divorce when there was a baby on the way, a baby that might bring them back together, he said. And finally, when Cary was nearing a year old, she'd explained about the mental photo, and he'd burst out angrily, "That's not fair! There were good things, too!" And that was true—there had been. But that was what she remembered, what came to her mind: She'd wanted glory, and he'd told her to make her peace with what he was willing to give her, instead.

Since then Sara had found the counselor's advice useful in other situations. When she'd signed the mortgage for her house, with Neil sitting across the table, smiling a little and raising his brows at her, she'd suddenly been irritated at him...it was as if he'd planned the whole thing, and she'd been tricked into thinking it was her decision. Sitting there, she'd brought up a picture:

Herself, years ago, a teenager, with Hal, out in the woods at somebody's farm, obediently holding a gun as the two of them waited for a deer to walk past the blind...waiting, waiting, and as Hal nodded silently towards a buck approaching in the distance, nodding back in acknowledgement but raising the weapon too fast and scaring the animal away. Hal knew what she did—to be fair, most of the time he went to the woods only to sit and contemplate and be at peace, himself. "Move slower," he told her, not in a disappointed way, and she shrugged. The routine happened once more, and he'd realized she had no intention of taking a deer: She too was there just to watch the animals as they went about their lives.

He laughed on the way home, telling her he wouldn't ask her to go anymore, he figured she had the same philosophy about boys right then, and that was okay. And when he'd wondered if *Rheta'd* like to try hunting, she'd told him it was nothing but dirt and blood and sitting and killing, and so, no thanks.

Sara always remembered what Hal said that day, and sometimes, especially after she backed away from Neil, she flinched at the memory of the words.

But Neil'd never seemed really to mind so much. Once in a while he'd show a flash of jealousy if he thought she was taking an interest in someone else; but mostly their relationship had been physical, superficial, and she had the feeling he wouldn't be too upset if she did go out with other people. And she would have felt the same about him.

But Ron was different. It was because they were older, she told herself, but she knew that wasn't true. Or it wasn't all of it. She'd thought he would have texted her again or called or something, and she realized she wished he would. She was afraid to bring up any picture in her mind this time—they hadn't known each other long, anyway, and it wouldn't be fair to judge him, or herself with him, just on those few months. But her mind did its own thing, and there it was: a picnic table, his hand resting on hers, and a bird picking up a piece of toast he'd thrown down, and the two of them laughing at his grouchiness.

And another one arose from somewhere: The two of them in bed, her hands in his unruly gray hair, what he said—"Please look at me, I want us both here..."

She shuddered and got up from the chair. It was only nine-o'clock. Rheta was right: A default decision, a choice made by not choosing, wasn't enough. She'd been shoving those things aside for days as if they hadn't happened at all, as if they meant nothing compared to everything else that had happened.

She missed Louise. Louise had scoffed at Cary's hint that she might like a gift: "We have a house full of our stuff. We don't need any more."

But, still... Resolved suddenly, she texted. *Okay if I come over?*

We're home so come on.

She headed downtown. Lynne's shop would have something handmade, a small quilt, a set of chair cushions, a seasonal wreath for a door...something Louise would like. And maybe she'd catch Lynne, and they could talk about the weekend, plan some kind of strategy.

But Lynne wasn't in. The manager seemed to feel it was his fault somehow, and apologized several times.

"She felt bad about what happened to y'all. She said she'd try not to involve you anymore. She left you something here if you came over. She text you about it?"

"No."

"Well, I guess y'all on the same wavelength, anyway." He returned to the register and fumbled around with several items, finally bringing her a sealed envelope. She read the note, a sense of futility settling over her.

"She told me she don't want nothing else happening to you," he added, trying to smooth down his tipped-blonde ginger hair that, he felt, represented him well with this local famous person.

She folded the note back into the envelope. "So it says." She bought one of the summer wreaths.

Louise and Harvey were busy painting the kitchen when she arrived, Harvey doing most of the work, running a roller across a wall according to Louise's instructions, and they were almost finished. Sara propped herself on a stool out of their way and watched. Louise scrutinized the wall up and down: "That's pretty good. I'll do the cleanup."

"You want me to wash out the rollers?" Sara stepped off the stool.

"They cost four dollars. Why'd I save 'em?"

"Well…I don't know why you would." She laughed, climbing back upon the seat, and Harvey laughed too.

"She's gonna go through all our money, Sara. She's spending right and left."

Louise arranged close-up jobs for him, and she took on the ones that required farther vision. He stored the paintbrushes in the cabinet; she took the empty paint can outside to the trash bin and swept the floor. They perked a pot of coffee in the freshly-done kitchen, breathing mild but not unpleasant latex paint fumes that mingled with the brew. When they all seated themselves at the table in the middle of the small room, Sara noticed Harvey holding Louise's hand.

Suddenly, she thought she had to leave, right then—"Have to go; got a lot of work to do—" She brought out the wreath and offered it to Louise, who made much over it and said she'd put it up later that day. Harvey held it close to his face—"Very summerish colors!"—and Sara asked them to come over next Saturday evening for a meal, and they said they might.

She locked herself in again at home and made a sandwich. She thought about calling Lindsay Mason and needling her to arrange a meeting…decided it wasn't worth it. She hadn't done anything at all with the fertility clinic since February, hadn't even thought about the literacy campaign since...well, since she'd contracted with MTE for the artwork. The predictable routine of her life had blown to pieces this spring, and she was a fragment of the debris, drifting along.

Her phone buzzed twice right after lunch: Neil, inquiring snidely if she was still pissed at him, and what she would make him do as atonement. Those messages she ignored. She pulled up the computer, remembered suddenly that Cary would be out of school early today, and went to pick her up, finding her giddy that only one more day had to be endured, and the long summer would stretch in front of her...and then she was quiet, contemplating how to fill *those* days.

"I'm tired, Mom," she said, watching Sara lock the door once again. "I didn't sleep much Friday night—it was all over the Internet, you know—and then I didn't sleep a lot Saturday night, either. Do you know people actually said bad things to us that day? They did. I guess it didn't matter that I wasn't their age, that I'm just a kid. So that night I had nightmares about everything. Anyway," she yawned, "I studied late last night, too, and I'm getting a nap."

"Need a snack?"

"Carson and I had a juice while we were waiting a while ago." And she threw herself on her bed, leaving her door open, and in a few minutes she was asleep.

SARA SPENT THE rest of the afternoon reading everything she could find on the Internet about Friday night. There wasn't much, actually: Mooresville police were still asking for tips about the identity of the persons who'd vandalized a local journalist's home. They hadn't published Rheta's address, but, hey, as she'd told Ron, you could find just about anything online, and if the newspaper hadn't, then other people could, and probably had found it. There wasn't enough evidence to be connected to anyone. The organization people suspected was behind it—Mooresville Association of Patriots—had declared they weren't involved: They wouldn't account for what individual members might have done, if they'd been pushed by the continuous misrepresentations of the media, but the group officially disowned the vandalism.

Countless replications of the TV station's original video—

edited, full-length, enlarged to show the lettering of the signs—had proliferated all over the web, into pages both mocking and condemning, vicious, hateful comments next to rational ones. Around four o'clock Cary stumbled groggily into the kitchen, asking for a cup of coffee: "Gotta study for one more exam." Sara made her a cup but diluted it with instant decaf. Holding the mug, Cary looked over her shoulder at the computer, still open to a news website. A strand of the purple streak hung near the right side of Sara's face.

"We should probably watch the news."

"Why?"

"Well, geez, Mom, you've got like umpteen tabs open. Look..." She brushed her fingers across the touch pad and found the page for the local TV station, and there it was: *Deborra Anderson Interviews Businessman and Journalist about Recent Vandalism. Watch at 5!* "I mean, really, you didn't believe she was actually going out with Mr. Matheson, did you, yesterday afternoon, trying to take your boyfriend?"

"What?"

Cary scoffed. " 'Local journalist', 'businessman'—who else? They probably arranged it yesterday while you were at Mass with me. So, I'm good for it. You wanna go to the living room or the office?"

"That's what it is—the 'office'?"

"Sure, why not." She shrugged. "Make yourself something to drink, we'll watch together. Since Deborra Anderson was kinda disrespected on Saturday, and Mr. Matheson, too, and of course Aunt Rheta— Well, anyway. They probably have a lot to say. I'll shut down your computer while you fix yourself something."

Sara hugged her—and she didn't look repulsed or roll her eyes. She hadn't told her where she herself had slept on Friday. Possibly Cary didn't imagine her mother would spend the night with a man. She could tell her Ron had loaned the cabin for her safety, and she could leave out the fact he didn't go to his own house; and maybe Cary would take that at face value. But she might not, and right now, just at this moment, Sara didn't want her to know everything about that night. Or maybe she just didn't want to deal with the idea that Cary might already know and had her own conclusions about it. Or maybe she herself just didn't want to think it had happened at all.

29

"TELL US WHAT you saw." There was actual concern on Deborra's face instead of the bland, fake interest she'd usually assumed in her periodic interviews with Sara.

Rheta brushed a strand of short black bangs off her forehead, did it again. "I'd been working on some things, set it aside, put on a movie. Maybe watched fifteen minutes, didn't even pay attention when a car went past, out on the street. There wasn't much traffic that night. So it was quiet. You know they didn't park in front of the house, but down the street, walked up, I guess. The first thing I knew, there was light flickering—"

"Torches." Deborra nodded.

"Yes. No noise. I looked, saw what it was, texted a friend to call the police—we had this arrangement, we'd been suspicious something could happen, hard for me to believe of Mooresville— so if either of us got into trouble, the other would get the ball rolling."

"For protection," Deborra commented.

"For protection, yes, police, somebody."

"And then?" Deborra asked, leaning forward.

"Well, I started towards the door as I was sending the message. I guess in the back of my mind, I thought I'd just go out there and raise hell at them. That was when the rocks came through the windows."

"Only they weren't rocks," Deborra said softly.

"No. They weren't rocks. They were bricks."

This was something Sara didn't know, and it took everything to a different level. You could walk out and pick up rocks, throw them impulsively; you had to plan on getting bricks.

"So, I hunkered down right there at the front door. There was glass all over the room, but I guess I was lucky: None of it hit me. I sent out some more messages, to my friend, my sister, but once the torches were lit, and I guess they made sure I wasn't coming out, they were gone. Nobody saw who it was; they were quiet, just like any other person leaving after a visit."

"It must have been terrifying. How long was it before the police arrived?"

Ron laughed in the background, and a second camera turned to him. Sara leaned forward, aware of Cary's quick glance at her. He wore a business suit and tie—uptight, she thought, a little over-the-top, compared to Rheta's slacks and pastel sweater; but she stared, remembered pressing her chest to his back as they slept....

"The police weren't in a hurry," he said before Rheta could answer. "They were out on the highway to catch speeders. Rheta texted her sister, like she said, who happened to be at MTE that evening at an event, with her daughter," he added smoothly.

"So...?" Deborra urged.

"Ms. Whitson, Rheta—" he gestured toward her— "told her sister to let me know what was going on—she'd been occasionally at our facilities in the past, and she knew I'd have security there."

"She asked you to send your personal staff?"

"More or less. To back up the local people. If there was a need." His tone was only slightly ironic. "But she didn't have to ask. When I found out, I sent people over. My security guys got there before the police did. Just a *little* before they did." He made a scoffing noise.

"Well, a good thing no harm came to you—" she spoke to Rheta.

"Yeah, I was grateful."

"You may know there's been social-media chatter, a lot of talk around town, about what it meant, means, in terms of Mooresville's presentation of itself, reputation." She hesitated. "Some discussion about how this could impact businesses considering locating here, and the election that's, well, actually very soon, isn't it? How it contrasts with the forward-looking general character of the election, why it happened now, at this time...."

She stopped, and Sara reflected that in an interview Deborra didn't usually editorialize with so many leading questions, so many loaded adjectives. The closeup camera that had hovered on Ron's apparently relaxed figure drew away, and another one showed the three of them together in an area of the studio meant to resemble a snug, friendly den. Rheta seemed frozen, her face expressionless. Ron and Deborra leaned in toward each other, solemn, even grim, and the moment went long for a television segment.

"I wrote an opinion piece for the paper, myself, a while back," he began. "You remember, I said the town has to come to terms with its past, has to move forward, has to get over itself, you'd say."

"Some people saw that as presumptuous. Like you were trying to take over the town," Deborra remarked, nodding, urging. "I saw the comments."

"Yeah. People want to believe that."

Sara remembered this broadcast wasn't live, it was from yesterday, and though she wanted to tell herself he was looking out at her, talking to her, it was a twenty-four-hour-old image of him.

And it was an unusual interview, she thought: They were so intense, and there were seconds of dead time, which hadn't been edited out. He sighed, visibly, on camera, as if he were weary, and continued. "On Saturday, Stephen Logan said nothing bad happened in Mooresville till I brought MTE here. There wasn't any division, everything was great. I hope that isn't true. I mean—I hope I didn't start it."

Deborra had caught back a remark, had almost shaken her head, but stopped, and, instead, said carefully, "Every town everywhere's had things."

Ron went on: "I don't want to be responsible for things going wrong. But I told somebody recently, a, a friend, and I've also said it to others, I'm invested in Mooresville. I like it here. I like all of you, or most of you, stubborn people, friendly people, and I'm not going to leave," he added gravely.

"But to use a farm metaphor, the old fields have to be cleared for the next crop." The second camera focused on Rheta's face a moment.

"I think Mooresville's at that sort of, it's a cliché, a—"

"—crossroads," Deborra said with him.

"Yes, that. I despise what happened to Ms. Whitson—" he gestured toward Rheta. "But I bet even she'd say if it takes that, she'd think it was..." He hesitated.

"Somewhat worth it," Deborra suggested.

"Yes."

Rheta's camera displayed her faintly nodding.

"She sure didn't want to agree with *that*," Cary remarked.

"Those other things a long time back, they were..." Matheson paused again.

"The churches that were burned. Let's go on and say it."

"Yes. And, you know, Mr. Moore, Ransome Moore, whose family gave the town its name, Ransome took his big equipment, I heard, and bulldozed those ruins, and helped start construction on new ones, and that's another metaphor for what should be done. We don't need, I don't want anything like what happened on Friday to happen again. We have to figure out how to stop it."

"You personally, yourself, you're going to be here for the long haul."

"I'm not a young fellow. I believe this was my last relocation, so I'm here, yeah," he said. Sara watched as he dragged his hand through the hair, which no doubt a makeup assistant had combed and arranged before the interview—wasted effort, she wanted to say, gazing at the TV screen.

"And I want things to keep moving forward."

"I understand the company's about to distribute a summer reading project to kids in town."

"And out in the country, too, anybody who asks for one," he said.

"And in the library there are new computers."

"Well, not all of them 'new.' But we donated some for the program, and their yearly one. A local artist did a lot of work for our project, and I think everybody's happy with the results."

"Would this local artist be someone who appears on this program from time to time?"

"Oh, now, let us have a few surprises."

Deborra smiled. "So none of these recent events'll negatively influence the company—you are here for the duration. You won't jilt us and move somewhere else."

Rheta looked down, shook her head, chuckled. He didn't. "Honest, Deborra, I'm tired of that, and you've said it twice now. No, it's fine," he waved off her apology. "I've heard it from others, and for a long time. I'm going to run with that, if you don't mind. Something I said recently, to one of your viewers in particular who'll understand. You've all seduced me, sort of. I feel like we own each other, good and bad. Should I've put that another way?"

Rheta interrupted: "You'll get roasted online again tonight, and this time you'll deserve it. Leave it in, Deborra."

Deborra laughed lightly. "Maybe we do own you. Our time's about up, and I appreciate your coming in to talk, both of you, and your ideas and thoughts on these issues. This interview," she added, facing her camera, "will be broadcast again on the evening version of the news." She flashed her warm, TV-personality smile, and the station went to a commercial.

Sara turned to find Cary watching her, raising her brows, that knowing kind of teenage smile on her face.

"Let me have your mug," she said and took the cup Cary silently passed to her. In the kitchen she tapped a message on her phone, looked at it to be sure, then laughed and hit "Send."

I'm too expensive for you to own.

HE DIDN'T ANSWER. She felt like a geeky adolescent with a crush on the high-school quarterback. She looked at her phone over and over for a while to see if he might have responded, but there was nothing.

Cary retreated to the room she'd christened the "office", flopped down on the sofa, and began studying again after they had a light meal. Sara cleaned the kitchen, looked at the door locks, texted Rheta to say she'd seen the TV segment, and was she OK at her apartment?

Thanks for checking. Window fixed. Good show, right? Later. Busy now.

SARA DIDN'T HEAR from Matheson because he'd silenced his phone earlier that afternoon. He'd told Ken Thomas where he'd be, what route he'd be taking, and ordered Eliot not to come along today, not to drive behind him, either, unless—he reflected—he'd done it at a distance. Which he might have. He knew he was the opposite of inconspicuous in that car, but that could cut both ways, and, anyway, he liked driving it. He'd updated things, installed a good sound system with a USB interface, subscribed to Sirius. Usually when he went out in the car, he played old hard rock, but now elevator music filled the silence. It was mindless. He didn't have to hear or interact with it, didn't have to sing along or bang invisible drums on the steering wheel; he could think of other things.

He tried to push away thoughts involving Sara; they made him anxious, and he wanted to concentrate on Ransome, and this new roll of the dice in Ransome's game. Rheta's idea hadn't made a dent on anything. They wouldn't know for days if the TV interview had moved the needle. So, Plan C. Would there be other players, or would it end up just him and the old man, and what would they do then?

But the Kenny G melody was playing, and somehow he remembered eating toast outside…a slow Saturday morning… He shook his head. Focus.

But his mind strayed: Did he want to do this again, did he expect her to? He wasn't a kid anymore. He knew you didn't helplessly, against your will, against your better judgment, fall in love, not at this age. You made that choice to submit to the prospect; it didn't force itself on you. You chose. Or you didn't choose, and that kept your life smooth and less complicated. There was an old song about that. "Desperado"…he almost reached to change the music: No.

So he could still walk away. So could she.

He'd married Meghan in his twenties. He'd loved her the way a young man could, at that time, at that age; but Sara was right, he'd had papa issues, and, fighting the war of father and son, he'd somehow come to view her as just one scene of the script he was busy shredding, and he'd torn out her part…and then she left. It had mostly been his fault; he knew it even back then. The two kids they had were never quite the same with him. They were old enough when it all went down to know what was happening. Only in the past ten years had his son started talking to him, trying to work things out. And that wasn't for his sake—he knew it—but because of his grandchild.

Then, several years when he played around at everything, thinking he could represent himself as a mold-breaker, an innovator inspired by all experiences that came his way, who couldn't be tied down by convention. People would throng around you when you wore that costume, he reflected now, as he made the turn off one highway and onto another.

A young couple waited at the stop sign in that intersection. The boy stuck his thumb up and flashed headlights at him; he acknowledged them with a wave and headed northeast.

And here you are, doing that rock-star stuff again, he scoffed, drawing attention to yourself, when you could've just left in one of the Hondas. The Thunderbird seemed to reawaken things in his mind that he otherwise managed to shut out. He'd wheedled Thomas into riding with him a few times, until one day when Ken objected, "No, man, I'm not getting in that thing with you again! You do some kind of stream-of-conscience shit—"

" 'Stream of consciousness'," he'd corrected.

"No, I mean what I called it! You get yourself all worked up for a confessional, and I'm the priest, and I can't get out while we're on the road, but I tell you what: Sometimes jumping out looks like a pretty attractive alternative. There's just something about this car that does it to you. I am not going there again."

It was true. He thought differently when he drove the Tbird. It was like writing with an old ink pen instead of using the computer.

He continued with the penance: Tasha—East coast, model-gorgeous, the trophy, as he approached forty-five, still subordinate to his father. And that one was his fault, too. He wasn't a great-looking man, he admitted it, and too irritable to be her ideal companion, so he knew she was intrigued more by the position, the money, that image he'd built for himself. They could've had a decent marriage anyway, but he was too busy angling for control of the company, and maybe there just hadn't been enough between them.... Her life was derailed when she'd married him, and he hadn't made it better.... Thank God there were no kids from that marriage....

But she'd been vindictive, wasn't happy about the prenup, and after those accusations (well, he conceded, nearing the bustling little town, "emotional abuse" might have been true at the time), he'd signed off on a settlement big enough to satisfy her desire for revenge.

Ransome would have cold beer waiting for him, he figured, but, driving the Tbird this far, he'd be drinking only water today. He maneuvered through the downtown area—it looked nice enough, had actually been on his long list when he'd considered properties, but it wasn't as pretty as Mooresville, he observed with a critical eye. He drove on into a residential section where the homes were new and the lawns professionally tended.

The other three relationships passed through his mind like short one-act plays. They hadn't been serious, and neither he nor the women had been upset when they stopped seeing each other. He had no reason to feel regret, but they left in him a mild distaste, like he'd had one of those sandwiches at that barbecue place Ransome had picked the other month.

Sometime along then he'd rummaged around and found his first wedding ring, from the marriage with Meghan, and put it on again. He'd never worn one with Tasha—another way of flaunting unconventionality. He knew people liked seeing a man of a certain age wearing a wedding ring; it was a signal, it conveyed the image of stability, told them here was someone who'd got past the impulsiveness of youth—he was safe, in a way, a man to be trusted.

When a woman of his same age went ringless, sometimes it was a prompt to wonder about her, maybe, for being old and having no one. He felt the unfairness of the double standard whenever he slipped his band onto his finger, as he did often in places where he didn't know the crowd and they didn't much know him.

But he'd come to understand symbols, knew their power. He had his little house built and bought a kiln, some tools, glazes, a wheel, because he understood now the thing of creating and not going through life tearing down, and leaving that behind as the summation of how he'd passed his time on earth. He spent weekend hours learning clay, forming misshapen objects, pounding them into lumps again, overwhelmed by the frustration of never getting his vision to take the physical shape he wanted. As the clay dried and he refined the things he'd made, he carved and molded his failures and regrets into the pieces. It was time spent better than he had for years, decades.

And, yes, Ken, not having a clue about their origin, had been mildly disgusted when he handed out copies of the thing he made, disgusted that he'd label them a "philosophy." He'd gone on and done it anyway, keeping to himself the secret of their genesis; so the staff had been indifferent, positioned them here and there, to pacify him if he asked, or maybe, like Michael Ivey, took them home to get them off their desks.

After a while, he'd realized it was just a comical interlude of the play, and by then he wasn't going to own it: Doing that would only inspire the sycophants to place their little pieces in a more visible spot, and the cynics to file them away as another of his wild hairs. He was too old to let either choice bother him.

All that had been for him an entr'acte in the drama, a well-timed rest before the second part, however that would be played out, but he didn't want Sara to be just one more short act—he couldn't stand that, not at his age, not after all those others. He'd rather be by himself. Even if she didn't want to be with him— "Even if she doesn't," he mumbled aloud twice. He enjoyed having somebody tell him off. Nobody did, much, except Ken. He thought about Cary—he'd be okay with her; and Rheta, he could get used to her, too, maybe, if she'd quit writing about him....

He buzzed the gate and, just to be sure, texted Ransome: **Here.** Then he silenced the phone; he didn't want interruptions. As he locked the Thunderbird, Ransome came out the side door, shaking his head.

"Man, one of these days some eighteen-wheeler gonna crowd you off the road, and that'll be it for that car, and you. Or some kid'll jack it out from under you. Why you wanna run the risk?"

He laughed. "You don't use it, what's the point having it?" They went inside and started the long talk.

30

AND, EARLIER THAT day, Rheta had unlocked the door and called, "It's me," as she went through the back of her apartment. She laid down a small bag of things she'd bought, and reset the locks.

Again: "Hey. It's me. Feeling better?"

There was no answer, and her pulse started racing the way it did so much now since Friday. Tiptoeing toward the front—past the half-bath, the laundry room, the guest bedroom—she realized she'd picked up a knife from the sink and had it in her hand. She'd chosen that apartment because most of the large windows faced north, away from the summer sun; and on the south side, the kitchen, it didn't matter much, because she tried never to be in the kitchen in the afternoon. But in the living room—where thick curtains covered the newly-replaced glass—everything was dim. She gritted her teeth and walked forward and saw he was asleep on the sofa, the light blanket she'd tossed over his legs kicked off onto the floor, his hand under the pillow she'd brought from upstairs.

She sneered at herself and eased back to the kitchen to lay the knife down. She put the ice pack into the freezer and left on the counter the prescription she'd picked up for him. *Look at you, hovering over a man, which you've never done in your life; stop it now.* But, instead, she shoved her phone into her pocket and crept back to the sofa and after a moment asked, "Feeling better?"

He opened his eyes. "Not much. Doc told me to expect a

headache and it's there, by God. I can't have any more meds yet, can I?"

"Nope." She wasn't used to doing this kind of thing, and that made her angry. Fidgeting for a moment, she sat down on the floor beside the sofa and leaned forward to look at him. He met her eyes evenly, unemotionally.

"I bought an ice pack. It's chilling in the fridge."

"Thanks." He continued watching her, and it was too much— she shifted uneasily on the floor. He started pulling the pillow from under his head. "Here, take this—not helping *me* right now."

"I'm good." She pushed it back to him. Another pause, and she asked, "You try to eat anything while I was out?"

"I did drink the juice, like you ordered. Quit fussing over me. I'm grateful it wasn't worse, and I appreciate you letting me come over so you could tend to me, but you're freaking me out. I'm used to hearing you cuss. Just cuss me. When we were little, if I fell off a swing—"

"Look," she said abruptly, angrily. "I said I was good—well, I'm not, I'm not good at this. I'm an old woman, and I never learned to be solicitous. And you don't have to remind me—"

"You'd come and yell at me, tell me to get up before you hit me," he plowed on. "Yeah, my memory wasn't injured at all. Don't make me laugh. It makes my head hurt."

She drew her knees up under her chin and rocked slightly back and forth, staring at him. "Too many bad things."

"You don't want anything else to happen to anybody."

"Oh, it *will*. It will."

He raised himself cautiously, slowly up on the couch into a sitting position, kept his eyes shut, leaned back. She stopped rocking and stared at him, watched as, blindly, he massaged his head.

"I don't like not having control over things."

"Nobody has control," he mumbled. "When have you ever? Not when we were kids, not now; you had no more control over what happened Friday night than I did, yesterday. We're just along for the ride."

She turned from him. "Don't say that."

"Sure, we are. We just hop in and let the Big Guy drive."

"And go with it, huh, that about right?"

"Go on and punch me, get it over with. You would've, once."

"Screw you."

He snickered.

After a while she checked on the ice pack. It seemed cool enough now to help, and she wrapped it in a clean dish towel so it wouldn't give him frostbite. She wondered if that could happen, frostbite? The package said it could, but she didn't think so. She removed the towel and laid it on top of his head.

He laughed, winced. "It can't help, there. Tell you what. Go fix the bed for me—" he gestured vaguely at the guest room— "I'll lie down for a while with that thing *under* my head where they shaved me, where I hit it, that might help."

"If you lie down, I am, too."

He opened his eyes and gave her another look.

"If you slip into a coma, it'll be on me, in my house."

He laughed again, a chuckle cut short by another grimace. "I won't slip into a coma, that's not gonna happen."

"I haven't been by myself since Friday night." It came out fast, and she scowled at him as if he had forced it from her.

"You and Sara sharin' her bed?"

"Just get your ass in here, and I'll check the front door."

"*Don't,* it's locked. You gotta get back to normal."

"This *is* normal."

He gingerly rose from the sofa and with one hand held the ice pack on the back of his skull; with the other he pushed her ahead of him towards her guest room. "This'll be fine. I can't climb stairs."

"Did the doctor say that?"

"No, I just can't imagine what that'd do to my head. So I'm not gonna experiment. Come on." She went ahead of him and pulled back the comforter in the tiny windowless room. He positioned the cool pack on the pillow and eased down on the bed, then, eyes closed, patted the other side. "I warn you, that better be good enough, because every time I move around, my head breaks open. So if you have to have company, be still, for God's sake. You're weird—didn't want this on Friday, when I *could've.*"

"And I still don't." She sank carefully beside him and pulled the comforter up over their legs.

"Take it off."

"I'm cold. I'll pull it over myself."

"You do that. Let's rest, okay?"

She would have been humiliated if she'd known Sara and Ron

had had the same conversation a few days earlier.

She tapped a quick answer to the message Sara sent just then.

Thanks for checking. Window fixed. Good show, right? Later. Busy now.

Then she lay awake thinking of what he'd said.

RON LEFT RANSOME'S house, the old man bristling and swearing. "You don't have to call anybody; I'll take care of it myself, dammit! Think I'm such a fossil I don't know how to do that? I did it all, back in the day. And next time leave that thing at home, because you stick out like a sore thumb!"

Ron laughed, buckled the seat belt he'd retrofitted into the car—no air bags, but he drove safely, and it was just one of those things you risked. It was almost five, and he probably should've offered to take Ransome out somewhere for supper—that clean, empty house was depressing, and he knew what it was to eat alone. But he didn't like driving the Thunderbird after dark, and if they'd gone to a restaurant, he'd be late getting back to Mooresville. So, another time.... He changed his mind about the easy-listening elevator music and chose rock for the trip back, checked the mirrors, rounded the semicircular drive. He stopped at the street, remembering the silenced phone, and turned it up, glanced down and saw she had just messaged him:

I'm too expensive for you to own.

What the hell did that mean? He navigated his way out of town, onto the quiet two-lane highway he'd come in on, still wondering. Was it that stupid joke about giving her a job at the company? That was long ago. Surely she wasn't holding that grudge.... Was it some strange way of saying she was getting rid of him and wanted to be with that piece of shit Neil Griffin, after all—

He slammed his hand on the steering wheel, laughed out loud. They must've aired the interview today. Well, yes; Ransome had turned on the TV as they'd headed out the door....

And then the funny side passed. He had more than another hour to drive, time to think. He didn't want to ruin this the way he sometimes still screwed things up unless they involved numbers and code. He needed to think about what to answer and how to say it and even when...whether to be serious or silly... Oh, God, no, *that* was all wrong.... He was still thinking, trying to work it out, still clutching the phone, holding it under his palm against the steering wheel, when the dog ran out in front of him, and he swerved. In five seconds the heavy old car had flown out of control and slid off the road into a ditch, taking with it a yellow sign and the poles the sign was attached to.

He'd locked the brakes—he knew better, but he'd done it anyway, not thinking, not concentrating, not focusing, holding the damned phone, and where had *it* disappeared? He sat motionless for a few moments, taking inventory of his limbs, his chest. Looking out over the long hood of the car, now buckled up exposing the engine. The radiator steamed.

It occurred to him that, before long, people would be stopping, and he didn't want things done by Samaritans he didn't know. He found the phone on the floor; the screen was cracked—why'd he held it against the wheel?—but it seemed functional. He dialed Ken's private number and told him what he needed. Ken reminded him it would be a while before the tow company they preferred got up there from Mooresville, and he agreed that he'd have to get a local truck: He'd have to ask Ransome for another favor. Ken coldly offered to send Eliot to retrieve him, but he could hear that tone, and turned down the offer. It was much closer to the old man's house, and he'd be delighted at having been right, thrilled at being useful tonight.

He made the call and winced at the words he'd known he'd hear, and then Ransome told him he'd get in touch with this fellow he knew, right on the south side of town; and since Ron wasn't that far away yet, he'd be there real fast. Ransome called back in a minute—the tow man was on his way; and he'd just put him up for the night, they'd get everything taken care of in the morning.

Two vehicles slowed down to pull onto the shoulder; a young guy approached. Ron decided he could no longer postpone getting out of the car. Pushing the heavy door open, he stood—well, he'd be paying for it for a few days, he thought, shifting his shoulders around tentatively. These old cars didn't take a shock like modern ones did—they just passed it right on to you.

"You okay?" the kid asked. But his eyes were on the Thunderbird, not on Matheson, and he was shaking his head sorrowfully. "Too bad about the car."

Ron closed the door and leaned against it; a shudder went through him as he pressed his back against the window. "I'm all right."

The couple in the other vehicle also got out and asked if he needed to go anywhere, make any calls, offered him a bottle of water. He was in the South; by now he knew people did that kind of thing here, but he still wasn't used to it. He was politely declining their offers when a tow truck, lights flashing, appeared from the town he'd just left, and the driver took charge and extracted the Tbird from the ditch. By then Ron thought he might've dislocated his shoulder. He told the driver to haul the car to Mooresville, paid an exorbitant fee with his card—but you shouldn't have driven it here, so suck it up, he told himself—and watched the flashing lights head south just as Ransome churned up the gravel on the shoulder next to him. Ron thanked the people who'd stopped, talked to the trooper who'd also stopped by then, and submitted to a breathalyzer: That would've been another story he didn't need in the news. Thank God he'd turned down those beers. He was fine, he told the man, and Mr. Moore was going to let him stay overnight at his house; everything was okay.

As they left he leaned back against the seat. "ER?" Ransome asked tersely, and he nodded.

"Just to be sure."

"What happened? Deer?"

"No, a dog. I didn't even hit it. Don't know where *it* went. Wasn't paying attention." The trembling of mild shock began; he knew what *that* was, too, but couldn't help tensing his legs and body to stop the shaking as Ransome sped back up the highway.

"It coulda been worse. Those antique cars, they don't take crashes like we're used to these days," Ransome said philosophically. "You gonna scrap it now?"

He turned to gaze at the old man in amazement and saw a twitch at the side of his mouth. "Well, what d'*you* think? Would you throw it away because you messed it up a little?"

KEN THOMAS DEBATED whether to let Sara know about Matheson's accident. He was glad it hadn't seemed to damage anything much but the man's car, and his pride, which could take a little roughing-up, in his opinion, and, besides, he wasn't sure exactly how Sara would react, hearing it from him. He thought about all of it for an hour before driving out to the big gate: He figured it would take about that long for the truck to arrive. Sitting in his office all that time, he'd slowly realized everything was quiet, eerily quiet, and he might as well wait at the road. He told the guard why he was there, parked, and lowered the windows.

He thought he might know more about the two of them than they knew about themselves, maybe, but there wasn't any reason for him to tell Sara; he'd seem like somebody arranging a blind date for his sister if he said anything. When Matheson returned in the morning, he could tell her himself, if he wanted to. Or he could do it right now; he'd called, so he'd had his phone with him, thank God. Sometimes he didn't take it along on his drives, wanted his privacy, he said. He had a thing about phones.

Thomas shook his head in disgust, picked up one of the trade magazines he'd brought to pass the time, but his thoughts went to the long list of things he stayed disgusted about. How many times had he lectured him not to go off far in that vehicle, or, if he just couldn't help himself, to have one of the security guys ride along, or behind, just in case. Ken had reminded him people could sue him, if there was the least kind of accident. He'd told him, again, he wasn't being careful enough with the finances, not that they were hurting, but he just disapproved of how the man seemed intent on turning every routine thing upside down, like a bowl with lots of stuff in it, just to see what would fall out. That's how it looked to Ken. And, then, he still seemed to have a teenager's view of his mortality. And everybody knew what he did once he had you trapped in the passenger seat, so nobody wanted to drive anywhere with him. Eliot would tolerate it once in a while, but only for short trips....

A recurring thought he'd had for a couple of years now resurfaced as he gazed out the windshield: He was tired, God, he was so tired of picking up after Matheson. He liked the man well enough, had liked him more after moving to Mooresville. Ron didn't patronize but appreciated him—but in the way a younger brother appreciates an older one who protects him. He wasn't Matheson's big brother, and he wasn't his father, either. By age, Matheson should be *his* big brother. He was tired of that role— "righteous fatherly Black man," that old trope. He threw it at Ron sometimes.

Ken let the seat back as far as it could go and tried to get comfortable. The late-May evening warmth slowly settled around him. He put the magazine aside—he'd known he wouldn't read it, anyway—and closed his eyes. Matheson had asked him more than once over the past few years how to get used to the Southern heat, the enervating humidity of the long summer, but it was something you couldn't explain in terms an OCD engineer'd understand—"nonquantifiable," was what he told Matheson. It was just a part of your routine during all those months when it wasn't cool. The joke went that in the South, you had two seasons: summer, and then the winter week. And it wasn't really much of a joke.

He'd undone a couple of buttons on the neat polo shirt, but still the sultry air brought a light bead of moisture to his forehead....

When the aggressive roar of the truck awoke him, he grabbed for the phone on the seat beside him: Well, he'd only dozed a few minutes. He stretched his arms as he spoke to the driver through the slats of the gate, opened it, told him to follow as he led the way to that garage building. The man maneuvered the Tbird into its place and then stepped out of the truck cab, eyeing Thomas curiously.

"The owner gonna fix that thing up? I might buy it if he don't intend to."

Thomas scoffed. "He'll want it. He's fond of it." He was ready to go home, ready for the iced tea Mary had waiting for him. But the guy scratched his head and frowned skeptically.

"What do *you* do here?"

It wasn't an unfriendly or suspicious question—but Ken had heard it before, phrased differently, sometimes *in* unfriendly, suspicious words, and just lately he wasn't in the mood for it. The man had sized him up—that shirt he'd unbuttoned in the heat, the color of his skin. He remembered even Matheson telling him last week, "Go cool off." What the hell did *he* know about it....

"You need authorization to leave it? Here's my card." He dug into his wallet and handed it over. It was always a guilty pleasure of his to see the manner change when he did that. Sometimes he felt bad about it, and he might today, when this guy didn't seem to mean anything by his question; but sometimes it was satisfying putting some redneck in his place.

The driver scrutinized the card and put it into his shirt pocket.

"I was told the towing fee's already been paid," Thomas continued.

"Yeah, he did it before I left..." The man glanced around as he climbed back into his truck. "Nice place out this way. More like a park than a business."

"Yeah, we like it."

He followed the guy out through the gate and onto the highway. He was thinking about the Thunderbird.... Matheson had messed the front of it up pretty good, and he himself would junk the thing, but he knew Ron wouldn't; that car did something to him Ken never would be able to figure out.... His thoughts stopped there suddenly, and when the first traffic light caught him, he dialed Sara's number.

She and Cary had had vegetables and French bread for supper and had finished the cleanup, and now she sat at the kitchen table, admiring the fading sunset that streamed through the back windows and colored the walls, thinking Matheson should've already replied with a smartass message. When her phone rang, she wondered idly why Ken Thomas would be calling at eight o'clock.

"Mr. Thomas—how are you tonight?"

He sighed. "Sara, really, it's time you just said 'Ken', don't you think? Whatever," he went on, "I'm fine. I may be stepping out of line. But I think you'd want to know. Ron crashed his car tonight."

"Oh, my God...is he all right?" Names and faces went through her mind in a flash—herself and Rheta, and Chris, and now Ron. "What happened? Did somebody—" Her voice thickened, and she couldn't continue right then.

He approved of her anxiety; it meant something. "He's okay—car's going to be in intensive care for a while, though."

"Was anybody else hurt?"

"Nobody else was involved. He was alone, on his way back from visiting Ransome Moore. He said an animal ran out in front of him. He ditched and hit a highway sign. I think Ransome's keeping him overnight. Probably lecturing him for a few hours."

Ken appeared to regard it as a minor accident, so she laughed. "Probably. And you said he's okay?"

"I guess so. He was making sense. You could text him to be sure." He paused and then added slyly, "I know you have his number, because I gave him yours."

"Hmm." She heard the remark, but her brain was running a loop of all the things that had happened since Friday. "You're sure it wasn't deliberate? I mean, after what they did to Rheta's apartment, and then Chris Liberto, I just have to wonder."

"No, this was on him, had nothing to do with Rheta." He

hesitated. "What do you mean, 'Chris Liberto'? What's happened to him?"

She explained about the fire.

"That's something I didn't know."

"They passed it off as a garbage-bin fire. No publicity."

There was a silence so deep then that she was able to hear an intermittent blip in the background before he asked, "You regret getting involved with Lynne's campaign?"

"No! No. If you're saying any of these things might've been for intimidation, well, it didn't work. I just hope she wins. She asked me…" she paused. "She asked me not to do anything else. She feels guilty this crap's happening to *us*, and not her. She feels like she brought it on us."

The background noise stopped; and he remained silent. He could tell her a thing or two, how it must've felt in the first place to ask for an endorsement, when your own qualifications ought to make that unnecessary; he'd been through it, he knew. But he wouldn't say those things on a cell phone. Maybe later, after the election.

"So you say the car's messed up?" she asked in the quiet.

"He got a man to tow it back here, and I saw it, and, yeah, he's gonna be unhappy."

"The company has good insurance, though, right." She was just making small talk now, and she wished Thomas would finish, so she *could* text…

"It wasn't a company car. It was that old one, his baby. You've seen it?"

"I don't think so…" Then a memory surfaced of months back, of her and Cary and Louise in the park, of a red vehicle rounding a curve that led out to the main street, of Louise paying attention because it was an antique, because, she said, Hal had had one of those, long ago…. "Oh, maybe I have seen it, once."

"He'll fix it up again, I know it, but if he listened to me, he wouldn't," Ken told her. She smiled at the disgust in his voice. There was background street noise, and she realized he was driving, and the blip must have been his turn signal. "But it's his personal obsession. So what can I say. He claims sometimes it straightens out his mind when he's trying to work on a problem. Does that make sense?"

"Maybe. A little."

"He's had it, oh, twenty-five years. Nobody touches that car but him. Nobody drives it but him. And if he ever offers to take you somewhere in it, after he fixes it back up—and, like I said, he will fix it—I warn you, you better say 'No', or bring along your headphones. I won't go anywhere in it with him anymore. 'Course, *he* won't be going anywhere in it for a while, so that won't be your problem or mine."

"If he's not hurt, that's the main thing."

"But *you* tell him that, when he gets a good look."

The color at the window had faded now to mauves and purples, darker blues. "Why was he up there, talking with Ransome Moore? Do you know?"

He paused again before answering, long enough to make her start to feel annoyed. Then: "I'll let him explain about that trip."

She sighed deeply to show her exasperation and said, "Thank you for calling me. I'll text him in a minute."

Cary was still studying in the office: Tomorrow was the last test she'd have to take, and then she'd be out for the summer. And then the driver's license. Sara reflected on what Ken had just told her, on how fast something could happen.

And then she laughed out loud, and Cary wandered into the kitchen to eye her. She gestured vaguely: "I just talked with Ken Thomas about something and, honestly, it struck me as funny. I'll tell you later, okay? Don't stay up too late."

Cary gave her another puzzled glance. "Sure, all right," and in a moment Sara heard her switch the lights off in the office, heard Cary's bed wheeze as she flopped down on it. Still she sat in the kitchen and smiled at the absurdity: Nobody but him ever drove the car? So he was along when Eliot delivered the sphere to her in the park, in February. She should've just followed Eliot back to the car and had it out with him then. It would've saved time.

31

HE COULDN'T GET comfortable. The ER doc had said it was only bruising where he'd hit the steering wheel, and the impact of the heavy old car against the pole, that made him think his shoulder was dislocated, and it might give him hell for a few days. Oh, and, "Plus, you're not as young as you were when this sort of thing wouldn't have slowed you down." He'd written a prescription for something Ron knew he wouldn't take—if there was anything he wouldn't do, it was get hooked on pain meds again—so Ransome had rounded up some over-the-counter stuff for him. And it hadn't helped much.

They'd returned to Ransome's too-clean house and sat up a while longer, going over the plan, second-guessing everything, trying to cobble together a couple of alternatives if the main parts didn't work. Ron had finally eased off the sofa and said he'd try to rest. "Feels like it *was* one of those eighteen-wheelers you talk about instead of just a little road sign," he groaned.

Ransome gestured at the hallway behind the den. "Second door to the right. Holler if you need something."

So he'd undressed and lain down, and the twitching and twisting began. He put the phone on the night stand, wondering if he should use it at all, because it looked pretty busted…. He tried to convince himself the twitching was because of the pain—there was plenty of that—but mostly it was because he was tense, worried about tomorrow, worried that the main actor wouldn't show. Or that they'd be charged with starting a brawl, if one broke out.

The text came as he stared at the ceiling.

When I said you didn't have enough $$, I didn't think you'd get depressed enough to wreck your car.

He held the phone in front of his face, realized his arms would go to sleep if he did that for very long—already they were trembling again. He tried calling her—straight to voicemail, and another text arrived: *No talking. Cary's last test is tomorrow. I think she's asleep. Don't want to wake her.*

Great, he thought, only words on a screen that looks like it's going to die on me. He gingerly sat up in the bed, stuffing a pillow behind his back.

All right. Don't want the other old man awake here, either. How'd you find out?

It seemed to him too long a wait before her response arrived. He read what she told him about Ken, laughed softly at the thought of the man trying to decide to call her. Before he could answer that message, another one arrived asking if he was hurt. He paused before replying to that one:

Bruised a little. Mostly the car.

Next time let somebody else drive.

The phone was sluggish, and the battery seemed to be dying faster than usual. He hurriedly typed: **No 1 drives it but me**.

I'M AWARE. That popped up on the shattered screen almost immediately. He frowned, stared at the message a moment or two, but something weird was happening with the phone, light flickering, touch not very responsive, so he told her, **Broke phone dying on me talk in the a.m.** And how would he talk in the a.m.? Maybe Ransome's phone—in which case he'd better get her number written down right now, because he didn't know it from memory, and Ransome wouldn't have it, he figured. He rifled through the drawer of the night table to find a pen and scrap of paper. The failing cell phone required him to punch harder and harder as he found her information and copied it. A winking emoji arrived as he laid the pen down. What the hell was that for? he wondered, but that was the end of the texting, because the screen froze and a few seconds later blinked off.

He arranged the pillows again and tried to rest.

SHE AND CARY both overslept Tuesday morning. "We'll get there," she said soothingly, shoving a peanut butter sandwich across the seat, and Cary glared at her:

"Yeah, you don't have to take this test. Just hurry, and if it means so much to you, I'll eat this thing." She took a huge bite, chewing ferociously.

Sara glanced at her. "You might brush your hair when you're done."

The first bell was ringing. Cary flung herself out towards the school entrance, where Sara observed that Carson had waited for her. "Remember I'm going to Allie's after this test," she yelled. Sara waved, but he and Cary scurried inside the building without glancing back.

She headed home, going much slower now. A text popped up on the monitor, from a number she didn't have in her contacts. She played it aloud: **Leaving for home. Using Ransome's phone**. Serves you right, she thought, remembering how she'd had to use his, how he didn't understand her reluctance in doing it.... She was turning onto the last set of quiet streets to her house when she noticed the Toyota, following at a distance that kept her from seeing who was in the car—but it was one person, she noticed, a man. She took a right down a random street, then a left, to make sure, then voiced a message to Rheta: *Left school somebody following me* Rheta's answer was fast: **On way w Chris**. Chris was with her after all? She made another left and was back to her own street again, reminding herself it was broad daylight, there were people up and about, should she stop away from her own house? and outrage overcame fear. By God, it was her neighborhood. She whirled into her drive and leaped out, striding to unlock the front, then turning towards the vehicle that came to a halt beside the sidewalk.

"You." She stopped.

Stephen laughed. "You don't hold back, do you. Can I come in?"

"You kidding me? You kidding me?"

"It's a pleasant morning, we can stand out front here, I guess, for everybody to see."

"Have you been hanging out at the school to find out where I live?" She realized whoever'd cleaned him up and slicked him down, as Lynne had called it, hadn't been entirely successful at getting him to hide anger. He jerked his head once before the mask came back up.

"That's over the top. Little paranoid."

"You tell your mob to stay home this time?" she scoffed. "Or will they be here, too, in a few minutes?"

That flash of irritation crossed his face again, and he forced another faint smile; she found that more disturbing than if he'd yelled at her. "I'm gonna ignore that. I told you I had nothing to do with it."

"Like you had nothing to do with the thing in Andy's shop, or with the churches," she goaded.

He took a few steps toward her. Her first impulse was to recoil, to dash inside that open front door and throw the locks, hide; but she planted herself as he approached until there was only about a yard separating them.

"Look. I was out, headed to my office—"

"Because it's so close to school."

"Okay, truth: I figured you'd be dropping your daughter off, and I wanted to talk to you, and I imagined you wouldn't answer a number you didn't have. I thought I'd catch you as you got here. And, by the way, I didn't *have* to follow you; you're not that hard to find. Most people—" he lifted his brows— "aren't hard to find."

"What d'you want, Stephen?"

"I was going to remind you you're on my list—" he showed teeth, but she saw no humor in his eyes as he added, "—of people I want working with me. A staffer."

"A councilman in Mooresville needs a staffer?" she scoffed.

He held up his hand and continued, "A consultant. Whatever you want to call it. Having you on board would..."

"Give you some respectability," she cut in.

"It's not like you've never done it. People know Ron Matheson got you to do that kids' thing to leech off your reputation. And I know those old ladies in that historical society, well, you let them do the same, too, before they cut you off. That kind of people always do, none of them think you're as good as they are, never have, never will. I'm giving you a chance to show them up for a change."

She stared at him, the words falling upon her, and she knew what had driven him long ago and now, what drove the people who supported him—that sense of never being the equal of another person—and she understood why people like him always had to have another group of human beings beneath *them*, because so long as there was somebody there, it meant you were not on the bottom yourself.

"The book's a community project."

He shrugged. "Whatever you say."

"And what I do with the preservation people—"

"Okay, anyway," he interrupted, "however you want to look at it, I don't see it's any different than *me* asking you to do it." A car passed, slowly, the driver turning in his seat to look back at them. "Wasn't planning to hang around outside."

"I don't want anything to do with the kind of people you attract."

"I'm not responsible for what somebody does on their own. I didn't tell 'em to do anything."

"You didn't tell them *not* to."

"Look, Sara, things'll be changing around here, and you can be on the winning side." His tone changed. "Neil's supporting me. You want me to have him talk to you about it?"

"You mean Neil Griffin. I doubt he's 'supporting' you— 'tolerating' you's more the word. And if I wanted him to talk to me about it, I could call him."

"I'm sure you can."

"What does that mean?" She hoped she sounded cold and dangerous. He took a step closer, and she straight-armed him, palm up, warned him off: "Keep your distance."

"I'm not threatening you. I know who you're with. And maybe you're working both sides of the street," he suggested with a shrug, "not necessarily a bad thing, you know. Just a little unexpected, from you. So if it's that, okay, I understand."

Up close, he looked rough, coarse, not smoothed-out at all, she realized. A part of her wanted to get inside the house, but fear, or stubbornness, kept her rooted in place.

"You better leave right now." Rheta's car hurtled around the final turn onto her street. "And don't come back, or I'll take out a restraining order against you, I swear to God, and we'll see what you say when *that* makes the news."

He flicked at his chin in a sort of involuntary, reflexive way, as if he were trying to bring the hand under control, and he leaned toward her. "You think Neil will write you one?" he asked mockingly.

"He's not the only lawyer in town."

Chris pulled himself slowly, carefully, out the passenger door, but Rheta leaped from the driver's side. Logan watched her, a wry twist to his lips. "Hey, Rheta," he said. "Trying to make up some more news? Sara and I were just talking about after the election. I guess she called you over, why, I have no idea." He strolled to his car, where Rheta intercepted him, crowding him, her hands clenched.

"Why're you harassing her?"

He looked up and down the street, exaggerating the turn of his head to left and right. "It's a public place. I got as much right to be here as you. I'm not 'harassing' anybody. You don't own this street. And why'd you come along—" gesturing at Chris. "Or have *you* two cozied up now? You making up a new story for her to put out?"

Rheta turned to Sara. "Get Ron to send a couple of his guys over."

"He's not back in town yet."

Chris glanced up, frowned, and she wondered momentarily what that was about.

"Call Ken Thomas."

"So here we stand, arguing like a bunch of drunks on a Saturday night," Logan said derisively, "drawing attention, and I guess some old busybody'll call the TV station or something, send in some phone footage they're probably recording. So y'all have a good morning."

Rheta stepped closer and tapped him on the chest. "Don't come here again. Don't send any of your thugs either."

"Matheson's 'thugs' are welcome, though?" A neighbor came out onto her porch, eyeing the group, holding up her phone. "All right, fine. But if you're trying to fit in with the folks that've always run this place, you ain't ever gonna—" He paused, "There'll be new leaders, and you won't fit in with us, either, and where'll you go then?"

He brushed past Rheta, got into his car and drove away. The woman next door glared at him as he left, unhurriedly.

"Afraid of us. Scared. Run off, Stephen." Chris laughed.

Rheta shoved ungently on his shoulder, and he stumbled, looked confused. "Jerk. If we'd wanted to, we could've beat the shit out of him. Maybe except for you. But Sara and I could've. So it felt good to you. It feels *good* to you, pushing him around. Knowing he couldn't do anything. Right." She shoved him ahead of her inside and locked the front door behind everyone. "We're all staying here, for now."

"IS EVERYBODY ON board or not?" Ransome demanded as he drove down the highway, carefully staying three miles over the speed limit, his eyes sweeping back and forth to watch for animals, cars pulling out from side roads, people slowing down suddenly in front of him. Ron felt ten years older than the old man. He'd reclined his seat to a forty-five-degree angle and tried to keep from tensing up his back muscles. Ibuprofen could only do so much.

He picked up Ransome's phone and looked through the messages again. Rheta'd sent just the one—**See you at 12**—but there was nothing else. "I guess we'll find out when we get there. You sure Deborra's on board? *She's* the one I'm wondering about, because Logan's right: The station *is* getting close to having to provide equal time."

Ransome's thick fingers gripped the wheel. "I know how to do these things. She says it's all right. It's not election-related. It's a news story."

"This's never bothered you—owning part of the local media, telling them what you want 'em to do?"

Ransome snorted. "You think, all those years, David Burkes didn't do it first? I just put my finger on the other side of the scales."

"Small-town politics. Shit." Ron was disgusted, and Ransome took his eyes off the road for one moment to glare at him.

"You have a short memory for somebody that's been on the receiving end of 'small-town politics.' Want me to remind you of all the crap you've been dealt since you got here?"

"You don't have to, no."

"So, anyway, Joe Sims's sending that kid, too—what's his name?"

"Jared."

"Yeah, him. Don't think Joe wants to come. Maybe he's constipated." Ransome's voice dripped contempt. "So, Jared, yeah. I'll remember it from now on. The more, the merrier. You can't say I pick and choose. I want 'em all there."

"What makes you so sure this is how to do it?"

"Well, we tried having you take the heat. Then, next, Miss Rheta and her civilized interview. Tellin' about the sonsabitches with those torches. Who knows if *that* helped." If Matheson had tried to speak, he couldn't have, as Ransome railed on: "If Joe'd done what I said to do, it'd've been taken care of, but no, gotta pussyfoot around it, *'maybe it's libel,'* can't have the poor boy upset." He shook his head in disgust. "Back in the day people paid attention. That wimpy bastard's got no balls. *'Maybe he could sue us.'* Gimme a break. I told all of you to wrap it around his neck, don't let him put a nickel in the meter without explaining it, but, no—"

"You can't print stuff you have no proof of, Ransome. It's not like the old days."

"Shit! Gonna rent Joe a room at Golden Acres and send him the bill."

In spite of himself Ron laughed at that idea, and Ransome might just do it....

The morning sun had warmed up the car, and especially the old man, as he drove south. He'd opened the vent and hadn't asked Ron if he wanted that much air blowing on his face. Inconsiderate old cuss. He leaned forward slowly, dramatically, to close the vent.

Ransome didn't notice.

Sara hadn't yet answered his last question—**Come to courthouse around noon?**—and he worried about that. Did it sound too demanding? He'd added the question mark to let her understand it wasn't a dictate but, instead, a wish, but maybe she didn't take it that way. He'd issued commands unthinkingly in the past—to his wives, his girlfriends, his children—and it never ended well.

"Sara coming, too?" Ransome asked as if reading his thoughts.

He grunted noncommittally.

"Don't know yet?" Ransome prodded.

"Hell, you old busybody, I told her to come to the courthouse at noon."

"You 'told' her?"

Ron leaned back again with his eyes closed. "No! I asked her, if you need to know. God, I hope I'm not as nosy as you are when I'm your age."

"Not long before you'll find out!" Ransome guffawed, glanced at Matheson. "You don't look so good right now."

"Yeah, I don't feel so good either. Thanks for the sympathy."

"You did okay in that interview. I watched most of it before I had to leave and haul your ass back to town last night."

Ron snorted. "But as you said, did it help?"

In a moment Ransome spoke again: "Maybe she thought you want her to go to the circuit clerk, get a marriage license."

"Shit!" He hadn't thought of that, and his reaction produced another raucous laugh from the man behind the wheel.

"Don tells me you two've got pretty close all of a sudden, and you're not getting younger."

"Don ought to keep his damn mouth shut!" He realized Ransome was baiting him in the same way Ken had started doing, and it made him feel like a teenager, and he was older than Ken, by God, and not that much younger than Ransome. —As the old man had just reminded him, several times, even. He adjusted his shoulders again against the thick, padded backrest. Well, the SUV's seats *were* more comfortable than the Tbird's, he admitted—and that made him think again of messing up his car, made his brain draw up a picture of that sign bending over toward him as the poles gave way…. He remembered what he was doing when it happened: sorting through his feelings about her, thinking it all poised on that one thing he needed to ask—*Was that "owning" shit a joke; can you tell me really what you're feeling?* And then he hadn't asked that—hadn't had time, because of that damned dog, and the sign, and the tow truck, and his busted phone, and now, he wouldn't, because he didn't want to forget to delete that kind of message on Ransome's phone.

His thoughts went next to Neil Griffin, and how she was going to feel about *that*. He figured the two of them had slept together— he didn't like thinking about it, but of course he'd long ago heard that gossip, even if nobody knew if it was the current state of things; and, anyway, he'd had *his* girlfriends. He didn't care about Matthew Wells, that wasn't his business—but that particular man....

He felt guilty, too, at the moment: What he and Ransome had planned, if it worked, was going to change things in town, mess up people's lives, and he ought to be concerned about that, right now, instead of fretting over Sara. And what had that wink and "*I'M AWARE*" been about last night?

—Dammit, he thought: back to her. He hit the button to raise the seat. Ransome gave him another questioning glance. "Pain?"

"Nope. Uncomfortable in other ways. I hope we're doing the right thing."

"We are," Ransome told him grimly. "It'll cause some trouble. But everything we did, then, informs what we do today. They tell you past don't matter? Don't believe it."

32

ON A TUESDAY, things were always slow, but then the lunch crowd hadn't actually arrived yet. Don wandered outside and adjusted a couple of umbrellas, glanced across the street, looked up at Neil Griffin's office. He hadn't noticed the man going or coming just lately, not since the past week, but then he'd been pretty busy himself, maybe so busy he'd just missed that. He grimaced and went back inside the restaurant. Since Sunday evening he'd been distracted. Chris would be okay, but Don had had too many reminders of mortality in his life to brush it off. And on the other hand, if Chris hadn't walked out at just that time, there could've been worse things....

Fifteen of twelve, and he noticed more people—people parking in the fee places, tapping phones to pay, people strolling down the streets, but not to the restaurant, although there was purpose in their steps. He texted Lisa: **What's going on today?**

Almost immediately she called him. "I don't know, but Chris asked me to be with him and Rheta at the courthouse. Well," she amended, "he said he was going with Rheta and he wanted me to be there for *her*. That's weird, isn't it? He didn't call or text or anything?"

Don ruefully remembered he hadn't looked at his phone all morning, but he wouldn't tell Lisa that. "I don't know what you're talking about," he hedged.

"Well, has she got herself into some kind of trouble, and he thinks she needs support? Have you heard anything around the tables?"

He shifted the phone to hold it with his chin against his ear and, agitated all of a sudden, wiped the glass on the front door, holding the cloth with both hands. "Nobody's said anything much," he began obliquely.

"Get Alison to hold it down for a while, she'll do fine, and run over to the courthouse. I can't get off work right now."

Lisa was right: Alison *was* capable of managing the place for a while, so he told her what to do, and left. He walked two blocks east toward the municipal building and stopped across the street from the people gathered at the base of the steps leading to the courthouse. There was a WREM-TV car out front. He scanned faces to locate Rheta or Chris, crossed over, and stopped at the sight of Ransome Moore lounging halfway up those steps, glad-handing people just like in the old days, and there was Ron Matheson next to him. In a moment or two they both turned and spoke a word to Deborra when she brought her camera guy near, and then Don noticed Deborra urging Chris to the top of the first landing. And as he stared, Chris reached out to shake the hand of a familiar-looking Black guy, familiar-looking, but he couldn't figure out who, at first. The two of them arranged themselves on the landing at Deborra's instructions, Chris occasionally turning and his newly-bald spot on his head flashing a circle of light flesh in his dark hair, a sort of monkish tonsure, Don thought. Deborra held a wireless mike. In another moment she began to speak, and

Don realized he'd have to get closer to hear her. But he knew what it was all about as he recognized Colbie at last, as he saw Rheta, several steps lower, clasp her tightly-wrung-together hands in front of her chest as she lowered her head and turned away, eyes shut. She looked as if she were praying, which—as he came halfway up the steps—Don thought was kind of funny, in a way, considering it was her.

HE'D ALWAYS BELIEVED he'd turn to stone, if this moment ever arrived, but, instead, relief and deep melancholy overtook him, as when he'd helped Chris pack and haul out Dominic's clothes when the old man died.

"Today WREM was asked to come to the courthouse for a statement from Chris Liberto and Colbie Jones about an event that occurred two decades ago." *Three*, Don mentally corrected Deborra, just as he noticed Sara on the steps at Ransome's other side.

Chris glanced toward Rheta's back, then confessed to having been in a car with four other boys long ago when they went joyriding on a sultry summer night and torched the worship places of people whom they not only had nothing against but hadn't even known. The small crowd hushed as he continued with details—the bottle of Johnnie Walker they passed around, their drunken hilarity as they realized none of them had lighters, the one who smoked producing a matchbook from his shirt pocket, which sobered them for a moment—were they really going to do it?—and they argued then about just going home and sleeping it off, until one of the boys started badgering, bullying the others, threatening to put them out on the dark road in the middle of nowhere, let 'em get back to town on foot.... When others joined in, the two fell silent and tried to think of a way to stop it before it happened. But the dirt miles rolled under the car, the dust roiled up behind them, and when they came to a halt at the first building, sitting stark white against the fields surrounding it on the moonless night, they stumbled out of the car with the other three and tried to look like they were enjoying the fun.

Don watched Chris tell it all, answering an occasional question from Deborra. Sometime or other Colbie laid his hand on Chris's shoulder and edged a little bit closer to him, and the crowd murmured, and heads turned, so that Don also turned, to see

Stephen Logan drawing near at a brisk pace, a stony, furious, maybe alarmed, expression etching lines upon his face. And behind him a few steps, his own face mask-like in another way, came Neil Griffin.

Chris continued: The second church, some miles away, was harder to set, and there was another argument, because what was the point of that? So they'd left and assumed it hadn't caught fire, headed back to town...and on the way passed Colbie, who was out walking, who stared at the faces in the back seat and then tore off through the thin patch of woods at the edge of the road.

Deborra wanted to know why he was saying this here, today, why not to the current sheriff or another investigator in a private setting, inside the courthouse, maybe, instead of outside; and Colbie held up his right hand to offer an answer himself. Colbie had thin gray hair now—this fact came suddenly to Don, and he self-consciously reached up and patted his own hairline. Deborra held the microphone closer to Colbie, who told then of being blinded by the bright headlights and getting a glimpse of a couple of faces belonging to the boys who weren't in the front seat, and then that car: Everybody knew who owned the car. And there he was, roaming around in the middle of the night, trying to work out his own problems, a Black kid on a dirt road in the country when a car full of drunk white boys went past him—he smiled wryly, though everybody knew it hadn't been funny then and still wasn't—and yeah, he'd run, but he knew who he'd seen. And, so, he finished, he was exhorting, with that religious word, out in the open air, exhorting the other boys, men now, to admit their own responsibility in the thing, as his friend Chris had just done.

"...Men like Stephen Logan," he added.

A few seconds of silence followed this, and then more mumbling as Logan pushed his way past several people and strode up the steps toward Ransome, Matheson, and finally the two men on the landing with Deborra Anderson. He halted a step below them, spoke loudly, angrily: "I hope the citizens of Mooresville see this for the election grab *they* think it'll be—a lame attempt to change the subject, throw a false narrative in, at the last minute." Her face impassive, Deborra moved the microphone toward him; he waved it off: "I don't need a microphone. Truth's loud enough on its own. I don't expect *you* to be fair."

Sara, fidgeting a few steps down, saw Deborra' mouth twitch

before she answered smoothly, "As a journalist—"

"Oh, you're a journalist," he mocked. "Well, everybody knows the way things're covered around here, paper, TV station, all of it. This is a blatant attempt to change an election, being supported and egged on by the media here—they're getting desperate," he railed.

"So, just to be clear, you're saying what Mr. Jones and Mr. Liberto are claiming is not true?" Deborra persisted.

He had taken half a step upward as if to join them on the landing. Colbie loomed over him, his face bitter, his disgust there to see, his hand still on Chris's shoulder. Stephen turned toward the crowd instead and gestured: "I'll see you in court! I've heard this trash over a month now, and the media, that thing they call a 'paper,' your TV reporters, you don't tell the truth about the outside influences taking over our town—I'll see you in court, but the election *will* go on and the people *will* have the final word about everything—" He paused, pointed downward suddenly toward Neil. "We'll draw up papers today, ask for an injunction against the station, to make you stop repeating this garbage."

Faces had turned toward Griffin, and he glanced around, when his eyes met Sara's.

"It's good being tight with your pal that helped you out years ago," Colbie remarked loudly. "Was he driving that night, or did he let somebody else have the wheel? I couldn't see that at the time."

Sara heard the collective, soft, "Ah!" from everybody around her, and she knew her mouth was open as she stared at Neil, who, after a moment, had withdrawn his own gaze from hers. This was what Rheta meant, what Ron had meant, and how many other people, she wondered, had known, and she hadn't? That very morning, after Logan left and they went into her house, Rheta had kept her eyes on Chris, her hand on his back, his shoulder, shoving him around, really, as if she thought at any moment he'd turn and run, and she was holding him there by force of will.

Then she'd got a phone call, and her face froze into hard stone, and she'd told him to move his ass, because *he'd* arrived in town.

Sara had thought she meant Matheson.

She looked across the steps to the other side of the concrete balustrade. Rheta clenched her hands, frozen, staring downward.

She gazed at everyone else near her: at Ransome, who looked the way you would if somebody started into a drunken speech at a wedding; at Colbie, who glared not at Logan but at Neil; at Neil himself, balanced on the second step and saying something she couldn't hear to someone beside him.

He beckoned towards Logan; Logan nodded, started down.

"Neil Griffin, why don't you do the right thing, for once?"

That was Ron, his voice loud, as when he'd called his picnickers down. Neil looked straight at her, squinted his eyes at her, just one brief flicker. She tilted her head to ask the question she couldn't say aloud. But he motioned at Logan again.

"It was a long time ago," Matheson continued, "and you were all just boys, but it would help bring us together if you just stepped up and did what this man did."

Neil laughed—" 'Us,' you and me? Bring 'us' together?" He turned, and with Logan walked briskly away, the small crowd parting to let them pass. Chris left the landing, shuffled down the next steps to where Rheta stood. Ransome appeared to rouse from his reverie all of a sudden and nudged Matheson: "Go on."

"In light of what you've all heard today, I hope everybody goes to the polls next Tuesday and does the right thing, since those two did not. I hope everybody sees that's *not* the face we want our town to present to the country." Ron paused uncertainly.

Sara could almost hear Ransome's snort—almost; but she *could* see his grimace right before he added, loudly, "Just get out and make sure that loser doesn't get elected!" Some older people snickered: same old Ransome.

People drifted away, typing on their phones; and others grouped into small units, talking. Deborra and her camera guy were conferring quietly with Ransome—as always, running the show. Sara heard him say, "Studio or where?" and Deborra answer, "Better there. Get him out of the sun, for one thing."

To Sara the last minutes had seemed like a deliberately executed dance, with Ransome sketching out the choreography— as usual. He talked with Colbie and Deborra, waved for them to descend some steps with him to where Chris had sat down on the concrete balustrade. Ron stood alone now, watching the group where Ransome held court, but he didn't seem to want to be part of it. Or maybe he felt he *wasn't* a part of it. Rheta was gone—how, so quickly? She realized Don had slipped away, too. She'd noticed him arrive, knew he'd eased up to several steps just below her, but then she'd forgotten about him, and now that he'd left, she wondered if he'd felt the same way she had, watching his brother do penance.

She went up the remaining steps, passing by the small knot of people who were carefully, slowly moving down to the sidewalk, descending at the pace Chris set. Ron watched her approach, but the stiff hug told her he too was having trouble today.

"God, a bunch of old men, all of us—Ransome's the spryest, and what does *that* say," he muttered.

"When you told me to come here, I had no idea it would be this," she said. "Let's use the wheelchair ramp."

He pushed her hand away as she reached for his: "No, if I fall, I'll pull you down with me."

She laughed and walked behind him, her hand on his back as they went. It was already hot; she could feel the light sweat as his shirt dampened.

"Ransome told me you might think I wanted you to go in and buy a marriage license," he said.

She couldn't tell if he was mouthing off or serious, and she couldn't see his face as he plodded downward. "Why would I think that?" she said carefully. "Why would you *do* that?"

"That was just Ransome. It was his idea yesterday to get Colbie to drive up, so Chris wouldn't chicken out—they must've been pals back in the day or something. And Colbie agreed to do it, met up with Rheta and Chris, but I warned 'em both, warned Ransome, without proof, what would they accomplish? And you watch," he said, turning at the switchback before continuing the journey to the street level, not looking back at her, "you heard it, that's what Griffin and Logan will say, that Chris's lying, trying to influence the election, and if he's not lying, well, let him take it on his own chin, because *they* weren't involved..."

They had reached the sidewalk when she took his hand. "You're really sore, aren't you."

"I've been better."

"You want to get lunch?" she asked.

"At Don's?"

"It's closest..."

He shook his head emphatically. "Not today. He'll be in the back, or at home—he won't be answering questions, I wouldn't if I were him," he added, "and I'm not really hungry. But I need some more ibuprofen, and I do want something in my stomach when I take it. Why can't you just fix us a sandwich, whatever you have at home, and that'll do."

"At home?"

"Something wrong?"

Well, yes, she wanted to say—letting you in there means I've let you *in*, and I don't know if I can; but she thought of Cary telling her, ***Geez, Mom, even teenagers figure it out***, and she thought of Louise moving out of her house to share a new one with somebody she'd decided was good for her.... "No, it's fine," she told Ron. "I was trying to remember if I have anything to eat. I haven't been out to buy much just lately, you know. I'm parked on Main. Can you walk there? Or do you want me to get my car and bring it here?" She paused: "Or maybe you need a wheelchair. There's probably one in the courthouse. Maybe the nurse would come with us."

He scowled at her laugh and picked up his pace. In a moment he spoke again: "Don knew it already, you know, and I wouldn't want him to feel like he'd have to look at us."

"He knew?"

"Well, sure, he's known all along. Ransome says he probably knew from the very first."

"Ransome's always said stuff."

"And normally I'd agree with that. But I asked Don, myself. Right before Joe endorsed Lynne. Right before the picnic—"

"Yeah, that," she broke in.

"Yeah. I had to know. I mean, by then, Ransome had got really pissed at all of us, said we were going to end up with Logan in office. Some weeks ago we had this secretive little meeting," he went on. "You couldn't imagine how many times this spring we've had conference calls, supper at Don and Lisa's house...but this was out in the country, this sleazy restaurant Ransome knew about where he figured nobody from town would go. He dressed everybody down that day. He ordered me to get Lynne involved. He asked Rheta..."

They had stopped at a cross walk with a few people gathering near them, waiting; he didn't say anything else until the light changed and they moved on. "He even tried to get Rheta to run, and you know she wasn't having that; and then he told me I should, which would make sure Logan'd get elected." He grimaced. "I wondered if he was just jerking us around, saying this shit to get us riled up, claiming he knew who'd been involved, to shame Joe into doing his job again."

"Joe was there, too?"

"Oh, yeah, when Ransome does his thing, he gets the right people, gotta give him that. I don't know how much Joe and your sister believed that day. I don't know when she found out the rest. Something in her face..." They passed another group of people, and he smiled faintly at them and again stopped talking until they had gone a few paces beyond.

"Something in her face that day told me to ask Don. Ransome wouldn't tell us it was Chris, only said he felt like at least one of them still had a conscience, that's how he put it, but that person'd have to decide on his own, Ransome wouldn't help him out with that. I started thinking about everybody I knew in town, eliminating people—"

"That's you: analyzing us..."

"Yeah. I knew Don would've given it up right away, if he'd done it—but he *wouldn't* have done it, he wasn't like Chris. But, then, Chris...I didn't know him so well, but after that fight you and I had at the restaurant— I ate there a few times after that, by myself, hoped I might run into you, if you want the truth, popped in at different times, ran into Logan instead. And I noticed some weird shit going back and forth between him and Chris. Because Stephen seemed to really enjoy jerking his chain, and I kept waiting for that famous temper Chris supposedly has to fire up. And it didn't. He'd just scuttle back up to the office.

"So I asked Don, and he told me Chris spilled it all to him a few months after it happened. Don said he believed his old man eventually found out, too—said Chris always thought it caused that heart attack...what a thing to carry around with you, guilt about so much. But Don hoped Chris wouldn't be the only one who stepped up."

"It was so long ago. What'll happen?"

"I don't know what the statute of limitations is on this. And civil-rights violation, that might not apply now, either. And then if Logan and Griffin keep saying it's a lie, and if Chris has no proof..." He shrugged.

He'd led them down the sidewalk opposite the restaurant, so that they walked past the building housing Neil's office. "You were right. I've been meddling. Like I said, it's my town, too. So what do you think?" He glanced at the lettering on the door.

"You mean about Neil."

He didn't answer. They passed the entrance before she said, "What do you want me to say. I don't think he'll ever admit it. And I wish I could say I don't believe...but. They were boys with too much free time. Too much money. Power over everybody else."

"They were kids, yeah, like I said at the courthouse—and now they're men. But I meant, what do you think *about* somebody like that?" he continued evenly.

"I wasn't in love with him, you know." She chose careful words. "He was...there, for me, when—"

"When you were vulnerable, and if there's anything he knows, it's when somebody's vulnerable." He nodded at the restaurant across the street, where the striped canvas awning hung festive over the windows, where people were assembling under the umbrellas, chatting with great animation. "Look. You got *that*, and you have those—" He gestured at the two buildings huddled on either side. "He tried to get Don and Chris to sell to him, first. He believed it would intimidate them. A clumsy way of doing it. So then he tried to get *us* to buy his properties from him—if we were willing to pay his price. I imagine he thought I'd pressure Don, later, to sell to *me*."

"Rheta got him to tell her that. That he wanted the block."

He looked at her gravely. "Yeah, he said it, but not what it really was—he wanted us to come to him, at his price, showing people he'd got the better of us, he still ran the place. And maybe another devious stab at intimidating them; who knows. Don't look so surprised. We listened to his pitch. Ken and I talked it over, figured out what was going on—he just wanted to be boss of his little world."

"Don's been here all these years. He wouldn't give in to Neil."

"No, he wouldn't, and it's bad business to sell when the location's fine; Don knows that. His grandfather, his pop, belonged here, and that'll hold *him*, and that's good, because he anchors the downtown. I ought to tell him that someday. He may not understand how important he is. When he stayed, Lynne stayed, and that brought those new places in.

"It all comes down to that: Neil Griffin couldn't keep his grip on everything the way it was one time. Ransome let loose, and moved on. But *he* never will. Well, enough of him," he headed back along the sidewalk. "He and Logan make an unhappy couple, wondering all the time if the other'll rat him out one day, and it'll never be over, for them."

She waited for him to ease into the passenger seat. "You're at *my* mercy today. And now I know what kind of driver you are."

"Smartass. Dig it in."

She made a few unnecessary turns to irritate him before he said, "I have an excellent memory. And anyway, I could find you on the Internet."

"Yeah, that's what Stephen Logan said this morning." She told him what had happened earlier; he listened without remark. She stopped in the drive at her house and unbuckled, but he stared ahead.

"Some people eventually redeem themselves when they start out wrong as kids. I don't guess he ever did. Have you heard from Lynne? Is there any way I need to help?"

She told him he'd done all he could do, should do, and repeated what Lynne had written in the note. "There's nothing else. There's just nothing. It'll fall on everybody else now."

She opened the door. He followed her into the house, glancing about. "You need help with the food?"

"I got it."

He sat at the table while she found a can of chicken and some condiments. In silence he watched her chop an apple, open the chicken, lay plates and utensils on the table. And she worked without wanting to talk to him right then, because she didn't know how to say it—that they were reverting to their lives now, Don and Lisa, and Chris, Rheta, Neil, Ransome and Colbie, all of them, the interruption and pain just a blip on a graph, and life would continue, while they awaited the next blip. This thing from long ago had drawn all of them together today, for the moment, but not forever: They'd move on. She didn't want to say that.

She brought the salad and a loaf of bread to the table. "Soft drink?"

"Water's fine."

She got that, for both of them, and took the chair across from him.

"Nice, cozy house."

"Yeah. But not too big. Just a *little* larger than your cabin." She took a breath, wanting to get this part over with, because he'd probably find out eventually, and better from her: "I bought it from

Neil after Matthew and I divorced. I'd rented it a while before I knew he owned it, and so when I found out, I told him I had to move, or he'd have to sell it to me. He chose to sell it."

"Your way of leveling the ground back up. And his, of having something to hold over your head. Vulnerabilities again." He took a bite of the sandwich and a drink of the water, asked for the ibuprofen, and took two.

"So what happened with the car?" she asked.

He shook his head, scowling. "A dog ran out, I forgot what car I was driving and over-reacted. It could've been worse, I guess. Nobody else was involved."

"I'm sorry. Can it be repaired?"

"I don't know. Probably. If I want to spend the money to do it," he answered glumly. "Every part of the damned thing costs twenty times what it originally did." He looked up when she laughed.

"Ken told me he didn't think you ought to, but he knew you would." And, there, she'd called him "Ken" one more time, so she might as well concede that, too.

"Well, he's right, I will!" He finished the sandwich, gestured "no" when she asked if he wanted another. "I was trying to think how to answer your text when I wrecked," he told her suddenly. "The one you'd sent, you know, about 'owning' you."

She sat back. "You blaming me?"

"No, it was me—I was stupid, not paying attention." He looked down at his plate, and she remembered how he'd been when he'd come to the cabin on Friday night, how he'd had the same expression on his face, as if he were staring at a jigsaw puzzle he suspected had pieces missing.

She dragged her chair closer. "Stop thinking about it."

He leaned his forehead against hers.

"You trying to head-butt me again? Don thought we'd been kissing that day. He preached at me like I really am his sister, like he had the right."

"Did you straighten him out?"

"I told him you'd bumped into me trying to grab something I'd brought to you. He didn't believe me when I told him there'd been no kissing, but a lot of arguing."

"So on Saturday when he saw us together, he thought you'd lied to him."

"He may have."

"Well, he'd be shocked, then, about Friday, right?" He grimaced when she pulled away. "What?"

She'd tried to think about it, and she knew the only thing she could say wouldn't sound good: "My life's been pretty uneventful, going along a road I've always known, planned out. I don't know *this* road, Ron. I didn't see any of this happening."

"I get that." He wasn't sure he wanted to know, but he asked, "Did you ever think about ending up with him?"

"Neil? No." She remembered sitting in the blind with Hal, deliberately not shooting anything.

"And Matthew. Why'd you two separate, really?"

"Matthew was fine with settling," she told him.

"Settling?"

"You know: This is what you've got, don't expect any more from me. Settling."

"It was easier not to make an effort. What's comfortable's always easier, even if it's bad." He took her hand and kissed the back of it. "This is the truth. Yesterday, I was trying to think about how to answer that crazy text of yours. It kind of shook me up, before I figured out what you were talking about."

"You know I was joking." She was relieved he'd changed the subject. She met his eyes, and he was in her house now, and Cary's words returned to her mind once again.

"You *are* too expensive for me to own," he said. "So I won't try that."

33

DEBORRA HAD ALMOST majored in theatre in college; it was a close second choice. Her flair for drama was something her journalism instructors and, then later, WREM-TV, hadn't encouraged much. Keep to the facts: That was the Gospel they preached...at first. Later, they saw the benefits of drama.

But today she envisioned Chris and Colbie walking *into* the little corner she'd had fixed up as a snug, friendly living room—not already seated, the way she'd done the interview with Matheson and Rheta Whitson; and she wanted the shaved circle on Chris's head to be a subliminally-featured shot as they entered. She wanted her viewing audience to wonder about it before she had him tell what had happened; it would be her first question—why did he have a head injury?—and that, she planned, would lead into other things. So she had the camera guys discreetly film them coming in, before they actually said anything.

She also didn't want him wearing anything nicer than what he'd had on at the courthouse. Colbie'd come in a tie, but she intended for him to take it off and undo that top button and look more like Chris.

"Better get this out of the way first. I don't go by 'Colbie' anymore. Well, I'll answer to it, if somebody calls me that," he corrected. "But I use 'Robert'."

"Why, if you don't mind saying?"

"Well, it *is* my first name. But I do have a common last one, and it've been easier to find a 'Colbie' than a 'Robert.' Lots of Robert Joneses around."

"You wanted to be hard to find."

"For a while I just didn't want any connection to this place, didn't want anybody trying to remember they'd had a connection to *me*."

Chris gently rubbed his temples.

"I got to where more people in Louisiana knew me as 'Robert' than people here'd known me as 'Colbie.' So I'm Robert now."

"If you don't care, though, I'm gonna use 'Colbie,' because that's what my audience will remember."

He shrugged. "That works."

She asked the producer to bring the men sandwiches from somewhere; Chris looked shaky, and since Colbie'd driven in that morning from Baton Rouge, he could probably use a bite, too. As she watched them eat, she sipped water, mentally reviewing the questions she wanted to ask. This segment couldn't be live—she was cautious about that right now, apprehensive about what either man might say. She figured she'd need it edited—she planned to have enough material for a couple of segments, actually. She discreetly signaled for the camera guy to roll again. She wanted the men comfortable, but there was an awkwardness between them.... Well, why not? They hadn't seen each other in decades. Chris finished the sub and made a joke about his meds, and did she want him coherent, or could he be partly catatonic? She laughed—but he did look better now, so she said maybe he could postpone those for an hour, couldn't he.

She asked about the bald patch. They made light of it at first, then became grave as Chris explained what had happened on Sunday. She asked which one wanted to start; they looked at each other and Colbie told her he wanted to give some context.

"You realize most people thought you'd died."

"Didn't know that for a while, no; but, yeah. Ransome Moore got me down to Baton Rouge, sent me there, just after that other stuff happened. For my own good, he said." Colbie scoffed. "Maybe so."

She nodded, tried to appear relaxed, but her muscles were all tense. The camera guy knew it was time to tighten in his frame.

"WHO'S GONNA TEND to the guinea pig this weekend?" The teacher always asked that on Fridays.

"You mean Liberto? Nobody wanna take care of the Wop."

Chris was stunned, ashamed as if *he'd* done something bad— twelve-year-old kid with swarthy features and black hair in a class where half the faces were Black and half white, and he somewhere in the middle. It didn't make it right when the science teacher turned red, scolded the other kid, and, later, said, "Hey, man, sorry for that, didn't intend it to go that way," and slapped his shoulder as if that reset everything. Chris fake laughed—"Sure, all right," because that was what you did as a twelve-year-old fighting the war that was middle school—and went through the rest of the day thinking the kinds of things that lodged in seventh-graders' minds like clods of mud swirling down a storm drain: Sometimes they washed on through, and sometimes they hung on until everything clogged up and a flood spread far and wide.

He and Don walked to the restaurant after school, to help out there before Dominic took them home later to finish schoolwork, before he returned, most days, to oversee the evening rush. Colbie rode the bus out to the county in the afternoons, out to the fields that stretched for miles to the horizon, Ransome Moore's fields of soybeans and corn and cotton and the other more exotic things: sunflowers, wheat, barley. But today Colbie caught up with Chris as they left the school—a "Guinea" and a "Wop" or two being called out, supposedly in a good-natured way, the testing way of teenagers who probe for weakness: Do you flinch? get mad? shrug and shrink, become invisible?

"Man, I need some help with that biology," Colbie lied. "You get good grades all the time. This next test gonna be awful."

Chris didn't really believe him, but gave him the home number, told him to call that night, because he knew Colbie wouldn't be likely to find a ride back into town. And, later, Colbie didn't keep him long—just a few lame questions about symbiosis which he claimed he didn't understand.

But that was the beginning, and over time they'd each protected each other, or if protection wasn't possible, they defended.

In a few years, as Colbie grew older and, then, angry and alienated at the way nothing seemed to change in the area, nothing got better but only worsened, he started avoiding Chris. *You're in town, man, where things happen, but out here, nothin' happens, people don't look down on you the way they do Black folks*: That was what he told Chris, and Chris would counter that Colbie didn't put up with the rich kids who dropped in downtown after playing tennis or golf, ordered a drink they knew they couldn't legally have yet, told him they'd get it at home, anyway, and enjoyed summoning him to their tables over and over for a napkin, a straw, something spilled.

One of them seemed to take pity on Chris one day, calling his friends down and speaking amiably as the others laughed and rolled eyes—asked him to ride around with a couple of them when he was finished at the restaurant.

Don warned him, but then Don somehow knew how to disarm the guys at school and these who came in to get ices and tiramisu. Chris envied him: He'd never been able to shrug it off.

It didn't take long to see he was useful as a scapegoat, somebody they could prod into doing mischief, the designated fall guy if one of the pranks went awry and they were found out. They could tell a cop they'd felt sorry for him, brought him along, and look what he did: Got drunk, went loco, shot those signs, penned that hog up in the public high school, egged those mailboxes—goes to show you can't be friends with just everybody, they were just trying to let him join in.

...Deborra interrupted with a nervous laugh: "Did you guys actually do all those things?"

Chris murmured the answer without humor: "Most of it. Well, we talked about some of it, thought about doing it."

"Do you want to tell what *was* done?"

That eyebrow-lifted glance again. "Not really."

…Colbie stopped talking to his friend who was running with those boys whose parents indulged their trivial misdemeanors and were able to buy silence and leniency if it came to it. That crowd wouldn't have let Colbie hang with them, anyway, and he was disgusted Chris would want to.

Deborra glanced at Chris, saw the deep sigh and averted gaze as Colbie told this part dispassionately.

Maybe Chris had got in and didn't know how to get out, she suggested. When you're a kid…

…And then there was Stephen Logan, who showed up at the restaurant after Dom sent word to his mother, Chris said. Dominic didn't like him, but had observed the persecution in his restaurant, knowing he couldn't intervene for Chris or it would get worse, and had heard of the same things going on with Stephen, knew the boy really needed work—maybe to help straighten himself out, maybe to help his mother feed him. In two or three weeks, Stephen was riding with them, ingratiating himself, fooling himself that he was one of them….

"Wait a minute," Deborra interrupted. "Will the others say this, too? They'll say you were with them off and on?"

Colbie and Chris glanced at each other, again, and Chris sighed and looked down, again. "I ran with 'em," Chris mumbled. "So did Stephen."

"Go on."

…And then Ransome Moore stopped growing soybeans. Colbie was mad. He said things he did believe at the time—he was a kid, kids see things through their own lenses, their hurts and desperation and anxieties reflecting back onto them, and reality's not always reality when you talk about feelings—an older man now, he knew that; didn't, then. He started walking a lot, just leaving the house, driving his mother crazy, strolling down roads all over the county, before the churches burned, before Ransome sent him out of town….

"So why'd Mr. Moore send you out of town?" she interrupted.

Colbie laughed a little, mirthlessly. She sensed a wall there, behind it something that neither of them would tell *her*; she recognized that sort of look. She started to ask again, decided not to.

...There was talk going around. Ransome took it on himself to do what he thought ought to be done....

She could tell it was a lie. Or, not the actual whole truth.

...That night Colbie was out walking a dirt road. His mother didn't know where he was some nights; he didn't tell her or even show up till the next day. And a car went past him, crowded him off the road. He couldn't see the driver or who was in the passenger seat in front; the headlights blinded him. It was a newer car, and nobody in his part of the county had one like it. But as it passed, then ground to a halt on the gravel, he did see two faces: Chris's and, in the middle of the rear seat, Stephen Logan's.

Chris looked shocked to see Colbie on a dark dirt road in the middle of nowhere. He turned his face away. Colbie decided right then to take a shortcut—it turned out not to be that, he was just running to hide, in the stubbly fields where the only crop now was waist-high weeds. The boys headed on back towards town; and edging through the tree line beside those fields, trying to stay away from the road in case the guys were looking for him, working his way towards home, he heard sirens and even saw the glow in the distance....

Terrible, heavy silence in the studio, the three people sitting in the contrived living room watching each other. Even the tech crew remained mute, just kept filming. Deborra said softly, "You didn't tell the sheriff? I've been told he was pretty good, for his time. He tried to uphold the law for everybody, not just some."

Chris remained silent.

Colbie crossed a leg over the other, looked her in the eye. "It's easy to be intimidated when there're important folks' kids involved. Ransome made arrangements to get me out. And I was mad. Like, they wanna run that town that way, fine, I'm rid of 'em. That's how I thought. Nobody from here ever asked me anything."

"But...you didn't see the guys do it?"

Colbie shrugged. Chris glanced away from him: "Look, I was *there*. The best I can say for myself is I did ask if they... But then I helped hold wood splinters for Stephen to light."

"But, Mr. Jones, you didn't see anything, really? You were hiding, and they went on, you say—"

"Yeah, that's it. A lawyer like Neil Griffin, he'd get me up there and ask me that, and I'd sound like I was rehashing every old grudge I ever had, airing all of them, opening up old wounds. So, yeah. I didn't really see them do it."

"But I was there," Chris insisted.

Again the room fell silent.

"I want you both to know how much I appreciate your coming in. When we put the segment together, I'll let you, if you want, take a look before... I don't usually do that for my guests," she added, "I don't let people I interview tell me how to present my information. But in this situation—"

"I want to say something else," Chris interrupted. The headache had been coming back for a few minutes, and now he was sweating, too. "The election's coming up."

"Yes," Deborra agreed.

"Well, I want everybody to think about how, this much stuff's known about one guy, they ought to vote the better candidate in, they should vote her in."

She frowned as his words tumbled out, jumbled and nearly incoherent in the scrambled mix of pain, not just emotional but physical now. Chris scrubbed his temples.

"Lynne Houston, you mean."

He nodded; nodding made his head hurt, so he did it gently. Colbie frowned, reached over to fumble with the microphone clipped on Chris's shirt. "We should stop for now."

"No, another thing, from me, just one more, okay?" Chris was breathing faster and his eyes were wide with headache.

"No, man, you ought to go to bed," Colbie argued.

"Just one more thing: You remember George Wallace." He paused. Colbie gave him a querulous look.

"I know who he was," Deborra answered.

"Well, later on in his life he went to John Lewis—you know who John Lewis was, right? So he asked for forgiveness. And John Lewis gave it. And so if John Lewis could do that, I hope the same can be done to me, here, everybody in town, Colbie, the church members, or their kids, their families."

"I have put that in the past a long time ago."

"So, really..." Deborra leaned forward, frowning, trying to comprehend a time before she was born, not sure how to ask the question. "I mean, really, why'd those boys want to do it, Chris? You said you were there, you knew them. Why?"

Chris shook his head and stared at the carpet, tapping a fast rhythm with his right foot.

"Because they could," Colbie answered for him. "They could, and probably nobody'd find out. And knowing they could…to show power, to tell people somebody could do that, and nothing would happen, and they could have their way. And it wouldn't ever matter what you thought or did about them."

"That," Chris said.

She looked at the tech crew, who, still recording, wore somber expressions.

34

RON GRUMBLED THAT the engineers were probably having issues with something; but she knew better. She texted Ken Thomas a head's up.

He wants to see that car. Bringing him now. Be careful who you send over.

And it went about as she'd expected. The tow driver had shown so much interest that Ken had Maintenance put a padlock on the door that morning. *He* wouldn't want the thing enough to steal it, and God knows there was security around; but, then, Matheson was a fanatic about it, so other people might be, too…. Eliot arrived to open the special garage and stood passively to one side while Matheson yelled and swore at the damage, flailing his arms about and using muscles he hadn't flexed in hours, opening the hood, crawling under the front end, slamming the driver-side door. After a while Sara had enough.

"That's it. Shut up. It's just a car."

Is Eliot deaf? she texted Ken. Then, *PLEASE tell me something he needs to do over there.*

She passed on the halfway-believable emergency he texted her. "And, by the way, quit acting like a child."

He scowled, took a couple of slow breaths; she smirked.

"Do you want to ride back with us?" she asked Eliot, but the man cut his eyes warily at Matheson:

"I'm good walking." He turned off lights and secured the garage.

Matheson settled back, eyes closed, as she scolded him the half-minute it took to drive the wooded lane to the main office.

"Really? Really? You put on that kind of shitty display to your employees all the time? I'm surprised any of them work for you."

"Sorry. I just hate what I'm gonna have to do."

"What? Shoot it and put it out of its misery? Send it off on a burning boat?" she scoffed.

"No, smartass, I'm gonna fix it, but having to shop for the parts will take up all my free time for a while."

"*Really*," she said coldly, parking near the door, and at that he turned a swift look at her.

"No. I won't spend all my time on it."

She glared at him, and he leaned over with a quick kiss.

"Shove off, and try to be nice to your people. I'll let you know about later. Now go. You'll see they all survived just fine without you."

"Yeah, thanks for telling me that."

She watched him walk inside, his gait stiff and gimpy—maybe she should've let him throw his fit a while longer and loosen up those muscles.

She'd have some time before he arrived to take her out for dinner—they hadn't decided where. Cary was staying overnight at Allie's. They'd make a decision later about where *they'd* stay, at the guest quarters on MTE's campus, or at her own place. They hadn't talked about that, but it was a decision hanging around to be made, and it was pleasant thinking about it.

A flask of Cointreau, a bottle of tequila, and a lime were on her kitchen table when she got back. And a note: ***Margarita on me. Probably better than the last one you had***.

She'd seen this handwriting before—many times. She didn't have to compare it, as she did those two notes of Ron's, to know whose it was.

In the still, sunny warmth of the summer evening, standing at her own table in her own house that Ron had called "cozy" just a few hours ago, she was suddenly petrified—as in a childhood nightmare when your feet wouldn't move but you knew you had to do *something*.

Had she unlocked the door when she got home? Yes. When they'd left, earlier, Ron insisted on keying the dead bolt himself, so she had to have unlocked it just now. Maybe she should text him, or Rheta, or somebody. Maybe she should ease out through the back again. But that was crazy.

So Neil had relocked the deadbolt himself.

If he was actually still here, she'd just shove him out. She wasn't afraid of him.

She reminded herself of that; but she prepared a text, then paused again. Ron didn't have a new phone yet, so she'd have to involve Ken once more, or go through the switchboard. Ron might have inherited all the problems of Mooresville—he might own those now—but he didn't have to own this. But she sent the text anyway, before she went through the rest of her house. Which didn't feel like hers, right now. It was just like him, keeping her off-balance, reminding her he could still steer her life. Thank God Cary was at Allie's. Would he have barged inside, even if she'd been here? Probably—for he couldn't have known for sure she *wasn't* home....

Her phone buzzed: **Wtf???**, sent through Ken's number. He would just come a little earlier than he'd planned, he added. Maybe she could get Griffin there for that margarita about the same time, and he'd have one with them.

Laughing softly at that suggestion, she thought he didn't seem intimidated—and she told herself: She wasn't afraid of Neil, either. She checked out the living room, office, her and Cary's bedrooms, the laundry area, the bathroom. A thought came to her, and she returned to the kitchen and hung the security chain across the back door: He wouldn't be easing in that way, without warning. Then she sent the text.

Come get this shit. And bring ALL the keys with you.

After she'd bought the house, for a few months—maybe even a year—she'd wondered sometimes if he still had keys; it wouldn't surprise her if he did. She'd never asked who else he'd rented the place to before she moved there. When she signed the papers, she mentioned it, pretending to joke, and he smiled and said something evasive like, "Wouldn't I give you all the keys to your own house?" —Not an answer; but then she'd just let it go. Drifting along. Settling.

She had a drill in the utility room. She could run to the store and get another dead bolt; she wouldn't have to deal with him at all today. Long ago she could've hired a locksmith to come and rekey the whole place. She should've had that done, anyway. She'd trusted his truthfulness. —No, even knowing what he *could* do, had shown he would, she'd just not wanted to admit he'd ever *do* it. She felt as if she'd just found out that something dishonorable, mildly indecent, she'd done in the past had been exposed.

She could even now just put the things outside the door, tell him to pick it all up and not bother her. But she needed to look at him, because it would be looking at herself, in a way. She poured a glass of ice water and leaned against the counter next to the sink, fidgeting.

But that was how he'd found her last time he'd been over. She wouldn't let him see her like that this time.

She bagged the bottles and lime and took all of it and the glass of water to the living room where she turned on the television, expecting something to be on the early local news; but there was nothing. She'd seen Deborra and her crew make the arrangements with Chris and Colbie, had heard Deborra tell them to get Chris out of the sun, over to the studio. Maybe they needed more time to do an edit. She texted Cary to make sure she was okay, sent Rheta a query about Chris.

He's medicated. Asleep on his couch right now. I fed him pills, took him home when they were through at the studio.

Something was missing. She frowned, composing the next question: *Is he OK by himself?*

Gotta learn to be, sooner or later. Sooner's better.

There was more, more she didn't know how to ask. She stared at the phone for a moment. *Did you know about him before today?*

The long pause gave her time to figure it out herself.

A while back I went through the possibilities. I didn't want to think it was him. So I didn't let myself go there every day.

Another text: **But actually he told me Friday when he was at your house. What better time to confess but in the middle of the night, when you're supposed to be supporting somebody else, right? Guess he thought I was so upset I'd just shrug it off. Or maybe I'd forget. I didn't.**

Cold, Sara started to say—backspaced that, tried to compose something else. Rheta beat her to the draw:

Ron didn't tell you, huh. And you didn't even figure it out on Sunday.

Sara texted a question mark.

Sunday night, after that fire. Cary asked why somebody'd target Don. Wasn't for Don so much as Chris. Intimidation.

You didn't put it together.

Did you know about Neil, before?

At least half a minute passed. Rheta was writing her a book, or having trouble with words, for once, and wanted them to be right…It was that: **Months ago.**

Why didn't you tell me?

This time the answer was immediate: **You already decided not to believe me. I practically did tell you several times. So did Ron. You didn't pay attention to either of us.**

She started to tell Rheta about the lime and the bottles—*Guess what: he's coming over, and I'll hand him his ass and shove him out*— But Rheta'd say she wouldn't do that; really, when *had* she? Telling her now would only cause the "I will! You won't!" kind of thing they'd yell at each other as kids.

The television played on, through national news, into the local segments.

Chris said 4 other boys. Him, and Neil, and Stephen. The other 2?

This time, waiting, she wasn't sure she wanted to find out. But Rheta was fast, and inexorable: **Jonathan Ingram.**

He died some years ago.

Convenient for the others.

The bitter words brought her up short once again, and another text popped in: **And Mark Mason, of course. Everybody's happy banker. Because you know you can be happy, with a lawyer guarding your back. And you've got his.**

She remembered Mark being in Neil's office sometimes when she was there, remembered the other week—only last week? It seemed like a year…. She didn't respond fast enough, and at last Rheta said, **Getting food. Talk later.**

What are y'all going to have?

Don't know about him. I'm doing what you and I did on Saturday. Can of soup, sandwich. Wanna join me? Then, **Never mind, you probably have plans these days.** And, in another four seconds: **Can you drive by and check on my apt once in a while for a few days, week, maybe?**

Hal would've told her to call. She called.

"I'm getting food, I said, gonna watch that movie I never got to, last Friday. What do you need? You don't wanna come by here, I'll get Jared to. No biggie."

"Where're you going?"

"I'll let you know when I get there. Hell, I'll even text you on the way, if it makes you feel better."

"Don't text and drive. But where are you going?"

"Smartass. I'm getting out, that's all."

"No, I'm ahead of you this time. You're interviewing somewhere, aren't you. Atlanta again?"

"Not there, God, no. I told you I stay away from places where I'll run into my exes. Don't know what it'll be. I'm just going looking. If I can't get something, I might end up back here. Probably not," she added in a mumble.

"He may need you."

"You know what? I don't care if he was a kid. I was a kid, I did the right thing, caught hell for it, for a long time. Is it because he's a boy, he'll be patted on the head—'boys'll be boys,' that shit? Why would I overlook it now? Oh, and I was wrong, so wrong, about what Neil was doing. He was trying to keep Don and Chris quiet, wasn't he. Tried to take advantage when times were hard and they were vulnerable. Get them into his debt then. But you know about that kind of thing with him, don't you."

The words cut.

"And Chris might've done it, but Don was stronger. *He* had the balls all along."

"That's harsh."

"Please. All these years, I felt so sorry for him, Dom dying, him stuck here…"

"You should still feel sorry for him."

"No, I shouldn't. You go feel sorry for Emily, or Colbie, or even Ransome, if you like, though I wouldn't for him. He knows what he did, and he'll pay for it till he dies, and that's about fair, and he knows that, too, and accepts it. Hell, you oughta feel sorry for *me*. Do you?"

"Yes."

"Well, good, I guess, but don't for too long. I confess to who I want to, and I'm clean. I tried to feel sorry for him," she added, "I did. I brought him over to my house yesterday, you know, kept him all day, bought him an ice pack." She laughed, a scoffing, incredulous laugh. "Put him in the guest room last night. Even after telling me that shit on Friday— I gave him plenty of opportunity, last night, today, to be repentant—"

" 'Repentant'? Why'd he have to repent to you?"

"To anybody! He was, 'Oh, well, whatever, just along for the ride.' He actually said that, those words. Those words," she repeated. "I just wanted him to, I don't know, say something like, 'I wish I'd done it before today. What can I do now to make it right?' "

"He did stand in front of the town."

"Yeah, dues paid, you think? You know what? I don't care. He gets all upset because something happens to me, to *me*," she railed, "and he spills his guts one night after years of not saying a goddamned word, and then, 'Oh, just along for the ride.' No. So can you drive by once in a while?"

"I will."

"Okay, and I'll text and keep up. Wanna hear about Cary and what she's doing."

SHE WAITED: IT was another part of the game Neil played. She remembered what he'd said about Don and Stephen; everything was a game to him.

She was still staring grimly, unseeingly at the TV when she heard the car pull into her drive. He rapped one time, at the front, as any other visitor would, and she left him there about half a minute before slowly, reluctantly, opening the door. "This is my house. Give me my keys."

He scoffed a little, wryly, dug around in his jeans pocket, and brought one out for her. "Can't I come in for a few minutes?"

She ignored the key. "You'd do it anyway—you *did*." She turned and motioned for him to sit on the sofa, muted the television. "Your pal Stephen invited himself in, this morning, just like you."

"I hope you treated *him* this way."

"He didn't get in. Count yourself lucky. But then you could, anyway, right?"

"Why'd he show up?"

She wanted to believe there was a little uneasiness in his voice. Maybe she just wanted that. "He asked me to work for him, after the election. Which he's sure he'll win, regardless of today, I'm guessing."

"I assume you turned him down."

"Yeah, because he's not gonna be elected."

"Hm." It was a polite, noncommittal thing you'd say to a child hoping for a gift Santa wasn't going to bring. He held the key out again. "Here."

"Doesn't matter, does it. You told me one time I had them all. You're probably lying again. Just put it on the table. For all I know, you may have ten more of them, and we could do this over and over, so tomorrow I'm having the locks reset. Should've, a long time ago."

"That's true. So why didn't you, if you thought I'd keep letting myself in? By the way, you oughta have a camera inside."

"Maybe I do. You wouldn't know." It was out of her mouth, a quick retort, and that brief little squint of his eyes told her he wasn't so sure for a moment.

He'd changed, of course—another move in his game—from the dress pants and business shirt he'd had on at the courthouse: soft blue T-shirt, now, and jeans...it suited him. She knew he wanted to look laid-back and chill and had picked that shirt deliberately. He probably remembered blue was her favorite color. He studied her solemnly, staying a few steps away; it reminded her of how he sized up a jury. There was no good answer she could make to his last question, nothing she could excuse herself with, and she didn't try now but reached for the plastic bag she'd set down on an end table and held it out to him.

"You can take this back. And, breaking and entering, you know, that's what you did. I could press charges."

"Nothing's broken. I did enter. But I did own this house once, and you and I were in a relationship, so it'd be hard to get anybody around here to believe I'm a common burglar."

"Yeah, that's the thing. You get by with stuff. You always have. And everybody in town does seem to know..." she paused, searching for a word.

"That we were lovers," he said.

It wasn't the word she wanted; "love" hadn't really played so much of a part in what they'd had. She knew he'd seen her flinch, but she went on: "Whatever...people seem to know it. Like *you* passed that around, maybe—because I didn't, and we weren't very open about it, after Cary was older."

"You always let people use your name, here and there. You used to ask my opinion about that, so...well, if I was asked if I knew you, I told them."

That was the second time today someone had brought up her endorsements, and both times it was nauseating, knowing they'd thought they possessed a slice of her in the deal. "What if Cary'd been here? You would've scared her to death, damn you, and she's had a rough several days."

"I knocked, very loudly. Nobody came to the door. When I opened it, I called. No answer. I didn't snoop around. I just put everything on the table, you know."

"No, how would I know? Why would I believe you?"

He laughed, the way he'd mock a witness, show he thought they were naïve. "You *said* you had a camera."

The very silence in her own house disturbed her as he stood there, that sardonic expression on his face. She went to the door—as much to walk away from him as anything—and slipped the bag handles over the knob, wishing she'd followed her instinct and put everything outside before he arrived. He hung his thumbs in the loops of his jeans and rocked gently side to side.

"I do occasionally tell the truth. So I kept a key. Big deal. I believed—hoped, I'd say, that we'd be back together at some point, and I'd be using it."

"What gave you that idea?"

He raised his eyebrows. "Well, you did. You were on the edge of it till Matheson managed to find his way into your—life," he changed something he'd started to say, perhaps, or maybe consciously chose those words, and that way of phrasing them. "I thought, with Cary about grown, it'd be another year or so, I figured it was because of her, for her sake."

"Wow. You've always been that sure of yourself?"

He considered that, shrugged. "Not necessarily. But there wasn't a rush. I was going to wait. You'd be worth waiting for." He glanced around. "I haven't been in this part of the house for a while. You've changed things."

"Yes. I've changed things." She said it slowly, to make sure he got that, but he turned around, inspecting the room, and then pulled the bag off the doorknob.

"Why don't I go on anyway and mix us a drink, and we can at least talk a little. I'll tell you my side of everything while we relax." He ambled toward the kitchen, but she moved ahead of him and blocked the door to the hallway with her arm. She wondered if he could tell that her knees were shaking.

"No, I don't want to know any more about that right now; I may know anyway. And even if you have something to say I *don't* know, it's late, for that. You should go home. Just, go."

He'd paused again a few feet away from her. Rheta's words: **You can't go to bed with somebody and not feel something.** She had only to sigh, or drop her arm a little, let her mouth soften, and he'd probably take those few steps toward her and, perhaps, lean very close to her face and she might lean in, too, and somehow she'd find herself back where she'd been. In spite of herself; in spite of Ron.

"Later?" he asked, "tomorrow, maybe, when we've—"

"No," she interrupted. "You have to go, because I've got an engagement tonight. I'm getting the locks changed tomorrow. Any other keys aren't going to do you any good now, so just throw away the ones you have."

He shrugged. "As you say, how would you know? —But I don't have any more," he added with a cool smile, as she grimaced. "That was the last one. Really. So you and Matheson have a hot date, huh?" He turned slightly and surveyed the room. "Well, the floor used to be comfortable enough, as I recall."

God, she hated him right then, and, leaving the doorway, she advanced on him until she could almost have touched him by taking a deep breath. "Just leave," she whispered coldly, her nose close to his chin, her gaze holding his. Peripherally she saw his empty hand reach up as if he intended to touch her, but he didn't; and, smiling at her, but not, and turning away toward the door, he left with what he probably meant to be a devastating final comment:

"Well, you have fun. And as it's that way, you probably should know I never was deprived when *you* quit sleeping with me. I could get that anywhere. You'll be tired of him pretty soon, and I'll try to work you in. I'll send you a bill."

WHEN HE DROVE off, she pressed the palm of her hand on the door, pushing upon it, leaning in. She remembered moving into the house with Cary, feeling accomplished after she assembled by herself the cheap bookshelves she bought for this room. She remembered the unease that crept into her as time passed and Neil had almost but not quite settled in. Sometimes he'd surprise her by bringing something to cook for dinner, and maybe he'd still be there in the morning, fixing breakfast for her and Cary. Sometimes, when Cary was a toddler and had fallen asleep in her own bed, she and he undressed in this very room and made love, like teenagers sneaking a quick one. He'd come and go, staying overnight once in a while, but never appearing to mind much when she started telling him she needed time alone, to work, to study, she needed space, because she'd never been on her own, really, to figure herself out, to get to know who she was. He'd said, "I got that; sure, take a while."

She'd never wanted to know him. And he'd never cared if she did.

It was near seven before Ron tried to let himself in through the back with the extra key Rheta had found and used on Saturday and had skeptically put back on the holder by the door jamb. Sara had given it to him earlier today, just for safekeeping, she told him lightly, as his eyes wrinkled up a little; and that was partly true: She felt better knowing it wasn't hanging up there for just anybody to grab, and he'd used it himself to lock the door when they'd left…. She was sitting at the kitchen table, sipping from the glass of water when he called softly, "It's just me," and she unlatched the chain.

"Let me grab my bag."

"No blood around anywhere," he remarked. "Or you cleaned it up very well."

She grimaced, made a scoffing noise. "Where have you been? It's later than you said."

"You didn't need me, and it was probably better for me not to be here."

She left to get the purse. In the bedroom she touched the blue sphere as she'd started doing whenever she left the house, as if it were a talisman. He'd wanted to see the rest of her house earlier that day, had walked gingerly through it, wanted the two of them to lie down for a while till the ibuprofen kicked in, and had noticed the sculpture there by the bed, asked her if she still wanted to smash it. She wondered—no way of knowing, either—if Neil had gone through the house, had found it there, sitting on top of the papers he'd given her, the ones about Matheson. He was right: She needed a camera.

They left in the company car he'd used.

"So where are we going?"

"I know this place out in the country. Pulled pork, all you can eat," he said, laughing at her exclamation of distaste. "Look in the bags," he relented, nodding toward several on the floor behind the driver's seat. "We can cook our own dinner, okay?" Then he drove to the cabin, where they made hamburgers and spent the evening watching a movie on the television he'd bought earlier to kill time before he picked her up.

35

"REALLY, MOM! YOU'RE talking about selling our house, after we just got through redoing that room?"

"That's when they say you should," she responded lightly, "when you've done a remodel."

Cary threw shade. "So since you and Mr. Matheson are going together, you start changing everything else, too?"

It was the next day—Wednesday. Ron had brought her back around eight-thirty that morning and gone through the house to make certain there were no new surprises from Neil. She pulled the chains over both doors, but she feared no unexpected visits today, and she called a locksmith who promised to come around before noon, and did. She texted Cary to find out her plans: Allie's mom would return her around one. It was after Cary had tossed her bag onto her bed and drifted back towards the kitchen, finding Sara waiting at the table holding out a new key, that Sara brought up the possibility of moving.

Now Cary glared at her.

"I haven't done anything yet," Sara reminded her reasonably. "I've been told by your Aunt Rheta I should've asked you a while back if you were okay with this place—"

"Aunt Rheta should mind her business!"

"—or if you thought maybe it was time to get something larger, or with more outside space, or newer. I can afford to now, whereas maybe a few years back…"

"And you expect me to think it doesn't have anything to do with Mr. Matheson." The statement was flat and sarcastic, sullen.

"No, I'm just asking. But I don't like that attitude, so we can talk about it some other time."

Cary eyed her resentfully. Then, "I guess you're also trying to make me believe it doesn't have anything to do with that crap on Friday and, well, just about every day since then."

"I'm not afraid of living here, if that's what you mean."

"That's not what I said."

"But it's what you meant. Really, I was just asking if you'd ever thought about— Look, we'll discuss it some other time. Tell me about your visit with Allie," she said.

Cary wasn't having it: "I'm fine being here. I had an okay time over there. I'm going to straighten my stuff now."

Sara heard the bedroom door shut, firmly, and sighed. *Look, I'm the responsible adult*, she wanted to tell her, *and I love you, but you don't get the last word about what I have to decide for us.* But she didn't say it. And Cary spoke truth more than she herself: She couldn't get past it, that sense of someone showing up around the corner with a brick in hand.

She wished again Louise were here to defuse things. A third person could do that. She might start shoving it on Ron.

LYNNE TEXTED "NOTHING" when she asked what she could do in the few remaining days before the election—a dismissive, hopeless sort of answer. Sara phoned her, hoping to tell from her voice how to interpret the word.

"Lady, if people don't know by now what's going on, there's nothing you or I can do, and maybe I wouldn't want the job, representing that kind of community."

"Cold."

"What else is there? I'm still speaking where I'm welcome. We just have to let it play out."

Depressed, agitated by her inability to help, she decided to sit out back in the newly bare area where Louise's overgrown impatiens and lantanas had been riotous. Maybe she should get some pebbles and large stones and redo the area as a rock garden. If she did sell the house, that would be desirable…people were into odd outdoor areas these days, feng shui, artful paths, water features…. It was probably inexpensive, too—she could do it herself, that would be a plus, give her something to keep her mind occupied….

In a while Cary came looking for her, laid Sara's phone on the patio table, slumped into one of the chairs. "It buzzed a few times.

'Unknown number.' Probably spam. It's hot," she complained, scowling at Sara as if she personally had produced the weather.

So who made you come outside? Sara wanted to ask, but instead, "I felt like getting some fresh air. Even if it is hot."

Cary squirmed in her seat, pulled the purple strand of hair forward and gave it a critical look, sighed.

"What about if I get some stones, make a rock garden here."

"Why'd you do that if you're gonna sell? Why go to the bother?"

It was a challenge, and Sara wished again Louise were there. Or that I had some newspaper ads I could shift around so I didn't have to look her in the face while I preached, she thought. "Make it more attractive to a buyer. Anyway, we're here now, and I don't want flowers again, and it is dog-ugly this way."

Cary lifted one leg over the arm of her chair, swung that foot. "Okay, I was snarky. To be honest…" She paused a moment.

"I mean, you were the one who told me several months ago we had a boring life," Sara reminded her. "Stuck in a routine, you said."

"Yeah. Those were the good old times." She gazed unhappily at the foot where, Sara noticed, she'd applied a henna tattoo.

"Nice. Did you and Allie go somewhere to get that?"

She glanced quickly at Sara, brought the foot back to the ground. "Yeah. Her mom took us last night. But, look… If you want to sell the house, I could live with that. I mean, this *is* the only place I've known." A slight frown. "But I could adapt." She grabbed her hair and flung it backwards.

"What sort of house would you pick, if you could, right now?"

"Newer than this one." Cary was ahead of her on it. She'd only got so far as wanting out of a place connected to Neil. "Something modern. And no knickknacks and stuffy chairs."

"I thought you liked what we did in the office."

"It fits this house—it matches. But, me, I'd just start over." She sighed again. They sat miles apart, miles lengthening as minutes passed. A car went by. They heard it slow down a little…another pet crossing the street? Someone unsure where they were? But they both turned toward the fence, where, on the other side, the noise was a dangerous mystery.

She rubbed her temples. "Cary. I need to get out, I'm not gonna lie. I never even thought about not feeling safe here, never entered my mind."

"At least you're finally admitting it."

"Downtown, the park, where?"

Cary hunched toward her. "Are you kidding? I'll never go there, just us, again! And you won't, either!"

She didn't deny it. And they were, once more, staring at one another. "Where, then?"

"Why don't you take a walk down the street like you used to?" Another challenge, and Cary's mouth was a grimace. "You won't do that, either, so here we are. Yeah, maybe we should move somewhere else." Her wide eyes held Sara's. "You know what? Michelle, you know, Allie's mom, she told me she was anxious about letting Allie stay overnight here for a while. Fuck all this," and she turned to the fence, her voice unsteady.

They sat that way for a while longer, some minutes, as the sun baked hotter and a few other cars passed by. It was fortuitous that the face-down phone signaled a text coming in: **Ron wants to run something past you and Cary. He's been trying to get you. Are you free to drive over?**

She sent a thumb's-up and chose careful words:

"That was Ken Thomas. He wants me to drive out for something. May be about the book."

"I'm not staying here by myself!"

She considered Cary's fierce expression. "No, he wanted both of us. I have no idea why. But you game?"

Cary gave her a weary, skeptical glance. "Sure, let's go, fine with me. Staying here doesn't seem to be helping either of us."

She sat brooding all the way, until they were almost at the gate. Then, suddenly: "It's all different. Everything. I don't even feel like the same person anymore. There's nothing you can say to make it better. Just, don't say anything. But I don't even feel the same." It hadn't been a week since they'd been here for the picnic, she reminded herself, and Cary was right.

The security man at the gate waved her through. So we're "official," she thought, and winced.

"So, really, why'd we come?" Cary stared at the entrance.

"He didn't go into it."

"You should've asked."

"Okay, but here we are, we'll find out in a minute. I had a thought just now. There's this guest house, they call it; they sent me to it Friday night, you might've seen that man driving over with me. To keep me off the road. You want to see it?" Cary turned an odd look her way.

"Don't expect me to live out here in the woods. I won't do it."

"Why would you think that? And I wouldn't do something like that without you having input. I would've hoped you knew."

Cary sullenly entered the office with her, and again they were waved past the secure reception area and started down the wide hall. But as she neared Thomas' office, Sara heard Ron's voice. The two men were studying Ken's computer, for a moment oblivious to their presence. She waited for one of them to look away from the monitor; Thomas did first, waved them in.

Ron smiled wryly at her. "Tried to get you earlier. But now, things have come up."

She realized who'd sent the texts Cary thought were spam. "Sorry."

"It came to me you don't have the number for this new phone."

"It 'came to him.' I *told* him," Ken said. Cary smirked.

"Whatever." Ron spoke to Cary. "How're you these days?"

"I've been better."

"Yeah, tell me. Well, summer's here, and maybe things'll quiet down after the election."

"Depending on how it goes, you know?" she answered fiercely. "I wish I could vote."

"Yeah, I wish you could, too. You'll be able to, sooner than you realize, sooner than your mother wants you to be grown." He came from behind the desk and propped himself against it, facing her. "I'll have to make this short. I had a better 'presentation,' but, no time now. This was what I wanted to talk to you about. Would you like to be the official face on our book program? Sort of the 'ambassador'?"

" 'Ambassador'? Really?" she scoffed.

"Whatever you'd wanna call it's okay by me. Deborra's gonna do a spot or two on TV next week, and it'd be better if she has a young person with her. We'll hang some posters here and there, on buildings, and I thought you'd be a good fit." He turned to Sara. "You object to this? Because it would be really public. And lately...maybe you don't want her to?"

"So what this is," Cary interrupted, "you're dating her now, and you're trying to please her, and bribe me?"

Bribe: that word. Ken squeezed his eyes shut in a grimace, and Sara saw Matheson squint at Cary just a brief moment. But he went on calmly: "No, I just thought you'd be a good spokesperson. If you want to." He shrugged. "If you don't, I can find somebody else. And what's between your mom and me isn't relevant. Or, really, your business, right now. You know? I just think you'd be good for what we have in mind. What do you think, Ken?" He turned to Thomas.

"Someone else would be with you—you wouldn't always do the ads, the interviews, by yourself," Ken told her.

"Who? Carson? Allie?"

"Actually, my grandson. He's young, too young to do it on his own, so you'd have to do most of the talking. We know you're a little old for a kids' summer-reading thing—we'll play it like a high-schooler remembering that she always loved to read, mentoring elementary kids. We already lined up my grandson but weren't sure about the other part, but I think you'd be just right. Old folks like us don't need to be the spokespeople," and he looked pointedly at Matheson. He glanced then at Sara, and she saw something in his eyes that told her he'd improvised most of that.

"And Deborra's also going to promote the library's regular program," Matheson added. "It has its place around here, too."

She turned to Cary. "Decide for yourself. But expect to get used to 'famousness,' like Louise would say."

"You did a pretty good turn in front of Stephen Logan's place last weekend," Ron told her.

A soft sound that might have been a laugh escaped her. "I'll think about it and let you know."

"So text me later."

She yanked the phone from her pocket and tapped as he called out numbers. "Now you have something even your mom didn't. Please don't share it around like the cops did my other one."

She sneered. "As if."

He hugged Sara, returned behind the desk. "Sorry, but we have to get back to this."

She nodded, paused. "Ron, could you let me show Cary the guest house, where I stayed Friday?" Cary glanced impassively at her. "She and I were talking about, maybe, moving some day, and she wants a more modern style…"

"Sure. Go ahead."

"Well, you know Eliot opened it for me."

He turned the analyzing look on her for a moment, considered. "Oh, the code—" Snatched up a sticky note, scribbled, passed it over to her. Last night he'd called out the number as he typed into the keypad, so she could remember; but she appreciated this act for Cary's sake.

As she drove along the lane to the cabin, passing the edge of the lake, the tall pines on either side, Cary remained silent. Sara eyed the spare building: the tall end almost all glass, the cypress siding on the other walls. It was the first time she'd really looked at it dispassionately. On Friday night and Saturday, it had been a refuge; last night, a comfortable place to spend time with him. Today she saw it for what it was: a Spartan building—solid, but like a vacation rental. They got out of the car and gazed at the lake in the distance for a moment or two; and, aware that Cary was watching, she remembered to glance at the note with the code as she opened the door.

Ron had turned the AC down when they'd left that morning, and the loft was uncomfortably warm by now; they scrambled back down the ladder after Cary took one fast look. Sara stood aside and let her poke her head into the bathroom under the stairs, the laundry nook. "Too small for us."

"No, it wouldn't work for us—we couldn't live in something this little. I told you I needed to be somewhere safe on Friday—that was here. But it's that austere style you were talking about. We could find, or build, something like this, maybe, bigger."

Cary gave her another look, and she realized soon she'd have to admit her relationship with Ron. Cary touched the controls that opened and closed the tall curtains, went back outside, and sat down at the shaded table. The birds were quiet in the still afternoon heat, the pine needles barely moving.

"It's hot," she complained again, started toward the car.

"Okay, then we'll go home. Honest, I was glad to get out, clear my thoughts. And, nice, that gig for the summer, right?"

"Yeah. The three of you work that out in advance, too?"

"No." She stopped in front of Cary, faced her. "I had no idea they were going to ask you about that. Complete news to me. When did you stop trusting me?"

"When you stopped telling me things."

She checked to be certain the door had locked—***Even here!***—and they drove past the guard who only glanced up as they went through the gate. Neither of them spoke for a couple of miles, Cary tapping away on her phone, unsmiling and focused on the buttons. The tapping annoyed her, but she said nothing.

At last Cary laid the phone down. "What's for supper? Why don't we get pasta? We haven't eaten at Don's in a while."

"Chris did bring food on Sunday. And maybe Don wouldn't want us there right now, with all that about Chris. And it might be too crowded."

"Sunday, wow. That seems so long ago…. Yeah, but it wasn't like eating there. It won't be crowded; it's Wednesday. And I don't think Don wouldn't want us. Anyway, we're family. It's like having a family meal. We've always gone there because of that, not because it's the only thing we eat, you know. And the boyfriend may as well come. I guess he'll be hanging around from now on."

She started to answer with something sharp, remembered how Ron had handled it in the office. "Well, in that case, you better figure out what to call him instead of 'the boyfriend'."

"We'll discuss it while we're all eating."

They were on their street when Sara thought about what she'd said. "Excuse me? What does that mean, 'while we're all eating'?"

"I mean, yeah, I have his number, so I texted him a while ago, and he said that would be good." She ignored Sara's exasperated gasp. "I mean, if he's one of *us*, now."

"So I guess I have to ask *you* what my plans are, what my schedule is, when we're supposed to go someplace?"

"He said he'd pick us up. I'm changing clothes."

She scampered through the door ahead of Sara but stopped at the hallway and turned back, serious. "Okay, when was the last time you were out there, at that cabin?"

The moment had arrived sooner than she'd thought. "Last night."

"I thought so. You might as well have just told me. I'd already figured it out."

Sara considered. "You came by here with Allie and I wasn't home."

"I wanted to show you my foot. Just to let you know: It's cool, the house—but it'd be better for *me*, when I get older, and maybe if I go to college around here, I could live there by myself. All that security would be nice. But *we're* not moving there." Cary's face was comically solemn. Sara felt a pang of loss over something she couldn't identify right then.

"No, we're not."

In a few moments Cary returned to the kitchen in leggings and another floppy tee. Her sandals were minimalist, to flaunt the henna tattoo. They waited for Ron to arrive.

IT SEEMED THE two of them had texted about more than just the evening meal. Cary said, "What do *you* want, Ron?"

Sara gave her a look.

"We talked, it's fine. I'm cool with it. Cary, you choose for us."

He stayed at her house till almost eleven, watching a movie also of Cary's choice. Leaving, he drew Sara to him and kissed her, possessively and long. Sara turned to find Cary watching with that teenage cynicism.

"He could've stayed," she told Sara.

"No, he couldn't."

Cary smiled and went to her bedroom, saying over her shoulder, "I have to be at the TV station on Friday, just to let you know, so don't go anywhere else that day. I'll need you for emotional support. Mr. Thomas' grandkid'll be there, too. You know how I am with babies."

EVEN WITH THE new people, Mooresville was still a small town. All the precincts tabulated election results electronically, and by eight o'clock a pretty good calculation could sometimes be made of winners and losers. This wasn't going to be one of those times.

Don Liberto told Chris to help that evening in the restaurant—really, he just wanted to keep an eye on him. When he'd asked Sara to bring Rheta along, she said Rheta was visiting an old friend somewhere. Don didn't like the sound of that—not the "old friend" part, but the "somewhere" part. But Sara stared him down, and he didn't ask anything else.

Around four Don had noticed a fair number of people striding purposefully into the building next door. That pissed him off. He called Lisa, and she took care of it.

Ron Matheson arrived with Sara and Cary, followed shortly by Ransome Moore. Other people who showed up seemed unsurprised to see Ransome, as if they'd all been there together two days before. Don changed the large TV over the bar away from the sports channel. The evening progressed, and some people left, but others congregated as the local news ran a crawler at the bottom of the screen, showing the vote tally. Don and Chris and the staff went about tidying up and shutting down. Don left the bar open: "But only sodas or water. No drunks leaving my business *this* night."

Light spilled out of the restaurant onto the sidewalk far later than it did on a typical Tuesday, and they saw comings and goings next door, too. Chris picked up his phone off and on for a while, then finally put it away, Sara observed. Before long, Lynne Houston, her daughter and her brother William, Ken Thomas and Mary, and Andy McGowan showed up, tapping quietly on the locked door, speaking softly to everybody as Don let them in, crowding around Ransome, who was in his element—though, Sara thought, with a nervous edge about him as he told his stories, his eyes going often to the television.

"Somebody should ask Stephen over here," Ken suggested gruffly after a while. Mary poked him.

"Didn't anybody invite David?" Ransome bellowed, and after a moment's pause in which the people of a certain age remembered, laughter echoed around the tables.

"Or Neil Griffin," Andy agreed, and then everyone except Sara and Ron chuckled again. "If they show up, you could open the bar, send 'em out to shoot up some road signs, get it in the paper." Ransome frowned at him, and he shut up.

Lynne scolded them: "It's not over. Y'all start that shit up, I may have to go home, leave you here by yourselves."

"You'd just sit there and watch your own TV, you know it," Ransome scoffed.

The tally went back and forth. Why weren't all the votes in, at this precinct or another? They argued about it, about the totals in some areas. At last, around eleven-thirty, the votes were called "complete," and Lynne led by twenty-nine.

They clapped, loudly, so perhaps the sound would carry next door. Cary found an air horn noise online, showed it to Ron, and he shrugged: "Go for it." She played it on her phone a few times.

Ransome was strategizing again, as he'd always done, huddled with Lynne at a small table: "There'll be a handful of absentees.

They could go either way, some for you, some for him. And he'll probably challenge it, I would, but you with a lead, he won't win, there won't be that many votes to challenge, that many absentees to make a difference, so that'll be that." He shook her hand, leaned over and hugged her.

Then they all shook hands and hugged, and slowly made motions as if to leave. William said he'd make sure Lynne got home all right, Andy asked Chris if he and Don needed any help closing up. Ron and Sara, with Cary lagging behind, followed Ransome outside to where he'd parked his SUV—of course, right in front, and there was a parking notice on the windshield: He'd neglected to sign in to the parking app. He guffawed and shoved the ticket under the visor.

They saw Lynne and William off, watched Andy walk down the sidewalk, and, in a moment or two, emerge from the alley next to his shop in his own vehicle. The air was balmy, almost coastal, a light breeze moving the leaves of the river birches. Ron asked the old man if he'd stay at the cabin that night instead of making the hour-and-a-half drive home by himself, so late; and to his surprise, Ransome agreed it would be a good idea. Chagrined, Ron glanced at Sara: He'd intended to stay for a while with her and Cary, continue their celebration, and now he'd be hosting an old man, listening to him snore downstairs in the open guest house, while *he* tossed restlessly in the loft and thought of Sara…. Well, it was fair: A while back, Ransome had put him up at *his* house.

The lights went out next door. For a couple of hours the restaurant crowd had noticed more people leaving than arriving, and now Stephen Logan stepped outside, locked up, and turned to see the silent group watching him. He smiled. "You know it's not over."

"Recount. I'd do that, too," Ransome told him jovially. Then his face changed as Logan approached. "But you know what? You're not gonna win. You're just gonna keep things riled up and then you'll lose, again. Go run for office somewhere else, some place that's got more people like you."

Logan turned a broad grin on Sara and winked at Cary, who grimaced. Then, to Ransome, he said, "Give it up, old man. You don't tell anybody what to do anymore. Tonight was a step backwards, but it's all good, because you won't be standing on this sidewalk in the morning."

Ron stirred, but Ransome, Sara realized, was still able to hold his own. "I might be here. How would you know? I might plan on being in front of this building every day until you decide to leave."

Logan shrugged a little. "I doubt it. You bailed out long ago when your own girl went out with somebody that made you squeamish. You won't be here. You left, *then*."

Ransome's face went blank, as if with a shock of suddenly-remembered pain or shame, and Ron now took a step toward Logan; but, holding up a hand, he shook his head and crossed the street, disappearing into the parking lot behind Neil's office, and in a moment they saw the tail lights of his Toyota becoming smaller, two red eyes glowing bright before they faded, as he left.

"I have to get Sara and Cary home," Ron said, breaking the disquiet of the moment. "Follow me, Ransome, and then we'll go on out to the office."

Ransome climbed into the SUV, but then he set one foot on the pavement, turned back to them. "I wish she'd won with more of a margin. It could drag out a couple of weeks, that asshole issuing challenges with the help of his *lawyer*—" he worked his mouth around— "but in the end she'll be okay. But it would've been good for the town if it'd been a bigger win. It would've meant something. This way it's not as definite as it should be, what it means.

"But a win's a win," and he brought the foot into the cab and almost shut the door. "You find that out as you get old. They don't come often enough, but when they do, you take 'em for what they are." He cranked the engine and waited for them to lead him out.